Collection Books 5 - 8

By

Esther E. Schmidt

Copyright © 2020 by Esther E. Schmidt All rights reserved.

No part of this book may be reproduced in any form,
without permission in writing from the author.

This book is a work of fiction. Incidents, names, places, characters
and other stuff mentioned in this book is the results of the author's
imagination. Cowboy Bikers MC is a work of fiction.
If there is any resemblance, it is entirely coincidental.

This content is for mature audiences only. Please do not read if
sexual situations, violence and explicit language offends you.

Cover design by:
Esther E. Schmidt

Editor #1:
Christi Durbin

Editor #2:
Virginia Tesi Carey

Cover Model:
Jeremy Allison

Photographer:
Golden Czermak / FuriousFotog

COWBOY
BIKERS MC #5

By Esther E. Schmidt

Colt

I'm a biker in an MC located at a huge ranch which breeds both longhorns and quarter horses. I'm not just a biker, a cowboy, or a rancher, but I am a man of many trades and talents. And one of those is to protect the one who captured my attention at first glance.

Kadence

Growing up as the daughter of an MC president, I'm well aware of the risks of running to another MC for help. But it's not like I had a choice. And neither did my heart when I fell for my best friend's brother. He's the one risking it all in an effort to change my life. Vengeance is bloody, and in the end, I might not be the only one who needs saving.

CHAPTER 01

COLT

My damn heart is racing and my lungs are screaming at me to stop acting as if I'm not out of breath. I definitely need to add more cardio to my workout. But I don't plan to race around like the devil himself is chasing me all the time, that's for sure.

"Hey, see Colt anywhere?" my VP, Roper, asks Ledger just as I sneak my way into the stables through the back door.

Ledger is about to reply but I make myself known as I step toward them, acting as if I was in the back the whole time.

"What's up?" I casually ask, suppressing the need to gulp a few extra breaths of oxygen into my lungs.

Roper narrows his eyes. "What did you do?"

Observant asshole. I'm not ready for him to know about my plan yet. The only one who knows what the fuck I've been up to is Alfie. And he agreed we need to keep it between us for now.

I hold Roper's stare and simply shrug. "Nothing. I've been in the back cleaning, while Ledger here took his time getting his horse ready. Oh, and I also rushed home to grab my phone, but that's it...been right here the whole time. What's going on?"

I'm lying straight through my teeth. I haven't been here and I didn't rush home to get my phone. What I did do was meet Kadence, my sister's former roommate and friend, at the spot I told her to wait for me. Then I kidnapped her and took her to the underground bunker that's connected to my cabin. I might also have spared a few minutes to gag her and cuff her to my bed.

I made sure no one saw me dumping the car at the junkyard the club owns, quickly throwing it through the car baler to get rid of it. And finally getting my ass back here as quickly as possible so no one knew I kidnapped the sister of the president of Deranged Hounds MC.

You can say this whole situation is complicated as fuck. And, really, it's not like I had a choice. This is also the reason why I couldn't spill any of my plans to my prez and VP. But I also won't do anything behind my MC's back, hence the reason Alfie knows what my intentions were before I put my plan into motion.

"Kay is missing," Garrett states.

Yeah, Kadence is not so much missing but no one knows that little fact.

I act my part and snap, "What?" Ledger voices the same thing right along with me.

"Alfie is going over the parking lot footage right now. May's car is missing too," Roper states.

The car has passed the point of existing since I made it disappear at the junkyard. But my sister, Mayven, is Ledger's old lady and I'm sure he'll sacrifice his car if she needs one, or I'll buy her another one. Whatever, the car needed to disappear.

And Alfie can watch the footage, we both know they won't see anything else but Kadence driving off as if she's leaving on her own free will.

We head for the main house which functions as our clubhouse with a large space for all of us and separate rooms in the back. I'm not a people person, therefore I have my own space at the edge of the ranch. A cabin I built years ago with an underground bunker and a small private stable and paddock where I keep my horse, Cavier.

Mayven rushes toward us. She's still on crutches, recovering from a gunshot wound to the leg because of the shit Deranged Hounds MC was wrapped in. Was. Because those guys who attacked us–while Kadence was on the back of my bike, and Ledger had Mayven on his when they started shooting at us–are dead and gone.

But there's still an issue at hand where Kadence's brother promised his own sister to one of his men to smooth over the fact he didn't pick the fucker to be the next VP. Now in my opinion, that's more screwed up than having fuckers chase you while spitting out bullets. Seriously. Who the hell whores out his own blood?

I had no choice but to kidnap Kadence. I did ask my prez, Weston, to interfere before I put my plan into motion, but we can't risk a war between MCs. We have kids, old ladies, and a ranch to handle and look after, along with a few other companies.

I completely understand it's not our problem since this woman is not related or linked with our MC for any reason other than Kadence is my sister's old roommate and her best friend. But fuck, the woman pulls on my every nerve ending and there's just something about her.

I can't stand to watch her cry or so much as see pain or discomfort on her face. I'm eight damn years older than her. She's way too young for me; and yet I threw everything to the wind and kidnapped the woman for her own safety, and my sanity.

"Any news?" Mayven asks Roper but locks her eyes on me next. "What did you do? I know you said something before you left. She cried. She hardly ever cries. What did you say?"

"Get in May's car, drive for a few miles and wait for me if you want to change your life." That's what I said before I left. She listened. I kidnapped. But it's not something I can share with my sister, even if Kadence is her best friend and the reason the woman crawled underneath my fucking skin.

In this case it's a good alibi; for the outside world it seems like we go head to head at every turn. Why would I have something to do with her disappearance when we obviously bump heads?

"I did, and said, shit," I grumble. "She's the one always running for the hills, so don't look at me."

Another thing making the part believable where she left on her own free will. Kadence ran from her brother's MC weeks ago, and came here to see my sister. It's working in our favor how she got in May's car again and hit the road.

Alfie stalks out of church carrying a laptop in one hand. "She drove off. She just got into May's car and drove off by herself."

Yup. I did mention solid alibies all around, right?

"So, she's not missing? Like I said…she runs. She did the exact same thing to her brother when she showed up here. Hell, she could have just headed home instead of waiting for her brother to show up. She knows there's no way out of the deal Rowen made and she knows she can't stay here." I shrug. "Now, can we all get back to work?"

I turn and head for the door.

"Just hang the fuck on, Colt," Weston snaps and I spin around to face him. "Are you sure you're not involved? You didn't tell her to run, or offer her a way out?"

I shrug, something I always do and it allows me to be indifferent or allows me time to either think about how to answer or not answer at all. In this case I need a few extra seconds to be aware of what words I offer him in reply.

Finally settling with, "I didn't tell her to run. I did tell her if she stayed, I would fuck her in every hole her body possessed. Maybe that sent her running."

Alfie barks out a laugh. "No shit? You really told her that?"

I shoot him a grin. "Sure did."

And I remember all too vividly how a shiver went through her when I whispered those words right beside her ear a few days ago. Yeah, for sure it sent her running; straight into my arms. I thought it would scare her off but she launched herself at me instead.

In fact, it was me who did the running…I turned on my heel and left the room. I guess in the end she turned the tables on me, and I fucking loved that. And the thought of having her gagged and restrained–waiting for me–in my bed is driving me insane. I need to get back to her.

"Oh, for fuck's sake," Weston grumbles and takes out his phone, jabs his finger against the screen, and holds it to his ear. "Rowen. Weston here. No. We have no damn clue. Security tape shows she got into May's car and drove off. Sure. Yeah. Want our help looking? Fine." He jams his phone back in his pocket as he mutters, "Fucking asshole."

"Everything okay?" Roper questions.

"Alfie, email the part where she gets in her car and drives off to Rowen," Weston orders before he directs his attention to Roper. "Yeah. All is good. Rowen said his sister's a brat who always runs when shit gets hard. She'll turn up sooner or later." Weston's gaze slides over everyone until it lands on me. "And if she does turn up here, we're going to tie her up and send her home. Understood?"

"Tie her up and bring her home. You got it, Prez," I tell him in all sincerity, since I've already done both…I have her restrained and in my home.

He turns his attention to Roper again and I take this opportunity to slide out of the clubhouse and head for my cabin. Time to see how Kadence is doing. I'm betting she's pretty pissed because she sure as hell didn't expect me to keep her gagged, restrained, and hidden in my bunker.

But with her being an unpredictable, headstrong, feisty, dynamite bundle of a woman, I really didn't have a choice in the matter. She's a proud one with a load of self-respect. I mean, you have to possess a lot of inner strength to pull through what this woman has endured for the past few weeks.

First, she lost her father, the former president of Deranged Hounds MC. He was murdered by a few of his own men who stole money and property from the club. Then her mother killed herself on the day of her father's funeral.

And then there's her brother, Rowen, who fucking gave his own sister to one of his guys to smooth over a dispute within his MC. Using it also as a way to tie Kadence to the club. It's insane. Degrading. Disrespectful, and in no way tolerable.

It takes a few minutes to get to my cabin. The first thing I have to do is put my horse, Cavier, into the paddock. He needs to stretch his legs. He's a very stubborn Cremello horse with blue eyes. I saved him when he was two years old. He was in an accident where the trailer he was in crashed. Fear is what I had to soothe out of him.

No one thought he would trust anyone or anything ever again. In my opinion all he needed was a load of patience and understanding. When you take a chance and offer something broken time to heal, you get a solid connection in return. And Cavier has been soothing the restlessness in my veins for years. We fit quite nicely.

It's the same with Kadence. First time I met her after I heard she became Mayven's roommate, I was set to threaten the hell out of her to make sure she wouldn't drag my sister in any MC shit her family was tied to. I quickly became aware she wasn't as involved with her father's MC. And she also knew Mayven was tied to one–through me–as well. Though May wasn't involved with my club either.

Well, she is now. All because my sister came running to me for help the day of Kadence's father's funeral. They held a gathering at the clubhouse where Mayven saw Rowen kill the rat who killed his father. She hightailed out of there and ended up here. Ledger, the fucker, fell in love and claimed my sister as his old lady.

Mayven and Kadence being friends–and the only other person she had and trusted–is the reason Kadence headed here when things went to shit for her too. That's when I had to see her every second of the day to protect my sister and make sure Rowen's club shit didn't land on our doorstep. Guess it was inevitable with Kadence being involved.

The young woman heats my skin and she never attempts to hide the lust she has reserved for me. Somehow, I kept my cool every damn day, and walked out on her without burying my cock inside her pussy. But when I discovered the situation her brother put her in? I still wanted to keep her at a distance–away from my cock–while fixing the trouble following her.

I guess I'm done with keeping her at arm's length since I kidnapped her. She didn't have a choice; it was either me taking her, or her brother would hand her over to Cannon. And like fuck I was going to let her slip away.

I'm simply going to stop overthinking shit; she's mine. I know I'm older and she should be with someone her own age, but she tears me up when I'm not around her. As if a match strikes and lands on the fuel inside my veins, lighting an inevitable fire. She's been burning me up from the moment I laid eyes on her.

I open the stall and slide the halter around Cavier's head to lead him into the paddock. The corner of my mouth twitches, knowing Kadence is right underneath the paddock. No one knows about the bunker. I built it myself, years ago, along with the cabin.

Therapy. Hard work with the sun on your back; best thing out there. And I have the result to enjoy and be proud of it on a daily basis. I love the home I built for myself. My brothers know not to come here unless there's a high priority issue. It's another reason why I am blessed to have this MC at my back; the support and brotherhood.

And of course, the hard work of the ranch along with my love to work with horses. I close the paddock and head inside the cabin. Washing my hands, I head to the bedroom where I stashed a secret hatch underneath the bed which leads to the bunker. I make sure to lock the bedroom door as a precaution, just in case Kadence manages to rush past me when I untie her.

Silence greets me when I step inside. The bunker is a large space with everything in one room. One corner contains a little kitchen setup, another corner is a couch and a table. A bed, along with a bedside table, take yet another corner.

There was a point in my life where I slept here each and every night. To make sure I was locked away from the world. Too much war was still vivid on a loop inside my brain causing the anxiety to overload on a daily basis.

My brothers pulled me through, giving me the work on the ranch needed to drain my body while mindlessly having conversations while we're at it. Cavier had a lot to do with it too; my therapy horse as I was his therapy person in return. I'm still a little fucked-up in my head, but I can push it to the background.

Kadence is still bound in place and her eyes are spitting fire. Satisfaction roars through my veins. I should stop the smile spreading across my face, but the woman before me lying in my bed is too good to be true. Her explosive character, smart mouth, and banging body have been making me painfully hard for quite some time now.

She's unlike other women I've encountered over the years. Her hips soft and round, built to grab hold and take a pounding without breaking. Tits lush and overflowing, her skin is light with a sheen of freckles spreading her nose and cheekbones. And the attitude fits her rich, dark, red hair. Yeah, she's a sight to behold.

"Let me make you more comfortable," I murmur and remove the gag.

"What the fuck, Colt?" she spits and fights her restraints. "Get these off of me, right now."

She indicates the cuffs but I have no intention of removing them. Not yet anyway. I should tell her to calm down, though I know it would be the wrong thing to say. Recent talks with Ledger have given me some added insight when he made my sister his old lady. He keeps blabbering about details where he fucked-up.

Normally I hate the forced interaction of hearing people yap about their personal shit, but in this case, I let him rattle and take in the added information. It's been helpful in some situations when it comes to handling this bundle of woman.

It's for this reason I neglect to comfort and address her

hysterical attitude and instead remain calm myself when I tell her, "Later. First you and I need to set some ground rules."

"Ground rules?" she hisses through her teeth. "What are you talking about?"

I return her furious glare with one of my own when I tell her in all seriousness, "I didn't risk my loyalty to the club to have you fuck it all up, understood?"

Though Alfie is aware of my actions, Weston and Roper aren't, and in this moment, they could see my actions as betrayal. Growing up as a club princess–the daughter of a president–she knows exactly what I'm talking about.

"Thank you," she whispers, but then adds in a firmer tone, "Uncuff me and we'll go over your ground rules."

I really want to keep her bound but knowing this woman, I would gain more compliance when I give a little instead of pushing my demands down her throat. It's for this reason I move quickly to remove the cuffs.

Instead of a thank you I barely snatch her wrist in time to prevent her fist from connecting with my face. With my next breath I have both her hands above her head, her delicious body underneath me as my face hovers above hers.

"Little spitfire, that's no way to thank the man who just saved your ass," I tell her but instead of looking her dead in the eye all my attention slides to her kissable lips.

Plump. Cherry colored all on their own and when she sucks her bottom lip into her mouth to sink her teeth in it, all of my sanity flies right out the door. I want to reach between our bodies, unleash my cock and sink myself inside her pussy.

I'm so damn hard for this woman and to think we're lined up perfectly. A little shift gives friction right between her legs making her release her bottom lip when she gasps a moan. Yeah, no matter the age difference, we fit damn well together.

Fuck it. I've been haunted by her lips for far too long. I've spent nights wondering how they feel, taste, move against mine. And when I crash my mouth against hers…life as I know it evaporates as a whole new expedition for living rises.

Years of dark and weary, muddling through while all I needed was a touch of brightness due to the fire this woman exists of. I can taste on her tongue how she's fighting for dominance. And as we clash with open lust she starts to submit so damn beautifully.

Her body soft and molding against mine, consuming the grinding of my hips and the way she moans in my mouth? I know for sure she's about to light up any damn second. Shifting slightly, I press my cock down right on top of her center, hitting the jackpot.

She tears her mouth away from mine and gasps for her next breath which comes out as a loud moan. The moan switches to a trembling plea of my name followed by another gasp for air.

I let my head fall into the crook of her neck, nipping the skin and sucking a sliver of it to brand her as mine. I've never felt the need to mark a woman, but I can't help myself. And I relish in the way she keeps grinding herself against me to prolong her pleasure.

Reaching between us I start to unbuckle but she suddenly freezes. Her nails dig into my back and it's not to urge me on. I pull my head away from her neck to face her and instead of lust, all I'm seeing is insecurity with a hint of fear. Out of all the things I thought this woman might be when I finally have her underneath me...insecure or frightened isn't fucking it.

CHAPTER 02

KADENCE

I let my head fall to the side and close my eyes. The delicious pleasure that was racing through me suddenly crashes to a halt before it fades completely. Why do I have to remember a moment from the past right freaking now?

Because it reminds you why you're here, and what happened the last time you were on your back and a man was on top, my mind easily supplies.

"Kadence." The way my name falls in a rumbled growl from his lips, drags my attention back to the man who's held my every thought since the first day I met him.

It didn't matter he came after me to threaten my ass if I got his sister in any trouble. I'm used to overbearing alpha males, slamming their chests and growling at anyone who dares to cross them. With my dad running a motorcycle club, it's all I've ever known for as long as I can remember.

My dad always kept me safe and for the last few years at a safe distance as well. He was trying to steer the MC to a more "law-abiding citizen" version instead of some of the illegal stuff they were wrapped in.

Well, not any more. Since it was one of his own guys who killed him. My mother couldn't handle his death and killed herself. And on top of losing both my parents within days apart, my brother thought it was okay to whore me out to one of his men.

A goodwill offer to soothe things over within his MC. And to put it in his exact words when he informed me of this little fact, "Your ass will be protected and linked with the club. You're my blood. The only family I have left; your place is right here."

Very fucking nice to throw me in the hands of a man I despise; Cannon. Who has wanted, and repeatedly tried, to get into my pants. Without my consent I might add. And he now thinks I belong to him. So, I did the only thing I could and ran to my friend Mayven. Because I don't have anywhere else to go. And I hated doing it because I don't want to pull others into the havoc of my life.

Yet, when Colt offered his help–even if I didn't know what he had in mind–I grabbed the chance with both hands. The whole "back to the wall, no choice, the hell with everything, I don't have anything left to live for," state of mind.

But I sure as hell didn't think I'd end up gagged and bound to his bed. Nor did I expect for him to finally make good on his promise and give me a mind-blowing orgasm. In the time I've known him he's done nothing but aggravate me. Pushing all my buttons just to get a rise out of me.

And for the first time, he's pushed the right button; lighting my body up with pleasure I have never experienced. Dammit. Why can't I have a normal guy? Or a normal fucking life? Hell, I'll even settle for a normal day with all this insanity hitting me from every angle.

The air rushes from my lungs when I'm pulled up into a sitting position. Colt cups my face as my eyes lock on his.

"There you are," he murmurs.

My cheeks heat due to shame. "Sorry. My mind thought it was funny to give me a short recap. It won't happen again."

I push my emotions back and lean in to catch his lips. The kiss he gave earlier swooped me away and made the world stop spinning for just a fragment of time. I need it. Hell, one taste and I'm not ashamed to admit to myself that I'm already addicted to this man.

He keeps my head in place, depriving me of a kiss as his eyes narrow. "What recap?"

Yeah, not going there. Time to shift topics. I rip my head from his hands and jump off the bed. "What's your brilliant plan, Colt? Keep me here locked up? Is that what you had in mind when you said 'Get in May's car, drive for a few miles and wait for me if you want to change your life?' Because becoming your personal sex slave wasn't the change in my life I had in mind. I already had that in my future, remember? Does the name Cannon ring a bell?"

He's in my face with my next breath rumbling, "Answer my fucking question, Kadence."

"I don't see why that's any of your fucking concern, asshole," I shoot back and place my fists on my hips.

His eyes hold an edge of darkness but instead of being hesitant at his dominating appearance, it draws me in. I've never been interested in any bikers due to being surrounded by them all my life, even if my father always protected me. But Colt is in a different league all on his own.

For one he's older than many of the guys of the MC my brother now runs. And Colt isn't very chatty or flirtatious either. If anything, he's grumpy, standoffish, and most definitely a loner. But damn, he's sexy. Dark hair always pulled into a bun at the back of his head. The sides are a salt and pepper mixture to show a hint of his age while his body is a solid youth of muscled strength.

His hand slides around my neck and he pushes me until my back hits the wall of the bunker. Leaning forward his lips brush my ear as his hot breath scorches my skin when he says, "If you want me to tell you what I have planned for the change in your life, you will spill your thoughts. If there's anything I despise it's lying and withholding information. And with the shit you withheld when you got here, I'd say you know this little fact by now."

I let my head slightly fall to the left as I close my eyes. The painful reminder of the shit I withheld—as he so kindly puts it—is the very reason why we're standing here right now. "Cannon tried more than once to crawl on top of me to fuck, okay? Your weight pressing down on me? My brain froze for a damn second or two."

"Did he rape you?" Colt asks through clenched teeth. "Did his fucking fingers touch your pussy?"

"No," I snap. "I managed to fight him off each and every time. My virginity is still intact."

Holy shit, stupid brain. Why did I let that little fact slip out?

A smirk slides over his face. "Well, what do you know…un-fucking-touched." His fingers tighten around my neck. "I should walk away. I'm so fucked-up you don't need my kind of crazy. Not to mention, I'm too fucking old for your virgin pussy."

My fingers tighten in his leather cut and I'm about to shove this asshole away from me but his mouth covers my earlobe before his teeth sink in, making me gasp from shock. Pleasure and pain mix as my body heats.

"But I'm done resisting you. You might have been able to fight off everyone else, but you won't be able to fight me, Kadence. I have fought many battles and never once came out on the losing end. But this isn't about winning or losing. This is about claiming what has always been reserved to be mine. And, Kadence?" His voice comes out as a rough growl when he adds, "I always take what's mine, no matter who or what I have to face to get my way."

A shiver runs through me due to the truth in his admittance. This man just challenged a brotherhood and is willingly risking a war with both MCs when he kidnapped me to keep me safe.

I know his MC can't interfere with my brother's club because there's nothing to be done since I'm the president's sister and Rowen picked a man for me. Personal issues, nothing more, nothing less. Colt's MC has nothing to do with it, even if it's fucked-up. It sounds like some twisted scene from a mafia romance. Minus the romance part, that's for damn sure.

"I hope you know what you're risking by not being able to resist me. And I can tell you right now I'm not worth it. You have to think about those little ones I've met. Weston, and Roper's kid too. My brother would go nuts if he knew you helped me stay away from him."

Fury washes over his face. "Not worth it? Then why the hell did you fight Cannon if you think you aren't worth shit? Are you willing to suck and take his cock in every hole to please your brother? Well, why didn't you say so? It would solve a lot of problems."

My fist flies out and lands on his jaw hard enough for him to step back and drop his hand, leaving me the space to kick his shin for good measure and dash around him.

"You asshole," I seethe. "I won't suck anyone's cock and surely not an asshole who cheats, stinks, and thinks my pussy is a damn prize to pop because he wants me for the title. A prize to be won for all to see and make him feel better and good about himself."

I try to land another punch but Colt grabs both my wrists and pulls me to him, making me collide with his hard chest.

"Glad to hear we're in agreement. You won't suck anyone's cock except mine. And I actually do have a plan, Kadence. But it involves a waiting game where in the end, I'm going to offer Rowen cash since your sick brother is all about making deals and whoring out his sister."

Fury flares hot through my veins. He tightens his hands around my wrist and slowly shakes his head.

"Don't get pissed, little spitfire. I hit the nail on the head about your fucked-up brother. It has nothing to do with you or the money I will happily cough up to buy your freedom, because that's how I see it."

"Buy my freedom?" I croak. "You really think my brother will accept cash if you offered? Cannon won't–"

"My plan involves Cannon dead and buried. And your brother is the president now, he needs to put the club first and his club needs money to survive," Colt simply states.

Laughter rips from me. I can't help it. The way he mentions Cannon's death as if it's part of a turd he needs to flush is hysterical.

His determined look stops my laughter, but the corner of my mouth is still twitching when I ask, "Okay, I'm curious...how do you plan to kill him?"

"Either Rowen will take care of it for me or the fucker will be stupid enough to undermine Rowen's authority, that will leave me to let him headbutt a bullet."

Headbutt a bullet. The way those three words fall from his lips in a deadly vow is making my heart skip a beat or two. There's something seriously wrong with me to find a man threatening to end another man's life sexy.

"Keep staring at my lips and I'll give 'em to you. But not to take your mouth, Kadence. I'll take the lips of your pussy in a kiss that'll make your orgasm explode on my tongue."

My pussy clenches at the mere thought of having this man's head between my legs. It has me wondering how his rough beard will feel when it slides along the inside of my thighs.

His breath heats my ear when he murmurs, "No use imagining how it would feel. And like I said...we're playing a waiting game where we have a lot of spare time to kill. I intend to spend most of it between your legs."

I have to swallow hard. Those aren't empty words and his big, calloused hands are slowly stroking me, stoking the fire his words already set aflame inside me.

The men I've been surrounded with weren't anything like Colt. Most might have been bikers but they took what they wanted, when they wanted. The only reason I'm still a virgin is because my father protected me–and threatened anyone who so much as looked my way–until the day he died.

Those other men didn't make promises. And Colt has done nothing but make promises and he kept them too. Even if I forced myself upon him by coming here and putting everyone at risk by doing so.

Colt called my brother and arranged for me to stay here for seven days after he heard my mother killed herself on the day of my father's funeral. And today, when those seven days were up and I had to return to my brother, Colt again offered me a way out; landing my ass here in his bunker.

And now he has another plan. Everything else in my life has fallen apart, and the one man who doesn't give empty promises is standing before me to offer me pleasure and a future along with it. I would be stupid not to accept.

"Okay," I breathe.

He hums in approval but it's clear he needs clarification when he asks, "Okay to what, doll?"

The way he says doll all husky…hell, a sandpapery voice… encourages me enough to go all in. I was already all in, but whatever; I want everything this man has to offer because I just know he's good for it.

"Okay to your mouth, the offer to buy my freedom, anything you have in mind: take lead and I'll follow." I'm prevented from saying anything more because his lips slam over mine, plunging his tongue into my mouth and letting my heart skip a beat to process what's happening to my body.

A low growl rumbles through his chest. His hands find the front of my shirt where he fists the fabric and rips; buttons fly through the air as his gaze lands on my breasts. My nipples harden against the lace of my bra. The man easily fingers the front clasp to free them but it doesn't last long because his hands are holding them hostage the next moment.

The heat in his eyes is giving me a power boost, as if he's enthralled and in disbelief. "Magnificent," he croaks. "More than a handful. I imagined them in my hands so many fucking times but this–" His mouth surrounds one of my nipples and the wet heat leaves me gasping for my next breath.

Another rumbled growl flows through the air before my body is swooped up, only to land ass first onto the mattress. Colt's hands are fumbling with the button of my jeans when a beeping sound starts and a red light flickers above our heads.

"Motherfucker," Colt groans and leans his forehead against my belly. "Someone is inside my cabin. I gotta go."

Fear makes my heart slam against my ribcage. "Who? Are they coming for me?"

He crawls up my body until his eyes hit mine. "There ain't nothing I won't face to keep you safe, doll. You're mine, you agreed. Now, sit tight and I'll be right back."

"Wait." I jump off the bed and grab his arm. "What if my brother is here? What if they are waiting out there to kill you because they know you have me locked up in here? You'll need backup. Let me help."

His arm lifts and when I follow to where he's pointing, I notice a screen on the wall.

"When someone enters my cabin, it activates the security system. Flipping on the screen, light, and alarm here in the bunker. Weston and Roper are the only ones inside, and I can handle both." He winces slightly and I know why.

"You shouldn't have done it," I whisper. "You lied to your brothers. Let me go up. I'll explain how I drove off to give a distraction and sneaked my way in here."

A sly grin spreads his face. "Smart thinking, but there's one flaw." He brushes his knuckles softly against my jaw. "There's no way you could have sneaked inside without me knowing. All my brothers are aware of the tight security system inside my cabin. I never leave room for errors and nothing major happens in this MC without my knowledge. Not when it comes to sneaking someone inside a house like you suggested. It's the reason only one other person knows you're here since he handles the security system of the ranch."

"You have an accomplice?" I ask with wide eyes.

He stalks in the direction of the door. "Alfie. But rest assured, he's had my back many times as I have his. He'd cut off his tongue before ratting me out."

The statement he just gave is the kind of loyalty these guys have among one another. It's way different from where I come from now that my father is dead. In the time I've spent here I quickly noticed how much more of a brotherhood and family this MC is.

Colt shoots me a wink before he disappears, leaving me with a pit in my stomach. Worry. Fear. And those two have nothing to do with me but everything with the man who sacrificed a lot for my safety.

I tie my shirt closed since the buttons are scattered on the floor and all I can do is wait for Colt. Hoping he once again sticks to his word and returns safely.

CHAPTER 03

COLT

The second I open my bedroom door and come face to face with my prez, I just know shit hit the fan.

"What's wrong?" I question.

"I'm giving you one fucking chance to explain, and you'd better have a damn good reason why your sister's car is a cube of scrap metal hidden away in our fucking junkyard." Weston's voice picks up volume with every word until the last two are bellowed in my face.

"Because I need time for my–" I cut off my answer as I quickly brace for impact.

Pain bursts through my head and my brain rattles from the hit to the jaw I just took.

I push Weston's chest to keep space between us, holding my hands palms up. "Let me fucking explain. Haven't I earned at least that fucking respect? I've always placed the club above everything else. Hell, above my own sanity, and you know it."

"You'd better talk fucking fast or my fist will end the discussion before it started, asshole," Weston snaps.

"I couldn't tell you anything about my plan because you would have reacted differently if Rowen called or anyone else showed up. Same goes for you, VP. I had to protect all of us so if things went to shit it would fall solely on my shoulders. But I did tell Alfie, and he knows I would explain to you guys and why I had to do this part on my own. He had my back while I set things in motion. Kadence is my old lady, but I also need to put my MC first and that means I had to take steps to keep us safe. And if you must know…I had her gagged and cuffed to my bed while I was talking to you guys in the stable. Only Alfie and I knew what was happening. And Kadence wasn't all too happy either, but I had to fucking do it. Rowen will do shit to get her back. He doesn't care about his sister and has enough on his plate with his MC barely keeping things together. First, they had to deal with rats, the money loss, the property loss. Which I just found out is their clubhouse, so they need to relocate by the end of this month. And then the fact some of the brothers doubt his leadership, Cannon being the loudest bigmouth and the reason why he promised his sister to that motherfucker."

"Fuck you, Colt," Weston hisses. "I told you we couldn't get involved. I fucking told you and you turned your back and saved her anyway."

Roper steps closer and places his hand on Weston's shoulder to push him slightly back and take his place to get into my face. "When you left our old ladies asked us to help search for her. They want to keep her away from her brother too. It's why I ended up at the junkyard since it's one of the places she knows from the lunch deliveries she helps your sister with. I did a sweep through this morning, you idiot. I noticed the extra cube of scrap metal as your sister's car right away."

A sigh rips from my chest. "Fine. I know how it looked, and I don't fucking care what you might think. I damn well have my priorities straight, I don't carry any regret and I'd do it again to keep everyone safe. I repeat…I needed all of you to give an honest reaction, then I had to check on Kadence since I had her gagged and cuffed. I was going to explain everything later, but I damn well couldn't do it right then and there. And I ain't going to make excuses for keeping my old lady safe…all while putting all of you first. I mentioned the gagged and–"

"Oh, for fuck's sake," Weston grumbles. "Do you have that wildcat still gagged and restrained?"

"I was about to eat her pussy but you guys felt the need to come here and scold my ass before I had the chance to fill you guys in. Because I really didn't think she would agree to be my old lady this quickly."

"She agreed?" Roper's eyes bulge.

Weston is giving me a smirk. "She's up to something. I hope she cuffs and gags you in your sleep and shoves a large dildo up your ass."

"Jeez, thanks for the well wishes. Fuckin' awesome, Prez. Quite the imagination you have there," I grumble and clear my throat to think of a way to turn the discussion back to the matter at hand. "Are we keeping it under wraps for now? I want her brother thinking she's on the run and stall to let time pass long enough for him to get desperate. Then I'll offer him money and a piece of property I bought a few months ago as an investment. I told my old lady I'll buy her freedom and that's exactly what I intend to do."

Weston rubs a hand over the back of his neck. "That actually sounds like something he'd jump to. It's an easy fix and it will save his MC. But there's only one problem."

"I'll end that fucking problem with a bullet if he comes near her again," I growl, knowing exactly what Weston is thinking about.

"Maybe Rowen might end the problem himself. Cannon was the one who let those two fuckers follow him, resulting in an attack on us. Your sister, one of our club's old ladies, was shot in the leg for fuck's sake and you, Ledger, or Kadence could have died. Not to mention Rowen was sloppy and pulled your sister unwillingly into a damn murder witness when he took care of a rat on club grounds. Your sister being in the wrong place at the wrong time was his fucking fault. That fucker owes us," Weston says, the anger in his words surprises me but it's a warm welcome instead of where we were a mere moment ago.

"Are we okay?" I ask, needing to know they are aware I acted in the best interest of all of us.

"You're going to keep her here in your cabin for at least a week before we tell the old ladies. Me, Roper, Alfie, and you will meet up tomorrow morning and discuss everything again to make sure we're not overlooking things."

I quickly nod in agreement. "You got it, Prez."

"I wonder which of the old ladies will figure it out before that week is up." Roper chuckles. "My money is on my old lady."

"What? No way, his sister will figure it out. She's pissed at him and will come over to chew his head off. Mayven will figure it out within three days for sure." Weston laughs.

"Are we taking bets? What the fuck, assholes? Get the hell out of my cabin and I'll see you guys in the morning. I have to get back to my old lady." I grab both their leather cuts at the shoulder and give them a firm shove in the direction of the door. "Out."

"Tomorrow, Colt," Weston warns before he leaves.

I lock up after them and head for the bedroom. Opening the hatch, I call out for Kadence to let her know it's safe. No need for her to stay in the bunker. My Prez and VP will make sure no one comes near my cabin so we might as well enjoy the normality of my home. I offer her my hand when she's reached the top of the stairs.

"Are you sure it's okay for me to–" She gasps and holds her hand close to my face. "Oh my God. What happened?"

"My Prez and VP found out before I could get them up-to-date about my plan." I shrug and lock the hatch, turning on my heels to head for the kitchen. "I need a beer."

"You and me both," Kadence huffs and I hear her footsteps behind me.

I grab a bottle and pop open the cap by holding it to the edge of the counter and give a smack on my hand, making the cap flip through the air and land on the ground. Lifting it to my lips, I down a few gulps of beer before coming back up for air.

Kadence snatches the bottle from my hand, drains the rest, and places the empty bottle on the counter. "Mind sharing another one?"

I grab a beer from the fridge and open it before handing it to her.

"Mind making some food for us?" I question.

There's a challenging twinkle in her eye but she nods. "It's the least I can do with you helping me out." She points at my jaw. "Need ice for that?"

"I've endured worse." I shrug and grab the beer from her hands to take a few sips, placing it on the counter when I add, "Let's go outside and grab some tomatoes and some other stuff from the vegetable garden."

"I can go outside?" There's vulnerability in her voice and I hate the position this strong woman is placed in.

"Yeah, doll. I have church set tomorrow bright and early to discuss everything. Weston and Roper decided to keep you being here to ourselves. It's the safest for everyone until we've gained some time to take my plan to the next level. And I know you and my sister are close and you've helped out with her setting up her business with lunch deliveries, but let her old man help out. For now, you need to focus on yourself. And with my cabin being remote and my Prez and VP making sure no one will come around, I'd say we're free to do what we please as long as we stay close to home."

I wrap my fingers around her wrist and pull her along to head out back. One of the things I love about my place is the fact it has a massive garden with a wide range of vegetables. With a large freezer filled with meat I can go weeks without shopping.

While Kadence was here with my sister, I noticed she spent a lot of time in the kitchen. My sister might have been the one with the plan to start a business that delivers lunch packages, but Kadence is a valuable asset. It's also why I've asked her to make dinner; to take her mind off the trouble coming at her at every turn.

"Oh. Wow. He's gorgeous!" Her eyes bounce from me to Cavier. "Now I know why you're living here and never let anyone get close. So freaking gorgeous. Look, he's practically glowing like a pearl or silk or–" Her ramblings stop when she reaches the fence and she holds out her hand.

Cavier might have had a rough past but he's nicer than me. And it might be the fact that I'm standing right next to her when Cavier immediately moves to get close. But when he skips me to sniff Kadence's hand, I have to agree with him…I'd much rather have her hands on me too.

"So soft," she murmurs with awe in her voice. "Can I ride him?"

I can't help the smile and pride spreading my face. "Yeah. Let me get a bridle."

It takes a few minutes but when I'm holding the rope and grab Kadence's ankle to help her onto Cavier's back, I get to enjoy the best of both worlds when I see my woman riding bareback on my horse.

She's not by any means an experienced rider, but I intend to change that little fact very soon. And with her showing interest like this? Fucking perfect. And to think she's only watched the other horses from a distance the time she's been on the ranch. One glance at my horse changes her mind from watching to actually interacting.

When I glance up at her my chest squeezes at the sight. Her hands are stroking Cavier's neck, eyes filled with awe, and there's a huge damn smile on her face letting me know how much she's enjoying something as simple as a ride on the back of a horse.

It's similar to a careless moment we shared a few days ago when she was on the back of my bike. She threw her head back and screamed at the wind, relishing in the feel at something so fleeting as a simple ride to enjoy yourself.

It was right before Cannon lead the two rats from their MC right at us, guns blazing and coming for Kadence so they could strike at Rowen by hurting his sister. Yeah, this woman deserves happiness in huge fucking chunks. And I'm dead set to make sure she gets it.

"How old is he? And how long have you had him?" she questions.

I keep leading Cavier around the paddock as I start to tell her a bit about his background. "You might say I saved him. He was two years old and a bundle of fear. He suffered through an accident when he was in a trailer. I caught his bright blue eyes and there was some kind of understanding between us. My head is more fucked-up than his so I knew he just needed time and space to mend his demons, along with a firm but loving hand and lots of fucking patience. He just turned six a few months ago."

"A firm but loving hand," she muses.

"Yep, and it's the exact thing that you need too." I glance back to shoot her a wink and relish in the way she narrows her eyes at me.

"I'll show you a firm hand when I get off this horse," she grumbles.

The corner of my mouth twitches. "Then I'd better keep you on the horse, huh? Needless to say, you missed the loving part. And if I remember correctly…and I sure as fuck do because I can still vividly remember how it felt to have your nipple in my mouth…you liked the loving part."

She completely ignores me and gives Cavier her full attention. Damn. I didn't know it was possible, but I might be jealous of my own horse. It's a good thing she looks magnificent right where she is or I would have to drag her off and into my bed.

Hell, I might do exactly that anyway. I bring Cavier to a stop. "Come on," I tell her and hold out my hands to grab her waist. "Off you go."

I shamelessly pull her against me and let her delicious body slide down mine.

"Please tell me we're doing this again later today, or tomorrow." The way she's staring at me–her state of mind depending on my reply–is gut wrenching.

Like I mentioned; this woman deserves happiness in huge

fucking chunks. And I'm dead set on making sure she gets it.

"Anytime, Kadence. Any. Damn. Time. If it's a ride on my horse, my bike, hell…my cock, fingers, and face along with it: it's all yours."

Her throat bobs and I love the little sharp intake of breath, making her mouth part slightly. How I would love to take those lips, drag her jeans and underwear down, and impale her on my cock. But I can't. She's a virgin and the first woman I've longed for and damn well claimed as mine; she deserves more. Much more.

I step back to take off the bridle to release Cavier, quickly wrapping my fingers around Kadence's wrist to lead her out of the pasture. I take a moment to hang the headstall before I head for the vegetable garden.

"We could make a salad," she muses.

And when I glance back–finally able to look her in the face now that I have my cock under control again–I see her palming one of the ripe tomatoes.

"Sounds good," I answer gruffly. "I could grill us a couple of steaks if you make the salad."

"Sounds good," she whispers, her voice carrying a cock-stroking tone.

The lust flowing through her eyes is something she can see mirrored in mine. My cock lengthens painfully against the zipper of my jeans and I damn well know we have to get out of here. Making dinner is a good damn start to put some space between us.

"Grab what you need," I tell her and turn toward the house.

And I swear I hear her mutter something in the line of, "Your ass."

But when I throw a glance over my shoulder, she's overly busy with picking tomatoes. To say the upcoming days will be interesting is putting it mildly. This woman triggers many things inside me I never expected to explore.

Hell, by the time I had my ducks somewhat in a row I was comfortable enough living on my own at the edge of this property. Feeling complete and satisfied. I guess I was wrong. One crucial part was missing and I now know because I just found it; found her.

CHAPTER 04

KADENCE

Ten things I love about my new life. I should grab a pen and make a positive vibes list. One I should keep in my pocket to look at a few times a day to remind myself I started a new chapter. But it's hard since the new life I started was only ten days ago and my future is still unsure.

I think that's the only thing going on the back of my list; the downside how the issue with my brother and Cannon is still unsolved. Though, Colt keeps reminding me how each day passing is moving forward to get things settled. He's so sure Rowen will take him up on his offer, but I don't know.

I mean, I never expected my own brother to hand me over to one of his buddies as some kind of peace offering to settle an uprising in his MC. It's safe to say I don't know my brother at all. And at this point I would be happy if I never have to see him again.

Yikes, here come the bad vibes. And to think I was going to make a "things I love about my life" list. Much better to focus on the positive. Colt being one to add a silver lining for sure. And I wish I could add hot sex to my list of positive vibes, but the truth is there isn't any.

How we collided in a heated, lustful moment in the bunker when he kidnapped me has now somehow been put on the back burner. Maybe it has something to do with me being a virgin or Colt's need to provide my future on a silver platter before getting fully invested, whatever; I have no clue.

Colt has these unreadable moments where he seems to be locked in thoughts. As if he suffered through darkness and sometimes still gets caught in it. And I know he has from what his sister has told me and let's face it; not many people decide to live in solitude like he has been doing for quite some years. Shit. Maybe that's it. Me being here, disrupting his serenity puts pressure on him somehow.

Cavier slowly enters the paddock and Colt closes the gate behind him. Needing to settle my rambling thoughts, I blurt, "Has it bothered you to have someone in your space all day every day for the last ten days?"

His eyes go thoughtful. "It should. But you're different."

Colt heads for the cabin and I tag along behind him. When I think over the last few days, I have to admit I don't think that he's lying. He doesn't seem agitated or avoiding me at every turn. He brings me out on the porch at night to enjoy the sunset while sitting together on a crib sized swing bed in silence.

And when you've lived in the city for most of your life there is quite a difference. But the serenity of the sanctum he's created at the edge of the ranch's property is like a little slice of heaven. I haven't missed watching TV for hours or jumping around to get things done.

Dusting or doing the dishes, sweeping the floors…it's…shit, I can hardly say "fun to do," but it really is. Maybe because the cabin isn't overly big, but it might also have to do with the fact it doesn't feel like a chore. There aren't many items in the cabin so it also takes me less time to clean.

And when Colt is doing stuff for the ranch or the MC, either heading out or sitting at the table behind the laptop to enter information or putting the horses up for sale, it allows me the time to read. It's a privilege to be here with him.

A tightness squeezes my chest. It's not only a privilege but a longing too. To have this slice of heaven to last a lifetime. And yet there's fear clawing inside my veins. All of this is almost too good to be true and I'm waiting for it to blow up in my face.

There are too many uncertainties, like the fact Colt hasn't touched me in any way or my brother turning up to drag me to his clubhouse, or Cannon for that matter. Though, I feel Colt and I have grown close over the last couple of days. Spending many hours talking, cooking meals together, him teaching me how to ride a horse.

Cavier is going on my positive vibes list for sure. I love riding and have reached the point where Colt isn't walking beside the horse but is giving me instructions from the middle of the paddock.

I seriously never want to leave this man or his horse. And I dread the day he's either sick of having me around or someone bursts through that door to end the dream I've been living in.

"Hey, why the sad face? You did great with Cavier." Colt turns the oven on where our previously prepared lasagna was waiting for us to bake.

Sad face? I wasn't aware sadness entered my features. All of this is dragging me down. And I've never felt as powerless as I feel now and maybe it's because of all of the uncertainties.

No. It's about the no sex part where I have no clue what Colt is thinking. He was quite clear when he had me in his bed, but those following ten days he has gracefully shared his sheets with me. Correction; he says he's sleeping next to me but there hasn't been one morning where I woke up beside him. And the falling asleep part happens on the couch so he carries me to bed.

My frustrations and doubts have grown and I know this situation isn't how either of us wanted to start out. And we might be getting along now but before he put his plan into motion, we were going head to head on a daily basis. While now all of a sudden, we're like an old married couple. Because while we might have shared comfort between us…the sex is lacking. Completely nonexistent.

"Cavier isn't the problem, I enjoy riding him," I grumble, and add underneath my breath, "It's you who doesn't want to take me for a ride."

"What was that?" Colt snaps.

"What was what, old man?" I snap, irritated by everything.

I stalk to the cabinet to grab two plates but I'm prevented from doing so when Colt's fingers wrap around my upper arm as he spins me around. His large, muscled body is caging me in, pressing me against the counter.

"Old man, huh?" he snaps with a harsh tone. But then his whole face changes and a fat smirk spreads his face. "I am. But I'm your old man."

"My old man?" I snicker. "If I had an old man my body would be aware of that little fact."

His hands leave my arms and are now placed on the counter as he leans in but in no way is the annoying man touching my body. I'm still caged in but everything about that fact leaves me cold.

"Ah. The root of the issue." Leaning closer he whispers next to my ear, "My old lady has needs."

My whole body freezes. Did he call me his old lady? I thought he was joking with the old man comment.

"I thought you needed time." He pushes off the counter and starts to pace the kitchen. "Fuck. I needed time. I've wanted you for so damn long and then to have you…I didn't know if I could handle it long term. And you being a virgin. If I would have crossed that bridge right at the start...if we didn't work out. Hell…if I couldn't handle having you around because I'm no good at this shit, Kadence. I'm not a people person."

"I know!" I snap, a little too agitated by his words and his anxious demeanor.

He takes two fierce steps in my direction. "The time I gave us was too much since I have no damn agitation or breach of privacy feeling when it comes to you. I fucking relish in the knowledge you can't go anywhere but here. One glance and my eyes can find you. The restlessness rooted in my bones faded to the background and I can sleep for hours just by holding you."

I close the distance between us and shove his shoulder. "Yeah? Then how come I never, ever, wake up in your arms or fall asleep in them for that matter?"

His forehead is pressing against mine when he says, "Because I hardly ever slept before you filled my bed. I never need more than a few hours but get double the sleep now so I'm an early riser. I make coffee and watch you sleep."

I jab a finger in his chest to punctuate every word. "Creepy. Fucker."

His head tips back and laughter rips out.

"It's not meant to be funny," I mutter, but am enthralled by the way this man is fully relaxed and offers me a genuine smile, freeing a flock of butterflies inside my belly.

This man has become the center of my world in rapid time and the mere thought of losing him threatens to shatter my heart irreparably.

I swallow hard and ask the very question that can squash my heart underneath the heel of his boot. "Do you still need time?"

"Fuck, no," he growls as his hand flashes out to wrap his fingers around my nape and pull me close to crash our mouths together.

His tongue brushes against mine and all of my earlier insecurities fall away. I guess the both of us were working through personal issues and needed the time to take the next step. I lean against his body and allow the heat of this man to scorch my insides until he sets my soul on fire to merge with his.

Soulmates used to be a mere word to me, but I completely understand it now. When a person's touch can seep through your body the moment of impact, lighting up every nerve ending to heighten the tingles spreading in your veins…I'd say I have found what most romance books write about.

A solid and unique connection. Understanding in more than

just the need for sex or closeness. We have the time behind us to prove there's more than lust, we have a foundation. Shared time is shared feelings which has eventually knocked down our hearts, causing us to simultaneously fall.

He's kissing me as if he is in fact giving me his heart and soul. His hands start to roam and are now on my ass, lifting me up as he walks until he can place my ass on the counter.

I keep my legs around his waist while his hands reach for my shirt and before I can speak up–remembering the last time–he's already gripping the fabric as buttons fly through the air. Some fumbling with my bra is the only hiccup he seems to have to set my breasts free.

His mouth surrounds my nipple, his teeth giving me a sweet erotic bite to make heat flash through my body until it settles between my legs. The throbbing of my pussy intensifies as he starts to suckle.

I can only squirm with pleasure. I swear this man can give me an orgasm just by spending all of his attention on my breasts. Yet, this time, I'm desperate to feel him closer; to feel him inside me.

My fingers pull at his belt in desperation. A growl rumbles through his throat and the man bats my hands away as he takes a step back. I'm about to curse his head off until I realize he's quickly stripping away all his clothes until he's naked in front of me.

He lifts me by my hips and onto my feet. His eyes are pinned on mine as he makes sure every single piece of my clothing ends up on the floor too. The Texas heat thickens the air but the shiver running through me has nothing to do with the temperature in the room but everything to do with the intensity of this man's gaze sliding over my skin.

"So. Damn. Gorgeous. Every inch of you. No matter if you're standing in front of me naked or fully dressed, riding my horse, or reading a book on the couch with your feet up. Watching you sleep in the morning with the settled serenity on your face as you hug my pillow the way you held me all night. Every. Fucking.

Day. And every fucking minute of our time since we changed paths from you being my sister's best friend to you being mine has been eye opening. I thought possibilities of starting a family of my own were a fading opportunity, but you…you set me aflame and cause a light so bright it eats away the darkness and gives me a glimpse of a shared future. Mag-fucking-nificent. That's you. In every damn way."

I'm still blinking and processing his words when his hands are once again on my waist to hoist me up and place my naked ass on the counter. He lifts my foot to spread me open as he places my heel on the edge.

Even as I see his mouth closing in on my pussy, there's no way my brain can process the instant pleasure and the visual to go with it. My head falls back and a low moan falls from my lips.

His tongue slides through my folds, flipping my clit, and moving to suckle on one of the lips of my pussy. The man knows how to bring me to the edge, and when I'm allowed to tip over and drown in a blissful orgasm. And it doesn't take long until he gives me what my body craves.

This time our eyes stay locked, a rumble of words vibrate against me when he grunts, "Come for me, Kadence. Let me taste your pleasure."

He shakes his head, his beard heightening the friction, pushing me over to surrender to the orgasm he grants me. His name falls from my lips in half a moan, half a plea for more. And I take my time to ride all the waves of pleasure. He slowly stands and crushes his mouth against mine.

I'm too wrapped up in the cloud of bliss he's created to care enough about the fact I'm tasting myself on his tongue. All because the pad of his finger is drawing small circles against my clit.

My pussy clenches when I feel the hot, blunt head of his dick nudge at my entrance. I might need to brace myself for the moment he surges inside me. Though, to my surprise, he's all tender with a passionate kiss, softly strumming my clit to keep the fire burning in my pussy while he slowly stretches me with every soft thrust forward.

A pinch on my nipple, his teeth sinking into my bottom lip, his growls, the gentleness of a slow retreat and filling me up again...it's everything that makes me plead, whimper, beg, anything to make him hurry to fill me completely.

The moment his hands grip my hips is when he slams deep inside me. A scream rips from my throat before I fall forward and sink my teeth into his shoulder to muffle my loud burst of discomfort.

His lips brush my ear. "If there ever was a place to call home and live in that place forever, this would be it."

Colt's breaths–like mine–come out in rough pants, as if it takes everything inside him to stay in place. The pain slightly fades and I feel his dick twitch inside me.

"You can...you can move now," I croak.

He pulls his head back to take in my face and after a few seconds he seems satisfied with what he sees because he connects our foreheads and pulls out until only the tip is being sucked back inside before he slides right back in.

A few more times starts a low burning sensation enough for me to meet his thrusts and let my nails rake over his back, urging him on. His hips pick up speed and force. The grunts slipping over his lips while his fingers dig into my skin almost feels like an animalistic, dominant, and possessive chase to make sure I'm his.

But there's no doubt in either of us. Not when he buries himself deep inside me at the same time stars appear in my vision, throwing me into a sea of pleasure only this man has been able to give me.

His dick lengthens and jerks inside me, warmth spreading everywhere while my name is being voiced with such tenderness and awe, my heart unfolds and accepts this man to his fullest.

The fingers gripping my hips loosen and slide around my waist. Colt lifts me off the counter and takes a few steps to sit down on one of the kitchen chairs, making me straddle him.

"So. Fucking. Good. But I'm going to need a minute to catch

my breath. Damn, woman. I don't think I've ever had the energy sucked right out of me."

A giggle escapes me and Colt's laughter fills the air along with it. I release a deep sigh of contentment.

"It's all systems go from now on. No holding back. Understood?" Colt says, all laughter has faded from his voice.

"The old lady thing? Oh. God. Condom. I'm not on the pill. Shit, Colt. Sorry. I didn't think but I haven't been able to take the pill ever since I ran, that's weeks ago. I'm not protected against pregnancy anymore."

Colt simply shrugs. "Like I said, all systems go. I have enough money for a large family. We have a roof above our heads with lots of space and a brotherhood at our backs. Starting a family sooner rather than later is fine by me. Unless you don't welcome any kids."

"I do. But–"

He cuts me off by telling me, "The situation you're in will be handled, doll. Don't worry about it."

Don't worry about it. Right. As if that's possible.

CHAPTER 05

COLT

I've roamed around for years in this fucked-up world. Seen with my own eyes how people slaughter one another for reasons unknown, or simply follow orders because you've been sent oversees to fight for your country.

It fucked my head up and made me distance myself from people due to the constant darkness absorbing my thoughts. Nonstop fighting my sorrows and falling asleep for an hour or two before waking up in a cold sweat.

I'm absolutely stunned to say those days are over. The darkness roaming around in my head is by no means completely gone, but it's somewhat subdued. And holding my woman at night–her warmth seeping into me–allows my whole being the level of calmness I need to sleep for a few hours on end. Waking up each day feeling refreshed is a new phenomenon and I owe it all to her.

I'm leaning against the doorjamb, sipping my first cup of coffee, on this early morning. Kadence is still sleeping, curled up in the blankets and looking ever so stunning with her dark red hair spread out over her pillow.

A hint of her curvy ass is exposed but the rest of her delicious body is covered. My cock twitches with the reminder of being buried deep inside her. Another element this woman has brought into my life; the craving of never having enough of something so damn sweet.

My phone indicates a message and when I check I see it's a text from Weston. He needs me and Kadence in church around ten. We've had a few meetings over the last few days and while I was the one who set a plan into motion, it's Weston, Roper, and Alfie who have taken over.

I don't mind since it gives me the room to spend more time with my woman. Teaching her how to ride has been rewarding for the both of us and it's another shared passion between us. We match in every way and even if I held her at a distance for so long because I'm eight years older than her, it's all moot now.

There's simply no stopping what's meant to be. And that's just it. There's also no stopping to face the issue that's still preventing us from roaming around freely. But Alfie informed me yesterday how Weston has taken steps to put it all behind us.

Seeing as the both of us are needed in church later, I'd say we're done hiding and everyone will now see, and know, Kadence is right where she belongs; by my side. I mentally cringe when I think about facing my sister, Kadence's best friend.

She's going to be pissed we withheld the fact that Kadence has been with me all along. Even though it was done for the safety of all of us, she wouldn't care. But I'm hoping the whole claiming my woman and making them sisters-in-law part will smooth things over.

"Hey," Kadence croaks. "Got any coffee for me?"

I push away from the doorjamb and stalk to the bed to place a kiss on her forehead. "Coming right up. Meet me in the kitchen when you're dressed. We're heading to the clubhouse in a few hours."

"We are?" she asks in surprise.

"I just received a text from Weston that our presence is requested. You get to see my sister and roam around the ranch since the cat will be out of the bag today. And thank fuck. You can come with me when I'm training the other horses and help Mayven out with her lunch packages and so on."

Her whole face lights up and it makes my chest fill with gratitude over the fact that this woman is all mine and is already connected with the things involving my life.

"Go, go, go. I need coffee. I'm diving into the bathroom to grab a quick shower and I'll be in the kitchen within five minutes." She waves her hands to urge me on and adds, "Go!"

A chuckle slips over my lips. "Excited much?"

"Uhm, yes! I'm going to see Mayven, Harlene, Muriel, Cassidy, and Joaquin." She throws me another beaming smile as she heads for the bathroom.

Her smile is infectious as she recites the names of all the old ladies of this MC. Well, Joaquin isn't an old lady, though in some way he belongs to Alfie. If he ever gets his shit in order.

Emotions are a funny thing and if I think my head is messed up, Alfie clearly has some issues of his own to work through. One being his possessive claim on Joaquin but needing a woman in between them to share and make his life complete.

I'm not a person who people seek out to have a heart to heart talk with, sharing feelings and shit. But Alfie has his way of springing stuff on you without leaving a choice to refuse. It's how I know these two have finally talked through their feelings and are now somewhat together but are searching for the right woman to make their relationship complete.

And knowing how unique one woman is to flawlessly fit in my life, and how damn special it is to find the right person…I can only imagine how damn hard it would be to find the right woman for two dudes. Yeah, talk about complications.

Kadence wasn't kidding when she said she'd be in the kitchen within five minutes. She's showered and dressed and sipping her coffee while following me into the backyard as I head for the stable to put Cavier in the paddock before we head out to the clubhouse earlier than planned.

The ride is way too short and I make a mental note to take her for a ride very soon because having her on the back of my bike, pressed tight against me, is another way to soothe the darkness in my head. Wind slapping around us, the scenery a colorful hint of life flashing by, and the road ahead of us which is never-ending. Fucking perfect.

Kicking the kickstand, I throw my leg over the bike and take the helmet Kadence hands me. She's practically jumping up and down with a boost of excitement. All while I'm on edge to get this over with. I have no idea what Weston's plan is or what we're doing here.

He's been the president of this MC for many years. Never one bad decision in my mind and he's led us from dirty shit into running this ranch fully on legal grounds. It's also why I feel some regret by dragging a possible threat to this MC.

We've all worked hard to keep out of the eye of the law and left danger behind us now that most of my brothers have started a family, kids roaming around, and they come first. And we've already upped the level of protection and loyalty this brotherhood consists of.

Hell, coming bare inside my woman was the best feeling ever, and the mere thought of getting her pregnant is a welcome possibility. I'm not getting any younger and there's no doubt in my head; Kadence is the one I want to spend the rest of my life with while expanding it to our full capability.

I lace our fingers and kiss the beaming smile plastered on her face. "I fucking adore you, woman," I murmur.

Her breath rushes out and she replies with so much happiness lacing her words. "And I fucking adore you right back."

Wrapped in a bubble of adoration we face the clubhouse, only to have our bubble roughly popped by the sights of Rowen and his VP, Koda, standing right next to Weston.

"No," Kadence gasps and the look she gives me is one where she thinks I brought her to the slaughterhouse my-fucking-self.

"I didn't know. Get behind me," I snap and quickly move her

behind me myself.

Reaching for my gun, I growl, "She's my old lady and she's staying right fucking here."

"Tone it down, Colt," Weston says. "Rowen agreed to your offer. Well, with a slight change but the result is the same. Kadence, as your old lady, is under the protection of the Iron Hot Blood."

I'm itching to know what the slight change involves but if Weston set this up—along with the statement he just made how Kadence is in fact mine—who fucking cares?

"Need us for anything else, Prez?" I question, needing to get my woman out of here.

Weston throws his thumb over his shoulder. "Head inside the clubhouse, we need to have a little chat."

I reach behind me and wrap an arm around my woman's waist to drag her close as we head for the clubhouse.

"Kadence, a word, please," her brother says.

I'm about to deny the asshole but Kadence says in an icy voice, "Fuck you, Rowen. You're dead to me."

Rowen's eyes carry sadness for a brief moment before it's gone. I shouldn't be intrigued but I find myself asking, "Prez, are the old ladies inside?"

Weston nods. "Harlene and Mayven, the rest will be here within a half hour."

I place a kiss on the top of her head and whisper, "Go inside, doll. I'll be right there."

She glares at her brother but disappears inside. I spin on my heels and face Rowen who is still standing right next to his VP.

"You and I, a word," I sneer and don't wait but stalk a few feet away from the clubhouse.

Rowen saunters my way and crosses his arms in front of his chest when he reaches me. "You're my sister's old man now?"

"She's always been mine," I simply state.

I would like nothing more than to bury my fist into his throat and keep hitting the fucker until he's no longer breathing, but this asshole is my woman's brother. No matter how angry she is at the idiot or the fact she just stated he's dead to her.

"All I wanted was for her to be kept safe and protected. With our folks both dead she had no reason to stay connected, and you and I damn well know you can't cut out a connection if you were once the president's daughter…and now the president's sister. Making her an old lady would have kept her close and protected. Cannon has always shown interest in her, it seemed like a good choice."

Fuck. He's right and yet so damn wrong. And Cannon was never a good fucking choice.

But in the end, it doesn't matter. "Sounds like your wish was still granted. She's my old lady and with it she's protected. I would say you can have some form of contact, but she's pretty pissed and hardheaded. You blew your chance of gaining her trust and maintaining a connection."

"Cannon seemed like the right choice: he's always wanted her," Rowen repeats and rubs the back of his neck and sighs.

"Always wanted to rape her you mean." I whisper the words low enough for only his ears.

His eyes flame with hatred. "What?" he snaps.

"Didn't know that little fact, huh? Not to mention, the fucker was the one who led those two idiots right to her a few weeks ago. She could have died that day when they came at us with guns blazing. My sister was there too and her old man. That's the kind of fuck-up you wanted for your sister? Your sister who has every reason to say her brother wanted to whore her out to one of his brothers. Did you ever fucking put yourself in her shoes, asshole?" My chest is heaving and it's fucked-up because I can always contain my emotions but I seem to fail when anger surges through me at the thought of what my woman had to endure.

Rowen nods. He looks defeated and deep in thoughts.

I should walk away but I surprise myself when I tell him, "I have your number. I'll be sure to text you pictures when our first kid is born and any others after that. Do you understand? She's mine. For-fucking-ever. No one will harm her or so much as make her feel like an object needing to be tossed around to be displayed since it would fit somewhere else better. For fuck's sake, man. What the hell were you thinking?"

I don't wait for an answer. I couldn't care less. But I probably shouldn't have risked one final glance at his eyes because they are filled with pain.

"Take care of her." His words trail behind me.

I raise my hand and give him a one finger salute. "A million times better than you did, that's for damn sure."

I would like to add the fact that this woman is mine to damn treasure, something no money in the world can buy. And when you realize you actually love someone it's then you understand the value of having something precious in your life.

But it leaves a bad taste in my damn mouth about the fact Rowen accepted the deal. Meaning he took the money and the property I told Weston to offer him in exchange for Deranged Hounds to fuck off and leave Kadence alone. Weston mentioned there was a slight change in the deal and I'm itching to find out what the change was.

First, I need my woman in my arms so I can breathe her in to obtain some sense of calmness. Stalking into the main room, I quickly scan my surroundings and see Kadence sitting at a table along with some of the women and Joaquin. With determination I close the distance and drag her into my arms to kiss the fuck out of her.

When the both of us come up for air, I nuzzle her neck and murmur, "You good?"

"Yeah," she sighs in contentment.

A little thrill flows through me and I pull back to cup her face and lock our eyes. "Stay with your friends, I'll be right back. I need to have a word with Weston, okay?"

Thank fuck the smile is back on her face and she rejoins the women. I turn to head for church but my sister is right in my face. I expect her to blow up about the fact I took her friend and withheld information–leaving her to worry about Kadence–but instead she launches herself at me to hug me close.

"Thank you so much," she gushes.

I wrap my arms around Mayven and hug her tight. I'm not much of a hugger and she knows it too. Add the fact I expected her to blow up and rip my head off, I'll take the hug any time of day.

I place a kiss on the top of her head. "You're welcome. Now go plan a wedding or something, I need to talk to Prez."

"You're getting married?" Mayven squeaks, making all heads turn our way.

I shoot her a grin and simply say, "I ain't letting her go, sis. Not ever. So, we might as well get hitched since she's already my old lady. And I'm set to knock her up some time soon."

"You're horrible," she grumbles, her eyes going to Kadence who is staring at us in shock. "You should have proposed in a normal way instead of throwing it out as if it's another thing to tick off your to-do list."

"Fuck normal," I mutter and head for church.

"Asshole," Mayven bellows.

"Ah, there's the anger I was expecting when I walked in here, sis. Good to know you don't disappoint."

She grumbles a string of curses but I'm already closing the door behind me. Alfie, Garrett, Ledger, and Roper are sitting at the table. The door behind me opens and Weston stalks inside.

"What a fucked-up situation," Weston says as he takes a seat.

"What part of the deal was changed?" I ask, needing to know every damn detail.

Roper throws a file on the table in front of me. "He didn't want the property you offered."

"Dammit. Why? They are about to be evicted, why turn down the property that could be a potential clubhouse?" I wonder out loud.

"Something about the location and space. They have issues with another MC and the property is close to a bar some of those fuckers hang out at. Rowen doesn't need the extra pressure. But Alfie gave him another option and he gladly accepted. They will sign the papers tomorrow, bright and early."

I nod in understanding of what Weston just explained.

"Rowen needs to pay that fucking dollar," Alfie snaps. "And you owe me, man."

"He's buying the property for a dollar?" I question.

Alfie shrugs. "We have it in black and white his MC will back off, and gave the well wishes to the happy couple and shit. Shit. We should have asked for him to make a video when he tells Cannon the joyful news."

"I hope he fucking chokes on it," I mutter.

Weston's face turns grim. "He might have mentioned Cannon wouldn't back away easily. But Rowen would handle it. Even if it meant killing the fucker. He was honorable, Colt. Once we told him what was going on between you and his sister. Rowen respects Kadence's choice and would have accepted if he knew, without the damn money offer but we put that shit on the table before we mentioned you claimed his sister as his old lady. So, the fucker got the money as a bonus."

"I don't care about the fucking money. Rowen should have killed the fucker the second he wanted my woman. He was blind not to see what kind of fucking idiot Cannon is," I snap.

"Calm down, Colt. Everything is handled for now, okay?" Roper shoots me a look of warning.

I hold my hands up. "Hey, I'm done. If you guys say it's handled, it's handled. We can move forward, no danger and shit."

"Why the hell did you need to jinx us with the 'no danger and shit?' You should never voice such things, asshole," Garrett grumbles. "Rowen still needs to bring the news to his club and control Cannon."

I merely shrug and glance at Alfie. "Let me know what you paid for the property you're selling to Rowen for one dollar. I'll make sure you'll get it in the next few days."

Alfie is now the one to shrug. "Don't mention it, we're good."

"We're good if I pay you. Text me or I won't stop nagging you until we're even."

"Fine." Alfie grins. "Three dollars."

"Fucking rich asshole motherfucker," I grumble and turn on my heels to leave the room. I have better things to do than being around these idiots.

Though I'm wearing a huge smile on my face, knowing these fuckers always have my back and made it possible to bury the past and spread the future wide open for me and my old lady.

CHAPTER 06

KADENCE

"Where are you taking me?" I ask with laughter in my voice since Colt is dragging me out of the clubhouse when we only just got here.

"I can finally show you something. I swear you can spend some time later with your friends but I have a surprise I've been working on."

A surprise? I keep my lips shut before I start to fire question after question. I won't be able to stop. Seriously, whenever my mother would buy me a gift I would harass her until I knew what it was or she would simply give it to me. I know, I'm horrible that way, but I'm just overly excited.

And along with the joy comes the sadness, hitting me straight in the chest. I miss my mother and father. Some days I still can't believe I can't pick up the phone and call them. They're really gone. It's another harsh realization how you can never take anything for granted.

The only family I have left by blood is my asshole brother.

And I have no need to see him. Besides, I have a load of new people surrounding me who have accepted and welcomed me with open arms.

Even if I brought trouble to their doorstep, there's not one single evil eye or rejection. That's a brotherhood. Blood or no blood, it's a true meaning of family. Every single one lets you know the important things in life and has their priorities straight.

It's one of the first things I noticed when I arrived here weeks ago. And it was a welcoming realization when I stepped foot inside the clubhouse a moment ago. The support of everyone is overwhelming.

"What are we doing in the stables? What could you possibly have hidden here to surprise me with?" I question, failing to keep quiet and wanting to get my head in the here and now to prevent myself from being sad.

Colt stops in front of a stall where a gorgeous deep brown horse with large white spots is standing.

"This here is Chucky. She's an American Paint Horse. A breed that fits you perfectly. She's twelve. No longer a rookie and I've ridden her a few times this week to get to know her since she used to belong to Alfie. She deserves more attention than he can give her but Alfie has three horses and he wanted to keep a new one he's breaking in now. I knew she'd be perfect for you and Alfie agreed. Otherwise he wouldn't have sold her."

"She's mine?" I croak, tears filling my eyes and I am grasping every bit of strength inside me to keep it together.

But I'm failing when I hear a sob, knowing it just ripped from my throat.

"Aw, dammit, sweetness. I didn't mean to make you cry," Colt mutters and takes me into his arms.

Maybe it's the overload of stress causing me to fall apart, or remembering my parents, or because a mere moment ago we heard the threat of my brother and Cannon has been handled. Whatever. The point is…I want to feel overjoyed with happiness. And I'm allowed to because in this moment I am wrapped in the embrace of a man who cared enough to kidnap me to keep my ass safe.

On top of it he's given me so much more than just safety or as he stated it when he gave me the choice of his help; wait for me if you want to change your life. Clearly the wait is over because this man has drastically changed my life and I can't imagine it any other way.

"Aw, she liked Chucky, didn't she? All sentimental and shit," Alfie says from behind us. "You better take good care of that little bundle of goodness. And I do mean the horse, not your old lady. Okay, clearly her too, whatever. You did mention about her mouth, did you?"

"I haven't had the chance yet, Alfie," Colt grumbles.

"What about her mouth?" I question.

Alfie steps closer and opens Chucky's stable. "She's too sensitive for a bit. It's why I only ride with her using a hackamore, the headgear uses a noseband to control the horse. But she's a real sweetheart and perfect for a beginner like you."

"Thank you," I croak and throw my arms around his waist to give him a hug.

It only lasts a fragment of a second before I'm pulled away.

"Yeah, not happening," Colt grumbles. "He's selling us the horse because he knows she's staying here on the ranch and will be well looked after. Not to mention, you're going to be riding her every day so she will get more attention."

"I could still need a hug for it, brother." Alfie grins.

"Like I said, not happening. Not from me and not from my old lady since you swing both ways. Go hug Joaquin and squash some chick in between."

I plant my elbow in Colt's ribs.

"Be nice," I tell him in a firm tone.

"I was being nice to suggest he go have a threesome instead of getting a hug from either of us," Colt grumbles.

"I could settle for you two hugging while I watch. But no tears this time. I hate it when people cry, it makes me uncomfortable."

"It's because you have no feelings, asshole." There's a low

rumble coming from Colt's chest before he adds, "Go watch Joaquin hug someone, weirdo."

Alfie places his hand over his heart. "I do have feelings. I have many." His hand starts to slide down to his crotch. "Especially when I grab–"

"We don't want to hear it. So, leave us alone. We're going to take Chucky home with us."

Alfie laughs. "Fine. Want me to bring your bike over later?"

"Yeah, thanks. Why don't you bring Joaquin along with you? Ledger and Mayven are coming by later too. We're gonna grill a few steaks, hamburgers, whatever."

"Will do." Alfie points at Chucky. "Take good care of her for me."

I give him a genuine smile and promise, "Absolutely. I already love her to pieces."

Alfie snickers. "No wonder you're with Colt. I was kinda worried with him not being loveable with his grumpiness, but I get it now. You fall in love that easy and all."

"Get the fuck out of here, Alfie," Colt snaps.

"Just kidding, grumpy." Alfie laughs as he stalks out of the stables.

"Come on, let's saddle up and bring her home."

I nod enthusiastically at his words and the both of us fall into a routine like we've done every day with Cavier whenever Colt had time to teach me how to ride.

We've almost reached the cabin when Colt asks, "Like her?"

"Love her," I tell him and look down at Colt but his eyes are set on the cabin in front of us.

We might have exchanged our feelings, but with Alfie mentioning how I fall in love easily, he made me think. Yes, I might fall in love easily when it came to the horse, but it was the same with Colt.

I thought he was extremely sexy the first time I met him and the attraction only intensified until it evolved into a solid bond between us. So, yes. It might be hard and fast, but it's real and something I haven't experienced before. And the way he takes care of me and goes through great lengths to make sure I'm okay and safe, I know we're equal in our relationship; it's where our strength lies.

I take a deep breath and let my gaze lock on our home as I voice the words, "I love you more, though."

A soft chuckle rings out and I feel him pat my leg. "I sure as fuck would hope so."

He didn't say it back is the first thing flowing through my head.

But then he stops the horse and says, "Come here, doll."

He curls his finger, demanding I lean over to close the distance. And when I do, he places his hand on the back of my neck and gives a tender squeeze before he takes my lips in a rough and demanding kiss.

He pulls back and tells me, "I'm pretty sure I love you more."

Colt is already taking the reign and leads Chucky around the cabin toward the stable while all I can do is stare at the man I know is mine in every way. It's still hard to believe–to accept–our future has only just blown wide open for us to explore and enjoy.

Cavier starts to neigh and Chucky gives a response. Colt chuckles. "In a moment, boys, you get to play."

"She's a girl," I scold, and Colt simply chuckles again as I dismount.

A few minutes later Chucky is in the paddock and both horses are running and making sharp turns to follow one another.

Leaning on the fence, I sigh and say, "I could watch them for hours."

"Cavier has been alone for a long time, but it seems he enjoys the company of a pretty lady."

A smile spreads across my face and when I turn my head, I realize Colt is watching me instead of the two horses.

"I guess he's the same as his owner." I step closer and lean my head on his shoulder.

His arm sneaks around my waist and pulls me closer. "You've brightened my life for sure, doll. I guess time has come for the both of us to shift gears and hit the throttle for better things."

"Is that why you've invited people here? I know you're normally the other way, keeping people away from this place."

I feel his body tighten and a grunt leaves his throat.

Lifting my head, I need to know. "What's wrong?"

A deep sigh slips over his lips as he steps away and points at the veggie garden. "Let's grab some tomatoes and get things started for our guests. They will be here soon enough."

I'm staring at his back as he heads for the tomatoes but my anger is suddenly rising; I know he's keeping something from me. It's the same reaction he gave when I questioned his grim face when he received a text right before we headed for the cabin. He simply said Garrett would be joining us for dinner later.

"Okay, buddy. Start talking. I know you won't lie but I also know you shutting down and not telling me shit means something is up and you refuse to let me get involved. Newsflash, asshole. We're together and this means we share. Good and bad. I thought this whole shitstorm we went through these past few weeks made that very clear."

"Shitstorms have aftereffects. True survival means balancing to keep your head above water and not letting anything scare you, not even fear itself. But I've also never had something clawing at my chest, and I know for fucking sure it's because I've never had an old lady. Something completing my life and losing it means the end of life as I love and now know what it was meant to be. So, precaution is what I'm going for. Eyes open, ears sharp, doll. Hence the visitors to soothe my worries and have some added bodies around us just in case."

I know he's right. And I might have been swooning over the fact my life changed for the better and how bad times are behind us, but I also know very well things can turn to shit in the blink of an eye.

And a cautious person is stronger than a careless one. And I also know not to let anything consume you and I trust Colt to handle this part for the both of us. It's been only a few hours since my brother accepted my future and I'm sure he needs to inform some of his guys who weren't at the meeting he just had with Weston.

And with Cannon forcing himself upon me a few times, it's not hard to realize how he will react when my brother tells him I'm never going to be his. This has to be the aftereffect of the shitstorm Colt just mentioned.

Letting my rambling thoughts go, I try to shift topics and ask, "So, we're getting married, huh?"

"I plan to knock you up, hopefully before we're married. Everything between us is a done deal, Kadence. Signing papers and make things official is just ticking another box off the list I have in my mind to make sure you're taken care of. If something happens to me…everything you see will be yours."

Crap. Here I thought to make light of things while I get some hard chunks of emotion thrown back. And it should warm my heart but I feel conflicted. Not to mention he's acting like he's going to expel his last breath sometime soon.

"What else is on that list of yours? Next to starting a family, getting hitched, and dying?"

Colt spins around to face me. "You're pissed."

A statement, not a question. Jeez, he's a real winner. I should give him a beer to toast his words of success.

"I plan, Kadence." There isn't a hint of anger in his voice, but a hint of vulnerability instead. "I'm not a young foal darting around on this fucked-up planet. I know what I want and how it needs to be in some form of timeframe because when I want something, I crave to follow through. And with you I want everything. Except for the dying part, that for sure as fuck isn't on my list."

Clearly, we're still exploring one another and more of our quirks and character traits will rise as we move forward. I know Colt has held off about us being together because of the eight-year age gap. But there's more to life than the little more than a handful of years in between us.

Yes, he might be more of a planner, something I never once tried or thought about. But it doesn't mean I won't follow his lead. He might be the one taking the next step forward but it's made with determination and absorbed with the thoughts for the both of us.

"Make sure it stays off the damn list and we will get along just fine," I mutter and try to stalk past him but he grabs my waist and drags me against his body.

My back is plastered against his front while his head falls to the crook of my neck to nuzzle my skin.

"Always ready to fight, but so fucking cute with acceptance. Your whole appearance and background screams recklessness. Yet, you have your eyes wide open, and one hell of a brain that's always crackling before settling. You're a brilliant woman I'm proud to call mine, doll. Just know everything I do will always be done for your safety and well-being."

I should swoon but his words make my skin prickle with awareness. Safety and well-being. Is there still danger I'm not aware of besides Cannon? I'm about to question him but the kisses along the line of my neck are very distracting.

"Screw dinner preparations," Colt says, his voice husky and laced with desire.

His fingers slide into my hair and he tightens his hand into a fist, giving me a bite of erotic pain. A gasp parts my lips. Lips he greedily covers with his own, diving his tongue into my mouth in search of mine.

Without breaking the kiss, he spins my body and grabs my ass. This man's hands roaming my body spurs my inner sex kitten to purr with delight. He breaks the kiss, snatches my wrist, and drags me off toward the cabin. Once inside he heads straight for the bedroom.

His fingers glide over the fabric of my shirt, pulling at the hem and lifting it over my head. We peel away the layers of clothing until everything is scattered around us on the floor. This man with his hair tied back, thick muscles ripping his body with strength is breathtaking.

His inked sleeves and chest make my mouth water and I know I will make time in the near future to trace every line with my tongue. I reach forward and wrap my fingers around his thick girth.

He's hard and there are veins wrapping around his length, pulsing and hot in my palm. The thick red tip is glistening from precum leaking from his slit. I rub my thumb over it and bring the digit to my mouth to taste him.

"Fucking hell, woman," he growls in a guttural tone.

I keep my eyes pinned on his when I sink to my knees in front of him. Guiding his dick, I part my lips and suck him into my mouth, earning another growl in reply. His hands slide into my hair, tightening to grip my head as he pulls me forward and rocks his hips to take control as he starts to fuck my mouth.

My pussy clenches as lust rises. Dammit, this man is everything and in this moment I gladly hand over my heart and soul because the way his eyes are staring down on me makes me aware I already own all of him in return.

CHAPTER 07

COLT

This woman stole my heart but when I glance down to see her take my cock into her mouth as she stares up at me in adoration and lust? Fan-fucking-tastic. Earthshattering and soul-scorching.

She's all mine and the trust she easily hands over as I take her head and start to thrust in her mouth is overwhelming. The tingle rises at the bottom of my spine. She just started sucking cock and yet I'm ready to blow from the mere heat and vision.

I'm debating pulling out because I want my cum coating her insides as I take her sweet pussy again, but there's no time. All that's left is surrendering to bliss as my cock thickens a fragment more before it starts to pulse and I shoot my cum down her throat without warning.

A guttural groan rips from my chest and in response she moans around my cock. I watch how her body trembles as she swallows down my cum and the way her eyes fall shut? I just know my woman had a damn orgasm sucking me off.

I repeat; fan-fucking-tastic.

Taking a step back I let my cock fall from her mouth and quickly hoist her up by the arms. I slam my lips over hers and plunge my tongue inside. Her hands roam my body and the way she drags her nails over my back reminds me of the same desperation of lust I saw in her eyes right before she got the both of us off.

That reminds me. I end the kiss and growl, "I need to taste that sweet pussy. You got yourself off, didn't you? Did you rub that little bundle of nerves while I held your head and fucked your mouth? You had your hands free. You did, didn't you?"

A husky smirk slips over her face as she walks back to the bed until it hits the back of her knees. She lets herself fall back... and fuck me...her hand slides over her pussy and she starts to rub her clit while the fingers of her other hand start to pump in and out of her slick pussy.

My cock twitches and starts to harden while I watch, enthralled by her skills. She might have been a virgin, my cock being the first one to take her, but it's very clear she knows exactly how to pleasure herself.

I palm my cock and start to stroke and squeeze. Stepping closer to the bed, I place a knee on the mattress. Her gaze is heated and locked on where I'm gripping myself. She won't be for long, though. I press my cock into the sheets and let myself drop to my forearms for a personal show up close of my favorite place on this planet.

Pink, puffy, and glistening. Her arousal is wafting around me and I'm unable to hold back. Her fingers are still inside her as I flatten my tongue and lick her from ass to clit. The little gasp followed by a needy moan goes straight to my balls.

Hell, I just came but I'm ready to hit her with another load of cum. Not yet. First, I need her to orgasm on my tongue before I let her pussy squeeze my cock with another rippling bliss for the both of us.

Fingers pumping in and out are blocking me from more of her deliciousness. A growl rumbles low in my chest as I flash up, grab both of her wrists and drag them underneath her ass. This allows two things to happen at once; her pussy to rise and her hands contained, putting her completely at my mercy.

Her legs are draped over my upper arms and the sight of her pussy spread open in front of me is a sight to behold. Unable to resist I lean forward and slide my tongue through her folds. I let my teeth graze her clit and right after cover the bundle of nerves to give it a full assault of sucking and flicking it with my tongue.

Her whimpers and breathy moans are rapidly filling the air, followed by, "Oh God, Colt! Yes. Shit. Fuck. Oh God."

Yeah, my woman isn't ashamed to ramble and scream out how I affect her body. Her taste intensifies and my name is moaned loud as she shatters in my hold. I let go of her wrists to grip her hips and press my face tighter against her pussy to lick away the remainders of her orgasm.

Her fingers are now tightening in my hair in desperation to either push me away or drag me closer, the way she's gripping me I have no clue. It must be because I'm teasing her swollen clit with my tongue and the little bundle is highly sensitive.

My cock is harder than it's ever been and I decide it's time to change things up. Getting to my knees, I easily flip her over onto her hands and knees. I grip her hips and make sure her ass is high up in the air, placing my palm between her shoulder blades to push her upper body into the mattress.

Sitting back, I take in the beauty spread out in front of me. Damn, what a magnificent ass. Unable to resist I lean forward and lick from clit to ass, letting my tongue tease her little hole. And the gasp of surprise is evident.

Though when she moans and presses back, I know for sure my woman is up for anything I have in mind. And there's a lot of dirty things I want to do with her and every single thing revolves around pleasuring her while getting my very own twisted fantasies soothed.

I grip her ass cheeks and spread them. The glistening mirage is making my cock twitch. Letting go of one cheek, I palm myself and let the thick head slide through her folds to coat it with her slickness.

Slowly pushing inside her pussy with gentle thrusts I try to pace myself, but my woman has other ideas when she slams back and impales herself fully. Fuck. I hiss through my teeth and let myself fall forward, placing a hand next to her head.

"Fuck, woman," I growl.

She moans in response. Fucking minx. Here I thought I needed to hold back a little since she's inexperienced but it seems she likes to dive in full force. And I should have known because this woman is all about dive in first, think later.

Regaining control has me lifting up while taking her wrists again, placing them in one of my hands on her lower back. And to make sure she stays in place I grip her shoulder and start to pound my cock deep in and out of her pussy. My balls curl around her clit with each thrust.

My grunts mingle with her gasps as her pussy clenches around my cock. Keeping her restrained as I tunnel through lust and haze. Thank fuck I already came once so I can last a little longer, but the tightness of her pussy rippling in a pending orgasm has me lifting my hand from her shoulder and heading for her ass.

My thumb strokes her tight ring, dipping down to where we're connected to lube it up. Her hands start to pull at my restraint but I tighten my hold as my thumb breaches her little asshole. My cock keeps pounding inside her pussy and through the thin layer I can feel myself inside her.

"Oh, fuck...oh...I'm gonna...oh..." Moans of pleasure are loud when she comes beautifully around my cock while I claim each and every inch of her body.

I let my thumb slide out, set her wrists free, and grip her lush hips to roughly fuck her until my balls draw up and cum rips from my cock in fast jets to brand her pussy all over as mine, and only mine.

I whisper her name as a silent plea, falling forward and unable to catch my weight. A grunt leaves her but she doesn't complain at all. I take a few harsh breaths before I can roll off, regretfully sliding out of her. Reaching for my woman I drag her close and drape her over my chest.

Both our hearts pound in sync as we try to catch our breaths. Lying on my bed, Kadence close, and our bodies well sated and slick with sweat is a moment in life which allows me to live in the moment and realize it doesn't get any better than this.

Hell, if it were only a fragment of what we have I would be a lucky man. But the way we fit is a match made in heaven on this fucked-up Earth.

I kiss the top of her head and regretfully murmur, "We have to get up. Visitors are about to arrive within…fuck. I have no idea. I lost track of time."

Her giggle spreads over my slick skin and causes an electric current to slide through my body. This woman. So damn perfect and my cock twitches with interest. No way am I able to start back up where we left off but the fucker sure has the thought of doing just that. It only proves I won't ever get enough of her.

She releases a deep breath and slides off me, pulling on my hand to tug me along. "Come on, shower time."

Hmmm. Shower. Now that does give some options to get my hands on her body. Knocking on the front door blows that thought to shit.

"Dammit. You go ahead, doll," I tell her and kiss the top of her head. "I'll handle our guests so you can get ready."

She rises up on her tiptoes to place a teasing kiss on my lips before dashing away into the bathroom. I watch as her curvy ass sways, but I am rudely ripped from my vision as the door closes and the pounding on the front door starts up again.

"I'm coming," I bellow and reach for my jeans.

Dressing quickly, I head for the door with newfound strength inside me. I feel lighter and my head is filled with new goals and plans, breathing in life itself and it's all because of the woman who completes me.

Alfie and Joaquin stroll inside as I head for the kitchen. "Make yourself at home, I have to get things set. Ledger and Mayven will be here soon. Garrett too."

"I might have invited Roper and Cassidy." Alfie grins.

"I think I heard Weston and Harlene were heading this way too," Joaquin quips.

The door swings open and Decker and Muriel stroll inside.

"For fuck's sake," I grumble. "Why are y'all coming here? We should have held a damn barbeque at the clubhouse."

Alfie snickers. "Dude, it's not every day you open your crib to people. Besides, we know how good your steaks taste."

Kadence strolls into the living room. There's a beaming smile on her face and her hair is pulled into a high ponytail.

"Hey, everyone. Head into the garden and have a seat, I'll be right out and bring refreshments in a sec," my woman says and strolls up to me.

She takes my hand and pulls me into the kitchen. "Can you grab some of the meat? I'll start the salad and put some bread in the oven after I've asked them what they would like to drink."

I respond by taking her mouth in a kiss. "Thank you," I murmur against her lips.

"What for?" she asks, a dazed look on her face.

"For being you," I tell her and kiss her nose.

I head for the fridge and hear her sigh in contentment, watching her ass sway out of the kitchen the next moment. Yeah, I will fight damn hard to keep her happy and will kill anyone who threatens to take away our happiness.

Time passes where food and drinks flow in a decent matter. I don't think I've had this many people visit me at the same time. But with my woman being the perfect hostess, I must say, it's not as much as a struggle as I thought it would be.

When it's well after eleven, the house is finally empty and it's only me and Kadence enjoying the late evening on our back porch. The sky is lit with stars and moonlight. We're sharing a beer and watch our horses graze next to each other.

She scoots closer and places her head on my chest. I have a crib sized swing bed we're lounging on. I love sleeping outside at times, watching my horse in the moonlight and hearing the sounds of nature. It's soothing. But falling asleep with my woman in my arms wrapped by the comfort of everything that enriches my life is a blessing.

Waking up by gunshots is a complete nightmare I need to wake up from. Shaking my head from the sleep, I blink to let my eyes adjust to the bright morning sun. Kadence's hands fist my shirt as our eyes collide.

"What was that?" she whispers.

Another shot rings out and our horses gallop wild through the paddock.

"Motherfucker," someone roars and if I'm correct it's Alfie's voice.

I reach for the table in front of me where I placed my two guns and a knife.

Sliding the knife into the sheath, I hand Kadence one of the guns. "Stay here."

She checks the gun and at this moment I'm glad she has an MC background. At least they taught her to handle weapons and not lock down with fear when things go to shit.

I grab my backup gun and stride around the cabin to get to the front where the shatter of glass and gunfire is still crackling in the air. Risking a quick glance around the corner I notice Alfie hiding behind my truck.

Fucking bullet holes all over my truck, but the blood in the dirt surrounding Alfie is what worries me. Silence falls and I now notice Cannon is standing near my cabin. He's reloading his gun and it's a wide-open chance for me to kill the fucker.

I don't know or care why the fuck he's here shooting up the place but he's going to meet his maker who can worry about that shit. Stepping out from behind the cabin I squeeze the trigger and fire off a few rapid rounds.

His body jerks but the fucker falls behind part of the cabin which gives him cover. I curse loudly but I need to dash back behind the cabin when a damn bullet whistles very close by my fucking head. What the fuck? Who is here besides Cannon?

"Who the hell is shooting?" Kadence whisper hisses from behind me.

I flash an angry look over my shoulder. "I told you to stay

fucking put."

"And I decided not to be a sitting duck but a participant. I can shoot, Colt. And I have steady and good aim."

We don't have time to fight because bullets are hitting my damn cabin. Another thing that worries me is the nonexistent return fire coming from Alfie. He's sagged against my truck.

I glance at Kadence and grab my damn heart in my hands when I ask, "Can you return fire if I jog around the cabin to surprise them from the other side?"

"Fuck, yes," she grunts underneath her breath.

I reach out to grab her neck and slam my mouth over hers to taste her lips in a fleeting kiss before I push my boots on the ground to race around the cabin. With my gun aimed forward I reach the corner and don't even glance around but jump out and start to fire.

Their eyes are still locked to where Kadence is firing, making them sitting ducks. A young guy with a prospect cut on with the Deranged Hounds patch is now getting drenched by blood from the bullets I fired into his back.

Cannon has a last breath to spin around and aim his gun at me but a bullet enters between his eyes and at the same time his skull shatters from the impact of a second bullet as my woman shoots the fucker as well.

Knowing the asshole is dead, I let my eyes travel over my front yard to make sure all threats are gone. Kadence comes rushing toward me. I holster my gun to wrap an arm around her and pull her close to inhale her sweet fragrance, making sure she's still with me and we're still alive.

Fuck. Alive. Is Alfie still breathing?

CHAPTER 08

KADENCE

"Alfie," Colt grunts and locks eyes with me. "Call an ambulance, right fucking now. Then call Weston."

He lets go of my waist and rushes off toward his truck. I now notice the blood coming from underneath his truck and the body behind it. Holy shit. That's Alfie? I grab my phone and am shouting for help before I disconnect when I know they're coming. Only to make a second call to let Weston know but he doesn't pick up.

I'm about to call Roper when I hear the rumbling of bikes and see the dust surrounding them up the road. Not knowing who the fuck they are, I rush toward Colt and Alfie and have my back to them and my gun raised at the bikers riding up.

I lower my gun slightly when I notice it's Weston, Roper, Joaquin, Garrett, and Ledger. But I shift my aim when behind them Rowen and his VP, Koda, appear. Filled with anger I fire off a round in the direction of my brother.

"Get the fuck off my damn property," I bellow.

My brother's bike comes to an abrupt stop. He kicks out the kickstand and jumps off his bike, holding both hands palms up.

"I called it in the second we knew Cannon was out for blood and wanted to drag you off. The fucker is insane, we had no clue he would go nuts when he heard he couldn't have you. He drove off with a prospect in tow and dropped off the radar. I swear we had nothing to do with it, sis. We drove like hell on wheels to get here because I was afraid he would go to you. When I couldn't reach Colt, I called Weston. I swear we didn't know."

I fire another round next to his boot. "This is all your fault."

"Noooo." The tormented plea coming from Joaquin rips straight through my chest.

Shit. Alfie. The blood. His sagging body. He didn't return fire. Joaquin's sobs.

He's dead?

I raise my gun to justify his death but the gun is covered with a hand as it's guided down. "You don't want to do that."

My eyes trail up the arm of who is preventing me from shooting another bullet at my brother. I let Weston take the gun from me and I mindlessly nod.

"I just…it's his fault. Alfie, he's…" A sob rips from me.

"From the looks of it, Alfie is still breathing. And I can't let you kill the president of another MC on club grounds," Weston says with a firm tone. "Even if the fucker is your brother. In the end he did do right by you. He stepped up and put you before the club, Kadence. He was ready to end Cannon himself but he was already heading here and couldn't get to you in time."

I let my head drop. He's right. "Sorry, Prez," I tell him, even if he's not my president, but in this moment–me being Colt's old lady–I know very well he is.

Not that I forgive my brother, but I trust Weston and the words he just gave me.

"Go help your man, the EMTs are here," he orders and I spin around to run toward Colt who is helping to keep Joaquin away from Alfie; the EMTs need to do their job.

I take Joaquin's face into my hands and firmly make him

glance at me. "Joaquin. Pull yourself together, you're not helping."

His eyes are still fixed on the ground behind me. I risk a glance over my shoulder and notice Alfie is awake and growling at the EMTs who are lifting him onto the stretcher.

"Joaquin," I snap, his eyes now landing on mine. "See? He's still alive. Now you need to swallow back the panic and go with him to the hospital. I'm going to be right behind you, okay?"

He stops struggling and closes his eyes a moment to inhale a deep breath. When he opens them there's determination flaring and he says in a firm tone, "You're right. I got this. He's got this. He's going to be fine and then I can spank his ass for almost dying on me."

"You're not spanking my ass, boy," Alfie grunts.

Joaquin releases a sound close to a mix of a sob and a laugh and I whisper, "He's a fighter. Go support your man. We got this."

Colt lets go of him and Joaquin rushes off to follow the EMTs who are loading Alfie into the ambulance. Colt opens his arms and it takes three steps before I let myself fall into his embrace.

His lips brush against my head. "Come on, let's go inside. I need some fucking coffee."

"You and me both," I croak.

Hours pass where we are faced with answering questions and cleaning up the mess that happened before we're able to head for the hospital. Once there we're told Alfie needed emergency surgery. He was shot twice in one leg, once in the shoulder, and twisted his ankle of his other leg.

He needs to spend some time in the hospital followed by weeks recovering but he's allowed to do it at home as long as he uses the wheelchair since his shoulder, and both of his legs are injured, and there's no way for him to use crutches.

Joaquin will look after him but I think the hospital will arrange a nurse. Whatever, I have no clue but he's getting help to change the bandages and care Alfie needs these upcoming weeks.

My head isn't functioning properly after this fucked up day and even if Colt and I are lying in the swing bed on the back porch–exactly where we were this morning when all went to shit–there's some form of serenity blanketing us.

As twisted as our day started, it's a valid promise our past is closed now. I didn't think Cannon would be nuts enough to bring a prospect to come and get me–guns blazing–because he had some kind of fucked-up idea I belonged to him.

There are so many things to say and yet lying here in Colt's embrace and watching how our horses are enjoying the moonlight settles my heart to know this is home. And yes, our house is now littered with bullet holes and we need to repair the windows but we will, because we have all the time in the world to do just that.

Colt reaches for the beer bottle and takes a long pull before passing it to me. "Maybe we should ask Ledger and my sister to build a cabin next to ours."

I have to swallow hard to prevent the beer from bursting out of my nose in surprise of what he just said.

"What?" I croak and clear my throat.

Colt chuckles. "If anything has been proven to me today it's that it's good to have a brother near. I can't help but think what would have happened if Alfie wasn't close and opened fire when they came for us. It's a good fucking thing he was checking the herd when Rowen called Weston about Cannon going rogue. And I also like the idea of having my sister live closer. She's been here on the ranch a few months now, but we hardly ever run into each other. She has her own company and me and my tasks for the ranch and MC and living here and all. And to be honest, I bet you'd love to help her with those lunch packages and having her close. Ledger isn't that much of an asshole: I could live with him on my property."

I place the beer back on the table and snuggle against his chest. "I think it's a great idea. And yes, I'd love to help your sister with her company. We could make the delivery rounds ourselves now that the danger has completely vanished."

"You two will always have a prospect trailing your asses. I won't ever leave you unprotected. But, yeah. You know what I mean."

A smile tugs my mouth and heart. "Yeah, I know what you mean."

He cares. He loves. As much as I care and love him in return.

EPILOGUE

Six years later

COLT

I guide my bike to the luxurious hotel I've booked for tonight. We always stay a night here when we visit Rowen and his old lady. Even after all these years Kadence still has a hard time connecting and opening up to her brother. But they're both trying and it's good to obtain some form of a family bond.

Rowen has reached out to her on a frequent basis after Cannon came for her. Though Kadence needed time to process all of it. He understood and gave her space to wait for her to reach out to him.

But when we received a long letter from the woman who was pregnant with Rowen's kid–and with Kadence being pregnant herself at the time–she opened up to the idea of restoring their family bond.

Though it had to be on her terms and since Rowen was happy with any form of a connection, he quickly agreed. It's why we ride upstate every now and then to meet Rowen, his old lady, and their kid. Sometimes we bring our own son, Walker, who is now almost five years old.

Kadence reconnecting on her terms meant she didn't want to have anything to do with the Deranged Hounds. So, we balance between meeting them for dinner every once in a while, or heading to an amusement park with the kids, or simply meet up to have a chat and a drink at a local diner.

We didn't bring Walker this time because our son wanted to spend time with my sister's kids. Mayven and Ledger have two daughters, Heather who is around Walker's age, and Rose who is almost three. Suggesting my sister and Ledger build a cabin next to ours has turned out to be one of my most brilliant ideas.

Not only do we enjoy their company from time to time but having our kids grow up close together, and always having a babysitter near is damn well perfect. Of course, a lot of my brothers also have kids, and the clubhouse is a good place any time of day, it's just perfect to live together on the edge of the property.

But for now, Kadence and I have the night all to ourselves. Maybe that's also why Kadence enjoyed herself today, but both Rowen and her got along great this afternoon. Her brother never forgave himself for the shit he's done–and let's face it, it was fucking disgusting. But he's also shown remorse for putting the club first.

He kept saying it was a desperate grasp to hold onto Kadence, made in a moment of grief of losing both their mother and father. He needed his only living relative close, especially at a time the club was falling apart. And he honestly believed Cannon had feelings for Kadence.

Stalker level feelings for fucking sure, the guy was twisted as fuck. And Kadence knows the weight Rowen had on his shoulders, and like I said…she accepts some form of family connection between them now. Though the life we built together is where true family has forged bonds strong enough to face anything.

The same thing can be said about the strong connection between me and my woman. Riding together, either horseback, or like now on my bike. Working at the ranch where she helps out during the time she isn't busy with my sister's company, taking care of the kids, our house, or enjoying the late evenings where we watch our horses silently graze in the meadow as the moonlight shines down on all of us.

Yeah, life is pretty damn good. And when we're finally locked inside our hotel room tonight…it just might get a little better since I have the whole night planned. Okay, I have just one thing planned, and that's the gift I have in my pocket.

It's not a wedding ring since we have been already married for five years now. But tonight happens to be our anniversary. I had a massive silver cuff bracelet handmade by a friend of my sister who she met through her company. My sister was right, the jewelry designer is brilliant and crafted the heads of our two horses on the cuff bracelet from a few photographs I gave her.

The resemblance is astonishing and I would have wanted it for myself as well, but it's made especially for Kadence. Though, I might have mentioned to the designer I wanted to have one with a thicker cuff made for me to match the one for my wife, but she said she was fully booked for the next couple of months. It doesn't matter. I have the perfect gift for my woman, and I know for sure she's going to love it.

"Did you want to run a bath first or have a beer at the bar downstairs?" She removes the hair tie and her thick, gorgeous dark red hair falls free in waves down her back. After all these years it still only takes one look at my woman to get me hard.

"I'd like to give you this first." I hold out the big black velvet square box and Kadence gasps as I tell her, "Happy anniversary, doll."

She covers her mouth with her hand and takes a step back. "Oh no."

Okay, that's not the reaction I was going for here.

Her hand goes in my direction, palm up as if she wants to stop me. "Hang on," she says and rushes to her backpack.

She pulls out the same fucking box. "Happy anniversary," she croaks and winces.

We swap boxes and open them simultaneously. I have no

fucking words for what my eyes are taking in. It's from the same designer for sure. But the cuff I'm holding is massive and made for a man my size.

Where I had one made for my woman's wrist with the heads of our horses, I'm staring at our horses running through a meadow while the moon is shining upon them and it's fucking magnificent.

Seconds tick by where we only stare at the same–and yet different–gift we gave one another. I know my sister had something to do with this and yet it's our personal touch what makes it so damn perfect.

I hand her my cuff while I take hers and the arm I want to put it on. She watches my moves and returns the favor to put the cuff on my wrist. I wrap my fingers around her nape to pull her close and lean in to kiss her.

I take my time to let our tongues perform a sensual slow dance. But I need more when I feel her nipples poking through the material of her blouse and bra. Or I might be imagining them because I know every inch of her lovely body.

Her blouse is damn frustrating with the tiny buttons. My thick fingers and my patience has blown to shit, causing me to grip the fabric and rip it apart. Buttons fly through the air as I'm dragging the fabric down her body and let it fall to the floor.

Her bra follows and my breath catches when I see her magnificent tits. "Take your pants off while I play with these," I roughly demand.

I roll her dark pink peaks between my fingers and tug them. Palming one breast I knead it slightly at the same time I lean in and let my tongue swirl around her nipple, sinking my teeth slightly into her skin.

She gasps and I damn well know how much she loves a little bite of erotic pain. Glancing down I'm happy to see she's naked and it takes me a few breaths along with a string of curses to rid myself of my own clothing.

But once naked I take her into my arms and grip her ass to easily lift her. She wraps her legs around my waist. Our mouths merge and I walk forward until I've pinned her between the wall and my body.

My cock is brushing her opening, flawlessly finding home. All it takes is a shift of my hips and I'm diving into a tight hotness welcoming me into bliss. We both moan and I start to sink in deeper and faster.

Our mouths disconnect when I slam into her body, making her head fall against the wall as she moans loud enough it echoes through my balls. Fuck, yeah. This right here is also the reason why we book a hotel every once in a while.

Mad fucking without the need to keep quiet for either the neighbors or a kid who doesn't need to hear those things. But fuck if it doesn't unleash pride inside me to be able to make my woman go crazy with lust.

Her nails trail over my back, silently asking for more as I keep tunneling in and out of her tight pussy. It doesn't matter what time or where we are, as long as we have each other we have the ability to fill our surroundings with all the love overflowing our hearts.

"So close," she gasps, making my cock a little harder to feel her pussy already starting to strangle me.

"You'd better come hard enough to take me with you," I grunt.

She screams when I change the angle and find her favorite spot. Knowing she won't last long if I keep hitting it, I roughen my thrusts and love the way we can tear each other up to shatter in a sea of pleasure, always being there to pick up the pieces and start all over again.

"Always," she grunts and takes another breath to fill her lungs with enough air to moan my name as she surrenders to the orgasm slamming through her body.

Two more pumps and her pussy is ripping the cum straight from my cock. My head falls into the crook of her neck while I try to hold my balance. Our hearts are racing in an effort to release the heat our bodies created.

"So. Fucking. Good," I whisper against her skin.

A giggle escapes her. "I won't ever grow tired of hearing you say those words."

"And I won't ever grow tired of voicing them, 'cause it's the damn truth." A grunt rips from me as I shift and feel my cock sliding out of her pussy. "Shit. My body does grow tired from all the hard fucking, though. Damn, I'm beat."

Another giggle leaves her as I carry her toward the bed, placing her in the middle and crawling in next to her. I don't care if the cum is leaking from her pussy. We're trying for a little brother or sister for Walker and I'm hoping tonight might be the night.

Would be fucking perfect with today being our anniversary. I can't believe it's only been six years since I gave in to the fact this woman stole my heart at first sight. And I can't believe I was foolish enough not to admit to myself sooner how I had to have her as my woman.

None of it matters because all of it led us to this point in time where we're in bed together. A solid friendship, a deep connection rooted within our relationship where we share the same goals for our future.

Freedom in every minute passing as we greedily enjoy what life brings us. Today, tomorrow, next year, decades, until we're old and gray where my woman is still the most gorgeous woman who holds my heart for as long as it beats.

"I love you so much," she murmurs, reaching for me as our silver cuffs connect.

I lace my fingers with hers. "Pretty sure I love you more," I reply to her sleepy face which lights up with a smile.

Yeah, we will always have the will to carry on together, our love is enough to face anything, and shall only grow stronger from here on out.

COWBOY
BIKERS MC #6
By Esther E. Schmidt

Alfie

I'm a biker in an MC located at a huge ranch which
breeds both longhorns and quarter horses. I'm not just a biker,
a cowboy, or a rancher, but I am a man of many trades
and talents. And one of those is to protect the two people
who need me the most.

Joaquin

Moving to Texas for my job allowed me to find
what my heart desires. Alfie and I are two parts of a
three way future, lacking one final part to make it complete.

Greta

Stepping into the lives of Alfie and Joaquin as
an undercover agent for the DEA is liberating and ultimately,
my downfall. We're risking it all in an effort
to change–and save–our lives.

CHAPTER 01

ALFIE

I open my eyes and the first thing hitting me again is discomfort and the awareness of how life is able to knock you on your ass on any given day. Every damn time I wake up I feel a dull ache and a sense of unease. It was worse the first few weeks when I was just injured, and it's getting less with each day passing, but it sure does something to a man's mood.

How did I get injured? I was shot, twice in one leg and once in the shoulder, and it isn't fucking fun I can tell you that much. Luckily the sprained ankle on my other leg I also endured is healed. Well, somewhat, since the pain is next to none. Maybe my grumpy state of mind is overriding the pain. Whatever.

Don't get me wrong, if I had the choice between stepping in the line of fire or not attempting to stop a bad situation; I'd do it all over again because I was protecting Colt and his old lady. No one fucks with any member or old lady of our MC; we live and die for the brotherhood.

I was the only one close enough when the call came in that

Cannon–a biker from Deranged Hounds MC–had gone rogue. I had to face him and a prospect he brought along all on my own. I held on long enough for Colt to jump in and help out. End good, all good.

But healing takes for-fucking-ever and the shitty thing is the fact I have to depend on others for help. And I fucking hate it. I'm always the one handling everything. I'm a damn leader; always on top and ready for anything. And now my ass has been in this bed for weeks.

Not to mention the one I share my life and house with is getting the brunt of my annoyance. Right at a time when we want to complete our lives; adding a woman. And lying on my back without being able to do shit or so much as run into a woman complicates things even more and makes my mind go in loops about all kinds of fucked-up shit. I'm a pathetic mess, but I ain't going to voice that thought out loud; I'd rather stick to being grumpy and annoy anyone who comes near me.

Laughter flows through the air and it's coming from the kitchen. It's Joaquin but there's someone else with him. A woman. Why the fuck is there a woman in our home? And why the hell is he laughing his flirtatious laugh he only reserves for me?

Yes, along with being frustrated, I'm also a selfish asshole who has laid claim on Joaquin ever since I saw him. But like Joaquin, I'm a man who likes to enjoy both sides and that means having a woman as well as a man in my bed to share my life with.

Joaquin is the opposite of selfish, and he too enjoys sharing a woman between us. Shitty thing is…we haven't found the right woman yet. And this brings me back to the fact of why the hell would he be flirting with a chick in our damn kitchen?

Unless…motherfucker. He didn't, did he? "That better not be a new damn caregiver you're talking to," I bellow, making the laughter in the kitchen come to an abrupt stop.

I hear the murmur of hushed words I can't quite make out until I hear footsteps closing in. From the hall I hear a woman's voice and I swear the angelic tone seduces me through the damn air as if she's already between my legs, sucking my cock when she says, "And what if he is?"

I close my eyes, because if I see this woman, I won't be able to stop myself from getting off this damn bed and ripping her clothes off to fuck her seven ways to Sunday.

It's for this reason I growl, "Get her the fuck away from me, boy."

"Not happening, Snappy," she whispers in my fucking ear and it activates my instincts to move fast.

My eyes fly open as my hands fist her shirt. I throw her over me in one fluid motion and onto the mattress beside me, pinning her in place with my body. My shoulder is screaming at me along with pain shooting through my leg, but I can't voice shit because this woman has her tiny hands wrapped around my throat in a choke hold.

One I can honestly say feels as if she's about to rip my damn Adam's apple right out. Do I care? Fuck, no. I'm staring at one hell of a beauty underneath me. Tiny, yet lush. Her hair is a dark, smokey gray ombré wrapped in a long braid, and her eyes are green yet lit with liquid fire.

"Back. Up," she snaps, but adds in a fake, candy sweet voice, "Please, sir."

I do not want to change positions for the sole reason her touch is leaking calmness through my skin. I can't explain it but this woman has a soothing effect on me. The way I let her guide me by the throat away from her body is telling the both of us I'm the one giving in.

My fingers are still gripping the fabric of her shirt and I'm the one guiding her weight; she's by no way in charge. Yet, I'd gladly let her take over if she wrapped her lips around my cock. Top or bottom ones; whichever is fine by me. Our eyes are locked and I swear I can see our future twinkling in her bright green eyes.

Instead of getting off the bed on the other side, she decides to straddle me first, brushing her fabric covered pussy against my very hard cock. I swear she wiggles first before she slides off.

For the first damn time in my life, I have nothing to say.

No joke, no dirty remark, no fucking order or a curse. Nothing. My throat is dry and I don't know if I should be angry, laugh, or grab my cock and rub one out. This woman is confident, straightforward, and not shy in going up against a man like me. I'm intrigued to say the least.

"Joaquin, can you grab my bag from the kitchen, please?" She might be asking but there's an edge to her voice to mold her words into a demand.

Joaquin has a knack for flawlessly following through if you curve your fucking voice and it's why he spins on his heels. My upper lip twitches in anger but this fucking woman gives me a little shake of her head. What the fuck?

I raise my upper body–ignoring the ache in my shoulder– when she closes the door and flips the lock. She stalks back to the bed and jabs a fucking finger against my injured shoulder. A growl rips from my throat but I can't voice shit because she cuts me off.

"You're a menace. I've read all about you and how you've managed to scare away four other caregivers over the past few weeks. That's going to stop because that man out there has a job too, you know. He needs to get his ass out of this house and you're going to let him. You and I are going to make sure we get along. I don't care if we have to fake it. I'll do what my job description requires me to do and will steer clear of you the rest of the day. If you put in the work it will only take a week or two until you're completely back to your asshole self. So, buckle up buttercup."

She turns around just as fast as she rattled out those words and heads for the door to flip the lock again. She lets Joaquin in who hands her a bag but looks at me with bewildered eyes.

I want to lash out at the woman and at Joaquin but the words she just voiced sink in. She's right about the other caregivers, and I couldn't care less. But what she said about Joaquin does matter. And again, I realize I'm fucking selfish since I let my frustrations seep through by giving him the brunt of it.

Which is always the fucking case because you lash out to those close to you. And Joaquin is fucking close to me. He's the whole love, devotion, loyalty. A concept fallen in three pieces and that's fucking it…we're two parts of a three way future, lacking one final part to make it complete.

Her angelic voice fills the air when she tells Joaquin, "Why don't you head over to the veterinarian clinic? I'll keep an eye on Alfie and fill out some forms I brought before going over the list of things you mentioned that needed to be done."

His eyes find mine. "Maybe I should stay."

"What you need is to get back to your normal routine and leave your worries about your friend for me to handle," the woman kindly states, rubbing me the wrong fucking way.

And speaking about rubbing something, she might as well get things straight. "What he needs to do is rub and suck my cock. Joaquin is not only my friend, he's one of my two lovers. Though we still have one position wide open, itching to be filled up by both of our cocks. Right, Joaquin?"

Yes, I admit, my dirty mouth is what scared away caregiver number one. Caregiver number two needed a visual of Joaquin actually sucking my cock to hightail out of the house screaming as she went. And caregiver number three couldn't take repeatedly walking in on me shamelessly masturbating. Maybe it was the sight of my pierced cock scaring her, whatever; it got the job done. And I think it was a mixture of all of that what sent the fourth one running.

This caregiver, though? She rolls her eyes and places her bag on the mattress. "I don't mind the two of you sucking each other off while I check the progress you made and if the injuries are still bothering you. Actually, it's something I wouldn't mind looking in on. I've seen, and done, more. Freedom of sexuality is exhilarating. So, by all means, suck each other's dick. Though, like I said…I might simply watch and not work, meaning I'd be here longer."

Her well-groomed eyebrow raises in a challenge and my damn cock twitches and starts to tent the fucking sheets.

Though she won't ever be looking in on that shit because, "I don't suck cock, Joaquin does. But we both like to suckle on a pussy if you're offering to spice things up."

"Twice now you've mentioned the request for a third party. I know you've been practically bedbound for a few weeks. But you should have healed enough to at least walk around the house on crutches or let Joaquin drive you around in the car. I mean, you can't be that desperate to offer the first…oh, my…all those other caregivers, they didn't accept your invitation either?" Shit. Even her sweet giggles are cock stroking.

"No," I snap. "We didn't offer. We might have shocked them by showing or telling them about our…how did you put it? Exhilarating sexuality. I guess that was shocking enough to send them running."

She looks thoughtful for a moment, opens her bag and says, "Their loss. Now, when was the last time you left this bed for longer than a pee break? Everything healed okay? No infections? No pain other than the soreness of using your limbs the way you should? Anything else happen in the time since they checked you over last?"

She's roaming through her bag while my eyes find Joaquin. There's a smile tugging his lips and he raises one eyebrow. I shoot him a wink in return. Yeah, the both of us more than like this tiny firecracker.

"Head over to Harlene and Cassidy. I'll play nice and won't scare her away," I tell him and his smile turns into a blinding one.

The man has a heart bigger than everyone on this fucked-up planet all together. He's been nothing but understanding while I've been here brooding in this bed.

"Are you sure?" he asks, but he already has one foot out the door.

"Get out of here. And don't bring any puppies or kittens home, dammit," I growl.

His hand is thrown in the air and he waves my concern away with a simple, "Pssssshhh. You'd crawl to the door if you knew

I was coming with a box of orphaned puppies." His look turns stern when he adds, "Behave."

"Don't I always?" I grumble, earning me a snicker as he heads out the door.

"You have yourself a sweet man there," she muses and checks my shoulder.

Wounds have closed and healed, but it's the damage on the inside needing the time to heal enough to function to a point where I was before a bullet ripped through it. I can't put my full weight on my shoulder or my leg yet. My other leg's ankle is practically healed but it's not fully capable of carrying all my weight. I'm afraid if I would, I'd have a setback for sure.

And she's right about Joaquin. "Sweet, sassy, annoying at times, but there's one flaw."

Her eyes narrow. "People have flaws. Everyone is special in their own way, it's the flaws creating the difference. If everyone had the same flaws, we'd all be the same dull person, lacking crucial elements someone would fall in love with."

"Christ, woman. Don't get all philosophical on me. I merely wanted to remark the man doesn't drink coffee in the morning. He's only been offering me orange juice or a spinach smoothie every fucking morning. I have to text one of my brothers, or one of the old ladies, to come and bring me some."

"Holy shit. You're kidding me? Who doesn't drink coffee in the morning? My brain doesn't even function without the black golden goodness. Ugh. I need at least two cups to get my eyes to fully open." She leans in and whispers while keeping her eyes on the door Joaquin just left through, "Are you sure he's human?"

She starts to slide her fingers over my shoulder and with her other hand moves my arm. Gripping the sheets, she tosses them off me to get to my leg. Her eyes aren't fixed on my leg, though.

"You can have a closer look, with your lips or tongue for instance." I can't help but chuckle when she's still admiring my cock with open interest.

"Nice piercing," she compliments and diverts her eyes and lets her fingertips trail over my legs to check on my other injuries.

"What's your name?" I question, suddenly realizing I don't know a single thing about her. "Mind giving me the file on you? Or just your name and you can hand me my laptop."

I'll run a background check myself or call Decker to do one for me.

"My file is in the kitchen, but let me give you a short recap. Greta Bostinger, twenty-three, single, high intelligence so I skipped a few grades, went from wanting to become a doctor to being an agent, to now standing here, being a caregiver and making sure I don't stare at your pierced cock. Very tempting, I must say. Does Joaquin ever let you leave the house? Hmm, is that the reason you're still bedbound? Is he keeping you under lock and key?"

"Miss Rattlepants. An agent? Explain," I demand in an even tone before I reach for my phone on the nightstand and text Decker the name, asking him to run a check.

"As a kid, I always wanted to become a doctor. My parents were both doctors and retired at an early age. Seemingly not early enough because they only got to enjoy their dream a few years before they died not long after each other. When they died, I realized me wanting to become a doctor was following their footsteps, their dream, not mine. And then I thought becoming an agent was my dream." She shrugs. "But it turns out to be nothing how I thought it would be. And like I said…I'm standing here, staring at that." She points at my cock.

Now it's my turn to shrug. "I mentioned you're allowed to do more than stare at it."

"Aren't you and Joaquin together? How can you offer to have sex with me? He was very sweet. I wouldn't do that to him, and you should have more respect for your man."

A snort leaves my body. "My man? He's mine all right, and we have a solid bond between us but if you want to wait until he comes home to suck me off, I won't complain. If you want to suck him off, even better, but only if I get to watch."

She drops the leg she was massaging and plunks her ass down on the bed beside me. "You like to watch? How does that work? Don't you get jealous to see him with someone else?"

"Hello, live porn. Why the hell would I get jealous? Joaquin is mine: he won't ever betray or leave me. We have an understanding. Others might not be able to wrap their mind around it, but we have our ducks in a row."

Sounds twisted, I know. But I meant what I said about Joaquin being mine and how we have a solid bond. It's grown for years and it might have started out as lust evolving into the craving to fuck a woman together, but we always moved on, the both of us…together, yet still looking for the one woman to complete us.

"That's special," she murmurs thoughtfully. "And ducks are cute."

"He is special," I agree, because if it was anyone else with a cock asking me to be in a solid relationship I would walk away. Joaquin's the only one ever making the craving flame inside me to break a relationship into three pieces of a whole.

CHAPTER 02

GRETA

"Lucky man," I tell Alfie and give him a beaming smile before patting his injured leg on purpose.

He growls low and I have to swallow my laughter. I know he's hurting and still recovering from the injury, but I also know pain can be a motivation and this man needs to get his ass off the bed.

"Come on, enough talking about your magnificent dick and that man of yours. I've brought you a surprise."

"You didn't bring me a surprise, it's always attached to you. Just open your blouse and show me those lushful looking titties. That's the surprise, right?" He rubs his hands in glee and I swear he's holding his hands out the next moment to size up my breasts and to get ready to hold and knead them.

Ugh. This man's head lives in the gutter and I've only met him a mere moment ago. But damn if he doesn't make my nipples tingle and beg for some attention.

"Sorry to disappoint you, stud. I brought crutches." I add

some sarcasm to my voice and add, "Surprise."

I grip my breasts and give them a little squeeze to give back what he keeps throwing at me. "These are not on your to-do list. Getting you up and walking is." I smirk.

"Give me those crutches and I'll fucking chase those two puppies with a speed you've never seen," he grumbles.

I laugh and shake my head as I stroll to the closet. "What clothes do you need? I'm planning to get you out of bed and into the living room. Once there we will have coffee and see how your leg and shoulder are doing before we add some other things on your to-do list."

"Sweatpants," he says and points at a drawer.

I take out a gray pair and throw them in his direction. "Put them on. And no, I won't kneel to dick-level and help you. There's nothing wrong with one side of your body and your ass can bend over to put on some pants. Make an effort, you'll feel better about yourself."

I head for the door and hear him mutter, "It's my back that bends, not my ass."

There's a smile on my face as I head for the kitchen, but it falls when I think about the reason why I'm here. It has nothing to do with getting Alfie Garmsons back on his feet again, but it's part of my undercover job nonetheless.

If I didn't hate my job before I walked through this door, I do now. Barely an hour into my first undercover case and I doubt the reason why I'm here. These two seem like nice and honest people. They're nothing like the MC the DEA thinks they're connected with.

My job really sucks, and I'm seriously questioning my reasons for doing the whole career shift. Though, the hating part of my job is mostly due to the guy I'm supposed to report back to. I should have never agreed to do this. But here I am, so not living my dream. But I guess life is all about moving forward one step at a time. And that's all it really is, another step to my next paycheck; I almost have all my debts paid.

I place my hands on the kitchen table and brace myself to

pull in a large gasp of air and hold it. I should walk away now. Drop everything and go for yet another career shift. It sure sounds like a necessity. I'm such a job-hopper. Maybe I should get my nose back in the books and become a doctor, a rehabilitation specialist.

I need more coffee to think over my crappy life, not to mention, I'm here and have to see this through first. Grabbing the crutches, I head back to the bedroom where Alfie is lying in his bed instead of sitting on the edge of the mattress and getting ready to slowly return back to his old life.

"Get up," I snap, making his head swing my way as I place the crutches against the bed.

Damn him. My life is crappier than his and he doesn't get to sulk. From what I've heard he's been sulking for weeks now. Enough is enough.

"I've read your file but I've also talked to Joaquin this morning and all of it tells me your ego got injured more than your body. Well, boo-freaking-hoo. Get up, grab those crutches, face the bite of pain your body gives and push through. I have coffee waiting for you in the kitchen." Anger is rolling off him in waves and remembering his flirty behavior, I might as well add a little something from his weirdo state of mind. "And if you make it to the kitchen? I'll flash you some boob."

Totally unprofessional but I'm here to get a job done, and my line of work requires to be willing to do everything to see things through. Well, if I would believe Matt, my DEA partner, that is. Such a promotion hungry workaholic asshole.

Alfie's eyes bulge. I don't wait for a reply but turn on my heel and head for the coffee maker. I make myself another cup of coffee and have one ready for Alfie when I hear a frustrated grunt and the sound of crutches on the dark red tiles on the floor of this cabin. Such a cozy home. You wouldn't guess two men lived here.

I'd bet money it was decorated by Joaquin. He might be a lean, handsome, manly man, but he wears black nail polish, and his clothes are neat. Like he just walked out of a fashion magazine. Oh, and the scarf he was wearing around his neck? Silk. I'm sure. Feminine and yet it looked hot on a guy like him.

And he was flirting. With me, a woman, that doesn't scream gay. Hell, if I didn't read up on these two, I wouldn't be able to figure them out other than Alfie is clearly the alpha in their relationship. And to think these two like to have a woman in between their hot bodies. My brain mentally slips off my drenched panties and dives right into the gutter. Yeah, getting in between these two hot guys would make any woman's inhibitions evaporate.

"Show. Me. The. Goods," Alfie grunts while he's leaning against the wall.

Sweat is beading his forehead and I know getting out of bed and down the hall to the kitchen cost a lot of his body. Joaquin mentioned how Alfie hasn't done anything other than leave his bed to go to the bathroom and back.

Without thinking I tear my blouse out of my jeans and pull it up, giving Alfie an eyeful of my breasts wrapped in a purple lace bra. When I tug the fabric back into my jeans and meet his eyes, I notice his hand rubbing his dick.

"Really?" I roll my eyes and move the coffee closer to him, shoving a chair out for him to sit on.

He shoots me a smirk and focuses to move closer to the chair. The man clearly needs to adjust to walking with crutches and the ankle on his bullet-hole free leg might not be fully healed either. But he needs to get his ass moving while keeping an eye on the pain.

Lying in bed for weeks on end is a huge change for someone who was very active in his life. It allows your mind to work overtime and fall into a hole one likes to hide in and it's hard to crawl out of. But Alfie is sitting in the kitchen, the first step to regain his active life back.

"There, isn't this better?" I tell him and take the crutches to place them within his reach against the chair next to him.

"Seeing a nice set of tits is always better. It's why Joaquin and I need a woman in between. Tits and pussy all day, every day."

"An eyeful of my breasts is all you're getting today, Mister," I tell him in a stern voice and take a seat across from him, grabbing my coffee in both hands.

"Fuck, you're strict. If you were mine, I'd spank that ass of yours a nice shade of red." He tilts his head. "Anyone ever spank your lush ass? It's made to wear a handprint by the looks of it."

I narrow my eyes. "The sex talk. It's your defense mechanism, right? Anyone ever smack you upside the head? Because my hand is itching if you want to keep that fucking mouth of yours running."

He grumbles something underneath his breath and if I can trust my ears it sounded something in the lines of, "I need Joaquin here to tame your ass."

We glare at each other while sipping our coffee. A thought comes to mind and I grab my phone from the table and snap a picture of Alfie, quickly sending it to Joaquin who gave me his number when he hired me on the spot this morning.

"What did you do?" Alfie growls.

I tilt my head. "Are you going to keep growling at me at every turn? I'm going to be living here for the next week or so, you could try to be nicer."

"I don't need a babysitter. Unless you do your job naked or topless, I could be persuaded to let you stay." The man shoots me a smirk and if I keep rolling my eyes, I'll be able to check out my own ass all day, every day.

"I'm not a babysitter, I'm a caregiver, there's a difference. And no, don't expect me to go naked or topless."

"What did you do?" He points at my phone and ignores what I just told him.

I shrug. "Sent Joaquin a picture of you sitting at the kitchen table."

My phone indicates I have a message and see Joaquin's response. And I swear I hear his voice in my head when I read, "Ohhh Emmm Geee. You did it!"

"Tell him about your tits. Better yet, text him a picture so he can forward it to me."

"For fuck's sake, Alfie," I gasp but can't help to throw my head back and laugh. Shaking my head and trying to get my laughter under control I mutter, "I think your head never leaves the gutter."

"Reality is hard enough to deal with, one foot in the gutter keeps shit real enough."

"Your foot isn't in the gutter, your ass and head are: you're drowning over there." I stand and rinse my mug and place it on the counter.

Alfie places the phone he was holding on the table. Both mine and his give an indication we have a message. I reach for mine at the same time Alfie checks his and a husky chuckle lets a hot zing spread in my veins.

I shake my head. "No wonder Joaquin is with you. Was he just as bad or did you infect him with your dirty mind when you two met?"

"He was already perfect when I met him." Alfie grins and there's clear affection in his voice.

"You two are cute together," I blurt. I clear my throat and add, "I need to pick up some of my stuff from my apartment later today and then I'll be here for the upcoming week, maybe two. From what Joaquin told me it's what he prefers since you won't get out of bed and do the work you need to do with your leg to get your body back to full strength. Plus, he works some nights for the veterinarian clinic, right? Well, if you do the work, I'm sure I'll be out of your hair in no time at all."

"I'm allowed to sulk," Alfie grumbles.

I grab his mug. "True. But you also need to get back on that horse. In a manner of speaking. But not. Well, you do train horses, right? Joaquin might have mentioned it when we had the job interview before he left for work."

"I do. Have you ever put your ass on one?"

Holding up the mug I question, "More?" He nods and I make my hands busy with making him another coffee as I start to tell him, "My parents loved all animals. I think it's also the reason why they retired at an early age and bought a small ranch. We had eight horses, two pigs, chickens, three dogs, and a cat. Sometimes I wonder what my parents thought of me because I rarely used to ride with a saddle. Hell, there were times I would just jump on and let the horse find its own way through the pasture." A deep sigh flows from my body as I fondly think back on the time I had with my parents.

"Without a saddle." Alfie's voice brings me back to the here and now and I turn to place the coffee in front of him. "Your parents still own horses?"

"Like I said, they retired at an early age but they were very career driven when they were younger. That is also the reason why my mother was forty-six when she had me, my dad was over fifty. They enjoyed their retirement and had all the time for me growing up. They died three days apart from each other. I think my mother died of a broken heart." I plunk down on the chair and slowly spin my phone around on the table with one finger. "My father had a bad heart. Both my parents were surgeons and decided to sell everything they owned, retire, and buy a tiny ranch with enough land to save animals and enjoy life for as long as they could. I was barely eighteen when I lost both. Rebuilding the ranch and giving everything up for the animals…by the time they died they had debts so everything we owned was lost and I had to do some weird damn jobs to pay off most of it."

"Sorry to hear that." His voice carries honesty and affection and it makes me connect our gaze.

"It is what it is. I do have fond memories, though. And hey, maybe you can speed up your recovery and offer me a ride on one of your horses. This ranch is huge from what I've seen when I drove up. And I only saw the pastures along the road to the cabin. You guys also own Longhorns, right?"

"They're a pain in the ass," Alfie grumbles. "But, yeah we do. And I'll be more than happy to give you a ride on my–"

"Do not say cock," I snap.

"You're no fun when you're stern. I rather have you flashing your tits at me again. Just give me a warning first. Joaquin is pissed I got to see them before he did."

"Ugh, you two are two dirty peas in a pod." I sigh and roll my eyes again.

But a smile tugs my lips when I hear his chuckle. The morning goes by in the blink of an eye and I do believe the whole back and forth banter is the reason Alfie is at least interacting and trying to listen when I ask him to do something. It's a personal win, though I'm not really here to make sure he gets back on his feet so to say.

"Are you going to be okay for an hour or two?" I ask and check my watch. "I'll be back later and Joaquin said he'd be here in about an hour."

"I've been alone from time to time over the last few weeks. I won't pee my bed or fall face first on the floor."

"Okay, Snappy," I mutter.

He was doing fine until I mentioned I had to leave and asked if he could manage for an hour or two. This man has some serious issues with asking others for help and getting back to fully functioning. As if it's a crime to be injured or something.

His eyes are set on the television and it's clear he's dismissed me. I slowly back out of the room and grab my purse from the table. Time to head to the apartment where I'm supposed to update Matt, my partner, and get back here to fully start my job to find out if this MC is in any way linked with some of the illegal activities Deranged Hounds MC was wrapped in.

CHAPTER 03

JOAQUIN

"When will she be back?" I question and try to scratch the black nail polish off my thumb.

Alfie bats my hand away. "Stop fidgeting and open the door. Weston will be here any second and you know as well as I do Greta will be back in about two hours. It's her routine since she always leaves once every two days for exactly two fucking hours."

"I don't like it," I huff and stalk to the door. "You should tie her to the bed and spank her ass like I told you to. I don't know why you have to bring Weston into this, we're perfectly fit to handle her ourselves."

Mister grumpy rumbles a growl and it vibrates through his chest. "She's been here ten fucking days, Joaquin. None of the other caretakers stayed. She's like the perfect little pussy taunting her sweetness in both of our faces. Your cock is hard, mine is hard, and she doesn't shy away. Not even when she caught us. You on your back, tied to the bed while your head was falling off the mattress as I fucked your upside-down mouth while jerking you off. She merely asked if I could support myself on my fucking leg with all the hip action. She ain't normal."

I grind my teeth and hiss underneath my breath, "She shouldn't be normal if we want her."

"Oh, for fuck's sake, Joaquin. Open your damn eyes. She isn't here to help me, something's up. And we need to get to the bottom of it seeing you're already wearing your rose colored glasses of love."

My hands clench into fists. Asshole. How can he not see the woman is sexy as hell, doesn't run away screaming when caught in a compromising position, and is intrigued by what Alfie and I have together? Though, I'm actually questioning what we have because he's such an undeniable, stubborn, hardheaded, grumpy, undisputable, horrific asshole.

Alfie sighs and steps closer to me. I want to turn on my heel and stomp out of the room, but I also see the wince on his face, due to the effort it takes by walking with just a cane. He cups the side of my face and lets his thumb stroke my jaw.

"Don't give me that look. You know I like those rose colored glasses on you. Always the ones with the big heart and massive trust. And I would like to have this little firecracker in between us, but not when I have my suspicions about her ulterior motives for being here. She's hiding things and that's unacceptable."

My shoulders sag. He's right. I always jump first and see where I land later.

"She's lying." I don't have to phrase it as a question, the look on his face is all telling.

Alfie's eyes shift and his hand drops, taking his warmth with him. Dammit. It's been a while since he's shown affection. Ever since he was shot, he's been withdrawn and even the sexy times we shared were lacking intimacy and basically me sucking cock, and him getting the both of us off quick and easy.

It's basically the reason why I called his doctor and asked for advice because he wouldn't get out of bed and sent the nurse away on the first day, the one who had to change the bandages and check his injuries.

I know he's struggling with the whole situation of not liking the restrictions suddenly laid upon him. And it's also the reason why I received the suggestion to try and find a caregiver. One who would stick around.

The first few, like the nurse, were easily scared away by Alfie. And then Greta showed up. I didn't even know the agency sent over a new one. To be honest, after the first few ran away screaming, I didn't think they would send over anyone else.

Weston walks inside and a lump is growing in my throat. I'm such a damn idiot. Alfie is right, I always get blinded by wearing rose colored glasses; seeing everything with a dash of roses and sunshine and expect the good in people. And it's weird because I come from parents who did nothing but kick me down all my life.

"Aw, fuck. Prez, can you please wait in the kitchen for us?" Alfie grumbles.

I close my eyes and pinch the bridge of my nose while I wave my hand in my face in an effort to cool myself down. I feel Alfie's strong, big hand with callused fingers wrap around my nape as he gives a harsh squeeze.

"Open your pretty eyes, boy. Give me the stormy gray."

I rapidly blink a few times to make the stinging go away. I hate crying and being emotional. I can't help it and most times it happens when I'm angry. All while people think I'm sad or pathetic.

"You and I will find out her intentions. Good or bad, we could always tie her to our bed and spank her lush ass, right?" The corner of his mouth twitches and now I'm getting a freaking lump in my throat because for the first time I'm seeing and hearing the affection in his voice and face which has been missing for weeks.

Even if this woman might have some ulterior motive we're not aware of, she is succeeding to bring the old Alfie I love back. And with what he just said…knowing how possessive he is and the need to be in charge when we have a woman between us. I can use this to challenge him.

Thinking fast I try to keep our connection going and say, "Only if I get to have her pussy first."

His head tilts ever so slightly and I can tell he's observing me. This is who he is; perceptive. And it's also why he called for this meeting and wants to question Greta. Always the protector and the dominant one.

His reply doesn't come as a surprise when he leans in and whispers beside my ear, "Only if I get to fuck your ass while you're balls deep inside her pussy. I'll make sure to control the good pounding you'll give her."

Rock. Hard. That's me. A few words from him and I'm ready to do everything he wants. First time I saw him I knew he'd be my downfall, but oh how sweet the ride has been. Though there has always been some nagging feeling of incompletion.

And it stoked my heart when Alfie brought up the same concerns one day. It led to a heavy discussion with the realization how the both of us wouldn't be complete without a woman. I've always loved both ways and it's also why my parents have practically declared me dead. But man, Alfie makes me feel alive. And sharing mutual goals while walking the path of life is all that matters.

Swallowing hard, I reach out and let my knuckles brush over the thick bulge in his pants. "I guess we have a deal. Now, let's head to the kitchen. We don't want to keep Weston waiting," I whisper in a lustful tone.

Alfie grabs my wrist and pushes my hand against his cock, leaving me to cup him as he rubs himself against me. "Don't. Taunt. You know what happens when you do."

Hell to the yes, I do. Hawt, raunchy, dirty as last week's socks sex. But we both wouldn't want it any other way.

And it's for this reason I give his hardness a nice squeeze before I dash away and add over my shoulder, "Talk to the ass, sexy." And I smack my own ass.

His rumble of laughter hits me straight in the chest. I quickly wave my hand in front of my face to get rid of all the emotions flowing through me. Seems I have my man back, and I know I have Greta to thank for it.

I don't even care what she's involved in or how suspicious her behavior is. Alfie and I have never been fully intrigued by the same woman. Desire to have random pussy in between us? Sure. We're both man enough to admit the sweet feel of sliding your dick into tight pussy is awesome, but feeling it while having it tightened by another dick? Mind-blowing.

It's also the reason the feeling of incompletion must be solved by adding a woman to our relationship. Not just any woman; Greta. She doesn't back down from Alfie's dirty remarks, joins in playful banter, and hasn't run away screaming. I'm going to make sure she'll be our woman.

"Joaquin." Weston nods and lifts his cup of coffee.

There's a rumble of voices and in stroll Decker, Roper, Garrett, and Alfie.

"Have a seat," Alfie says and sits in one of the chairs, hooking his cane on the table to keep it close. "Coffee?" he asks me with a raised eyebrow.

I should say, "Yes, add some sugar for me, hun." And plant my ass on a chair too. But the truth is…I like caring for others and to make them feel good, it gives me satisfaction in return. It's why I make my hands busy and hand everyone a cup before I join them with some tea for myself.

"She's too clean," Decker states. "And I'm not getting the full background details on paper you told me about. There are no other family members named Greta who she inherited the name from like she mentioned to you. I think this woman is undercover but spilled personal shit by accident. Which means she's a rookie or she might not like her job all that much."

"Fuck," Alfie grunts while my heart sinks. "And to think she told me right to my face she was an agent, but I thought she meant before she was a caregiver."

Weston checks his watch. "I expect a text message any minute from the prospect we put on her."

"I have information from a buddy of mine at the FBI," Decker states. "But this needs to stay between us."

We all nod. I know I'm the odd one out at this table since all these men are brothers through the MC they're all a part of. I'm not a biker and other than being with Alfie, I have no connection. Through the years I've earned my place, though. Trust and loyalty are what we're all made of and it's the reason why I'm sitting at this table among them; fully accepted.

Decker leans back and lets out a rough sigh. "Our MC is under investigation. DEA. He couldn't say anything else but it's safe to say we have an undercover DEA agent nosing around in our MC."

"Motherfucker," Roper grumbles.

Garrett curses while Alfie is locking eyes with me. Unbelievable. The woman who has been around us for the last few days has been lying to us and trying to put us in jail? Oh, gosh. They don't think I have anything to do with it, do they?

I feel my eyes widen but Alfie slowly shakes his head. "Breathe, boy. You don't have anything to do with opening our home to the DEA. You might have hired her but she showed up on our doorstep responding to a job opening you placed through a legit company."

Decker snorts. "As if. You're a big ol' softhearted, loyal man, Joaquin. We know you wouldn't have anything to do with it. The DEA is smart and took the opportunity of the job opening you guys had. And they're targeting Alfie for some reason."

"Not just some reason," Weston says as he places his empty mug back on the table. "It doesn't require a high IQ to wonder why, since we're clean as fuck. Up until the day before Alfie got shot."

"Deranged Hounds MC," Garrett grumbles. "Those fuckers didn't have their shit in order. The rats who stole money and property, this is a backfire from all of that, right?"

"I was the one whose name is linked through the property I sold to Deranged Hounds in order for them to back off and leave Kadence, Colt's old lady, alone." Alfie groans. "That's the link. Kadence is Rowen's sister. Rowen is now the president and is trying to steer the club into legal shit but it might not be quick enough. And for us to be infiltrated? Fucking hell, this is bad."

Weston shakes his head. "We don't have anything to hide. They might think we're in the same shady shit, but we're not. You selling property to Rowen for one fucking dollar might have triggered the DEA to get the idea our MCs are in bed together."

Fuckety-fuck. Sounds logical. Kadence is tied to Deranged Hounds MC since she was born into it. Her father was the president until he was killed by a few of his own men. Rats who stole money and somehow the property which was their clubhouse. They lost a lot and with Rowen becoming the new president, he needed a new VP.

That asshole Cannon–the one who shot Alfie–thought he would become the new VP. And since he had the hots for Kadence, Rowen promised him his sister to keep her close to the MC. It's a whole bucket full of craziness because Kadence and Rowen's mother committed suicide on the day of their father's funeral.

Kadence came running here since her best friend is Mayven, Colt's sister. Colt fell in love with Kadence and wanted to offer Rowen a deal; money and new property to save their MC. Rowen accepted Colt's claim before they offered him a deal so the whole money and property aspect was a bonus.

Cannon didn't accept his president's order and went rogue. He came here, guns blazing, in an effort to take Kadence. It resulted in his death and getting Alfie shot. And now yet again it all blows back on us.

Oh, lordy, I say us because I'm a part of this MC and their problems are mine too. I accepted it the day I accepted Alfie's claim. And it sucks big freaking monkey balls to find out Greta is an undercover agent because I really thought she was the one for Alfie and me.

A big hand covers my thigh underneath the table and gives me a hard squeeze, bringing me back to the discussion at hand. "How would you like to handle this, Prez? I hate to say it, but the woman is the reason why I got my ass out of bed every morning the past few days."

Garrett chuckles. "I thought you guys wanted her in bed… along with you instead of getting out of it."

Alfie's hand on my thigh keeps me in place. The man flawlessly knows when my body is tense and I'm about to blow. But I'm also not surprised by the anger in Alfie's voice when he says, "Watch it, Garrett. The woman hasn't done anything wrong yet."

"Except lie and stroll into our MC under false pretenses," Roper mutters.

"Oh, for fuck's sake, Roper. The rookie is doing her fucking job, have some respect." I shoot a thankful smile at Decker who just stood up for Greta.

Even if I feel betrayed, Decker speaks the truth; Greta is just doing her job.

Weston crosses his arms in front of his chest. "What if you two woo her? Try to find out if she'll spill the beans and work from there. If she closes up and stays away? Nice job too. We have nothing to hide and for sure as fuck we're not going to warn Rowen. I want all connections severed until this shit is cleared up. And Roper? Talk to Colt. Even if Kadence hates her brother right now, I want to make sure there is no contact at all. Understood?"

Heads bob and I don't realize I'm picking my nails again until Alfie's hand engulfs both of mine.

"We'll push her and see how she'll react." Alfie shoots me a wink. "Right?"

He knows damn well I can't say no if he shoots me a wink. He always makes me swoon when he does that. Besides, I really like the woman who has been staying with us for the last couple of days.

"You betcha." I grin, already looking forward to the pushing part. Hoping it involves my hips doing the pushing in her warm and welcome pussy.

"Okay, let's head out before she comes back. I don't want her wondering why all of us are gathered here. And for now, keep her away from the clubhouse and the other old ladies along with our kids. If you want to get back to working with the horses, Alfie? Be my guest, but shoot Colt a text first so he can make sure to keep others away." Weston stands and nods at me. "Thanks for the coffee."

I trail behind all of the men and close the door behind them. Turning toward the kitchen I see Alfie leaning against the door jamb.

"Ready for some fun?" He grins.

I purse my lips. "I thought you'd never ask."

CHAPTER 04

ALFIE

"Any suggestions on how we're going to get into her panties? I'm thinking you're going to have to take the lead. She's friendlier toward you and thinks I'm the asshole. This calls for some good cop, bad cop action. You being the good one."

Joaquin snorts. "And she being the cop."

There's that jab in my chest again. I have no damn clue why it strikes me so hard to become aware this woman has been playing with us. My phone vibrates in my pocket, when I check I see Weston is calling.

He starts to rattle as soon as I answer. "The prospect I put on her just called me to report there was an incident. She's on her way to you guys, or he thinks she went your way since he decided to follow the guy she had an argument with. She threw the first punch but the fucker hit her back. She got in her car and left, so this is your heads up. I'll check in later when the prospect has more info on the fucker."

"Thanks," I grunt and end the call. I connect my gaze with

Joaquin and give a short recap of what Weston just said.

He's about to say something but I notice her car coming through the gate. I point at the window. Joaquin turns and curses underneath his breath.

Her smokey gray ombré hair is pulled back into a braid but some strands have fallen out. Eyes puffy and one side of her face is clearly more red. I can't fucking believe a guy hit her, even if she was the one to strike first.

Without thinking I head out and stalk right up to her car to open the door. She's still sitting there, trying to get a grip before entering our house. But suddenly nothing matters except the need to comfort this woman.

She gasps when I pull her out of the car and into my arms. I kick the door shut and stalk back into the house, letting Joaquin close the door behind us. I take a seat on the couch and place her on my lap.

"You shouldn't put too much weight on your leg," she croaks.

And it's then I realize I didn't even reach for my cane or feel the discomfort I usually have when I put weight on my leg or arm.

I take her head into my hands. "Some things are more important and it lets you bite through the pain to deal with important stuff first. So, mind telling me what happened?"

Her eyes are all puffy and red and her bottom lip trembles before she sinks her teeth into it.

"Oh, come on, baby girl," Joaquin says with liquid comfort in his voice. "We're here for you whatever you need."

She's fucking torn. Her eyes are bouncing all over the place and there's such pain running through her it's lashing out and hits me right in the chest. And that's exactly where I pull her against and slowly rock her from left to right while Joaquin strokes her back.

"Fuck it," I growl and pull her back. "Who was the fucker hitting you? And I hope to hell the punch you threw was hard or I'll have to show you how to get a better jab in next time."

She covers her face with her hands. "Oh, no, no, no. Dammit,

I should have known." Her hands drop. "You had me followed?"

"More than that, sweet cheeks. More than that. But whatever it is, we can handle it." Joaquin brushes his thumbs underneath her eyes to gently wipe her tears away.

"No, you can't." Her eyes go down and I take this moment to draw Joaquin's attention.

Our connection has always been one on a deeper level. I can sense how he feels and in return he knows exactly how to handle me or knows what to do or what needs to be done. Like now. Our gazes collide and I give one single nod and the crinkles around his eyes show me he understands the hint I just gave him.

His well-groomed eyebrow raises and I am very aware what I'm asking him to do and I can't help but give him a smirk before I nod. Hell yes, I'm sure. And it's rare because we might have fucked a woman together in the past, but since the day I claimed Joaquin was the day I didn't want him to kiss another person.

Suck a pussy, sure. But tongue fuck another person? Hell no. His mouth is mine and I explained it very clear how all his kisses are mine alone. But in this moment? She needs it and though I'm dying to taste her–circumstances be damned–I can't be the one who kisses her first.

I'm holding her and know very well I'm too dominant to take her. Joaquin's kisses are phenomenal. The man can swoop you away with his tongue and draw you in where only surrender is the option you gladly take.

He places a finger underneath her jaw and tips her head slightly back. Leaning forward he catches her lips in a kiss right before my very eyes. It's as if he's sucking my cock. I can't describe it any other way than I'm getting hard by the view of his lips brushing hers and knowing how good it feels.

I've always been a man who enjoys watching. But this? I've been plugged into their moment where sparks fly as they land on my skin to scorch me with the heat they're creating. I'm unable to resist and place a kiss on her shoulder and move my way up to her neck.

She moans into Joaquin's mouth and by now I've passed the point of rational thought. Her hand slides in my hair, nails scraping my scalp and I make sure to sink my teeth into her earlobe to give her a spark of pain mixed with pleasure when I lick the sting away.

She's still sitting on my lap but she's facing Joaquin, who is thoroughly ravishing her mouth. Working on the buttons of her blouse, I sneak my hand in and knead her breast. Instantly she pulls my head closer and whimpers.

So damn responsive. I have the sudden need to feel both our cocks slide inside this woman at the same time. Lust like never before slams through me and it makes me tear at her clothes, ripping away her bra so she's now naked from the waist up.

Joaquin breaks the kiss and he's wearing a big smile as the both of us see the desire swirling in Greta's dazed look.

"You have to taste her. Enchanting. She kisses like the first rain on a summer's day and all you want to do is fucking dance in it," Joaquin croaks.

He gently guides her head toward me and I follow his lead to crush my mouth against hers. She instantly opens for me and I thrust my tongue inside, colliding with hers allowing the electricity to bounce off our connection.

She gasps into my mouth and I don't even have to pull back and see why because I instinctively know Joaquin is sucking her nipples. We flawlessly know how to please a woman and yet it feels like everything before now has had the sole purpose of perfecting our skills for this woman.

There's slight frustration pulling at me due to the little room we have and the way all of us are in this, we might as well take this party somewhere else to finish it. Though, first I relish in the comfort of her kiss before regretfully pulling back.

"Joaquin," I murmur.

He lets go of her nipple with a plop and glances at me. He gets to his feet, allowing me to stand and hold Greta in my arms as I make my way into the direction of our bedroom. Every step I take there's a sliver of fear Greta will regret our little kissing session on the couch but it doesn't come. In fact, she snuggles closer and places a sloppy kiss against my neck.

By the time I place her on the bed, Joaquin is naked and crawling on the mattress to capture one of her nipples again. Her hand goes to the back of his head, fingers sinking in his hair to keep him in place as her eyes start to undress me.

She catches every move I make to get rid of my clothes until her eyes widen. Yeah, she damn well knew I was pierced. She might have even had a glimpse of it over the past few days, but to see it right in front of her while my cock is hard as fuck is a complete different visual.

I palm myself and slowly stroke up and down, letting my thumb slide over the barbell poking from underneath the head straight through the slit. Precum spills and I step closer to the bed. Placing one knee on the mattress I inch closer to her mouth and without thinking her tongue sneaks out and fucking licks me.

"Motherfucking hell," I grunt and the air rushes straight out of my lungs.

Joaquin huskily chuckles. "Play with the barbell. Flip it with your tongue underneath the head."

I watch from the corner of my eye how he crawls down her body and nestles himself between her legs.

"I'm clean. Joaquin too. You?" I grunt as her tongue swirls around my cock.

Her eyes hit mine. Placing a soft kiss on the head as she says, "Clean and on the pill."

I fist her gorgeous hair. "Suck her pussy good and hard, Joaquin. But don't let her come. Not until I tell you to. Open up, babe. I'm going to fuck your mouth."

I tighten my grip. She gasps, causing her lips to part and I take advantage by feeding my cock into her hot mouth. I know Joaquin is spearing her pussy with his tongue because she fucking hums around my cock as if a jolt of pleasure is releasing from her into me.

I keep her head in place while I slowly let my hips do the

work. Sliding in and out of her mouth while my eyes bounce between both of her lips. The ones sucking my cock and the other ones getting sucked on by Joaquin.

Fucking perfect. Sharing is caring and magnificent when it's between people who share the same mindset. All a-fucking-board. Because what lies before us is a destination we're all heading for with eyes and hearts wide open.

"Joaquin," I grit, feeling our woman suck my cock so damn good my balls already start to tingle, and I need a distraction and my curiosity fed. "How sweet?"

The lines around his eyes crinkle and my man lifts his head, mouth and jaw glistening. He crawls slightly up her body and lets our lips meet. That's fucking it. Her taste on my man's tongue while she's sucking my cock. Bliss. Utter satisfaction where I'm the one in control and have these two lovers tangled with desire to make sure pleasure hits all of us.

I reach down with my free hand and lean forward, getting the cooperation of Joaquin as he lets me guide his dick to nudge Greta's entrance. Letting him slide through her folds and spreading the wetness while I deepen our kiss, knowing I'm tasting the place I'm shoving his dick inside.

He groans and Greta moans around my cock, vibrations flowing through my veins, making my eyes roll into the back of my head while I fight like hell to hold my orgasm back. Fuck.

So.

Damn.

Good.

One of my hands is gripping Joaquin's neck while the other is still fisting Greta's hair. All three connected. The two of us ramming our cocks into her willing body as she shakes with pleasure. Her lips tighten around me, her head bobbing and trying to swallow me whole.

Usually I can watch Joaquin getting pleasure for a long time, relishing in the visual but now? The way her tongue is playing with the underside of the head where my piercing is as she switches it up by taking me to the back of her throat and damn well swallows? Utter perfection.

Sweat is trickling down Joaquin's forehead. His thrusts are rough and choppy. I know he's close and so am I. Letting go of his neck I let my fingers slide down between their bodies in search of her clit.

"You'd better clench that pussy hard and rip the cum from his dick, you hear me, Greta? I'll let you come if you take our cum inside you. Understand?" She whimpers while I ram my cock deep down her throat, keeping her head in place by the tight grip on her hair. "That's it, baby. Come for us."

Slow circles around her bundle of nerves, I press down right on the center and feel with my other fingers how Joaquin's dick is being rewarded by a rush of her arousal as she comes beautifully.

Greta moans around my cock. I can't hold back when I hear Joaquin grunt as his body jerks. I keep Greta's head in place and throw my hips forward, letting a roar of satisfaction slide out of my chest while slowly pumping her mouth to make sure every drop is ripped from my body and spilled into her.

I untangle my fingers when she slightly leans her head back. Her whole face screams fully sated as she glances up at me before letting her eyes connect with Joaquin. My gaze is set on where his dick is still lodged inside her pussy. Slowly pulling out, he shifts and curls his body against her back.

They leave room for me and her hand reaches out as she drags me down against her. She's so tiny, she fits in between our bodies perfectly. Her head lies on my chest while I can easily reach for Joaquin to give the man a lazy sloppy kiss for the sake of perfection.

There's only a slight twinge in my shoulder and leg. Mind over matter you might say or the pain of the last few days was a mental one I needed to shake. I know for damn sure my body has had enough time to fully heal from the injuries it sustained and Joaquin and Greta might have been right to think my ego was mostly injured.

None of it matters because we're lying in one bed, all of us sated and perfectly aligned. I know very well we have a long road to cover until the dark clouds hiding our future are dissolved enough to dream ahead. But we're on that fucking road and I'm taking the wheel to guide us to a clear and better one.

CHAPTER 05

GRETA

Completely sated and wrapped in warmth and comfort. It's a hard contrast of what I was feeling hours ago when my asshole partner tried to blackmail me. Shoving the incident, my job, and the decision to quit to the back of my mind, I snuggle against Alfie's chest and reach behind for Joaquin.

Two men. A wild dream and another stark contrast of what I've once experienced back in my college years. Clearly, back then the two men I was with didn't know what the hell they were doing. Not to mention it was as if during that encounter the two men needed to prove themselves to each other.

Rivalry, jealousy, the whole "my dick is bigger than yours, and I know how to use it" while in the meantime I get the brunt of their alpha male chest banging and it wasn't anywhere near what I've just experienced.

Joaquin was an extension of Alfie, where Alfie took the lead, and yet made sure not to interfere with the pleasure of either of us. Holy shit, I don't know if this was a one-time thing or if I just needed to be swooped away from a screwed-up state of mind…but I could go for a second round if they're up for it.

I'm about to spill my thoughts about being up for more of this action when they both pop out a question.

"Have you tried anal before?" Joaquin asks as his hand slides to my ass.

"So, DEA agent, huh?" Alfie rumbles.

Shock fills me and how comfortable I was a moment ago, I'm now strung tight as a string. And in all honesty, I'd rather answer the anal question and leave the DEA agent statement. Holy shit. I now realize they knew I was a DEA agent before we ended up in bed together.

How can they be so freaking kind and caring while they know I'm DEA and my job is to investigate their MC? Though for all they know I could be an evil bitch wanting to do anything to get them behind bars.

"Yes." I clear my throat. "If done with the right preparations, anal is enjoyable." I cringe at the reminder of my one and only previous experience many years ago, and for the fact that I've managed to answer both their questions at the same time.

But the "right preparations" statement is true because I've had pleasurable encounters with butt plugs. Somehow, I know being with these two men at the same time–either double penetration involving my pussy or ass along with it–wouldn't compare to anything I've ever encountered.

Alfie places a finger underneath my jaw and tips my head back to make eye contact. "Talk to me, and not about your tight little hole because we'll handle all the preparations you need to take the both of us at the same time."

"I'm on a case involving your MC and Deranged Hounds. We need to know if the Iron Hot Blood is involved in criminal activities too. There was a link between you and them, Alfie. You sold them the property where their new clubhouse is now located. A dollar, really? It screams shady business," I scold and push myself upright.

Dashing off the bed I start to pace in an effort to shake the anger. This is screwed up, no matter what angle I look at it. Not only my private life, my work environment, my insane partner I'm forced to work with, this case, and these two men who gave me the best time of my life a mere moment ago. And now everything is twisted beyond repair.

"Her ass is so cute when she strides."

"Her ass? You know I'm a big boobs man. Have you seen them bounce? She needs to take a ride on my cock while my face is buried in sweet heaven," Alfie groans. "I just had a visual. Greta on hands and knees, you bounce her off your cock while I'm lying underneath to ping-pong my gaze back and forth between tits and you guys being connected. Yeah, let's do that. We need to make a list. My cock in her pussy, yours in her ass. The both of us simultaneously rubbing dicks inside her pussy. Fuck. The list is never-ending."

Damn that man and the visuals he just planted in my head.

"Focus!" I snap and point a finger in Alfie's direction. "Why one dollar? And why the shooting? Did you owe them more than the property? Did they force you? Are you involved in any of their business?" I close my eyes and shake my head. "I can't see why. The days I've been here it's all work involving the ranch and Joaquin works hard at the clinic. What does this MC do? Deranged Hounds was involved with drugs and guns. All links to tie to them until recently. Then you guys get into the picture. Alfie, you were in the hospital…gunshots get reported, you know."

"You done rattling?" Alfie grunts.

"No! My asshole partner wants me to plant evidence since I told him there is no connection and you guys along with your MC are squeaky clean. He was pissed and still thinks you're dirty but hiding it better and wants to nail you. He wants a promotion and needs to put you guys behind bars to get it. He doesn't care about truth or lies. He deemed you guilty while all you guys talk about, and do, is ranch stuff. Longhorns, maintenance, training horses, getting more livestock. And dickhead Matt, my asshole partner, thinks I can easily transfer some files onto your laptop. Hell, hide some drugs in your cabin and plant some over at the clubhouse while I'm at it. And if I didn't? He would make sure I didn't have a life left to return to. He blabbered a detailed story about how he's done it before and how the woman ended up dead. He laughed in my face and it made me feel as if he was a vile criminal instead of an agent. He said I wouldn't dare defy him because it's easy for me to do since I am fucking easy. He has the pictures to prove it. Hell, he said I probably take both your cocks at the same time because it's my thing. Oh. My. God. And I did, didn't I?"

I cover my face with my hands and start to furiously rub my eyes as I start to ramble to myself, "How the hell did this day go from bad to worse in supernova style? This morning I was certain I had enough information to round up my report and explain how there was no link or illegal activities involving the Iron Hot Blood ranch. Heading to my partner for a check in I reported my findings and then he went nuts. He raved about an upcoming promotion and how he would lose it if he didn't have this major bust. The idiot showed me a picture on his phone. It was from a photoshoot I did years ago when I needed money to clear away a huge part of the debt my parents left behind. He insinuated I had sex with those two men who I did a sexy lingerie shoot with. Yes, he was right, but it was none of his business. And the shoot happened before I became an agent. It doesn't interfere with my career, it's in the past and it should stay that way."

I swallow hard and let my hands drop. "Until he swiped his finger over the screen and I saw in a flash how there was a photo of those two men having sex with a woman. It couldn't have been me. My face wasn't even in the picture. When I had sex with them it was at their house, they were roommates. But a second of doubt running through my head was enough for Matt fucking Carlinck to jump to the conclusion he had something to blackmail me with. He started to push me mentally and that's when I hit the asshole. He threw a punch in return and I left. Like I said, I don't even know if the photograph is real…but it doesn't matter. The photoshoot is enough to spread doubts. And if I have to work with assholes like him? I'd rather–"

"Suck our cocks and quit your job? Because I'm rich and Joaquin and I will both support you as our woman. It's why I sold Rowen the property for one dollar because I couldn't give two shits about money." Alfie grins and all I can do is stare at him.

"You did not just say that," I hiss.

Joaquin scrambles off the bed with his lean, naked, and sculpted body. He reminds me of my own nakedness. Dammit, my head is drowning with all the issues surrounding me while I need to focus and find my way out.

"Come on, sweetheart. Come sit. Alfie's head is always locked in the gutter but he also sometimes manages not to think with his dick. He's the kind of man who can handle anything. Let's all take a breath and focus. Alfie will know what to do, won't you?" Joaquin pierces Alfie with a hard look while he guides me to the mattress and sits down next to me.

Alfie stalks to the closet and throws on a pair of jeans. He doesn't seem to use his cane anymore, though I can't help but notice the slight limp. The leg still bothers him but he's made great progress recovering from his injury.

He throws a pair of light blue jeans in Joaquin's direction and grabs a shirt. Before I know it, he's pulling it over my head. The shirt swallows me since Alfie's much bigger than me but it's also comforting to be wrapped by his clean scent.

Alfie lets his knuckles slide over my cheek. "I can't think straight if I have those magnificent tits on display. Now. One more time. This Matt, your asshole partner. He tried to blackmail you into planting evidence because he wants a higher position with the DEA? Am I correct?"

I give a faint nod.

"It sounds too simple if you ask me," he states and rubs a finger over his jaw.

Anger surges through me but I don't get to say anything since Joaquin prevents me when he whispers in my ear, "Let him ramble for a bit. He's not talking to you or me, he's getting things straight in his head. Believe me, I've tried to talk when he's like this, but he doesn't even listen when he gets to this stage."

I lean into Joaquin's embrace, giving up on the havoc and deciding I'm too drained with my head spinning while I don't see an option to get out of this loop I'm stuck in.

Alfie stalks away and comes back holding his phone. "Decker, can you get me info on Greta's partner? His name is Matt Carlinck. And make sure to dig deep when it comes to his career. I want to know if the fucker has ambitions and every step he took climbing up the ladder and who he kicked out of his way to get where he is. Okay. Thanks."

"What's going to happen now?" I question.

"Now we're going to get properly dressed and head for the clubhouse. I need to talk to Weston." Alfie grabs a shirt and throws it on before putting his leather cut over it.

Joaquin gets up and runs his fingers through his hair. He looks uncertain, as if he wants to bring something up but doesn't know how to address the issue he's clearly struggling with.

Alfie sighs. "I know. Weston ordered us to wrap her around our finger and keep her away from the clubhouse. But she spilled details without thinking. I get the feeling she's open and honest about everything she told us." He pierces me with a harsh look. "And if you are lying, we'll find out soon enough and deal with it."

"I'm not lying. My report about you guys is in my car, glance it over if you don't believe me. After Matt tried to blackmail me I thought on the drive over here about everything and decided to quit my job. I've made a career shift before: I think it's time for me to crawl into a corner and lick my wounds. But I'm too pissed, dammit. I normally don't let anyone walk right over me but what choice do I have? Those pictures are out there. I did the photoshoot and had sex with them too." I let my head drop into my hands. "I'm such an idiot."

A growl rumbles and my hands are pulled away. "I don't want to hear you call yourself that ever again. You gave into your sexuality and you provided for yourself. Those photos gave you the chance to pay off a great deal of your debt. And you shouldn't quit a job over a fucking asshole who thinks he can force his way onto you. He shouldn't fucking be in a position if he thinks he can handle his partner this way."

Joaquin strokes my back while I face Alfie's furious gaze. These two. Harsh and sweet, muscled and lean, they are so well balanced it's perfection from both worlds. My eyes sting and I can't help the first tear from falling.

"You shouldn't growl at her when she's vulnerable," Joaquin scolds.

"Then she shouldn't be taking this too fucking hard. It's that asshole Matt's fault, not hers."

"Sorry," I croak and try to wipe my tears away. "It's all too much right now and with the two of you being so sweet to me… I'm so sorry to come into your home and–"

Another growl rumbles from Alfie's chest before I feel the bed dip and his strong arms surround me. "You're doing your job, Greta. Even if it involved going undercover. Clearly, we don't have anything to hide and we're not pissed. Weston might have said he doesn't want you anywhere near the clubhouse and he's right. Inside the clubhouse you'll get to meet the old ladies, their kids, all of the others while our brotherhood revolves around trust, friendship, and loyalty. And I think you know as well as Joaquin and I do shit between us has shifted. If us sharing a bed wasn't clear enough, we want you to be ours."

Hope blooms inside my chest but I try to push it down. "You guys can't. I'm not–"

I'm prevented from finishing my sentence when Joaquin grabs my jaw and turns me to face him before he takes my lips in a harsh kiss.

He pulls back just as quickly. "Do not finish that sentence. We don't want grumpy dragging you over my lap so I can hold you while he spanks your sexy, curvy ass."

A tiny bark of laughter slips over my lips.

"You and I both know the only reason you're telling her this is because you want to be the one giving her ass your handprint," Alfie mutters and this time it's not a tiny bark of laughter but a full-blown one ripping from me.

It must be the whirl of events leading up to this moment, but by laughing with these two there's also a large weight falling from my shoulders. Maybe it should be as easy as quitting my job and letting these two enter my life. A guaranteed turnaround.

One where I would get to ride a horse again or maybe own a dog or a duck. I've always loved animals. But due to my job and the apartment I rent not allowing any pets, it's been very lonely.

"What thought entered your brain, darlin'?" Alfie questions. "The one making your eyes twinkle with longing."

I sigh and think about spilling my thoughts. I might as well, I have nothing to hide or lose at this point anyway. "I miss riding horses. Miss animals surrounding me like I used to have when my parents were still alive. And I really, really would like to have a pet duck. The building I live in doesn't allow any pets. I never had one. And they look so cute and fluffy."

"For sure as shit you're going to be riding very soon. I have three horses and am always breaking in new ones or training other quarter horses we breed and sell. The ducks, though? We don't have a pond. Maybe Joaquin can pick up a puppy for us, or a stray in need of a home. He's been nagging me to get us a dog. Those things are cute and fluffy enough for you too, right?"

"They are cute and fluffy," Joaquin says with a hint of laughter in his voice. "But like Alfie says, we don't have a pond. Maybe we could let him swim in a large tub, until we have a–"

"No fucking ducklings. Get a damn dog. One of those large breeds and not the kind we need to carry either. If we leave it to you, I bet we'll end up with one we need to hold like a second handbag or something," Alfie grumbles.

Joaquin huffs and I can't help but smile. These two are so different and yet they fit perfectly together. I should be thankful they open their arms to embrace me. They don't judge why I came into their lives or about my past.

"You two really are something." A sigh rips from me and I add with determination, "Even if I won't ever get a duck, I'd gladly settle for having the two of you."

"Geez, I don't know if we should be thankful or crushed. I mean, I'm cute...not fluffy...but at least I get picked over a freaking duck," Joaquin huffs overly dramatic.

Alfie snickers. "You are all cute and fluffy, boy. Besides, she didn't pick. She embraced the two of us. We're her ugly dicklings."

"Oh. My. Gosh. You did not just make an ugly ducklings penis joke." Joaquin rolls his eyes and laughter yet again fills the room.

Yes, I'm guessing my life is barely starting with this massive change. And if the contentment and carefree feeling is the promise of a future with them? I'll gladly jump into this new adventure and see what life with Alfie and Joaquin has to offer.

CHAPTER 06

JOAQUIN

I can't stop touching her. I've always been an all-hands-on-snuggle-bear, something Alfie doesn't mind when we're home. And he also doesn't mind showing affection when we're in the presence of his brothers, but it's different and brand new with the woman who is snuggled tight against me.

She laced our fingers when I threw an arm over her shoulder to pull her close. It's a right in your face statement and Cassidy is so happy for me, she's practically a puddle on the floor. She and Harlene are both my best friends. We go way back and also work together at the veterinarian clinic Harlene owns.

They've never judged me and accepted me for who I am; a weirdo with a strong will to carry life at the tip of my finger and twirl it around. Though I might seem as if I feel comfortable in my own skin, but it's taken a lot for me to get there.

Both my parents are still alive and yet they've declared their own son dead to the world. I had to drop out of veterinarian school because I couldn't afford it and it was made impossible to get a job with my father boycotting me whenever I applied.

All because I don't fall in love with a gender but a person. Or the fact my heart has always been big enough for more. But maybe it was because I liked black nail polish or act overdramatic, or even girly on some occasions. Whatever. I left all the negativity behind me. The people I'm surrounded with now accept me for who I am.

Harlene and Cassidy accepted me before that and when Harlene's father and brother died and she took over the veterinary clinic, she offered me a job and we all moved here. All while she knew I didn't finish my education but again she saw my worth and accepted me as an assistant.

As if I was born to do this job and it amazes me how life has a way of sliding into place after it's been shaking on its foundation. I help keep the clinic running smoothly and even get to assist in some of the cases; it's all I've ever dreamed of.

Well, that and Alfie. First time I saw him my jaw hit the floor and slid right back due to all the drool. Hawt. Rough. Oozing sex and to top it off…he was interested in me. Me. The weirdo with his own twisted look on life.

If someone would have told me I was going to end up with two sides of love I would not have believed it. It's the whole soulmates, white picket fence dream society dictates while in my head one soul shattered in three parts until it was set aflame to be merged into one the second Greta walked in the door.

I don't even care if she's DEA and came to us to investigate the MC. Okay, it's bad, I know. But you have to accept the rain and the sunshine to be able to see rainbows shining in the heavens above. And she is utter sunshine while our grumpy man might be compared to the rain.

And hey, I could be heavenly while we three create the rainbow. See? My mind works differently but being accepted for who you are is a warm blanket after walking home in a thunderstorm.

"Still don't want a leather cut, Joaquin? I mean, you could

be allowed in church right now since I overheard Alfie's claim," Garrett says. "The man got you riding a bike and you're already one of us, you've proven yourself loads of times in the past."

I can't help but snort. "The man also got me riding his dick. It doesn't mean I need to wear something special to be able to be a part of something. This is all him, Garrett. I'm happy sitting here with the old ladies."

Garrett shoots me a grin. "Ah. I get it now. You're an old lady, Joaquin."

"People and their labels," I mutter under my breath.

Greta squeezes my fingers. Alfie explained it to us when we walked to the clubhouse together. The second he strolled into church and was among his president and VP, he would claim Greta. Seeing he did the same for me, our triangle is plain, clear, and accepted for everyone in this MC.

And mostly for us; equal sides and united as one. I take a deep breath and let it all sink in deeper, still not fully believing this is possible and how lucky we are to have found one another. And it's not just us; we're a family now.

"You know," Garrett starts. "Back in the day they would call it a backup system. If something happened to one dude, the woman would still have the other man to take care of her and any children they might have."

"Don't you have to be somewhere?" I question. "We just found each other and you're rambling about a safety net in case one of us dies. I thrive on positive vibes and you're messing with our vibe, now shoo."

"Shoo? I'm not one of the animals running around the clinic, Joaquin." Garrett chuckles while I glare. He holds up his hands. "Fine, I'll leave you old ladies alone."

I shoot him a dashing smile and tell him in all sincerity, "I hope you get an old lady soon, one who will tie your balls with barbwire before she yanks them off."

"Harsh, Joaquin." Garrett shakes his head. "Fucking harsh for a man who has a nice set of balls himself."

"What the fuck, Garrett," Alfie growls from behind him. "How do you know he has a nice set of balls?"

"You should soothe grumpy before the vein on the side of his head blows," Greta whispers underneath her breath.

"You soothe the beast, I'll do it the next time," I whisper back.

Greta rolls her eyes and stands. Glancing back at me she says, "You don't want to do it because you like seeing him go alpha on anyone who makes a remark about you."

I shrug. "It's sexy."

She plunks back down next to me. "Yeah, you're right."

"I said get them in here, not go head to head with Garrett. Now, dammit," Weston bellows from the doorway of church.

All heads turn his way and Alfie steps toward us. "Come on, you two."

We follow him into church and he closes the door behind us. Greta's hand slides into mine and I keep our fingers linked as we take a seat at the large table. I've been inside church once or twice before.

Even if only members are allowed, Weston does let others sit in during a meeting if they're either involved in business at hand or needed for crucial information. But the look on their faces show no interest for information.

"The guy is clean," Decker says the moment Alfie takes a seat on the other side of Greta.

I can feel her body going tense and I give her hand a little squeeze of reassurance. Whatever happens, happens. I've been through my share of shit in my life and I can't speak for Alfie but I won't let this woman slip through our fingers. And deep down I know she's honest and telling the truth.

The way I see Alfie place his hand on her knee underneath the table tells me we're all fully in this together. My heart skips a beat. This is really it, something we have desired for years now and finally things have fallen into place. Well, we do have some bumps in the road to hobble over.

"I'm not lying," Greta says with a firm tone.

She might have been all tears and open emotions when it was just the three of us in our bedroom, but now she's the strong person she is, fighting for justice in her own way.

"He wanted me to plant evidence. He blackmailed me. Hell, he even mentioned he's done it before with another chapter of Iron Hot Blood." The whole room falls silent when she voices the last sentence.

Weston narrows his eyes and says in utter calmness, "Mind expanding a little about the last fact you threw on the table?"

"I don't know all the details of that case. He only mentioned he had a woman plant evidence before and how it was easy enough since bikers only think with their dicks. Videos of dog fights. No. Wolf fights, I think he mentioned wolf fights. And he made another threat on top of it. Well, I think he did because he said the woman who planted the evidence for him turned up dead. It made me feel as if he had a hand in it instead of the bikers she was betraying. Either way he put me on the spot, he thought I didn't have a choice. If I didn't plant the evidence, he would spread the picture of me naked with two men along with some of the pictures and details of the lingerie shoot, and with it ruining my career and my life. Or I'll end up dead."

She clears her throat and before my eyes she grows a little taller as she says, "I've been deep in debt. I've put every ounce of dignity into a box and endured what I had to do for me to be able to crawl out of debt and kept my head high while doing my job. I might not be able to keep my apartment if he ruins my career but I refuse to fall to my knees for a man who justifies actions for selfish reasons and drags good men into the dirt to step on their backs to get there."

Again, only silence fills the room, until Weston breaks it with the words, "Roper, get Figor on the phone and ask him to come down here."

Roper stands, grabs his phone and stalks out of church to make the call.

"You just gave us vital information and with it, confirmation. I now know with a hundred percent certainty you're not lying. I know what you're talking about with the mention of wolf fights and the setup along with it. The woman in question, the one who planted the evidence? She did indeed turn up dead. But I fucking swear no chapter of Iron Hot Blood would harm animals in any way. But they do own a special breed that looks ferocious, though they are highly trained and for sure as fuck don't participate in any dog fights. The president was arrested for the murder but it didn't stick since he had a solid alibi, not to mention he was innocent and like you mentioned…he was set up, both with planting the evidence and trying to pin a murder on him he didn't do. We need him here to talk this through because if it is the same fucker we're dealing with? We will need the backup and all the information we can find since he got away with it once, and I'll be damned if he taints me, you, or any one of our MCs." Weston stands at the same time Roper strolls back into the room.

"He'll be here in about two or three days," Roper states. "He and his VP are getting on their bikes as we speak but it's quite the distance he needs to cover to get here from his ranch to ours."

I lean in and tell Greta, "Nevada and Texas aren't right next to each other."

Greta nods and turns her head in Weston's direction. "Do you need me to do anything? I might have hit Matt and he punched me back, then I left. I don't know…he might have already sent the pictures like he said he would."

Alfie shakes his head. "He wouldn't. If he's done this before he'd wait to see what you would do before taking action."

"Alfie's right. He's done it before and feels confident and superior. I think you should send him a text. Somewhere in the lines of asking him not to send those pictures and what he expects you to do. He might not reply over texts, maybe he will if he's that stupid. Anyway, it's a first move to keep this warm before we can burn this fucker," Weston growls out those last words in anger.

Greta takes out her phone, types what Weston just said and turns it to show him. He nods and a second later Greta presses send. It only takes a handful of minutes before her phone vibrates.

"He replied back. He says he'll meet me at the same time and place in a few days and to wait for him to text me."

Weston and Decker both give her a tight nod.

"This gives us time to plan. We might not even need a few days to wrap this shit up. But we do need Figor, and not just for backup. This man smells trouble from miles away and he's dealt with this asshole before."

"Is she okay to roam around till then?" Alfie questions, and I'm sure he's referring to the previous order where Weston explicitly told him to keep Greta in our house and away from the rest of the ranch and the old ladies.

Weston rubs a hand over his face. "Why the fuck do all of you need to claim a woman wrapped in trouble?"

"Hey," Roper snaps. "I resent that. My woman wasn't in any trouble when I claimed her. In fact, she was the one who recognized trouble heading our way instead."

"Whatever," Weston grumbles and glances at Alfie. "She's shown loyalty, you claimed her, it's your responsibility." His gaze slides to Greta. "You do understand our dynamics and what it entails for Alfie if you betray us, right?"

Greta places her hand over Alfie's and gives our linked fingers a little squeeze. "I understand very well. And I would never turn my back on the men who welcomed me into their lives, even if I walked into theirs under false pretenses. Acceptance might be a word in the dictionary and for some a mutual agreement, but for me? These two who I now realize complete me, and who have a family surrounding them, who don't judge and stand strong? I will never walk away into loneliness and solitary emptiness after being wrapped with warmth and adoration they gave me. They showed a glimpse of a possible future and I have accepted them, and all of you along with it."

"A simple yes would have done the trick," Weston grumbles.

Roper chuckles and slaps his chest while I quickly wipe away a tear leaking from my eye.

I lean in to kiss her cheek, Alfie treating the other side of her face with his lips while I murmur, "Thank you for touching my heart."

Waving my hand, I try to steer my emotions back on track. Gosh, I can be such an emotional mess. But it's worth it. Like Weston said, a simple yes would have done the trick but she opened her heart and gave us a look inside.

"Okay, that's it. Joaquin is about to spread the waterworks. We're done here and I'll call church once Figor arrives." Weston turns on his heel and heads out the door, Roper and Decker slide out of the room too, leaving only the three of us behind.

"I won't let you near that asshole again," Alfie suddenly growls. "We'll wait for our other chapter to get here and handle it before the meet. Then we'll clear out your apartment and you're moving in with us."

Greta reaches out. "It's okay, Alfie. I'm an agent, remember? I am trained to handle these kinds of situations. The breakdown I had might have given you the impression I'm weak, and maybe I was in that moment when I was caught off guard by a partner who should have had my back instead of dragging me to the other side of the law and throwing away everything we as agents stand for. I am strong when I'm not blindsided and need to function and do what I was trained to do."

"You didn't have a breakdown, sweetie," I tell her. "You simply switched from being an agent to being a woman who needed to be comforted by her two men to get through the shit life threw at you. We all have our moments where we need others to lean on. Heck, you're the one who managed to drag Alfie out of his wallowing cloud of self-pity he was in after he was shot. See? Even the mighty stumble every once in a while."

"I didn't fucking stumble, I took three damn bullets," Alfie grumbles.

"Yeah, yeah, whatever you say, sugar." I roll my eyes and notice the smile and warm look sliding over Greta's face.

"Keep rattling that mouth and I'll shove something in there to shut you up," Alfie says and my dick goes from flaccid to rock-hard.

"You know damn well I'd still be able to hum with a mouth full of cock," I huskily reply.

Greta's full-blown laughter fills the air and with a load of affection she states, "You two are so freaking adorable."

Alfie drags her to her feet. "You're not too bad yourself, baby," he mutters and takes her lips in a scorching kiss.

Seeing them together flames up desire inside my veins. There's no room for jealousy in a relationship where sharing is a main necessity. You know what you want for yourself and it's this part you offer the other person. In our case we receive double the load right back and it only makes my heart swell even more.

CHAPTER 07

ALFIE

"Joaquin, lock the door," I order and take a seat in the chair while I keep Greta caged between my legs and the table.

I unbuckle my belt and slide the zipper down to free my cock. Palming myself I tighten my grip to give some relief. Damn, this woman has me on edge.

"Off with the pants, Greta. You're going to straddle me and take my cock. I'm dying to know how well your pussy is going to feel hot and tight around me. Then I'll ask Joaquin to join me. It's up to you to decide where you want to feel him. Are you ready, baby?"

Her dilated eyes are spilling lust and desire and I can taste it in the air crackling around us. I push myself, and the chair, back to create some room between us and the table. Greta's jeans hit the floor along with her panties. She's already straddling me. Joaquin appears behind her and I notice his hand sliding through her folds.

"Wet and ready." Joaquin groans and adds, "What do you

want, sweetie? His piercing hitting a spot deep inside you?" He glances around her and finds my gaze, palming my cock the next instant and lining it up at her entrance. "I don't think we're going to leave it up to her. Let her wrap her tight pussy around you and I'll put my mouth to work and see how she flowers open."

I hiss from the heat of her tightness sucking my cock down until she's impaled and I'm balls deep inside a place where the sun doesn't shine but the warmth is radiated in the same fucking brightness.

And as if that's not enough, I feel Joaquin's experienced mouth latching onto my balls. My eyes cross and I'm seconds away from detonation. If this is all that heaven will allow in this fucked-up world…there's no other place I'd rather live than in this moment where the three of us surround ourselves with pleasure.

I grab her ass and as I let her slide up and down my cock, I make sure to spread her ass cheeks, allowing Joaquin to play with her tight ring. When she lets herself drop and buries her face into my neck while she moans, I know for a fact she's treated to a finger sliding into her ass. I can feel him stroking me as I lift my hips from the chair. Damn.

So.

Fucking.

Good.

"You're drenched, Greta," Joaquin croaks.

The sound of a zipper cracks through the air and I let go of her ass cheeks, knowing Joaquin will take over. Right now, I don't want her head buried in my neck; she needs to be right in the center and pulled in every direction to throw her off focus enough to make her shatter into bliss.

I sink my fingers into her hair and pull her head back to capture her lips with mine. She gasps when I feel Joaquin's cock touch mine as he slides up and down her flesh in an effort to coat himself with her cream.

She's pushing back, searching for him and thank fuck an

experienced, unrestricted woman is the one who belongs to the two of us, allowing our instant connection to merge our bodies to their full extent.

I swallow her moan when Joaquin gently starts to nudge his cock against her pussy while he keeps pumping his finger in and out of her ass. One out, two in, preparing her to take his cock. Oh, fuck. Maybe she'll take us both into her greedy pussy because I can feel the head of his cock sliding against mine as she pushes back.

"Yes," she gasps and I grip her hips to keep her in place.

"Slowly, darlin', let Joaquin do the work," I tell her and I can feel her clench around me in response.

"Fuck. You guys," Joaquin groans. "You should see what I'm seeing." He hums. "Lean forward some more, sweets. Alfie?"

I wrap my arms around her and plaster her against me, sliding somewhat down to give Joaquin some more room to work with. And I can feel how wet she is by the way her juices slide down my balls. Joaquin's cock disappears but I can feel his hot breath the next instant.

He's going to lube us up some more and the way my balls are drawing up, I won't be able to prolong my orgasm for very long. The mere thought of the both of us possessing her is enough to make me spill my cum deep inside her welcoming pussy.

A gush of wind and the heat of the head of his cock gives me the knowledge Joaquin is standing, ready to line up and…

"Oh, God," Greta whimpers. "Please," she urges and moves slowly up and down my cock to work another one inside her body.

"Fuck, fuck, fuck," Joaquin grumbles. "You fucking minx, sucking the head right…fuuuuuck."

He slides deep because Greta is moving in between us. That right there shows her craving is as heated as ours and letting her lead allows her body to adjust. And hot damn, adjusting it does perfectly. I let my hand slide down to her ass at the same time Joaquin tries to grip her for balance, covering my hand.

Being connected, intimate, united, together. A special kind

of adoration doesn't begin to describe what's going through me. No matter our pasts, this right here is our future and it's laced with perfection.

Her pussy strangles my cock. She throws her head back and I watch–enthralled by the way her whole face washes with pleasure–as she comes beautifully at the same time cum rips in hot jets from my cock as I feel Joaquin's dick jerk inside her ass through the thin membrane. Pleasure thickens the air as we all try to catch our breath.

Her head is on my chest and I slowly stroke her back as she groans due to Joaquin gently pulling out of her ass. "I know I'm repeating myself, but you should see what I'm seeing. So damn hawt. My cum is sliding out of her ass and all over–"

"I can feel it leaking over my balls, boy. I don't need the damn visual."

Greta giggles and the sound is like bells ringing on Christmas morning, but it also makes my cock slide out of her pussy, adding my cum to the shared release.

"Come on." I smack her bare ass. "Let's get dressed and head home. I think it's time for some shower sex."

"We just had," Greta starts but her face shifts when she glances at my bare cock.

And it's not the size nor my piercing giving her the worried look.

She bites her lip before letting go and whispering, "I know I'm on the pill but that isn't always full protection against pregnancy. And with the both of you coming inside me…we haven't mentioned…what if…I mean," she stammers.

"Alfie and I have had long discussions about possible children in our future," Joaquin starts.

I tuck myself back into my jeans and let her know, "We both would like to enrich our lives with a large family. Adopted, all his, mine, none of it matters except for the love and devotion to give a solid home and future to whatever lives would expand our family."

She covers her face with her hands. "You guys," she

grumbles through her fingers and I don't know if she's horrified or happy.

Thank fuck Joaquin steps closer and pulls her hands away. "What's wrong, baby cakes?"

"Nothing," she squeaks. "You guys are too freaking perfect and I'm waiting for the bubble to burst. How are you two still single? Womenless. Ugh, whatever!"

A chuckle slips over my lips. "'Cause, we were waiting for you, Greta."

"Yes, we were," Joaquin murmurs and gives her a sweet kiss.

I step closer and he hands her to me so I can take her mouth. I end our kiss way too soon and when we're all dressed and ready we head out of church. Not paying any attention to all the eyes focused on us, we drag our woman out of the clubhouse and head for our cabin.

Two days pass where we enjoy our time together without any interference. Joaquin was able to take the first day off from work so we could be lazy and stay in bed most of the time. The second day I brought Greta to the stables and showed her my horses and the ones I worked with.

The woman looks absolutely gorgeous on the back of a horse and it's even more sexy to see how she handles a fifteen hundred pound horse between her legs. That's how Joaquin found us when he finished working at the clinic. The two of us leaned on the fence, watching how Greta enjoyed riding bareback.

It's a stark contrast to what I'm feeling now. There's a large pit in my stomach due to uncertainties and I want them dealt with. I left Greta and Joaquin in the cabin. They're watching some sappy movie because Garrett texted me the president and VP of our other chapter arrived at the ranch.

Stepping into the clubhouse the feeling of unease slides right off and I feel like a better man. The clubhouse is filled with my brothers and a handful of men from our other chapter. Weeks ago, I was in pain and bedbound. With solid determination from Joaquin and this bunch of crazy I managed to heal to a point where I needed Greta to give me the last push.

Standing here, seeing my brothers laughing, and knowing I have two loving people waiting for me at home makes me realize a person like me isn't better off alone. There are times when life gets crazy, balancing on a ship drifting toward disaster, a renegade with a loaded gun, living on the edge, or feeling like an outsider in the dark. But it only takes one moment in life to connect on a deeper level.

I'm thankful for everything I'm connected with. And I'll fight like hell to keep it this way. If I have to take more bullets to make sure everyone I love and care for are safe...so. Be. Fucking. It.

"Alfie, you remember Figor, right? Ash too," Weston says as he waves his fingers for me to get closer.

Yeah, I remember Figor alright, but damn.

"You've grown, brother," I grunt as the fucker grabs me in a man hug and slaps my back.

My shoulder screams at me. I might seem completely healed, but there's still tissue inside overcoming the damage that was done due to a bullet ripping through it. But there's no denying the friendliness of Figor.

He might be as big as a house and as strong as a primal animal ready to face any enemy, but he's also one of those people who can be a friend for life once you've gone through a moment where you really get to know one another.

And we did, a few years back when we were still wrapped in illegal shit, until Weston pulled us out. But right when we were confronted by a rival MC, amidst bullet rain, in swoops Figor along with a few of his men and his trained dogs.

Don't let him catch you calling them dogs. According to him they are a special breed which are descendants of wolves, only bigger and stronger. Anyway, if it weren't for him, his men, and pack, we wouldn't have survived.

We've met up a time or two since and I've even showed Joaquin some of their dogs since he loves animals and these are special and highly trained.

"Long time, my friend," Figor rumbles.

He's almost twice my size and that's something since I'm a big fucker myself. I'm glad I left my heart at home so I don't have to worry about him asking about either of them. I swear these guys are dipped in pheromones because if I remember correctly, all the women fell ass first to the ground with their legs spread wide wherever they made an appearance.

I glance around and now realize none of the old ladies or hangarounds are in the clubhouse. I can't help but snicker and shake my head. "Weston, did you rid the house of women to let these guys focus on the job at hand?"

Weston gives me a hard stare.

Ash snickers. "It was the first thing I said too. I was looking forward to some new sharable pussy."

Figor sticks his nose in the air and inhales deep. "Smell that? Alfie here reeks of two different people. Fucker has it made. Finally settled down completely, did you?" He shoots me a grin which I return.

Damn, the fucker either is good at guessing or has the same nose as his dogs, to be able to smell both Joaquin and Greta on me.

He slaps Ash on the back. "You'll be drowning in pussy soon enough when we're back home, brother. We need to deal with some business first. Which shouldn't take too much of our time because the lack of sharable pussy indicated you guys have more old ladies and less free action."

"And not a single regret," Roper grunts.

Figor holds his massive hands up. "No offense there, VP. It's all good. Hell, I envy you and yours. I'll kiss the moon on the day I gladly hand over my balls when I find my mate for life."

"I hope you find your old lady soon enough," Weston states. "Life changing. Not to mention the pain in the ass nights sitting up with babies and shit. But I wouldn't want it any other way."

"I hear ya," Figor grunts. "Now, let's get to the point. This fucker who put a rat bitch in our midst is now targeting you guys?"

"Yeah." Weston takes a seat on one of the couches in the

main room.

Since the large space is filled with only brothers, there's no need to head into church. Besides, with the handful of bikers from the other chapter, church would be overly crowded.

"Colt claimed the sister of another MC's president and that's how shit got started. The DEA had the Deranged Hounds MC under a microscope and when I sold them property–which was part of the deal we made with them to get Deranged Hounds to back off and leave Colt's old lady alone–for one fucking dollar, it triggered the DEA to set their eyes on us. Even more when one of those Deranged Hounds fuckers went AWOL on a suicide mission in an effort to get to Colt's old lady. I interfered in time but took three bullets and had to have surgery."

"Ah, hospitals report gunshot wounds, and you selling them property, it's a direct link. But from what Weston said, this issue you guys have now is the same fucker who wanted to plant evidence with us? And he's now trying to do the same with you?" Ash asks.

"Matt Carlinck," Decker says and hands Figor a file which he quickly glances over.

"Same asshole," Figor grunts and hands the file to Ash. "The woman he used with us was a fucking rookie. I could smell her fear from miles away. All it took was one harsh look and my fingers wrapped around her throat before she started to rattle how he blackmailed her into planting evidence. She didn't get a chance, though. We let her go but the next day the DEA was all over our club grounds and hauling me off to prison for murder. Even if we had solid proof the woman left healthy and alive and none of us left the clubhouse that night, it took weeks for them to release me. And if you ask me? I think the fucker killed that woman himself in an effort to pin that shit on me."

"It earned him a bonus of some sorts. And now he's looking for the same thing…higher up the food chain and he's using Alfie's old lady to do it," Roper quips.

"We should have killed him but it was a club decision to leave it alone," Ash grumbles.

Figor gives him a hard stare before locking eyes with Weston. "At the time we couldn't use the heat. Shit was fucked up with me thrown in jail and them thinking we had some sort of dog breeding factory for dog fights or some illegal shit. All accusations were dropped and if we did kill that fucker we would have risked everything."

"Yeah, and with Matt getting a bonus, he got what he wanted and left you guys alone," Decker sighs.

"Exactly. And we have enough shit to deal with." There's a sly smile spreading his face. "Though, now we have everything rolling smoothly and some time to kill. I guess we can use it to visit a mutual acquaintance for old time's sake."

Weston leans forward. "I don't want a slaughterfest on our grounds."

"I have something else in mind." Figor swings his head my way. "Your old lady, she's the one working with Matt, right? Her partner?"

I'm not liking the sound of this, and yet I don't have another option but to nod.

"She up for helping us or are you keeping her locked away?" Figor questions.

A surge of pride hits me. "She's willing to help."

"Good." Figor grins. "Because I believe she's the key. We'll do everything by the book and this time…it will be Matt who's going to be swimming with the fishes while everyone thinks he simply ran off to escape prison time. Because for sure as fuck are we going to expose the fucker and send him running from the law. And then we'll take care of the fucker."

I have to admit, "I sure am liking the sound of that."

Figor grabs my shoulder and gives it a rough squeeze. Fucking hell why does it have to be my recently injured one?

"Then let's get to it," Figor grunts and drops his hand.

I sigh in relief when the sting in my shoulder fades and hopefully it's the start where every shitty thing our lives are wrapped in will start to fade from here on out. Because I need the future clear and wide fucking open to enjoy the hell out of it now that I found the right people to embrace life with.

CHAPTER 08

GRETA

"Do you want to go over it one more time?" Decker questions and the man sitting beside him is staring at me too.

I swallow hard and give the both of them a confident smile. "No, it's all clear."

"Sorry we can't be in the room with you," Nick, the FBI agent sitting next to Decker, says.

Decker snorts. "Me and Alfie will be in the bathroom and through the crack of the door we'll be able to see and hear everything. We're right there if things go to shit."

"I would be more at ease if we could do this the official way," Nick grumbles.

"You owe me," Decker simply says.

Nick shakes his head. "As a former agent you did a favor for the FBI, a protection job and you end up marrying the woman, Decker. I'd say you owe us. But it's all good, we're happy to take out a rotten person in a crucial position. I still can't believe a DEA agent thinks it's okay to plant evidence. Fucking hell."

"That's the reason we're here, to take out the trash so everything can go back to normal. Funny, though. The DEA sticking their nose into our business to check if we're into some shady shit. Yet we're the one to wrap up the bad seed within the DEA."

"Don't remind me," Nick grumbles and rubs a hand over his face before he shifts his attention back to me. "All we need is his admittance to you planting evidence he's supplying. As soon as those words leave his mouth we're pulling you out. Understood?"

"Understood." I glance down at my chest where underneath my shirt the tiny high-tech equipment is hidden.

They're going to be listening in on every word voiced and any sigh expelled. Dammit. My palms are damp and my nerves are shot. I seriously wish I could fast forward this day and know all will be well.

What I wouldn't give to have this shit behind me so I can go riding with Alfie and Joaquin. Either on the back of either of their bikes or take the three horses out for a long ride. Alfie has three horses and though I adore all three, my favorite is the brown quarter horse which is the youngest of the bunch.

He's dynamite in a muscled package and he keeps me working every second I'm on his back. It's no wonder Alfie named him Dev, it's short for Devil. But he's such a joy to ride and sweet as sugar when I'm grooming him.

But right now, my mind doesn't need to dwell on all the joys my life has been wrapped with these days. It needs to be sharp and ready because the details I've been told about my partner gives me the creeps. Those bikers from the other chapter think Matt killed the other woman he tried to force into planting evidence.

I'm not in the mood for dying. Even more when I feel life has just started. But I'm ready to face him. I've been trained to do this. I might be quitting after this is handled, but I'm not weak; I can, and will do this.

"Okay, we're going to leave but we're right outside in the

white van," Decker says.

Nick leans on the table. "Don't hesitate. He might be your partner but if he's dirty he's just another criminal who needs to be behind bars. Understood?"

I give him a tight nod and both men walk out the back door. The place where Matt and I meet to discuss the case we're working on is a tiny, one-bedroom apartment on the ground floor. It has a garden leading to rocky grounds, typical rough terrain but it does give a nice view of the scenery.

"Nervous?" Alfie says as he comes up behind me.

I tear my gaze away from the view and spin around to seek his comfort. "It would be crazy not to be nervous. Being relaxed and overly confident can get you killed."

"That's our girl," Alfie murmurs and places a kiss on my temple.

Our girl. It's never 'my girl,' even if it's just the two of us here. That reminds me, "Did Joaquin message you?"

"Nope," Alfie chuckles. "He's pissed at me for making him go to the clinic. He wanted to take the day off and sit in the van, but I told him he needed to go to work. He's been taking too many days off with me getting injured. And I know how much he loves his damn job and he misses working with his two best friends."

I give him a small smile, knowing the reason why. "You wanted to keep him safe."

"It's hard as fuck having you in the line of fire. Even if I know you're qualified and a damn agent, but my mind simply can't cope. And Joaquin has proven to handle himself perfectly. Did I ever tell you about the time Cassidy's ex came by the veterinary clinic and kept Joaquin at gunpoint? Fucking hell. Decker and Roper went in to save them and the fucker almost shot them but Joaquin grabbed a fire extinguisher and blasted the fucker. They took him down because of him. And there was another time where we jumped on our bikes to confront fuckers who came after Colt's old lady, guns blazing, he just dives in no matter what. He's capable, reliable, fucking strong and fierce…

but I can't have the two of you at risk all at once. And fuck. If something happens to me…he needs to be there for you."

I crash my lips against his to silence all his worries. He opens and swirls his tongue against mine. Throwing everything out of harm's way and giving us a frozen moment in time to fall into tenderness right before havoc threatens to crash our lives.

His fingers slide into my hair and he pulls my head back to break the kiss. "Whatever happens next we will be moving forward. No regrets and no looking back, okay? Live life…two if tragedy rips us apart or three for perfection. Living is one day after the next and don't fucking dwell on shit you can't change. Dying isn't what we want but if shit takes a turn…you move forward, get me?"

I drag a deep breath of air through my nose. "Dying isn't what we want so in a few hours we're going to pick up Joaquin from work, have dinner at the diner where they have these magnificent hamburgers Joaquin brought home last week…and then we'll all go for a ride. Bikes. Horses. Each other."

"Each other," Alfie croaks. "And I kinda promised Joaquin you'd ride on the back of his bike for the next week as compensation for him heading into work today."

He winces and pouts right after and it makes me chuckle. "I'll be on the back of your bike soon enough."

"You'd better be," he grumbles and places a kiss on the top of my head.

His phone vibrates and we both know it's showtime.

"Stay strong, and like Nick said, don't hesitate. If the fucker pulls a gun on you…aim to kill that asshole."

"Will do," I promise right before he disappears into the bathroom and leaves the door slightly ajar.

I wipe my palms on my jeans and focus on the entrance. Matt is bound to walk in any second and with Alfie getting a message on his phone, we know he's arrived.

Without knocking Matt strolls in and shuts the door behind him. He throws a USB stick my way. "Get that on that biker scum's computer."

"What? You want me to put what on his computer?" I ask, making sure I sound confused since I need him to say the actual words.

"Just do what I tell you, it's not that hard," Matt snaps. "And you can print some of those files and spread it around."

Great, more random words.

"What evidence do you want me to plant, Matt?" I sigh, getting agitated. "What's on the stick you threw on the bed? It's not like you can put random information on a computer or put papers on a desk and that's it."

"You," Matt growls. "It's you who is planting evidence, Greta. Not me."

The asshole laughs right in my face.

"And don't think you can grab that stick and run to our boss either. Everything is made on your computer and will be a direct link to you. And when I tell them about your little fuck session with those two models you did a photoshoot with, all your credibility will be blown to shit. I've worked years for the DEA and you're just coming around the corner. A fucking rookie trying to suck cock and grab a quick score. Yeah, who do you think they'll believe, me or you? Right. Now get your cunt over to the bed and grab that stick and do what I say. And if you must know, the files contain information about dog fights."

He takes a step closer to me. "The last time I covered my tracks and I'll do it again. That bitch was tainted by those bikers and needed to keep her mouth shut, just like you. One swipe with a knife across the throat to silence her before her dirty cunt landed in a ditch. It's the exact way all of them treat women. Biker scum are all outlaws and think they can do anything to earn a buck and fuck whomever they like. Easy targets. Their profile fits and who knows, maybe I didn't kill the woman and maybe those bikers you are with now did. But you make sure not to get caught, you hear me? Or you'll find out what I'm capable of. I don't care if you have to spread your legs to get it done. Hell, you'd probably do it anyway since you enjoy it, don't you? Maybe you should suck my cock too before you head out and plant the evidence."

The door swings open behind us. "Freeze, FBI," rings out loud.

Before I can grab my gun, Matt has launched himself at me and throws an arm around my neck to use my body as a shield.

Oh, for fuck's sake, such a cliché, my mind offers. But his arm tightens and makes it harder to breathe.

"Let her go," Alfie says in a deadly tone.

Matt's words flow in a rumble through his chest when he says, "Get the hell out, all of you. We're DEA and you're interfering with a case we're working on."

"FBI, Matt. Put the gun down and we'll talk," Nick says.

There are three other men behind him and they're all dressed in black with bulletproof vests. I, on the other hand, along with Alfie and Matt aren't wearing any protection. Matt slowly drags me back as he heads for the back door.

"Stay there," Matt growls and keeps swinging his gun from Nick to Alfie.

Neither do anything and let Matt guide me toward the back. I know they can't risk my life and I'm also very much aware they didn't put anyone in the back yard since it's surrounded by a gate left and right and all there's left is the rough terrain out back which leads to a rocky nowhere.

I slightly stumble and Matt spits curses in my ear, calling me a bitch and a stupid cunt as he drags me out the door and into the daylight. I can feel his head glancing left and right in an effort to search for a way out. What a stupid idiot; there is no way out. Not unless he can climb rocks anyway.

Matt fires his gun, the sound echoes through my ears as I see Nick jump out of the way while Alfie keeps standing tall as if he's bulletproof. Dammit, Alfie. I'm about to scream for him to get down when I notice Nick who has his eyes wide as he takes a step back.

I don't know what's happening but something slams into us from my left and it makes both Matt and I crash to the ground. Pain bursts free in the upper part of my arm where my body takes the brunt of the fall.

A thick, black paw enters my vision as growls reach my ear. Wetness sprays on my face and I scramble away on my hands and knees. Risking a glance over my shoulder I barely manage to catch a flash of black fur dashing over the rocks like a feather bouncing in the air. The animal heads for a man I recognize as Ash, a biker from another charter Alfie introduced me to earlier today, before the both of them disappear out of sight.

I'm stunned and still staring when Alfie's hands surround my face. "Are you okay? Are you hurt?"

I tear my eyes away to make them collide with his. "Was that a dog? A wolf? No, a dog. There are no wolves in Texas. Are there?" Looking over Alfie's shoulder I see Matt's body on the ground, his neck is ripped right open. "Holy shit, oh yikes, that's nasty. Though a bullet can do more damage, but…yikes."

"How in the fuck am I going to explain this, Decker?" Nick rumbles. "I thought you guys didn't own these type of dogs?"

"Hey, don't look at me, it's not my dog," Decker states. "I have an Australian cattle dog. And I don't know what the hell that breed was, but thank fuck it was here and ended the hostage situation. Fuck, that would have ended badly otherwise. Neither of us had a clear shot. Matt had nowhere to go and nothing to lose."

"I hear ya." Nick puts his gun away and I hiss from the pain when Alfie tries to pull me up by my arm.

"Oh, fuck, I'm sorry." Alfie turns his head in Nick's direction. "Call an ambulance, I think she dislocated her shoulder."

Decker kneels beside me and I hear Nick talk into his phone.

"You should call Joaquin," I tell Alfie. "He must be going crazy."

He reaches into his pocket and taps his phone before he's holding it in between us. He's put it on speaker and on the second ring I hear Joaquin's voice.

"Is it over? Are you guys okay?" The worry bursting from those words is evident.

"I'm fine. Matt isn't though, he's dead." My eyes almost

slide to the body but I don't need another visual of a ripped-out throat.

I take a deep breath and hold it, the pain in my shoulder is tormenting me. The adrenaline rush I was riding must be fading.

"What the fuck am I hearing, boy?" Alfie growls and my attention goes back to them.

"Nothing," Joaquin says a little too quick.

"Right. Well, I'm taking her to the hospital. I'll call once we're there, okay?"

"Talk later," Joaquin quips and ends the call.

"What was that about?" I question but at the same time EMTs come rushing my way.

Alfie's lip twitches. "Nothing you should worry about. I might spank his ass if it is what I think it is, but you'll love it."

"I think you two would love the spanking part too," I mutter underneath my breath, making Alfie laugh.

And even if the pain is hard to breathe through, hearing this man laugh soothes my soul and warms my heart. Knowing Matt and the situation is dealt with we're now able to really have our mutual shared future wide open for the taking. And I'll be sure to grab hold with both hands.

"Fuck, that hurts," I grumble and glare at the EMT who I know is only trying to help.

I guess we have to swing by the hospital first before I'm able to grab hold of anything.

– JOAQUIN –

I pace the room until I finally hear a car approach. Stalking to the door, I swing it open and patiently wait for Alfie and Greta to get out of the car. Her arm is in a sling and my heart squeezes knowing how much it must have hurt.

She will need to take it slow for a few weeks. Alfie called and talked me through what was done. The doctor gave her a sedative and was able to maneuver the shoulder bones back into position. And it takes around twelve to sixteen weeks for it to heal completely but the next two weeks she will have it in a sling and will be pampered by the two of us.

As soon as she steps over the threshold, I have her face in my hands to give her a kiss. I need it as much as her. To make sure my body and brain knows she's still right here with us. She moans into my mouth and it's music to my ears. But I have to end it all too soon.

"I would like nothing more than to take you into my arms and squeeze you," I sigh in regret, knowing I can't because I don't want to hurt her. "But I guess we can wait. I do have a surprise for you."

"I thought we agreed–" Alfie starts but I shoot him a glare to silence him.

"We agreed to disagree on the pond you're going to dig." I turn and guide Greta toward the couch where there's a box.

"A pond?" Greta questions and when her eyes lock on the contents of the box she gasps.

Tears form in her eyes and she takes a seat right next to the box with the ducklings.

"You got me a duck," she croaks and places her hand in the box, gently stroking a finger over one of the fluffy bundles.

"Seems he got you three. And what the fuck is on their heads?" Alfie grumbles.

I roll my eyes. "They're Crested Khaki Campbell ducklings, they have a mohawk."

"Great, not only do we have three ducks, we have three weird ones," Alfie mutters underneath his breath and I once again shoot him a glare.

"Who wants normal?" Greta says in adoration as she swoons over the ducklings.

"Normal is overrated," Alfie agrees as he takes a seat on the other side of the box. "If we're also getting a dog…we should get one without any hair. Or one who has a mohawk to fit in with the ducks and all our weirdness."

Greta giggles and I laugh right along with her.

Her face grows serious. "We're not getting a dog like the one that attacked Matt."

She visibly shudders.

"That was a special breed, no buying those," Alfie states. "And didn't you hear me? We're getting one with a mohawk." He reaches out and brushes his knuckles against her jaw. "Don't worry about the dog, sweetheart. He protected you, like we all will. Me, Joaquin, our MC, along with every chapter of Iron Hot Blood. No one dares to mess with us. Not now, not ever."

Alfie stands and places a kiss on the top of Greta's head. "I'm going to grab the ice cream I promised you."

He stalks off into the kitchen and Greta whispers, "I might have been a big baby before they shoved my arm back in place. I whined about needing ice cream to make me forget all about it."

A chuckle slips past my lips. "You deserve all the ice cream, woman. Even if we have to hand feed you. Are you sure you're okay?"

She nods and I'm happy to see the small smile on her face is an honest one. "Yes. Though the whole dog ripping out Matt's throat was something I could have done without. But on the other hand, the dog saved my life. Not only mine, who knows what might have happened if he didn't take Matt out. Yikes. Do you think the dog is okay? Is it normal for a dog to do that? And why would a dog save me and run away the next instant? Why didn't Ash stick around? I saw the dog ran to him, is it his dog?"

"Some dogs are special trained ones. Like those K9's the

police use. Those guys from the other chapter that were here have this fan-freaking-tastic breed." I grab my phone and have to scroll way up to where I received pictures from Alfie when he ran into them a while ago.

I click on one of the pictures and turn to let Greta see. She gasps and grabs the phone. "Holy shit, I think this was the same one. It looks like it. Thick black fur, blue eyes, and the size… this was the dog."

"They are highly trained if I remember correctly. I bet those bikers helped the FBI. Didn't Matt try to frame them too? And killed that woman who he ordered to plant the evidence with them? Yes. That might be it. I've heard their dogs are great at tracking too."

"Don't worry about the dog. They are trained but not to kill or do this shit on a daily basis. The dog was going for the hand holding the gun but missed and got the throat instead. Lucky for us he accidentally killed Matt in one go. Besides, what's the damn difference if Nick put a bullet in his head to save you from this dangerous situation? The fucker is dead either way, end of discussion," Alfie says as he strolls into the room. He hands me the bucket of ice cream and a spoon. "Put that phone away and help our girl to some ice cream. Everything is behind us now."

"Only if you put the ducklings back into the cage I have set up in the corner with a lamp to keep them warm." I shoot him a grin and hold out a spoonful of ice cream for Greta to wrap her lips around.

"This shit about taking care of furry things is already landing in my lap," Alfie grumbles but takes the box and gently puts the ducklings into the space I've created for them until we have their outdoor place set up.

My heart warms when I see Alfie handling those fluffy bundles, knowing how strong and fierce he is. Seeing him sit down next to our woman who gives him a welcoming smile and the adoration twinkling in her eyes is showing there's more to our connection.

The warmth flowing through my heart is letting me know

it's love and it's in all of us. Complete and as one. Finally able to put things behind us and have the choice to be free and have a shared future.

Today I am thankful. Tomorrow I will still be thankful. And every day that follows is one to treasure when you've reached a point in life where you feel complete, inside and out.

EPILOGUE

Eight years later

ALFIE

Sitting here in our backyard, throwing peas and corn at our three ducks, always has a peaceful vibe at the end of a busy day.

"But I really think we need a baby cat," Silas says and tries to give me his best shot of puppy dog eyes. Or in his case, fluffy kitten eyes.

I slowly shake my head and try to soften my voice when I tell our four-year-old son, "We have many animals to take care of and we can't add to all the responsibilities. Besides, we have to leave some animals for other people to take care of, right? Otherwise they will be sad if they can't find a kitten to love."

His head instantly bobs in understanding.

I. Am. Brilliant.

"Daddy, Daddy, Daddy," Reese screams at the top of her lungs.

Our daughter is six and such a blast of energy.

"Calm down, sweetheart," I tell her and shift Luke, our two-year-old son from one knee to the other.

We have three kids and while Reese is the spitting image of her mother, Silas has Joaquin's nose while Luke here has my eyes. We don't need paternity tests to show others in black and white these are our kids.

We're a family. One who might not fit in any box or follow the standards of what society dictates. But we live. We love. And we share tears, laughter, and the joys and burdens each and every person encounters when they find the one they love and share their lives with. In our case, we found more than the one to love, and it might show our hearts are a fragment bigger to carry all the love we have for one another.

"Decker and Muriel are throwing a cookie sleepover and we're invited." Reese grins and looks at Silas. "Except for you, you can't go."

"Reese." I add a little snap to my voice. "Be nice."

"I am nice, Daddy." Her gaze drops to the ground and she whispers, "I heard Dad tell mommy Silas couldn't eat cookies."

Kids. Always picking up on half a conversation and thinking they know everything. And then, my favorite part, they always say what they think. Doesn't matter where they are, they just blabber out their thoughts. Right in your face and no sweettalk or softening a blow.

And Reese here is one nosy little lady.

I give her a stern look and raise one of my eyebrows. "Have you been eavesdropping?"

"Maaaaybe," she says, throwing her arms to her back to hold them there while rocking her body left and right.

"Silas can't have certain cookies because we found out he's allergic. But he can have others. We just have to pay attention to some things."

She nods thoughtfully. "I can pay attention."

I can't keep the smile off my face. See? Such a smart and helpful little girl.

"That's very sweet of you," I compliment.

"Hey," Decker says as he steps into the backyard.

I lift my chin and hoist Luke to my hip when I stand. "You're having a sleepover with all the kids?"

"Yeah, all of the kids are coming over to the large barn. We've transformed it into a movie theater and Muriel and Mayven, along with Kadence wanted to get all the kids together and do a marathon of cartoons or something. Along with cookies. Colt and Ledger are joining me to keep things in line. Luke can come along too and we'll keep an eye on Silas. Muriel called Greta and she just explained about Silas being allergic, gluten intolerance, right?"

I'm nodding while Luke holds his tiny hands up. I absolutely love the brotherhood. Our kids not only have two dads and a mom; they have a large as fuck family. Surrounded by brothers and their old ladies and children where everyone is comfortable and welcome in their own skin.

In less than twenty minutes, all three kids have their stuffed animals in hand and are joining Decker to head over for a few hours of entertainment. I did tell him I'll come and check on them later because Luke might want to sleep in his own bed. He's been fussy these last few weeks and I want to make sure everything is okay.

I'm standing on the porch when I see Joaquin coming down the road. He's on his bike with Greta warming his back. Such a great sight. For the outside world these two are married by law, though there's three people wearing a wedding ring.

It was a mutual decision and we wanted to make sure everything is set in case something would happen to either of us. There are a lot of people who might not accept who we are, our reasons, our motivations, but they are what they are; ours.

"Did you have a nice day at work?" I question as Greta dismounts and sways her curvy ass my way.

With the shit happening within the DEA, Greta decided she wanted to make another career shift. She took classes and is now a rehabilitation specialist and she loves it. Having three kids doesn't stop us from chasing our dreams.

Joaquin works at the veterinary clinic three days a week, taking care of our children on his days off while Greta has other days off and I can adjust my schedule here at the ranch to fill in when needed.

"I did have a nice day, but I get the feeling it's about to get nicer." Her lips find mine and it's the homecoming any man and woman crave after a long day.

"Take it inside, folks," Joaquin chuckles and I tear my mouth away from Greta to smack his ass just as he passes by.

He yelps and rubs his ass while shooting me a glare. I raise my eyebrow in challenge. If he thinks he can glare at me, he's got another thing coming.

"I think someone needs a good spanking," Greta whispers huskily beside my ear.

I direct my attention at her. "Someone, huh? I have two hands sweetheart, and they're both itching."

The giggle slipping over her lips just as she dashes around me and into the house goes straight to my cock. Yeah, it's about to get nicer indeed with the promise of getting some sweet ol' lovin'. And it's a good thing the kids are taken care of and out of the house for the next couple of hours, allowing the three of us the freedom to explore the bliss our bodies can give one another.

Stalking into the house and locking the door behind me, I notice the array of clothing littering the floor as I make my way to the bedroom. I lean against the doorjamb and let my eyes feast on the two bodies before me.

Greta's large breasts are pressed against Joaquin's lean chest. Mouths are exploring, tongues battling while hands roam. I take my time to peel every inch of clothing from my body until I'm naked and palming my cock.

Slow strokes while I rub my thumb against the piercing. This right here is what expands my soul into the wide-open heart my body holds. Never afraid to love big and chase what makes me whole and complete.

Greta's heated gaze lands on me. She loves being watched. It's as if Joaquin's hands stroke her body for the both of us to make her pussy drool with the attention she craves from both our cocks.

Joaquin has always been a gentle lover, all tender strokes paying attention to every inch of her body and exploring every rush of air flowing from her lips as he tries to find new ways to light up her body.

Foreplay is most times the pleasure of watching for me while these two heat the room. But as the musky scent of our woman teases my nose I'm barely able to hold back. Joaquin suddenly spins her around, raises one of her legs to allow her to put her foot on the bed while he palms his dick and lets her wetness coat the fat head before sliding inside her with gentle strokes.

Fuck. There's an urge of desperation and I stalk forward, coming around them to watch Greta's face filled with pleasure. My gaze slides down to where they are connected. The slick lips of her pussy surrounding Joaquin's dick as he moves inside her.

I drop to my knees in front of them, my face right in front of her tight heat. Enjoying the way she's being fucked. Their scent envelops me and I'm unable to hold back as I lean in and let my tongue tease her clit.

Her hands dig into my hair to hold me close as I lap her juices, touching both of them at the same time. I might not suck cock but licking them both simultaneously heightens an animalistic craving and almost makes my balls burst.

"Don't fucking come, you hear me, boy?" I rumble against Greta's flesh.

Joaquin moans in response, his thrusts slightly faltering when I cup his balls as they curl around Greta's sweet pussy.

"Fuck," he grunts while our woman moans.

She's close. And when I suck that bundle of nerves between my teeth to nibble and give the right pressure, she lights up beautifully. Screams of pleasure fill the air and it's mixed with curses ripping from Joaquin as he desperately tries to hold back his orgasm.

I rise and stalk to the bedside table, getting the lube before walking around the both of them. "Make her lean over the bed but don't let your cock leave her empty," I order.

Joaquin keeps sliding in and out of her body as he slowly

shifts to turn their faces toward the bed. Greta places her hands on the bed and I let my hand glide over Joaquin's back, pushing him forward.

His sharp intake of breath goes straight to my cock when I drizzle some lube between his ass cheeks. I make sure to add some to my hard length before throwing the bottle of lube on the ground.

"Bury yourself deep," I roughly growl.

Greta groans as Joaquin's dick pins her in place. I palm myself and knead Joaquin's ass with one hand, opening him up to line the fat head against his tight ring. Both of us slick with lube, I only have to fight some of the tightness before I watch, enthralled how he takes me inside him.

Joaquin slides out of Greta and slowly impales himself on my cock by doing so. All of us groan while he moves in between us, pleasuring all of us with slow thrusts. Sexual tunes surround us, the visual of what lies before me, one, all, fucking completion at its best.

I can't hold back and thrust forward, making Joaquin slam into our woman. I pound his ass and with it fuck both of them at once. Guiding. Controlling. Being there for both as they are there for me. Greta is the first one to launch into pleasure.

I know when she starts to strangle Joaquin's dick to rip the cum from his body as he starts to pulse inside her the way his ass is clenching tight around my cock, taking me along with them. Bliss. Utter bliss fills my veins.

– JOAQUIN –

My heart is racing while I'm surrounded with heat. Greta underneath me and Alfie's body against my back. He gently slides out of me and his hands skim the side of my body. He might be rough around the edges, massive muscle, and a dirty mouth but when it's the three of us he's all tenderness with a wide-open heart.

There's a loud slap along with instant heat flaring on my ass cheek. "Ass in the shower, boy. And bring our girl, the night is still young as our cocks are hard. Let's see how many times we can get her to orgasm. What was our last record?"

Greta groans and mutters underneath her breath, "Holy hell, this again."

A chuckle falls from my lips as I take a step back, regretfully pulling out of her sweet, hot pussy.

"I believe it was six, but I might have lost count from being crossed eyed due to holding back my own orgasm," I easily supply.

Greta grumbles some more and I hear Alfie turning on the water. I scoop her into my arms, making her yelp in surprise as I carry her into the large bathroom.

"We have two down, what do you think? My fingers next or your mouth?" Alfie wonders out loud.

"What about my own fingers while I watch Joaquin and you?" Greta boldly says and lets her teeth sink into her bottom lip.

Yeah, Alfie might not be the only one who likes to watch. And none of us will ever hold back to let the others know what we want, what we need, what we crave; each other.

Alfie wraps his fingers around his dick and cleans off the soap before he steps away from the warm spray of water. He's playing with the piercing and my mouth waters at the mere sight of him growing hard again.

Even after all these years we can never get enough and I do hope we get to enjoy ourselves for many years to come. And as I fall to my knees, my lips automatically part, while my eyes connect with Greta. It's then our connection is yet again completed by the moans of all of us filling the air.

– GRETA –

Our bodies are heated and it's not from the steam surrounding us but from the level of love mixed with lust flowing through our veins. Watching the men who stand by me adore one another makes my heart spill with intensive joy.

I'm forever grateful life gave us this destination. Even if nothing ever goes as planned and it's always a struggle to keep your head up and walk the path of life as brave as you can…because no one knows what lies before us…it's in these moments you realize you can only adapt and follow your gut.

I step closer to Alfie, needing my lips on his while Joaquin takes his dick into his welcoming mouth. The way Alfie moans, allows me to swallow his sound of pleasure. His fingers dive into my hair and he pulls my head back.

"I believe you were given an order," he rumbles and hisses as his eyes slide down.

We both enjoy the visual of Joaquin humming around his dick and I can't help myself when I wrap my fingers around Alfie's thick girth. My other hand cupping Joaquin's face and gently moving him back to control the pleasure of both of them.

Joaquin knows flawlessly what my intentions are when he stands, allowing me to slide in between my men. I take Joaquin's dick and stroke both of them simultaneously.

Both their mouths go to my neck, lighting my body on fire and there's no way I can deny either of them. The way they surround me with their love and devotion, being there for our kids, and embrace every single moment life grants us with is the kind of perfection one can only dream of.

And maybe that's it; all of it is a dream come true. Because as I bend over to take Joaquin into my mouth while instantly feeling Alfie's pierced dick nudging my entrance as he slowly starts to fill my pussy, really does feels as if all of my dreams have come true.

Family. Love. Devotion. Loyalty and complete trust. None of those things you can hold or touch and yet you feel every inch of it. Warm, protected, the sense of belonging. Everything is worth fighting for when you have your mind set and your heart full.

Sounds of pleasure fill the air, bodies filled with bliss and release as we all surrender to one another. Now, tomorrow, and every day we're granted with after the next one.

COWBOY
BIKERS MC #7
By Esther E. Schmidt

Garrett

I'm a biker in an MC located at a huge ranch which breeds both longhorns and quarter horses. I'm not just a biker, a cowboy, or a rancher, but I am a man of many trades and talents. And one of those is to protect the one who captured my attention at first glance.

Raney

I exist and that's about all I can say. The only thing I live for is the horse I love more than life itself, until my father sells her without my knowledge. No one has ever stood up for me, until the biker who bought my horse gave me a choice to get out of a situation I was born into. Am I really free to dream about a future? Or did my situation only shift, pulling innocent people underneath the destructive thumb my father has been keeping me under?

CHAPTER 01

GARRETT

"Care to explain why you bought that horse? You do know we breed damn fine ones ourselves, right?" Oak, one of my brothers, questions.

I shrug and keep up my pace. "Saddle breaking age, nice bloodline, and the mare was totally calm, even with the sound of a truck backfiring."

"True, but still–"

"Give it up, Oak. My money, my decision. Hell, if you don't stop nagging like a bitch, I might get the feeling you're pissed I got myself a sweet deal, one you wanted instead. Besides, we sold the three horses we brought, club business is done, and we have an empty trailer going home. I might as well take advantage and get myself a new mare." I slap Oak on the back. "Be a good pal and help a brother out by getting my horse into the trailer while I handle the rest of the paperwork."

"Fine, but you're driving home so I can sleep," Oak grumbles.

I wave my hand in the air as I walk away from him. I don't mind driving the six hours back home. I've never been one who needs loads of sleep anyway. I'm up at the crack of dawn even if I only had my eyes closed for four hours.

Hard work and dedication provide the kind of satisfaction you need to fuel your will to live another day. It also gives you the opportunity to reap the fruits of your labor, and that's what I'm doing today; buying a horse as a present to myself.

Like Oak mentioned, I could have my pick from the horses owned and bred by the club, but it's different. Something about the easy road giving less resistance. While now I'm getting myself a horse I haven't bred, raised, or trained.

And there's something about this mare. She caught my eye when they brought her into the auction. I was about to turn away and head home but the Palomino stood out with her gold coat and white mane. Add the serenity of her presence and it triggered possibilities inside my head to train her as my main horse to both work with while herding livestock but also enjoy early morning rides.

You can clearly see someone gave this horse love while she was growing up. I get the feeling this mare is worth every penny I just paid. The paperwork is handled quickly and I'm walking back to the trailer when I notice a small commotion.

Oak has his arms crossed in front of his chest and is blocking the entrance of the trailer as if he needs to guard it. I can clearly see the mare is loaded up and the way Oak is now pointing at it and leaning into the tiny person in front of him, I'd say the commotion is about the horse.

"What's going on?" I rumble and come to a stop behind the woman who is facing a man twice her size.

She spins around and lets her gaze collide with mine. And damn does it collide. It's more of a full front collision with lust sparking on impact. The brightest of green eyes, high cheekbones, puffy lips, and the fire in her gaze is most definitely intriguing to say the least. And all of it is framed by long black hair. Fucking stunning.

"This man here is taking my horse," she says and jabs her finger against Oak's chest.

Shit. Talk about a missed chance to act on the whole sparking lust thing I just experienced because we're about to face off.

Now I'm the one crossing my arms in front of my chest when I tell her, "I bought this horse at the auction. She's mine, everything is in order."

"Everything is not in order," she hisses with a slight tremor in her voice and steps closer.

I now notice how her face is showing a hint of despair. She's either not used to standing up to someone or this is a matter of the heart with the way emotions are slicing through her eyes.

I soften my voice and tell her, "I can show you the papers."

"That won't be necessary. Don't mind my daughter, she's overdramatic." I turn to face the man who rumbled out the words and watch how his face turns into a menacing glare as his tone hardens when he tells the woman, "Get your ass away from those men and into the truck, girl. We're leaving."

Girl? She might not be wearing any make up and is tiny as fuck, but he's talking to his daughter as if she's twelve while I'm pretty damn sure she's a grown-ass woman.

"No." The word might be a denial coming from her lips but the two letters are on a breath laced with a hint of fear.

I tear my gaze away from the man and assess the woman who has her hands turned into fists–knuckles white–while she waits for her father to respond. And the way she's bracing herself lets me know the man has a track record of talking to his daughter by using his hands.

"Ass. In. The. Truck." The man spits out his words one by one and each of those make her fucking flinch.

There's clearly something going on between these two. I step in front of her and face the man.

"Mind explaining why she thinks I'm taking her horse?" I calmly ask.

"No need." The man reaches around me to grab the woman by the arm and pulls her forward. "This one's always been on the stupid and crazy side. Thanks for the sale. Have a safe ride home."

He starts to drag her away but she rips her arm from his grip. She shoves her hand into the back pocket of her ragged jeans and holds out a rumpled piece of paper for me to take.

"My father sold her to me before she was born. I've worked my entire life at the ranch without asking for one damn thing and I've earned her by doing extra chores. I paid for her with hard work. He wrote a contract. See? You can't take her, she's mine." Every word tumbling from her cherry-colored lips is one of despair and it slices through my damn chest.

I take the paper from her and let the words of her so-called contract sink in. It takes everything inside me to stay rooted and not punch this fucker in the face. Keeping my anger at bay I shove the paper into my pocket.

The man has the nerve to smirk and give me the words, "Kids. Always a fucking pain in the ass. As you can read." He slides his attention from me to his daughter. "There is no issue. My daughter and I are going to take a little walk. Raney. Come here."

Instead of taking a step toward her father she backs up closer to Oak and gets behind me. I have to give it to her, from what I'm experiencing in this moment there are a few things very fucking clear. One, I'm almost positive the woman can't read. And two, she's not as stupid as her father thinks she is.

"Raney," I address her but keep my eyes on her father. "Instead of taking a little walk with your father, would you mind having a little chat with me in private?"

"Not going to happen," her father snaps.

I put a load of steel in my voice when I tell the asshole, "Not your call cause for damn sure it's going to happen. And if it's not? It won't be because you're throwing out demands but about the fucking fact that the lady has a choice. Now, Raney, can I talk to you about our horse?"

The timid "yes," flowing through the air behind me is enough for me to slightly turn and face Oak.

"Keep an eye on things, brother." I don't have to ask him to have my back.

We're both members of the Iron Hot Blood MC. A solid brotherhood located on a ranch where we breed and train horses along with other livestock.

"I said," the woman's father starts but Oak is stepping toward him.

I take the woman's hand and guide her around the trailer to create some distance and privacy.

As soon as we're out of earshot from her father she asks with a tremor in her voice, "What did the note say? It wasn't a contract, was it?"

As I figured; pretty sure she can't read.

"How old are you?" I question, needing to know this for what I'm about to do next.

"Twenty-one." Her eyes are searching mine. "Why?"

"You're right. The paper you gave me wasn't a contract."

Her shoulders sag and she looks as if life itself just shattered in front of her. "Figures."

"I have no clue about your situation, but if I had to guess it's not good. So, I'm going to offer you something, okay?"

Her eyes find mine and she tilts her head. "Offer me something?"

I tap my finger on the patch of my leather cut. "I'm a biker but our MC is located at a ranch. I have a small cabin with a spare bedroom I'm offering to you. No strings attached. You can get on your feet, away from your father, whatever. I'll even pay you if you want to take care of the horse. I wasn't planning on buying a horse today since we train and breed horses ourselves. But I recognize a good horse when I see one. That being said, I have my own work to do and could use the help. So, what do you say? Free room and board, earning some cash and stay with your horse while you're at it."

"She's my horse," she fucking croaks and might as well rip my heart out along with it.

"Like I said, come along and I'll give you a job. Hell, I'll throw in the option to buy her back while you get your shit together. Deal?"

She narrows her eyes. "Are you going to give me a real contract?"

"Yes, you have my word," I reply through clenched teeth. "One thing I will never do is lie."

Her head tilts. "I should question whether or not you're a con-artist, a serial killer, or a rapist, but I guess it's a chance I have to take."

"Fucking hell," I grumble underneath my breath and take off my Stetson to run my fingers over the buzzcut I'm sporting before answering. "I'm none of those things. And for you to add it's a chance you have to take? Woman, for you to say that shit makes me fucking angry."

She flinches and blurts, "I'm sorry."

I have to inhale deep and slowly let that shit out because my anger is all-consuming. She's apologizing for the bad situation she's in–and for my anger due to all of it–while nothing is her fault.

Deciding not to dwell and move forward, I throw out the question, "Do you need to go home and get a few things?"

She looks down at herself and shrugs. "I only have one other pair of clothes. If I earn money by working for you, I can buy some new ones. Till then I can wash these before I go to sleep and have them dry by morning."

One pair of… another deep breath and I manage a few more when I really take in the woman standing before me. She owns a single change of clothes, is tiny as fuck, and has minimal meat on her bones but still stands strong as if she can handle a heavy load. I'd say she's been working her ass off all her life for nothing more than one meal a day.

"Hungry?" Shit. I keep asking her question after question.

She bites her bottom lip. "I could eat."

"I bet you could," I mutter. "I gather we have a deal then?"

She quickly nods and holds out her hand. "We have a deal if you give me a job and Izzy back."

"Izzy?"

"Our horse." She gives me a shy smile.

"Our horse," I echo. "You move in with me, work for the cash I'll pay you for taking care of Izzy, and I'll give you the promise she'll be yours soon enough."

"Soon enough," she murmurs.

I take her hand and it's the same as when our eyes collided the first time; an explosion of lust slams into me. Into the both of us if I can judge by the sharp gasp tumbling over her lips and how her pupils dilate.

Not something we need in this moment and it's for this reason I tell her, "Get in the truck, front seat. I'm driving and Oak will be in the back seat."

Her head bobs and she walks around the truck to get in while I head for the back of the trailer. Before I reach it, Oak steps out from behind the trailer.

"Ready to go?" he questions.

I look past him. "Yeah. Where did her father go?"

"I told him to piss the fuck off. She's coming with us I assume?"

"Yeah," I repeat. "The fucker left without so much as a peep?"

Oak rubs two fingers against his jaw while his upper lip twitches in anger. "Not so much as one. I might have punched him once in the face and threatened to gut him if he didn't get the fuck out of my sight. I might not know what the hell is going on between the father and your girl, but even a blind man can see that shit ain't pretty. What did the note say? The one she gave you?"

Your girl. Those words roll easy over his tongue. Just as easy as they sound damn right in my ears, and I barely know the girl who I met mere minutes ago. But like hell am I ever going to share with anyone what was written on the damn note.

"It doesn't matter." I smack his upper arm. "Thanks, man. I owe you one for getting rid of the fucker. Come on, let's head home."

"Sounds good," Oak grunts and gets into the back of the truck. I make one final round to check if everything is okay with the trailer and my new horse before I get behind the wheel and head home.

I for sure didn't expect to return home with a new horse, let alone bring a woman back to my cabin along with it. But it seems life has a way of throwing things in your path when you least expect it. And to say I'm intrigued by both animal and woman is an understatement.

I can't wait to get to know the both of them. The horse might have to wait but I'm spending the next couple of hours with the woman sitting right next to me. So, I guess it'll be a crash course getting to know her since I kinda lied about having a spare room.

Hopefully she doesn't mind sharing a bed, otherwise I'll be sleeping on the couch in my own damn house. But I guess that's the angle of shit thrown in your path when you least expect it. And sleeping on the couch or not, I know I did the right thing by offering her a way out. The damn note is still branded inside my head.

I am such a dumb fuck, I can't even read.
If I could, I would know this note is a load of bullshit.
Nothing is promised and nothing is owned.
I am stupid and I will never achieve anything.
I will keep working for my father for as long as I live.
My name is Raney and I'm an idiot.

The note is clearly written and signed by her father. I recognize the signature I just saw on the property papers of the horse. Wiley Bolcord. Fucking asshole. How the hell can you call yourself a father when you degrade your own daughter like that?

My knuckles are white as I grip the wheel. It's a good thing Oak handled her father because thinking this shit through…I would have done more than punch the fucker in the face and tell him to get the fuck out of my sight.

"You okay, dude?" Oak questions from the back seat.

"Fine," I grunt.

Oak snorts. "Sure you are. Okay you two, I'm gonna sleep for a few hours. Wake me up if you stop to eat something, otherwise don't wake me unless we're back home."

I give another grunt and watch through the rearview mirror how he settles in before I let my gaze slide back to the road in front of me. Silence hits the truck and to be honest? I need it to let my thoughts settle.

Glancing beside me I get a hint of the woman's profile. She's wearing a tiny smile and has her hands folded on her lap. I would like to know what she's thinking. She doesn't seem scared or sad. To be honest it looks like she's hopeful.

Fucking hell, for a young woman to be hopeful while she just left her father, twenty-one years old with no possessions, sitting in a truck with two complete strangers while she agreed to come with me…to my house…promises that might as well be lies to fuck her over.

Yeah. Desperate situations call for desperate decisions and choices taken with your back against the wall. No fucking wonder she's hopeful. And it makes the need inside me rise to make sure this woman gets everything she desires and more.

But I guess I have to tackle the little lie I told her first…about the spare room…all while I mentioned to her I never lie. We're already off to a good fucking start.

CHAPTER 02

RANEY

My heart is pounding in my chest, each beat fills my body with a fragment of hope. Hope for a better future. Any type of future as long as it's different from my past. But mostly one where I have a space for me and my horse. That's all I ask. I don't need much. Not to mention, I've slept in the stable for as long as I can remember.

I've never had a lot, never complained, and work hard to keep the stress and aggravation to a minimum. Keep your head down and get through the day meant spending the night with my horse for the past three years. Only to find out my father lied once more and betrayed me.

I shake my head in an effort to clear my thoughts. I want to leave it behind me. I should. I'm in a truck with two strangers but also with the one thing I love more than my own life; my horse. She's in the trailer and I'm thankful for the man driving the truck to allow me the chance to hopefully have the future I desire.

Glancing over my shoulder I try to keep my laughter at bay when I see the awkward position Oak is sagged into while he's snoring loud. I shake my head and shift to look out the front window again.

I blurt out my thoughts, "He's going to wake up with a sore neck."

Garrett glances in the rearview mirror and back to the road in front of him. "Nah. We have these kind of road trips every once in a while and the idiot always sleeps like that. You can say he's used to it, or he just doesn't complain about being a human pretzel when he wakes up."

I risk a quick glance at Garrett. He introduced himself and Oak when we were a few minutes into the drive. Garrett Verhams. A name I won't simply forget. He not only bought the horse I loved even before she was born, but he also stood up for me. Something no one has ever done.

There has been one other moment in my life where a guy should have stood up to my father and helped me, but the guy in question zipped-up his pants and ran. Though getting caught in the barn after having sex with the son of one of my father's men wasn't as humiliating as what I experienced when Garrett discovered I couldn't read the note I handed him.

Embarrassment hits me again and his reaction makes me more ashamed due to not knowing what was written on the note. There were complete sentences on it and it looked like a contract of sorts because I did recognize my own name and my father signed it; I've seen him place his signature a load of times. Here I thought he wrote down how Izzy belonged to me.

Gathering mental strength, I ask with a very thin voice, "Please tell me what was on the note."

He gives a curt shake of his head. "It's not important."

"It is to me. I want to know," I press.

"How about this…I'll teach you how to read so it won't happen again."

"I'd rather have you read it to me," I grumble and turn my head to face the side window to add underneath my breath what my parents told me many times, "Besides, the reason I can't read is because I'm too stupid to learn."

"What the fuck, woman?" Garrett snaps. "No one is too stupid to learn."

"I am." I can clearly hear the words echo inside my head from both my mother and my father telling me repeatedly I'm only capable of working with my hands. "You don't know me. But no worries, what my head can't learn, I'm more than able to make up for with my hands. I can work. No reading necessary."

"I might not know you but I know people. You can learn anything you want as long as you want it badly enough. It's all about the effort you or anyone else around you are willing to help out with. No matter how slow or fast, taking one step after another is moving forward. And some might indeed not be able to study or become something out of their reach, but everyone has their own qualities in life. That's why there are many jobs and professions."

My cheeks heat from shame. I would love to be able to read but this man already offered to help me in other ways, I can't be a more of a burden than I already am. "I'd rather work with my hands. I love animals, so no worries about helping me to learn how to read. You have your job and I'll work for you. See? No reading required."

"What if I hand you a list of things I need you to do?" he easily replies.

A sigh rips from me. "You can tell me, I have a good memory."

There's a smile in his voice when he replies. "See? You're smart. So, don't ever let me hear you calling yourself stupid or dumb ever again, understood?"

"You can be very annoying," I mutter.

A chuckle flows through the truck and my eyes are instantly drawn to him. His jaw is smooth and nicely shaven. The leather Stetson he had on earlier–which showed years of wear but it adds to its character–is now off for the drive and shows the man has a short buzzcut.

The broad shoulders and thick, muscled forearms give the impression he's strong and most definitely doesn't have a desk job. The roughness of his hands and fingers also shows this man works with his hands. One hand is covered with a tattoo, going up and underneath his sleeve and I wonder how far it travels up.

"I am," Garrett says and pulls me from my ogling moment. "And I'm pretty sure we're going to get a crash course getting to know one another since we'll be living together for the time being. And...I might as well tell you I kinda lied earlier. I know I said I wouldn't lie and I didn't exactly lie."

I turn slightly in my seat to face him. Dread fills me and I push out the words as my heart starts to slam against my rib cage, "You're not going to let me earn Izzy back?"

"What?" he grunts. "No. That's not it. I lied about having a spare room. I only have my bedroom so we either have to share a bed or I'll crash on the couch."

Relief washes through me. "Oh, thank heavens. You scared me there. No worries about my sleeping arrangements, I'd be happy to sleep in the stable with Izzy. I actually prefer it since I've always done so."

"Always...fucking hell. I keep repeating your words when you spew things that shock the fuck out of me. You know it's not normal to sleep with your horse, right? I mean, once or twice for fun or if we have a mare who's close to giving birth–" A strangled growl rumbles from his chest. "From now on things will be different."

He presses a few buttons and I hear a call connect through the speakers.

"Hey Cassidy," Garrett quips.

"Hey yourself, are you guys on your way back?" a female named Cassidy asks in a sweet and kind tone.

A burst of jealousy hits me and I have no clue why because Garrett isn't mine. I hardly know him or the woman. Shit. I just assumed he didn't have a girlfriend. Maybe he's married, has a handful of kids, who knows.

"We'll be home within a few hours, but could you do me a

favor?"

"I'm not cooking anything and neither are the other old ladies," the woman huffs and I have to bite my lip not to laugh when I see Garrett rolling his eyes.

"It's not about food," Garrett grumbles. "I'm bringing a woman with me."

"Ooooohhh. Seriously? Wait. Don't tell me it's a mare or I'll kick your ass. You're talking about one with breasts and who can really talk and walk, a human woman, right?"

Now I can't help but bark out a laugh and quickly slam a hand over my mouth to cover the sound.

Garrett glares at me for a breath or two and drags his gaze back to the road as he answers, "Actually, I've found myself two women, Cassidy. And I can ride them both, but the one with the stunning rack and two sexy legs she walks on is why I'm calling."

I instantly choke and start to cough.

"She's there? She heard…dude, not nice. And why are you calling? Oh, hey, Garrett's woman. I'm Cassidy, his VP's old lady."

I remove my hand from my mouth and take a calming breath. "Hi, Cassidy. I'm Raney."

"Don't you sound like a sweet thang. Can't wait to meet you."

"Yeah, yeah. Can you get her a few things? It was a spur of the moment thing for her to come with me and she didn't have time to pack a bag so a change of clothes would be nice."

"I'll call the other old ladies and we will organize a little something, no worries. It's going to be a few hours until you get here, yes?"

"Yes, but I'll get her whatever she needs tomorrow…for now she just needs some things to–"

"Shush, Garrett, we got this. See you later." The woman simply hangs up on him.

I have no clue who she is but she sounds sweet and like a good friend.

Many questions rise inside my head but the one I would like to know the answer to the most is the first I blurt without thinking, "Do you have a girlfriend?"

He doesn't glance my way when he answers. "I wouldn't have offered you to stay with me if I did. And most definitely wouldn't have mentioned sharing a bed."

"What's a VP's old lady?"

"I'm a member of the Iron Hot Blood MC. Like I mentioned, we live on a ranch and all work together. Cassidy is my vice president's old lady. My VP is Roper. He's claimed Cassidy, she's his woman and with it protected by the club. You can compare it to getting married…biker style. My president is Weston and his old lady is Harlene. Decker has an old lady too, Muriel. And then there's Ledger, his old lady is Mayven. And you're also going to meet Kadence, Cold's old lady. And let's not forget Greta, she belongs to both Alfie and Joaquin. But I'm sure the old ladies will fill you in soon enough with all the details and the dynamics of the club."

I try to process everything he said and all the names he threw out. I know a ranch is a lot of work and no one can manage it alone, it's why my father always had a few men around to help him and why I was always working my ass off.

But there's one thing he just mentioned that stands out. "Greta has two men?"

Garrett snickers. "Caught that didn't you? No worries, like I said, the old ladies will fill you in soon enough."

My curiosity spikes. I've always been a person who asks too many questions, or so my parents always told me. Over time I've learned how to either keep them to myself or find the answer another way. But it seems Garrett doesn't mind if I fire one question after another.

The hours quickly pass through our easy chitchat and before I know it my nerves spike when Garrett brings the truck to a stop at a huge ranch. Night has fallen but that doesn't take away the beauty of it. Horses and Longhorns are grazing in different pastures, lit by the moonlight it's rather captivating to take in the amazing view.

"Gorgeous," I gasp and open the truck door.

"Rise and shine, Oak, we're here," Garrett snaps and slams the door shut behind him.

I stroll over to one of the pastures and lean my forearms on the fence.

"I'll show you around in the morning," Garrett says as he comes to a stop next to me. "Want to help get Izzy settled in?"

I give him a radiant smile. "Yes. Stable or pasture?"

"Stable. She can take the one next to the other two horses I own."

Confused I step back. "You have more horses? Why did you buy Izzy?"

He places a hand on my lower back and guides me toward the trailer. "One of mine, Cal, is twenty-one and I don't want him to do the hard work anymore. I also have Kayla, she's sixteen, but when I saw Izzy I kinda wanted a horse for myself to enjoy besides work. And while Cal is enjoying her somewhat retirement, I'd like for him to have a buddy. I noticed Izzy not just because of her beauty but also the calmness of her character."

"Where I was thankful to have one horse, you now have three…such luxury," I blurt and realize it's none of my business and quickly add, "You are right about Izzy, she'd make a great buddy for Cal. She's calm by nature but she's used to a lot since I've always had her trail along with me every second I could."

Garrett smiles. "How does that work, the trail along part?"

"Izzy's mom died. My father didn't want to spend the money on a vet but the men who work for him guessed it was either a tear of the uterine artery, causing a small leak,   or an infection, or both for that matter. Thankfully Izzy did get a good start with the colostrum and we had another mare who gave birth a day before Izzy was born who somewhat adopted her. Izzy and I have spent every day together ever since. Me fixing fences… her darting around me, cleaning stables, her darting around me. Helping out with training horses, she'd be by my side. She's actually crazy enough to want a scarf around her neck when it's snowing."

I shoot him a grin at the reminder and realize I might come across as a stupid kid, making the happiness instantly fall flat.

"Mind sharing why the drop in happiness?" the observant man questions.

Remembering his mention of not to call myself stupid, I might as well keep it vague instead of lying because I can't let him know I value his opinion. Not only because I'm thankful for him stepping up for me, but mainly since I think he's insanely sexy. And I'm feverishly attracted to him. But dreams are like a puff of steam; semitransparent and easily evaporated.

I've never allowed myself to dream. And it's not like Garrett would see something in me as a woman to build a future with. I mean, he owns three horses and a cabin and works at this gorgeous ranch and has a group of friends. And then there's me, owning only the clothes I'm wearing.

Shit. I just met the man and my issues are piling up. This morning when my father and I left for the auction I didn't have any issues going through my head. All I did was work and sleep, day in, day out.

I thought we were headed to the auction to sell two horses. When we arrived, my father sent me to handle something. I didn't even find out my father had brought Izzy until I saw her standing in the ring, sold off without a second thought.

"Raney." Garrett's voice draws me back to the here and now.

A burst of female chatter rings out and six women and a man come strolling our way. All gorgeous with curves, unlike me. I'm more boyish and a stick-like figure. Yeah, dreams about having a future with the man who is looking intently at me are going to stay dreams for sure.

CHAPTER 03

GARRETT

Raney is clearly not used to attention from other women. Her eyes hold slight panic and she's wringing her hands while half of the time her head bobs in answer instead of giving them actual words.

I left her with the old ladies for the time it took me to put Izzy into the stable. The second I knew she was settled I headed back out and found Raney still rooted in the spot where I left her. Taking the bag Cassidy has beside her, I swing it over my shoulder and hold out my hand for Raney to take.

"Thanks, girls. Appreciate y'all coming out to welcome Raney and get her a few things, but we're gonna head for the cabin now. Catch ya later, tomorrow or whenever 'cause Raney is going to be here for a while. It's been a long day and I'm sure she wants to see where our horse is staying."

Raney slides her hand in mine.

"Our horse? As in yours and hers? How did that happen? Or did you buy one and got one free?" Kadence snickers.

I can feel Raney tense up, her cheeks heat and I can practically read the embarrassment in her eyes.

"All you need to know is that the mare belongs to both me and Raney and that Raney needed a job and I offered her one along with a place to stay. Like I said, it's been a long day."

The girls complain against our backs but I couldn't care less and drag her away to head for the stables.

"I figured you wanted to see how Izzy is doing before we take care of you."

She mindlessly nods as her eyes widen. Her head whips around to take in the stables.

"I'm guessing you like Izzy's new home?" I give a low chuckle because I'm stating the obvious.

"I don't think I could ever clean my parents' house as clean as this place," she muses.

Her answer strikes me as odd and I can't help but question, "How about your home? Did you live with your parents? Have your own space?"

She rolls her eyes. "My home was the barn: it was anything except clean."

My chest squeezes when I see her wince from blurting the truth. Her gaze hits the ground and I'm not liking the way she hides herself from me.

Tipping her chin up to force her to look into my eyes I tell her, "The past is something no one can change. The future, though? Wide open. Remember that."

Her throat bobs and her voice is paper thin when she whispers, "But I don't have anything, what kind of future do I have?"

"One where someone gives you a chance, an opportunity. You already grabbed it with both hands. So, I fucking say you have a future. The rest is up to you."

Gratitude washes over her face and she surprises me when she grabs my leather cut and lifts herself on her toes. Reality sets into my brain at super speed and I for sure as fuck don't want a peck on the cheek, putting me in the damn "friendzone."

Flashing my hand to the back of her neck, I curve her

movements slightly and capture her mouth with mine. Yeah. Fuck friendzone. Life is too short for long runs and darting around shit. When I see something good, I tend to dive right in. And chatting with her for hours during the long ride home and the way electricity sparks between us? No way I'm passing up this opening shot.

The tiny gasp of surprise allows me to swoop my tongue over her lips and taste her. At first, she's tentatively swirling her tongue against mine but when I squeeze her neck and shift the angle of her head to deepen the kiss, we go from soft to frantic.

Her hands slide over my chest and up to my head. I'm vaguely aware my Stetson falls off but her nails trailing over my scalp feels damn fantastic. Dropping the bag I was holding to free my hand, I instantly grab her ass and drag her against me, making sure she feels what one kiss from her does to me. She moans into my mouth and it spurs me on to kiss her harder.

"Look at that. Garrett, my man. Come home with not one nice lady but two, huh?" Alfie's words reluctantly force me to break the kiss.

I'm still holding her body tight with one hand cupping her neck and the other one possessively on her ass. Guiding her head into the crook of my neck, I keep her close and our connection vibrant when I answer Alfie.

"The horse belongs to both me and Raney. I'll introduce my woman to the club in the morning after we're settled and had a few hours of sleep. And if you'll excuse us, we're gonna check on Izzy real quick and head for my cabin right after."

Alfie snickers. "Anxious to get her alone, are you, eh? All right, I'll leave you two to it. I'm done with my chores for today and am itching to get home. I'm told there is a blow job in it for me from my man while eating my woman's pussy, ain't gonna pass it up just by talking to you guys. See you in the morning. Have a good night, I know I will."

He turns on his heel and walks out. I brace myself for Raney's reaction because Alfie doesn't have a damn filter. He also doesn't shy away to let everyone know he has both a woman and a man and how they are living happily together.

She's shaking as I pull her from the crook of my neck but when I check her gorgeous face, I see she has laughter written all over her. "That's the one you told me about? Who is in a relationship with another man along with a woman?"

"Yeah," I wince. "I should have given you a bit more of a heads up how Alfie blurts out whatever is on his mind. Needless to say, most times it's about sex."

A giggle slips over her full lips and it's cock-stroking. I need to focus. All I want to do is drop to my knees, rip off her pants, and lick her pussy to find out if she tastes as sweet as she seems.

"As long as the work gets done, who are we to judge what another person does?" The twinkle in her eyes shows she's still laughing on the inside but her attention is drawn to Izzy.

I scoop up my Stetson and put it on while we stroll closer. The horse is eating some hay and seems completely at ease. We take a few minutes to watch Izzy until Raney finally says, "I could use a shower and a nap. With getting everything set, the long drive to the auction, the auction itself, then the whole incident, and then you…I'm drained."

"You put me in that long list as if I'm also–"

She quickly places her finger on my lips to silence me. "No, no. You've been the best thing that's happened in forever. No one has ever stood up for me. There was this one time where I thought a guy would…well, obviously he didn't. So, for you to stand up for me against my dad, saving Izzy and allowing me a chance to get away from where I've always been? I never had a chance or opportunity, and believe me when I say I've wanted to get away many times. But you can't really plan when you have no money and no place to go. So, I can't start to explain how much it all means to me."

"What was the one time a guy didn't and should have?" I question, my curiosity might be drawn but anger is scratching my brain to know why a man wouldn't step up.

Her eyes stay on Izzy when she says, "A few years ago my father walked into the stables and caught me and a guy getting dressed. My father took one glance at me and knew I just had sex. Let's just say I expected Ted to stand up for me when my father started to give me hell, but instead he left."

She doesn't say anything else and I hate filling in the blanks so I have to know, "Did your father hit you?"

A deep sigh flows over her lips along with the whispered words, "Hit, kicked, pushed, ordered me around, and if I wasn't within reach, he would find something to throw at me. I've learned to be compliant all my life but as a teenager I did act up from time to time until it was beaten out of me. What other choice did I have?"

The distant stare isn't a look I want to see. I experienced one incident between her and her father, heard a few words spoken about her past and I'm torn between wanting to know everything for some sweet revenge, and letting go so she can move on. Though, I should leave the past in the past and make damn sure this woman will only know pleasure and positive experiences from here on out.

Knowing more talking will cause her pain with the hurtful reminders, I choose the most sensible option. "Come on, let's get you that shower."

I snatch the bag from the floor and hold out my hand. She laces her fingers with mine and I take the short walk to my cabin. It's small but cozy and holds everything I need. Unlocking the door, I usher her inside and place the bag on the couch.

"Are you a movie fan?" Raney's eyes trail over the old western movie posters I have hanging on the walls of the living room.

"I ordered them online, better than empty walls or posters of naked women." I shoot her a grin and she rolls her eyes. "But, yes. I enjoy watching classics."

I point at a rack filled with old movies and she strolls over to let her fingers slide over the titles. During the ride here we talked for hours and I know she's not completely oblivious to everything going on in the world, though there are some things clearly kept from her.

"Feel free to watch some TV when you're done with your

shower. I have to head over to the clubhouse and have a little chat with my president. We sold some horses at the auction and I'm sure Oak brought him up to speed, but I also have to check in."

"Sure, no worries. And I would like to watch a movie with you. I haven't watched one in years. My mother would allow me to see a movie when I was younger but you know how it is with work…up at the crack of dawn and when every task is done, you're drained. Besides, I wasn't allowed in the house after the Ted incident."

Her eyes go to the floor again and the words she said earlier hit me full force again.

"You weren't allowed in the fucking house?" I grunt in anger.

She starts to wring her fucking hands as she gives a faint shake of her head. Yeah. I need to take a breather or I'm going to plant my fist into a wall. I close the distance between us and lift her gorgeous face by placing my finger underneath her chin.

"You left all of it behind when you got into my truck, you hear me? From now on you keep that beautiful head high. This is your home now where I'll take care of you and where you're free to do shit you like to do. No more sleeping in stables or being deprived of basic necessities. And I'll make damn sure you'll have days off to watch a fucking movie or go with the other old ladies to have your hair or nails done or some of the shit women do. Pedicures. Yeah, you're gonna paint your toenails and shit."

Her cheeks heat. "I've never had a pedicure let alone painted my toenails."

"I'm going to rat you out to the old ladies," I murmur right before I give her a slow and sensual kiss.

She needs tenderness and the time needed to adopt to the changes in her life. I allow the both of us to enjoy our kiss for a few more heartbeats before pulling away.

"Time to show you the bathroom and give you some privacy. I won't be long but take your time. I'll make you some food when I'm back, okay?"

"Sounds like a dream," she shyly says.

"Woman," I growl. "You are the fucking dream."

My mouth covers hers in a rough kiss and it takes every inch of strength to pull away.

"Bathroom is over there. Towels and shit too. Fresh clothes in the bag. I'm sure you'll manage. I have to go now or I won't stop kissing you and most definitely want more but it's not going to happen."

Again, her head falls and the anger inside me makes me snap, "I told you to keep your head high." The words are out before my mind catches up with the realization why she dropped her head.

Releasing a deep sigh, I tell her, "You and I are happening, Raney. If you don't want there to be anything between us just tell me now and I'll bunk with one of my brothers and give you the space you need. But if you do want there to be an us…we will take it slow. You have been through a lot from the shattered parts I've heard you mention. And I don't want you to feel obligated or do shit with me as a damn thank you. Understood?"

"I want there to be an us. And not just because I'm thankful." There's a truckload of determination in her voice and it's stroking my ego for sure.

"Thank fuck." I chuckle and let my fingertips trail over her jaw. "Go shower and relax."

"Will do." The two words tumble from her lips and I turn to head for the door because if I don't, I'll end up kissing her again.

The walk over to the clubhouse is way too short for me to process my rambling thoughts. This morning I didn't have a woman or so much as the need to have a damn relationship yet now? I want to tie Raney to my bed and keep her there each day to the next.

I've seen men fall for the right woman. It happened to my president, my VP, and a handful of my brothers. They all gave their heart to a woman so it shouldn't come as such a surprise. And it feels right between me and Raney but things about her background are unsettling to say the least.

Stepping inside the large room I notice a few of my brothers sitting at the bar enjoying a beer. Decker strolls out of the office and is holding some papers. He comes to a stop when he sees me and points at church.

"Did they call you?" he questions.

I give a curt shake.

"Come on, Oak filled us in and I called a friend of mine to do a quick check."

Fuck. My blood pressure spikes at the thought of what the results of that check is. Decker used to be FBI and still has those connections. We head into church where my president, Weston, is sitting in his chair with Roper, my VP, right next to him. Oak and Colt are sitting at the table with them along with Spiro.

"Did you get her settled?" my prez questions. "Oak filled us in to make sure we know what we're dealing with and I asked Decker to run a check."

I take a seat across from Oak and lift my chin. "Thanks brother." Oak nods and I direct my attention to Weston. "Everything about this makes me fucking furious. Some of the things she shared about her past? Watching her reaction to some of the shit and what Oak and I witnessed?" I swallow my anger down and shake my head.

Decker takes a seat next to me and pats my back. "Take a few breaths, brother. Because it's going to get a lot worse."

Roper rubs his hands. "Let's hear it."

"Itching to handle something other than your day job or changing diapers?" Weston raises his eyebrow.

"Shut up, you've been elbow deep in diapers too and it's been awhile since we faced some danger. And I just heard our old ladies gush about the new face Garrett brought. Are you going to tell your old lady there's nothing to worry about? Or will you tell her all the fleshy details they want to know because they'll drag them out of us one way or another?"

"I don't want anyone else to know," I snap and glare at each and every one of my brothers. "She's embarrassed enough as it is. Fucking uncomfortable and hasn't slept in a damn bed for fuck knows how long. Hell, she doesn't even know how to read and her fucking father is to blame for everything."

Silence fills the room.

Eventually it's Weston who places his forearms on the table and pierces me with a hard look. "My old lady asked me to make sure Raney felt at home here. You have nothing to worry about when it comes to her being embarrassed or uncomfortable. If anything, I think it's better if everyone is aware of some delicate things so she won't be embarrassed. You're barking up the wrong tree here, Garrett, and you know it. It's the anger talking, so rein that shit in and let Decker tell us what he found out so we can make arrangements if necessary."

"Sorry, Prez," I grumble.

"I hate to disappoint you guys," Decker starts. "But I've got nothing about Raney."

"Nothing?" Spiro whistles low. "Let me guess, it makes this shit more fucked-up."

"Seems like it." Decker places papers in front of him. "But there's nothing about Raney. She simply doesn't exist. No birth certificate, no social security number, no record whatsoever of her being born or her mother being pregnant. Now her father on the other hand, he does have a record. Fraud, theft, assault, and even murder charges. The murder charges were dropped due to lack of evidence and the body missing for that matter."

Roper releases a string of curses. "Do we have all the details on this guy?"

"Not yet. Nick…well, he's gonna put it on record so the FBI is going to dig a little deeper. He only gave me a quick rundown but will get back to me as soon as he knows more."

Weston nods at Decker's words. "Church in the morning when you have all the details. And Garrett?"

"Yeah, Prez," I grunt.

"Maybe it would be best to have Raney join us tomorrow morning. She can fill in the blanks. And don't start about her being uncomfortable or embarrassed, she needs to know she has a voice here, okay? From what Oak has told us she…how shall

I put it?"

"Has been suppressed all her life? Born to be a slave and work at her father's ranch? No choice, no education, no humanity or equal rights, no fucking nothing? Yeah…she needs to hear and listen to her own voice when she has a say in all of it," I easily finish for him.

Slaps on the table ring out in support while my brothers grunt their agreement. We talk for a few more minutes until there's nothing left to discuss. Time to head back to my cabin and settle in for the night. I have no clue if I'm going to be able to sleep because it's going to be a long damn day tomorrow for sure.

CHAPTER 04

RANEY

"What in the hell are you doing?" a voice barks from behind me.

I drop the cloth I was holding and place my hands over my racing heart.

Gasping for my next breath I tell Garrett, "You scared the crap out of me."

"Good. Now tell me why you're scrubbing my kitchen floor instead of relaxing. Did you even take a fucking shower?"

I scramble off the floor and shake my head. There's only silence greeting me and I dare to risk a glance in his direction. Shit. He's pissed. I glance down at the floor I was cleaning and think of what to do or say but come up empty.

Whenever my father was pissed or needed someone to blame, I would just stand still and let it wash over me. I guess in this situation I'm opting for the same thing and let my mind wander to Izzy while I wait for him to rain down his wrath. One breath after another flows in and out until I see his boots appear in my vision.

"Eyes, Raney. Give 'em to me." How can his voice carry softness while it held anger a moment ago?

Slowly I meet his gaze and stare at his face which is filled with kindness.

"Care to explain why you're on your knees working when you mentioned you were drained and were going to take a shower and relax?"

"I'm not sure how to explain it, other than the fact that work has always cleared my mind, and my body for that matter. Everything is messy inside my head and then you and your kisses and I couldn't stop thinking, and I saw the muddy prints on your kitchen floor and–" I catch my bottom lip between my teeth to stop my ramblings and cut off my brain before I make more a fool of myself than I already did.

He surprises me by sliding his arm around my waist and pulling me against his body. I can feel him inhale deep and release his breath over the top of my head.

"It's going to be hard as hell to give you your damn life back," he murmurs. "You're falling back on routine. It's work for others while it soothes your restlessness. And the crazy part is…you don't even know it's fucked-up. Just like how you mentioned it's okay if you needed to sleep in the damn stables with Izzy." He pulls back and cups my face to connect our eyes. "No matter the effort, how uncomfortable, awkward, hard, or unthinkable… we're going to make it work. The most important angle in all of this is your happiness. And to be honest, happiness is different for everyone, so who am I to judge if cleaning the floors is what you need to soothe your brain. For me it would be either go for a ride, bike or horse, or put my feet up and watch a movie for the hundredth time."

"I have to keep my hands busy. If I'm with Izzy after the work is done for the day, she lies down and I'll pet her. Most times I also create braided rope halters, lead ropes, and reins. I like braiding rope."

A grin spreads his face. "Braiding rope, huh? I think that

could be considered a good hobby."

This might not be a good time to mention my father pressured me to make a few a week and some on demand because he sells them. His finger gently slides across my forehead and in between my eyes.

"Why the lines of worry?" he murmurs.

"I do enjoy making those but it can also be considered work because my father sold them."

"All you ever did was work and earn money for someone else. Yet you have no social security number, no birth certificate, no bed, no money, no clothes, no nothing...even the horse he agreed for you to have after the hard work you did, turned out to be thin air. Fuck." He steps away and releases another string of curses.

I have no clue how to answer or if I even should. My eyes travel to the cloth and how it left a watery stain around it. I'm about to reach for it when my head is being gently cupped and I'm staring into Garrett's soft and gentle eyes again.

"No cleaning for you. You're going to take a shower while I calm down and clean up here. I'm not angry at you. All my anger is rising because of the situation you were in but we're handling it, okay?"

"Okay," I whisper and keep my gaze on his lips.

They curl into a smile and move when he gives me the words, "We're not going to handle it by kissing because I might not be able to resist you when I'm feeling this pumped up. Go on, sugar, enjoy your shower and I'll fix us something to eat."

He spins me around and smacks my ass before pushing me into the direction of the bathroom. I can feel a smile spread my face and stroll into the bathroom, flipping the lights once I'm inside.

This cabin might be tiny but every inch is used to its full extent. The bathroom not only has a large shower but also a bathtub and a sink with a towel rack and a small cabinet. A pile of blue, rolled up, fluffy towels sits on top. I lock the door and strip my clothes before stepping into the shower stall and brace for the cold water.

Grabbing some of the bodywash in my hand I start to quickly wash but am happily surprised by the warmth of the water. I hardly ever have a warm shower. My mother always told me they have bad pipes when I was allowed to take a shower.

But this? I have to adjust the water a bit because it's too hot and it's ahh-mazing. I don't have to hurry and instead I take my time to soap up my body, realizing I'm covering myself with Garrett's scent. I take the shampoo bottle and take a whiff. I keep smiling while I wash my hair.

I suddenly realize Garrett might want to have a shower too and I'm stealing all his hot water. Quickly finishing up, I turn off the shower and grab one of the fluffy looking towels. Heaven. Sweet smelling fluffiness like sunshine being wrapped in the softness of bright blue clouds. I never thought a towel could be this soft.

I rub my body dry and make sure to get most of the water out of my hair and it's then I realize I didn't bring the bag with the clothes Garrett's friends brought me. I wrap the towel around my body and slightly open the door.

"Garrett?"

He steps out of the kitchen with half of his body. "Yeah?"

"Can you please hand me the bag? I forgot to take it with me."

Garrett strolls over to where the bag is and snatches it up. He closes the distance between us and hands it over. His eyes never leave mine and he doesn't so much as steal a glimpse of my body, even if it's mostly covered by the towel.

"Thank you."

He shoots me a wink and spins around, letting the words, "Hope you like spaghetti or else it's just a sandwich," over his shoulder as he disappears into the kitchen.

I close the door and squat down to open the bag and check what's inside. I can't believe my eyes when I pull one piece of clothing after the other from it and they all look new. There are even tags on the panties and sports bra. Most of the clothes are too big but I'm absolutely thankful to receive these gifts; it's more than anyone has ever given me.

Except for what Garrett gave me; a chance, an option, a future. I remove the tags off the clothes and pull on a fresh pair of clothes. I'm drowning a bit in the leggings and the shirt falls mid-thigh but at least it's clean and new.

I follow the mouthwatering scent of spaghetti and stumble onto Garrett who has his back to me. A very naked back with a large tattoo of a horse. The very sexy man is only wearing his jeans and like me he's walking barefoot and somehow it makes him more attractive.

"Have a seat," he says without turning.

I now notice he's set the table for two and I slide into the chair facing him. Garrett carries a large pan over to the table and puts it down between our plates.

"I hope you're hungry." I don't have time to give him words in return when he starts to fill my plate.

He serves himself and takes the seat across from me. I watch how he snatches up his fork and shoves it in the noodles, twirling to roll them and ultimately bring the bundle into his mouth. I grab the fork and mimic his moves.

My mother taught me how to cook when I was growing up. Some things I learned the hard way and I have the burns on my hands and arms to prove it, but I'm mostly good at it and enjoy baking as well. Though most times I wasn't allowed to eat what I made, but that's beside the point. Though the food hitting my tongue is delicious.

"This is really good," I groan and quickly fill my mouth with another load.

"There's enough to feed an army so feel free to eat as much as you like."

"That's a first," I mutter between shoveling another forkful into my mouth.

"My house is yours, my food, my bed, anything you need. And when you're finished, we'll order some stuff online."

The fork freezes on its way to my mouth. "You don't have to

do that: your friends gave me enough."

Garrett gives a sharp shake of his head. "You work for me, remember? I need you to wear proper clothing, as your employer I'm responsible."

I keep staring at him and blink a few times. "Are you serious?"

He leans back and crosses his arms in front of his chest. "Employees and employers each have responsibilities, rules, and obligations. The whole world thrives on them for that matter. And I hate to say it but when I went to the clubhouse to meet with my president, Oak already debriefed all of them about what happened at the auction. Decker, one of my brothers who used to be FBI, did a background check. He found out you don't even exist."

I place the fork down, suddenly I'm not that hungry anymore. "I…I don't exist? What do you mean?"

"When someone is pregnant, they have health checks and shit and when the baby is born you file for a birth certificate. You get a number from the government…you need it for a lot of stuff like getting jobs, it identifies you. From what Decker found out there is no record of you. No record of your mother being pregnant, nothing. There is no Raney Bolcord."

"But why? Why would they? I don't understand."

"I should have waited to mention it to you until after you've eaten." Garrett glances at the spaghetti, his gaze softens when his eyes land on mine. "My guess is as good as yours but with the glimpse of your life I've gotten, I'd say he created a free dedicated worker to earn money on his ranch."

I mindlessly nod and pick up my fork. All I've ever known was work. The braiding rope halters was something I saw in a horse magazine one of my father's men gave me. It had step by step pictures, making it easy for me to learn the basics. Most of the other stuff I know I was told by either my parents or the men who worked for my father.

And it was not like they chained me up, I sometimes went with my mother to the store to carry the groceries. I'm not a complete idiot. I also went with my father to sell horses and other stuff; working at the ranch and around the house is all I've ever known. But my father did tell me once or twice how I would never get anywhere.

Mostly he threw those words at me when I felt rebellious and wanted to see the world and live on my own. Okay, that was a one-time thing right after he ran off Ted. But I now understand what Garrett is saying. My parents put me on this earth for one reason; to use me. Deep down, I've known. Deep down, I knew there wasn't a way out. Not until I met Garrett.

But it also raises the question, "Now what?"

He points at the food in front of me. "Now you eat. Catch your breath, take your time to build something for you while you let us help you. You're not alone, okay?"

I grab my fork and poke at the food.

Garrett's big, tattooed hand covers mine. "It's a lot to take in and with everything that happened today I just want you to know everything might be all fucked-up, but it's also a turning point. One day you're going to look back and remind yourself of the long road you came from compared to the fruitful life you built for yourself."

"Fruitful." I snicker and shove some spaghetti into my mouth, completely oblivious to the taste.

"Bad choice of words, maybe. Just know we're all here for you. Take it one day at a time and tomorrow is a day you'll spend with Izzy. No work, no obligations. And that reminds me, did you start to break her in yet?"

A smile spreads my face at the reminder of Izzy. "I haven't yet but she's used to a bridle and to a saddle. I don't think she needs much work."

"Let me know when and how and we'll make a plan together."

A flock of butterflies assault my stomach and a happy smile spreads my face. "I would like that very much."

"Deal, now eat." He grins and points his fork my way.

My appetite returns and I even grab seconds. With a full

belly we wash the dishes and clean up after ourselves. After another discussion about the sleeping arrangements, we settle on sharing the bed.

It's big enough for the both of us and it's silly for him to give up his bed and sleep on the couch. We're both adults and besides, I might be drained but I'm not used to sleeping in a bed. I'm used to sleeping in the stable with my eyes on Izzy.

And I miss her. It's the middle of the night, darkness surrounds me while Garrett is in a deep sleep beside me. My eyes are burning and it's impossible to sleep. I've been tossing and turning and I'm afraid to wake up Garrett. Sliding out of bed, I tiptoe down the hall and out of the house.

I'm almost at the stables when I hear, "Mind telling me where you're sneaking off to?" rumble through the darkness.

A scream rips from my throat and when the man steps closer, allowing the moon to shine a faint light on his features, I instantly recognize him.

"Oak. You scared the crap out of me."

He doesn't so much as twitch and is still looking at me expectantly.

"I can't sleep. I don't want to wake Garrett. Would it be okay if I sleep with Izzy?"

His eyebrows shoot up. "Sleep with Izzy? As in sleeping with a horse in the stable?"

My cheeks heat and I wring my hands as I whisper, "I haven't slept in a bed in years. I can't sleep."

"For fuck's sake," Oak grumbles underneath his breath. "Come on."

I follow him into the stables and feel some of the restlessness slip away when I see Izzy. Oak opens the door for me and I step inside to let my fingers slide over her coat.

"Here you go. And you better not run off with Garrett's property, ya hear? Look."

My gaze snaps to his.

He's pointing at black orbs on the ceiling. "Every inch of this ranch has eyes on everything at all times, understood?"

Feeling embarrassed by his suggestion I would steal from Garrett and run off with Izzy to go…where? Back to my parents because life was awesome? The things I've experienced today were some of the best things I had in years. The food in my belly for one, not to mention my horse is still with me and well taken care of.

All of it makes me snap, "I wouldn't betray the first good thing that entered my life. I don't expect you to understand but I will see it for what it is and thank you for standing up for your friend. I would be thankful to call him or you that one day too. Though I like to think he already is my friend for the way he was the first person who stood up for me."

Oak doesn't say anything in return and merely shakes his head and strolls away. I take a deep breath and close the stable, taking a seat in the corner in the warm bedding and lean my head against the door. My eyes fall shut and with each breath I regain calmness with the scent of Izzy as I drift off to sleep.

CHAPTER 05

One week later

GARRETT

Oak opens the stable for me and I step inside. Izzy doesn't so much as twitch when I scoop Raney up who once again slipped out of the bed and into the stables. It was exactly one week ago when Oak woke me up to tell me where Raney was. I have been dragging her back to bed every single night since.

At least she's been waking up in bed every morning, but falling asleep in it plagues her mind. During the day she's the complete opposite. Maybe because all she knows is working at a ranch, but she falls right into the routine of helping and working. With the horses as well as the other livestock, along with every chore around the ranch.

Hell, she helped me rebuild part of a fence as if I had one of my brothers assist me. And when I gave her different kinds of rope a few days ago, she braided a stunning rope halter for Izzy. One Alfie, along with many other brothers, wanted and have asked her to make one for each of them in return for money.

I carefully place her on the mattress and she turns to curl into herself. Thankfully she keeps sleeping as I stare down upon her. Not only does she fit in here on the ranch, she's also been working very hard to take steps in learning how to read.

Six days ago, I had a meeting with my brothers in church. We discussed her whole situation. They wanted her to join us but I decided to keep her out of it. In my opinion she didn't need the added stress of everyone discussing her life and the details Decker found out.

The first night with her taught me that; she had enough demons clawing at her brain. What she needs is a clean break. It's the reason I burned the note she thought was a contract, making sure she wouldn't ever be able to read it. I don't want her to read or hear things that can hurt her.

And I knew I made the right choice when Spiro questioned if Raney wasn't scamming me. Knowingly being in on the stuff her father was a part of where sometimes he would sell horses and later come back to steal them along with a few others, forging papers to sell them again. I lunged for Spiro's throat and it's a good thing Oak held me back because I was ready to kill a brother over this woman. That's how deep she's already managed to crawl underneath my skin.

I slide underneath the covers and pull her against me. She snuggles closer and puts her head on my chest. It pains me to know how she seeks me out in her sleep and is comfortable to snuggle close and yet the restlessness and lack of inner trust draws her to the routine of falling asleep in the stable.

But then I think about how well she's progressing with learning letters and reading. After the meeting I had with my brothers almost a week ago some of the old ladies came to me and asked to help Raney settle in. I took my brothers' advice to save her from embarrassment and shame and spilled some details, one of those being her lack of reading skills.

They jumped right in and bought her a stack of flashcards with letters and words on one side and illustrations on the back to help her. Shit kids use to learn and to be honest? I didn't even think about doing this or have any idea where to start. The old ladies took over, and in a way, it made her also adapt into their group as well.

A few days ago, I asked if she needed my help with the cards, pulling random ones and letting her tell me what letter or word. Her cheeks turned red and I had no clue why. Until she quickly grabbed a stack of cards with words on them and they all tumbled onto the floor.

Seems Kadence made an added stack of cards to teach her dirty words. I got a good laugh out of that and couldn't help but tease her. She ended up slapping my chest and ordered me to pick up the cards since it was my fault they ended up on the floor. I did and couldn't help but hold up each card to make her read it out loud for me.

What has also been helping is the phone I bought her. After explaining how it worked, we started texting and the smile on her face was priceless when she read my first text out loud. One simple "Hi," never held so much meaning. And it was the same when she texted me back the same word.

Progress takes time and not every angle has the same speed. But for now, I'm damn proud of my woman and I hope she feels and knows how far she's already come. My woman. I relish in the way this statement sounds inside my head and realize she's actually rooted deeper underneath my skin than I originally thought. I kiss the top of her sleeping head and release a deep breath, content to finally fall asleep with my woman in my arms and safely in my bed.

The sun shining through the curtains wakes me up way too early on my day off and I realize my arms are empty. A groan ripples through me and I slant my arm over my eyes. The softest of laughter enters my ears and I take a squinted peek from underneath my arm. Raney is sitting crossed-legged, staring at me with a smile on her face.

"What's so funny?" I question and close my eyes in an effort to catch some more sleep, though I know it's futile.

"You," Raney quips and I automatically smile and let my arm drop from my face when I hear her blurt, "You make me happy."

Her face turns red and her eyes go wide but I love her honesty and the way she always catches herself after blurting out her thoughts. The redness tinging her cheeks always shows her innocence. She might think it's either shame or embarrassment but I think it's endearing.

I jolt up and cup the side of her face, letting my thumb trail over her heated cheek. "Good," I murmur. "Because you make me damn happy too."

I decide to pop a question at her to create a distraction because her eyes still hold slight panic due to the thoughts and feelings she just shared.

"Are you ready for today?"

The smile sliding over her face is blinding.

Yes," she says with determination. "We have another hour before we're meeting the others. We're going on your bike, right?"

"Yeah." I feather my lips softly against hers.

These last few days we've only stolen some kisses here and there. I was determined to give her space to get on her feet but it's been difficult not to strip her naked, drag her against my body and have my wicked way with her. But I guess with our admittance–the both of us being happy with one another–it's time to take the next step.

The next step being sex. I make a mental note to buy some condoms since we're headed into town with my prez and VP– along with their old ladies–later today. It's why I asked if she was ready for today.

"Let's get this day started with some coffee. I'm sure I'll need a cup or three to wake up. Damn it feels as if I skipped sleep completely," I grumble and swing my legs off the bed.

"I'm sorry." Her soft voice flows through the air and I spin around to face her.

"What for?" I reach for my jeans and pull them over my boxers.

I take a few steps in the direction of the bathroom when she says, "For sleeping in the stable again."

Her eyes are fixed on her hands while she's plucking at the bedsheet.

Stepping closer to the bed, I lean in and lift her chin with one finger to make sure she sees the truth in my eyes when I tell her, "Some things require a process. Old habits can also take longer to break, even more when feelings are involved and it's been a routine for many years. I don't care if I have to keep dragging you back to this bed, spread horse bedding all over our bed, or bring Izzy into our bedroom for that matter. One day you will allow yourself to fall asleep in our bed. And that day will be fucking perfect because it will mean I will get to hold you while we fall asleep together."

Her hands are gripping my head the next instant and she merges her lips with mine. Her tongue slides past my lips and I greedily take what she gives. Our kiss turns feverish when I sneak my arm around her waist to pull her body flush against mine. Fucking heaven.

She's still the one in control with her hands cupping my head and I relish in her boldness to take what she wants. My dick is hard and luckily safely locked behind the teeth of my zipper. It's a good thing otherwise I'd rip off her pants and bury myself deep.

Condoms. My job for the day is to buy condoms and a large damn box to make sure we have enough for the foreseeable future. Raney breaks the kiss and buries her head into the crook of my neck.

"You really, really make me happy, Garrett." Her words are a soft whisper against my skin.

A groan rips from the back of my throat. "Wait till we have a box of condoms, we'll add a few more reallys in front of the 'make me happy' statement."

She giggles against my neck and I give her a tight hug before letting go and tell her, "I'm gonna make some coffee. I'm sure the women will be here soon."

"We agreed to meet in the clubhouse fifteen minutes before

we leave. Harlene and Cassidy had to go to the clinic to handle a few things, we couldn't meet up sooner or they would have been here already." Her eyes slide to the bed and she takes a step closer to me. "We could…kiss some more…and more."

"Good to know." I shoot her an apologetic smile. "But I don't have any condoms, and believe me when I say we're going to rectify that as soon as we head into town."

"Good to know," she echoes.

The longing and lust in her eyes is making my dick harder. I have to clear my throat and adjust myself, trying like hell to think about anything other than burying myself deep inside her sweet pussy. Yeah. Not helping.

"Coffee," I croak. "We need coffee."

"Good thing we're both off today and only have a few hours planned in town for some shopping. That leaves the rest of the day to spend together."

I have to blink a few times but my heart fucking jumps about the fact she's straightforward and wants this as much as me, that's for damn sure.

"We might need more than the rest of the day," I murmur and step closer.

She tips her head back to look into my eyes while her arms slide around my waist.

Her voice is a mere whisper but it rings loud inside my ears when she says, "Maybe tonight I'll be too sated to leave your bed."

"Now there's something to dream about." I brush my nose gently against hers, giving her the words, "We're saving the best for later. Come on. Coffee, before I say the hell with it and knock you up so you won't ever leave me."

Her eyes go wide and she jumps away from me. "We can't. I never even gave it one single thought about having children, becoming a mom, a parent. I don't even know what parents should be like since mine were clearly twisted. It's…no. I'm–"

I know it's a shitty situation but I can't help it when a slight chuckle rips from me and I point a finger in her direction. "Why do you think I'm still wearing pants pressing for the both of us getting coffee? We have all the time in the world, sugar. No rush, no pressure, no kids for now, just us."

She closes the distance between us and I know we're going to end up tangled in a hot kiss that's going to make my dick un-fucking-breakable.

"Coffee," I croak once more.

Her eyes lower to my crotch and she swallows hard. She wets her damn lips before biting down on her bottom one. If she keeps this up I'll blow my load inside my pants; that's how much I crave her.

I spin on my heels and head into the bathroom to freshen up, locking the door behind me to be sure I have time to cool down. When I've handled my business and stroll back into the bedroom, I find it empty.

Pulling on my boots, a shirt along with my cut, I go in search of Raney and find her in the kitchen. She holds out a cup filled with steamy black goodness. The corner of her mouth twitches and it's a look I love on her; relaxed and happy.

"Have you made a list of the things you'd like to buy?" I question as I take a seat at the kitchen table.

She joins me and pulls a piece of paper from her jeans pocket and hands it over. Instead of words she drew the items she needs. As agreed I've kept my end of the deal and gave her cash for the first week she worked for me. I have talked her salary through with Weston, not wanting to cut her short or make her uncomfortable if I gave her more than necessary.

The look she gave me yesterday showed me she wasn't expecting that much money while it was still at a normal rate. Raney might have been kept underneath her father's thumb but she's damn smart. It shows in all the things she does and how quick of a learner she is.

And the money I gave her is safely kept in a jar in our bedroom while she took out a small cut she's going to spend. And the smart part? She's buying necessities to braid halters and ropes she received orders for since everyone on this ranch loves her creations.

Passion, relaxation, whatever; braiding is another way for her to create an income. She's doing all of this to buy Izzy back, the way I promised her. But to be honest? The horse has a value beyond recognition and she won't be able to afford Izzy because Raney is tied to her and I'm not going to give that woman up; she's mine.

The thought of her being my woman settles my raging heart and the pounding need rushing through my veins. We just discussed future stuff like kids and throwing out feelings and solidifying there actually is an us.

This leaves me one more thing to do today; voice my claim to my prez to officially make Raney my old lady.

CHAPTER 06

RANEY

I have my own money in my pocket and my arms wrapped around the hottest man alive. Not to mention, we're on our way to buy condoms because there's an us. This is a moment I will remember and treasure for a long time.

Any moment spent with Garrett is one to remember. From the day I met him I've only experienced good moments. There's just one hard part in all of this and that's falling asleep. I'm absolutely exhausted but the restlessness in my bones doesn't allow me to fall asleep in the bed next to Garrett.

I do wake up in the bed next to him and it warms my heart to know he cares enough to get up and drag my sleeping body back into bed with him. I know it's not the sleeping part I have issues with but I guess I'm afraid to fall asleep and realize my life was a dream…not wanting the day to end and wake up in the hell I have been living in. Or whatever the reason for me not being able to fall asleep in a bed like a normal person.

Hopefully one day. It warms my heart how he mentioned

he'd even cover our mattress with horse bedding or drag Izzy into our bedroom if it would help. He really has all the patience, strength, and ability to help. He cares. And in return I adore him. Every day I fall a little more for this man and it's both scary and amazing all in one go.

And I absolutely love this bike ride. Garrett controls his machine flawlessly while I hold on as I'm plastered against his strong back. He skillfully guides the bike around the corner and comes to a stop right next to Weston's bike. Harlene dismounts and gives me a smile.

Another thing I enjoy about living with Garrett; I now have a whole group of friends. And it's not about them being nice because Garrett told them to; their intentions are real. I've noticed it the first few days when they offered to help me with learning how to read.

The laughs and spending time without so much as a complaint and wanting to meet up again and again…everything shows these people like me for who I am. I return the smile and wait for the bike to stop roaring. The vibrations die and Garrett pats my thigh, indicating I can get off.

My legs are wobbly but I've very much enjoyed the ride and can't wait to get back on again. But first we have some shopping to do. My cheeks heat at the reminder of Garrett mentioning we need a few large boxes of condoms so we won't run out any time soon.

I've only had sex twice, and neither time was worth mentioning, but I get the feeling it will be very different with Garrett. For one because I'm physically drawn to him and have developed feelings, adding to the need to be with him; to feel more connected. But mostly due to our kisses rising more excitement and heat through my whole body than I've ever experienced.

Garrett places his hand on the small of my back and guides me toward Weston, Roper, Harlene, and Cassidy. We all head into the hardware store where I pick up the items I jotted down to make different braided halters.

The guys have to swing by the butcher next for the meat

order they placed. We're having a barbeque on Friday and most of the shopping will be done tomorrow morning but the girls wanted to marinate and prepare the meat and that's why we're picking it up today.

Weston places a kiss on Harlene's lips. "Call if something is up. We'll meet you guys in front of the store, okay?"

Garrett leans in next to my ear. "I'll go into the store when we're done at the butcher so I can grab a few boxes of condoms."

My cheeks heat and I bury my fist into his leather cut to keep him close and cover up my red cheeks. The bastard chuckles and places a kiss on the top of my head.

"No worries, I'll get enough to keep us going for–" His sentence ends in a grunt when I plant my fist in his gut.

"Enough," I grumble.

Laughter falls from his lips and he pulls me close to give me a kiss, one where everything around us falls away until a few throats clear behind us.

Garrett breaks the kiss and tells me, "Stay with the other old ladies. You can always call if something is up."

"I know, no worries," I promise him and the girls drag me toward the shop while the guys head for the butcher.

I have a backpack for the stuff I already bought so my hands are free to do some more shopping. Taking a shower has now become a routine and using Garrett's bodywash is nice but getting my own scent would be amazing.

It's the first task the girls take very seriously and I think they've shoved eight different bottles underneath my nose before I can so much as take one whiff. And they all smell amazing. I still haven't made a decision when Kadence and Harlene check out the other products in the next aisle.

I finally find a bodywash I like. It's a vanilla and raspberry scent and I'm grabbing similar shampoo when I hear my name being hissed from an aisle behind me. A chill runs up my spine when recognition sets in.

Holding the shampoo and bodywash against my chest I spin around and face my father. He's ducked behind the different products on the shelves and his eyes are set over my shoulder. A quick glance lets me know he's watching Harlene and Cassidy.

"Time to come home, Raney," my father hisses underneath his breath. "Playtime is over."

Fear grips me and I refuse to let my father ruin things for me. For the first time in my life, I feel like I belong and every day is filled with joy and happiness. I'm not giving up my life with Garrett; he reminds me every day I have a choice to live life my own way without taking orders from anyone.

I take a step closer and hiss back, "There is no playtime, I have my own life now."

His eyes go hard and he releases a sinister laugh. "Stupid girl. You have no life. You only have what I give you. And if you think that man you're fucking gives a shit about you, you're wrong. He might like to fuck you but you're not the only one he's fucking. He'll grow tired of you and kick you out and you'll have nothing."

"You made me think Izzy was mine and you sold her. I had nothing when he offered me a chance to start over," I snap.

"That stupid horse was never yours. Your job is to take care of the horses so I can sell them when they're ready. That horse was ready to make me some money and you had others to work with waiting for you, you ungrateful bitch." His eyes focus over my shoulder and he slightly crouches while his voice lowers some more. "Get your ass home. Work needs to be done so stop being selfish by thinking with your cunt. If it's the fucking you want, I'm sure I can get one of the men to do you or maybe you can work that job nights so we can make more money. I'll even give you some too. And that's me being nice. I've been watching you, Raney. I know your every move. I meant what I said: you have no life, only what I give you. And if you stay here? I'll kill every single one of them, one by one and I'm going to start with that guy whose bike you were on, and then I'll kill all those chicks you laugh around with." His chin jerks in Cassidy and Harlene's direction, making my blood freeze. "And I'll make sure to shoot that horse you pine over. Don't think I won't. Remember Ted? That bastard who kept you from your work? He didn't live for very long after I caught him. Your cowboy biker will follow in his footsteps and end up in the ground as well. I gave you everything, even life itself, you ungrateful bitch, and I'll take it all away. Home. Now."

He turns and rushes out of the store. I'm frozen to the floor while my head is spinning. Ted. The guy he caught me with and who I never saw again. Did my father just insinuate he killed him? How he is going to kill Garrett and every single one of my newfound friends? Kill Izzy? My chest feels like I'm being crushed between two walls and there's no room for me to take my next breath.

"Was that man bothering you?" Harlene stalks toward me while Cassidy runs out of the store, probably to go after him.

"I want to go home," I muse, the things my father threw at me are still slicing through my brain.

I'm clutching the two items with one arm and shove my free hand into my pocket to reach for my phone. It only takes a few swipes of my thumb to call Garrett.

"We're almost there, sugar." His voice is warm and soothing and I close my eyes to let those words calm me down. "A handful of minutes and we'll be buying those condoms and heading home."

This is what I needed; a distraction to pull me out of the darkness my father threw at me.

"Hey, is everything okay? Is Cassidy there with you? Harlene?" he questions, the words holding concern.

"She's here." I glance at Harlene and she takes the phone from my hands.

"Hey, Garrett, it's me, Harlene. Where are you guys? Okay, we're going to pay for our stuff and meet you outside. Yes. Okay."

She hangs up and gives me my phone back.

"Come on, let's get out of here. The guys will be here within five minutes and then we'll head home."

Cassidy stalks toward us, she's slightly out of breath. "The dude was fast. What did he say to you? Do you know who he was?"

I mindlessly nod as we head for the cashier.

"The guys will be here in a few minutes, we're going to head home," Harlene tells Cassidy.

"The guys are here," Garrett rumbles and pierces me with his gaze. "Are you okay? What happened?"

"There was a creepy guy—"

Harlene starts, but I cut her off. "My father, he was here."

"Fuck." Garrett releases another string of curses and pulls me close.

"I'm okay now," I croak.

He pulls back and glances down at me. "Yeah, you are. Come on, let's get back to the clubhouse."

I stay rooted to the floor while Cassidy and Harlene walk over to Roper and Weston.

"What's wrong?" Garrett asks.

The concern is vivid in his eyes and it makes my chest squeeze to know how much he cares about me. Such a stark contrast with my father, and I now clearly see the lies he has been telling me. Not to mention how stupid I've been all my life. Why didn't I see how my parents basically chained me to them to work while giving me nothing in return other than a roof above my head and some scarce food to keep up my strength?

"Nothing is wrong," I tell him with determination, fighting the fear so my father won't ruin this thing between Garrett and me. "I would like to pay for these and we need—" I lower my voice and whisper, "Condoms. Let's not let my father ruin everything."

He gives me a smile and cups the side of my face to give me a soft and quick kiss. "Yeah, you're absolutely right."

Garrett takes the bodywash and shampoo from my hands and adds three boxes of condoms. He pays for them while I try to object and pay myself but the cashier has already put the items in a bag and gives him the change.

We head for the bikes and I should feel worried due to the confrontation with my father and yet Garrett's protective arm around me offers me all the comfort and strength I need to keep my head high.

I don't ever want to go back to where I was. Every day since I arrived at the Iron Hot Blood ranch has been one wrapped with warmth and fun in a relaxed environment. No matter the hard work I also participated in. Somehow none of it was a chore and I did it with a huge smile on my face.

Not to mention, I had Garrett's company through all of it and the knowledge Izzy was well taken care of and I could go to her any time of day. And the hot showers, the food, the friendships, all of it is such a stark contrast to what was once my life. So, I'm going to fight for what I want; my dream.

The ride back allows me the time to let my brain settle with the decision to leave the past for what it is. My father has told me many lies and the one about Ted must have been one too. He's just angry I'm not doing all the work anymore and he has to do it himself or hire extra people to do it for him.

We arrive at the ranch and I expect Garrett to take me to his cabin but instead he guides us into the clubhouse. Cassidy and Harlene both shoot me comforting smiles as Garrett guides me into the room they call church.

Roper and Weston stroll in behind us and Decker, along with Oak step inside as well before the door falls shut behind them. Garrett pulls out a chair and takes one for himself right next to me. The other men take a seat while the silence in the room is deafening.

I know this is all about me and what just happened. Here I was ready to leave the past in the past and yet I realize it's just running with my head tucked in my ass because there is no escaping your past unless it's resolved.

"Can you please tell us what your father said?" Garrett starts.

His tone might be soft and supportive but the looks I'm getting from all the other men feels like I'm a threat in the room they need to extinguish. And I realize they're right. I am pulling all of them into my past where my father is coming back to haunt me.

I was stupid to think I could live the dream because it felt like it was within my reach with Garrett at my side, but it was foolish. My father won't rest until I'm back and who knows what lengths he'll go through to get me back.

Would he? Am I willing to take the risk and put all of their lives on the line? Because what if there's the slightest chance he did kill Ted and will kill Garrett? I never saw Ted or Ted's father again for that matter. My father has hurt me many times. He would. Sadness and fear hits me hard. If something would happen to Garrett or any of my new friends, I could never live with myself.

"I'm sorry. All of you gave me so much." I stand and turn to Garrett. "Thank you. For everything." My eyes start to burn and my throat clogs up. I have to force out the words I need for him to hear before I start to sob and turn into a mess and can't speak. "I don't want to buy Izzy back because she loves it here and is in good hands with you, I can see this now. I…I have to go. Thanks. All of you, from the bottom of my heart."

Tears are streaming down my face as I dash through the room, swing the door open and head for the exit.

CHAPTER 07

GARRETT

I rush after my woman and manage to grab her by the waist. "Now wait just a goddamned second."

She pushes away from me and with tears streaming down her face she yells, "No. I can't. You have to let me leave. Forget about me, Garrett. There is no other way."

"Fuck that," I growl and snatch her wrist to pull her toward me.

I bend my knees and shove my shoulder into her belly to hoist her up and carry her–fireman style–back into church. I kick the door shut and slide her down my body. Cupping her face with both hands I keep her eyes locked on mine. Even if she sees me as a blurry mess, she needs to hear what I have to say and know I mean every damn word.

"I won't ever forget about you because you're rooted underneath my goddamned skin. You're mine, Raney. Mine to care for, to protect, to cherish, and mine to damn well claim right here in front of my brothers. Whatever you're facing you're not alone. So, no. You're not leaving, and there's always another way. You don't have a wall behind your back with no way out, but a solid brotherhood who protects no matter what."

The tears keep flowing over her cheeks and are wetting my hands. My heart is near bursting just from the look of gratification mixed with adoration and warmth. She crashes her body against mine and wraps her arms so damn tight around me it's hard to damn well breathe.

"I don't want to lose you," she croaks between sobs.

I rub her back and kiss the top of her head. "You're not getting rid of me this easy, sugar."

She pulls back, face red and wet but she's still breathtakingly gorgeous and all mine. "My father threatened to kill you if I didn't go back. And at first, I thought it was all lies. He's lied so many times…but then he mentioned Ted, and seeing you guys all together…it just hit me…what if there was a slight chance…I can't risk you getting hurt." Her head swings to the right to face my brothers. "Any of you for that matter. You've all been sweet and kind. I can't risk your lives."

"Good, 'cause we're not risking yours either, doll," Decker states. "A friend of mine will be arriving any second. He contacted me today about a few things concerning your father. The day you got here two brothers looked out for you and we took it to the table. We have been trying to get things set for you to help get the paperwork done. My friend, Nick, who is FBI, mentioned your father has been a murder suspect but the charges were dropped due to lack of evidence and a body. But Nick reopened the case this morning. You mentioned your father said something about Ted? Mind explaining what that was about?"

Her eyes return to me and the red on her cheeks deepens. Fucking hell, she's ashamed of the situation she's in and talking about what she mentioned to me isn't helping either; confessing to it with a room full of men.

"You didn't do anything wrong, love," I murmur and raise my voice to let my brothers know, "Her dad caught my woman and Ted after they messed around. Ted didn't stand up for her or face her father. She simply never saw him again."

"He was the son of one of your father's employees, right?" Weston questions and Raney nods in reply.

Roper clears his throat to gain my woman's attention. "Anything else your father threaten you with?"

She shakes her head a little too quick for my liking.

I put my finger underneath her chin and let our gaze collide. "You can tell us anything. We will never judge you, okay?"

Her eyes go down and I really hate the fact this woman has to feel ashamed on many occasions. We will put all of this behind us as soon as possible so I can make sure she'll never have to suffer discomfort inflicted by her parents.

Her words are a mere whisper but I easily pick up on them. "He mentioned if I was with you for the fucking. He said he could put me to work for that too…make more money and how he would give me some of that."

"Motherfucker," I growl and drag her against my chest.

Curses flow through the air and by the anger written on my brothers' faces I say they easily picked up on her whispered words as well.

"Garrett, take your old lady home. She's your number one priority. And for now, she's on lockdown because we're not taking any chances. We don't want that fucker coming anywhere near her and we have security cams all over the ranch so if he comes here, we have him on tape. As soon as Nick gets here we'll discuss how to ban him from her life for good."

I'm about to thank my prez but Raney beats me to it when her voice soft and small croaks, "Thank you so much. I don't know what else to say but know this means a lot. I…this…so much."

"You're family now, Raney," Weston simply replies. "Let your old man take you home."

Her head bobs as I guide her out the door. She seems a million miles away when we step inside the cabin. There's a knock on the door and I check before opening it but notice Harlene standing on the porch.

"Here." She hands me the bag of stuff we bought and also Raney's backpack. "I thought she might like these. You know, if she wanted to braid something to relax or shower with her own scent. She took a long time picking the one she loved the most."

"Thanks." I give my president's old lady a smile. "Appreciate it."

"Make sure she knows we're all here for her." She raises her voice and tilts her head to look around me. "You hear me, Raney? We're all here for you and now that you've found us, we won't let you go. You're our friend, friends stick together."

I'm pushed to the side by Raney's body when she launches herself at Harlene to pull her into a hug. With all the tears streaming down her cheeks in church, I would think she doesn't have any left. Yet these seem like happy tears and I have to say, Harlene adds a few of her own as well.

After a few minutes and when most of the tears have dried, Harlene pulls back and rubs Raney's upper arms. "I heard you're Garrett's old lady now."

"News travels fast," I grumble underneath my breath.

Harlene shoots me a smile. "President's old lady, remember? When my friend walks out of the clubhouse looking like she did? You can damn well expect me to ask my man what the hell happened."

"Appreciate you looking after her," I honestly tell her.

Raney slides her arm around my waist and leans against me. "You guys really are something."

I give her a squeeze. "You fit right in since you really are something too, sugar."

"I'll leave you guys to it. Call me or text if you need anything." Harlene waves as she walks back to the clubhouse.

We should go inside but the change from being miles away to leaning against me with a content sigh and slight smile tugging her lips suits me better after the short visit Harlene brought us.

A black SUV comes down the road and I can feel Raney's body freeze.

I give a comforting kiss on the top of her head. "Relax, I

recognize the SUV, it's Nick. Like Weston said, let them handle it. Your job is to relax."

She glances up. "Mind taking a shower with me?"

"A shower? With you?" I'm instantly rock-hard at the thought of being naked and in close proximity of one another.

She gives me a shy smile and her cheeks pinken adorably. "I bought new bodywash and shampoo and I would like to know what it feels like to take a shower with my own stuff. As a couple we could shower together, right? Because you're mine too, you know…since I'm yours."

I let my lips meet hers and slide my tongue inside her mouth to take hers on a sensual dance. One of her arms sneaks up and around my neck as she presses her body closer to mine. I grab her ass and she's as light as a damn feather as I hoist her up.

I walk into the cabin and close the door, flipping the lock to make sure we have enough privacy. I only break the kiss to search for the bag and take it with us as I carry her into the bathroom where I place her down on her feet.

Turning on the water, I take out the shampoo and bodywash before I start to strip away all my clothes. Raney's gaze is on me while she rips off her clothes and lets them fall to the floor. Her eyes might still be puffy but they carry a load of heat.

And where there were different kinds of emotions taking the upper hand back in the clubhouse, right now they're burning with lust, adoration, and a deeper meaning. One I also feel inside my bones and pulses through my body with every squeeze of my heart.

I hold out my hand and she slides her fingers over my palm. Stepping underneath the water, I take her with me and let my hands roam. She grabs the bodywash and squirts a fair amount on her hand.

There's a twinkle of mischief in her eyes when she says, "I've been smelling like you for days, I'd say it's time for you to smell like me."

I hold my hands out. "By all means, I'm yours."

And damn does it feel magnificent to get soaped-up by my

woman. There's no trace of stress tugging at her brain, no worries of the world pushing us around; there's only us. Her hand slides down and a groan rips from my throat when her delicate fingers start to fondle my balls.

More fingers join the party and wrap around my hard length. My arms flash forward to brace myself against the tiles, my woman caged in between as I surrender myself to the feelings she draws out deep inside me.

If she feels this good with her mere hands, I'm dying to know what it would be like to bury myself deep inside her pussy. Her movements might be slightly inexperienced but glancing down at her face, eyes intrigued and filled with desire, it's sexy as fuck.

It catches me by surprise when my orgasm hits. Cum shoots out over her hand and her stomach. A fucking straight aim to brand my woman as mine. Her hands fall away when I step closer and cage her between my body and the tiles. A gasp tumbles from her lips, probably due to the cold tiles.

I take advantage to slam my mouth over hers, teeth clashing from the force of uncaged hunger she erupted inside my body. I might have blown my load but I'm nowhere near sated. And it's exactly what this kiss is telling her when my tongue starts to fuck her mouth the way I want to dominate her pussy.

She clings to my body, raises her leg to curl around mine so she can press her pussy against my cock and it's damn near heaven. My mind is triggered by the warning how we need a condom because it's too damn easy to shift my hips and sink balls deep.

A frustrated groan rumbles from my chest and I turn the water off, keeping Raney close as I stalk out of the bathroom and head for the living room to grab the bag. I'm balancing her ass on one hand and with her legs locked around my waist I easily carry her back to the bedroom.

I let her bounce on the bed. I rip the box of condoms open and the things go flying all over the place. Snatching one off the bed I rip open the foil and quickly cover myself. My eyes find my woman.

Waterdrops still sliding off her body, hair plastered against her skin, and eyes wide with desire. Her pussy is glistening in a warm welcome and it draws the need to taste her. Leaning in I do just that but I'm stopped when she's holding my head.

Eyes wide she gasps. "What are you doing?"

A sly smile spreads my face. "Gonna taste my woman. Eat your pussy and suck out an orgasm before I bury my cock inside you over and over again."

"That's not. You can't." She swallows hard. "Really? Kiss me…there?"

I blow a hot breath over her wet flesh and watch how her whole body shivers, and it's not from the fucking cold.

"Yeah, really. This pussy is all mine and judging from your reaction I'd say I'm the first one, and most definitely the last, who will taste you."

Her hands linger for a few more breaths until they fall away. Her eyes stay pinned on me when I lean in and flatten my tongue against her pussy, licking her from ass to clit in one go. She tastes as good as I imagined and I slide my arms underneath her ass to tilt her hips and settle in.

"Oh, gosh. That's…oh. Garrett." My name on a long moan while she releases short gasps in between words is ego stroking to know I'm bringing her pleasure no one else ever gave her.

It doesn't take long for her taste to intensify. A few combined nibbles with my teeth grazing her clit, sucking on her pussy and spearing her with my tongue lights her up like the brightest of stars on a dark night. She screams my name and holds my head in place while grinding herself against my face.

I should give her time to come down from her high but I'm too damn close to blowing my next load into a condom while I haven't even felt her pussy wrapped around me. She's driving me absolutely insane and I relish in it.

Tearing myself lose from her tight grip, I surge up and place the blunt head of my cock against her hot and puffy lips. Balancing on one hand next to her head I watch closely as I start to thrust. Her nails dig into my back, eyes locked on mine, lips parted and the sexy as fuck gasps break my restraint as I throw my hips forward and slam inside.

"Fuuuuuuck," I growl at the ceiling. "So fucking tight and good."

I slowly tip my head down to watch my woman and she gives me a shy smile. Her face is flushed and this time there's no shame or discomfort; only pleasure.

Without a second thought, and drunk on lust and desire, I spill my real feelings. "Feeling this good when we're connected, it makes me adore you more than life itself."

"If this is our first time, I think we might do better the next time," she replies tartly.

A bark of laughter makes my hips falter but I quickly overtake the pounding I was giving her. I don't think I've ever laughed during sex and this woman manages to bring out every single element into our moment, making it special and unique.

Exactly what her pussy feels like; special and unique. I already came once in the shower and it should allow me to last longer but when I feel her walls start to strangle me, head throwing back to voice my name on a moan as pleasure consumes her...I have no other choice but to follow her into a sea of bliss.

And if it's this intense our first time, it has a load of promise for the future.

CHAPTER 08

RANEY

I watch Garrett's tight, muscled butt head for the bathroom to dispose of the condom. I can't believe this handsome, sexy, strong, muscled, tattooed man is all mine. The fierce way he dragged me back once I told him I couldn't put any of them in danger really stole my heart.

And the way he acted makes me think I won't ever get it back. Not that I'm worried since I'm pretty sure I stole his just now. Sex is ahh-mazing. Mind blowing and orgasm-shattering. I've never experienced pleasure coursing through my veins the way this man took hold of me and worshipped my body.

I simply don't have any other way to put it. And I feel deliciously sore and sated as I watch Garrett stroll back to the bed. He leans in and brushes his fingertips along my cheek so tender and loving, it makes my heart skip with joy.

"I like this look on you," he murmurs and leans in for a kiss.

I eagerly kiss him back but he pulls away with a soft chuckle.

"I don't think your pussy is ready for a second pounding yet, sugar. And I should be sorry for going a bit rough on you but you dragged me into the moment where I could barely breathe unless I chased an orgasm for the both of us."

"I'm not complaining. I'll never complain about something that feels so good." I push myself up and sit on my knees to be on eye level with him since he's still standing beside the bed.

"Good," he gruffly replies. "Wanna do something fun before we go for another round?"

Deciding to live in this magical moment where not only my body but my whole life feels great, I simply hum, "Hmmm. Something more fun than we just did? Count me in."

He gives me a goofy grin. "Nothing beats sex with you."

"That we can agree on," I admit in all honesty.

His head tips back and laughter rips out. I watch how this strong, naked man tightens his muscles while he's completely relaxed.

When he faces me again, he grabs my wrist and pulls me against him. "Don't ever change and don't let anyone tell you how to live your life. You know damn well what you want and enjoy so grab every second like it was yesterday and live for the now."

I slide my arms around him. "I'm already living in the now. It happened when you stepped in my path and guided me into the whole 'too good to be true, dreaming while being wide awake' road of life."

"Our road of life," he murmurs and places a kiss on my lips. "How about we go check on Izzy or go for a ride through the pastures to check on the livestock? We have to stay on the property, though."

I quickly nod and step away to grab some clothes. When I'm fully dressed he takes my hand and we head out through the back.

"What would you like to do? Check on Izzy or go for a ride?" he questions.

"Both," I instantly reply. "We check on Izzy first, saddle up and enjoy the afternoon on horseback."

There's a large van in front of the stables and the side door is open but no one is around.

"Weird," Garret mutters. "I know the farrier is supposed to swing by this morning but he always comes inside the clubhouse first so a brother or two accompanies him into the stables and yet no one is around. And it's afternoon, he should have been finished and out of here already."

I glance around me when Garrett takes out his phone and puts it to his ear, pulling me toward the stables to look inside. "Weston, didn't Seger leave yet? He was only here this morning, right? Why is his truck still–"

His voice is cut off at the same time Garrett spins around and roughly drags me out of the stables. I risk a glance over my shoulder and see a lifeless body on the floor.

"Oh, no," I gasp.

"Dead body in the stables, Nick still there?" Garrett grunts.

"Hang up," a voice snaps hard enough to make my heart jolt.

Garrett pulls me behind him and is no longer holding his phone when he growls, "Get the fuck out of here. This is private property and you're trespassing. Not to fucking mention there's a federal agent on our grounds who will arrest you on sight."

My fingernails dig into Garrett's leather cut while I risk a glance around him to watch my father point a gun at us.

"No," I snap, realizing he's here for me, for what he said he'd do and I can't let that happen. "I'll go with you, just let him go."

"Stay behind me, Raney," Garrett says with a load of domination and demand in his voice.

I take a step to the side but Garrett's arm swings back to keep me in place. A shot rings out and I scream as Garrett grunts.

"You're going to die slowly," Garrett snarls and I notice how his body is leaning to the side. Blood is soaking his pants and I realize my father must have shot him in the leg.

"This is none of your business. You bought a horse from me and nowhere in those papers or during the auction was mentioned you could freely fuck my daughter and make her a whore to do your bidding. It was a horse you bought, not a goddamn money cow along with it. Raney, get your ass in that van. Now." My father raises the gun and aims it at Garrett's head. "Or your fuckbuddy is going to get his brains mixed with the dirt underneath our feet."

"Big mistake coming here." I recognize the loud snapping voice as Weston's. "A bigger mistake to use the farrier as a cover to get in here unseen."

I glance behind me to see Roper, Weston, Oak, and a handful of other bikers standing next to each other.

"Private property, asshole. Look up and to your left and to your right. Hell, spin that fucking brainless head of yours three-sixty to see your little fuck-up has been documented. The security feed will send your ass to prison for a long damn time," Roper adds.

"You stole from me. I'm merely retrieving what's mine," my father bellows.

A man I don't know steps around the van and is aiming a gun at my father. "I beg to differ, Wiley Bolcord. You see, the woman standing next to Garrett Verhams is a ghost. She has no birth certificate or social security number. And I'm sure if I ask her if she belongs to you or wants to go with you, she'll scream 'no fucking way.' Am I right, Raney?"

I'm stunned how this man I don't know seems to know all about me and weirdly enough stands up for me.

"Yeah," Harlene's voice flows through the air. "She's no one's property. Well, she's Garrett's property but he claimed her as his old lady, and that's different, so–"

"Too much rambling, Harlene." Cassidy cuts Harlene off and adds, "But she's right. Raney is our friend and no one will ever hurt her again."

"Or we'll kick your ass," Mayven growls and my eyes sting to see Muriel along with Greta and Kadence standing fierce behind the row of bikers.

Each and every one of Garrett's friends…no. They have become my friends too in the short period of time I've been here. They are all standing up for me. They have my back while there's a man facing us with a gun in his hand. He just shot Garrett and can hurt a lot more people and it's all because of me.

This man standing before us might be my father but he only took things from me. He never cared anything about me. He only wanted the money I could make for him and the work I could do to help him.

He lied. He was cruel and not only in words but depriving me from a lot of things and basically robbed me of living. It was only when I got out from underneath his thumb when I realized he was basically suffocating the life out of me. It all ends here. I can't go with him because I just got a taste of how living is supposed to be.

"No fucking way," I say those words with my heart and soul. "I belong where I am, and that's right here on this ranch along with my friends and my old man."

My father's face turns furious and I've seen it many times. I know what's coming; his wrath. I try to push Garrett out of harm's way but not before a gunshot blasts through the air. My grip on Garrett fails when he launches forward and takes my father with him to the ground.

Another gunshot, and I watch how Garrett punches my father in the face. He's straddling him and lands one punch after another. I grab Garrett's leather cut and try to pull him off but it's useless.

"Stop. Please," I scream. "Please, Garrett, stop. I don't want you to end up in jail."

His brothers are surrounding us and manage to pull Garrett away. The man who I don't know but stood up for me anyway is kneeling down beside my father and is cuffing him.

"Don't worry, Raney. Garrett isn't the one going to jail, this fucker is."

I now assume this must be Nick, the one working for the FBI.

"Thank you," I croak and feel Garrett's strong arms surround me.

"Are you hurt?" His gaze slides over me.

Realization sets in. "You're hurt! He shot you. Someone call an ambulance."

"Already on its way," Harlene says as she rubs my back. "Come on, let the guys bring him inside so he can sit down and get his leg elevated instead of standing here in the dirt."

I step aside to allow Roper and Colt to each grab one of Garrett's arms to throw it over their shoulder as they balance his weight to get him to the clubhouse. I don't even give my father a second glance.

The people who I only met a little over a week ago mean more to me than a man who I have known all my life. Hell, strangers gave me more than he ever did and it's a hard contrast to balance my past and future. But I'm determined to put everything behind me and focus on a future where I'm in control of my own life.

We step inside the clubhouse and Joaquin comes rushing toward the couch where they are putting Garrett. He holds out a glass of water and places a medical kit on the table. Harlene and Cassidy both jump into action and pull on gloves before they cut open his jeans to assess the wound.

They might be vets but it's better than nothing. Hell, I don't even know what to do but they work together effortlessly to try to stop the bleeding and cover the wound. Sirens blare from outside and I release a deep breath when I finally see EMTs come rushing in.

Time passes where we head to the hospital to take out the bullet. He's so damn lucky from what I've heard. The bullet didn't do any real damage. But I heard more than one shot and it turns out one of those belonged to Nick who shot my father's hand in an effort to mess with his aim. Thankfully he did so when Garrett knocked them both to the ground, he wasn't shot.

He could have died.

I could have lost the man I love.

I know it might be too soon to talk or think about love but my heart and gut doesn't lie. What I feel for this man is beyond comparison. When you're wrapped with kindness, feel comfortable in silence to enjoy each other's company, share the same interest and passion in the hard work each of us does on the ranch; you know deep down it's a match made in heaven.

He is a slice of heaven right here on earth. My savior from the second I laid eyes on him. Everything feels right. And when you know what it's like when your body lights up at the sight of your man who is still alive and just woke up from a surgery to retrieve a bullet because he once again saved me from my father; you grab hold and never let go. You give meaning to that feeling and label it for what it is; love.

"Hey," he croaks and winces when he tries to sit up.

I carefully grab his hand and give it a squeeze. "I was afraid I would lose you."

He gives me a faint smile. "Not a chance, sugar."

The door of Garrett's hospital room swings open and Decker stalks inside. "Is your lazy ass still in bed?"

"Shut up, asshole," Garrett grumbles.

"I just came in to let you know Raney's father is heading to jail and according to Nick it's an open and shut case with everything we have against him. He won't get out any time soon. And it's not just what that fucker did today but Nick also had a breakthrough with that other case. They–" His eyes go to me and he clears his throat. "Sorry, I can't tell it any other way than they did some kind of sonar thing when the dogs indicated they found something when they had a warrant to search the property. Nick is pretty sure they found a dead body buried on your dad's ranch. It must be from Ted since he's been missing and he did mention it to you. But we'll know more once they've recovered the body and such. We'll keep you up to date but I thought you guys would like to know everything is handled. He won't bother you again, Raney."

Tears are yet again sliding down my cheeks and I can't stop them. I'm not sad but they are happy tears.

"Thank you," I croak. "I'm so thankful to have all of you in my life."

Decker points a finger in my direction. "Meant to be and

shit like that. You fit right in with the other old ladies and don't even mind the hard work around the ranch. And don't forget I placed an order, huh? You're damn good at braiding rope and I'm sure you know your father sold your stuff. You knew about that, right?"

I nod. "I knew he sold them. He had me sometimes make special orders."

"Well, you being the brains and actual hands behind those great items–" He cuts his sentence off and shoots me a wink. "You could sell them yourself. Make an online shop and get it up and running. You'll have a way to support you and do what you like for yourself. And I'm sure one of the guys can help you set up a website or anything else you need."

"Enough with the hints and tips. My woman is free to do what she wants, when she wants. Now go hunt down a doctor or nurse and ask when I can get my ass home," Garrett grunts.

Decker chuckles. "All right already. Don't go anywhere, I'll be right back."

Garrett curses while Decker's laughter fills the room as he heads in search for medical personnel.

"Come lie down next to me." Garrett scoots to the side.

I glance at his leg. "But you're wounded."

"Don't care, I need to feel you."

How can I ever deny him when I want the same thing? I carefully crawl into the bed with him and sigh in contentment. I want to tell him so badly about what I feel for him but I can't; it's too soon. Lying in this bed and what we just went through might cause for him to think I'm telling him those words for different reasons.

But my heart skips a beat when he murmurs, "I fucking love your scent, your body against mine, and the way I feel when those bright green eyes of yours land on mine. I could say I love you but then you'd probably blame it on my dozed-up state. But I really do. You're so damn special. The second I laid eyes on you it was as if you jolted my body into awareness. And we now have the time to explore everything we want without having to look over our shoulder. Free to dream about a future, one where I do hope we have kids one day who also enjoy working with horses as much as we do."

"These days I can't seem to stop crying," I croak. "But I won't blame it on the medication because I love you too."

"Thank fuck. Shit. I don't think we can have sex today. Unless you ride me, that won't require me moving around as much."

A giggle escapes me. "We have all the time in the world and many positions and places to have sex. I have a feeling we won't ever grow tired of exploring things together."

He brushes his knuckles over my nipple. "I'm ready to start exploring when you are."

I gasp and jump off the bed when a nurse stalks into the room. Garrett chuckles and I shoot him a glare but it quickly turns into a smile when I remember what he just said, what we said to each other.

He loves me. He really, really loves me and offers me the world, one we built together with mutual respect and surrounded by friends. One where I will be sure to make my dream a reality. And I already have my knight in shining armor at my side.

EPILOGUE

Two years later

GARRETT

I glance at the empty spot beside me and realize Raney isn't in bed with me. I don't know why but the memory of the first few days together two years ago assaults me. One where she would be restless and not able to fall asleep in bed and had to sneak out to the stables to sleep in the damn horse bedding with Izzy.

It changed the day I got out of the hospital. I have no clue if it was the change in life knowing she was completely freed from her father–since he's rotting in jail with a lifelong sentence–or her worry to make sure I was okay since I couldn't walk, let alone carry her back to bed like I did every day. Fact is, as of that day she slept in my arms every night.

Except now. But there's a logical explanation for it. I push myself up and notice my wife standing in front of the window, her eyes are glued on the darkness of the night. She has her hands on her back and she's twiddling with her wedding ring. I chose a golden band with a floral carved design and it looks very delicate around her finger.

"Any change?" I question.

She spins around and stalks back to the bed. "Did I wake you?"

I give a little shake of my head. "By standing silently by the window? Not a chance, sugar."

A tiny sigh flows over her lips and she slides between the covers to snuggle close.

"Fuck," I grunt at the feel of her cold feet brushing against my leg.

The giggle caressing my chest as she snuggles close is awakening my cock. Her hand slides over my abs and a moan tumbles from her when she wraps her fingers around my dick. I close my eyes and relish in her touch. Her mouth lingers on my neck, a sloppy kiss, making electricity dance over my skin.

After years she still manages to set my body aflame with desire while my heart holds hers. We share the same dreams and hopes, and it's for this reason we've only just decided it's time to take the next step in our future. Last night we threw all the condoms away and we're going to let fate decide if we get to expand our family.

And when I open my eyes and stare into hers–filled with the same amount of love and devotion as mine–I'd say we're more than ready to embrace any children we might be graced with. She's come a long way and is so damn strong and determined. She's managed to teach herself how to read with little help from me and her friends. She'll be a great mother. She's kind, loving, caring, devoted, overly protecting and I know all of this because I know her.

But mostly because Izzy is going to give birth any day and Raney has been sick with worry. It's the reason why she was standing in front of the window, keeping an eye on the stables while I'm sure she checked the feed of the camera we have set up to watch the mare.

I'm drawn out of my thoughts when Raney straddles me and places the head of my dick at her entrance, slowly sinking down to impale herself. I hold my breath and try to keep the tingle in my balls on a slow burn.

The sight above me is enthralling. Perfect tits peeking through her long black hair but it's her gorgeous green eyes that draw me in. We found love when we least expected it and were thrown into each other's path to move forward together; perfectly paired.

Her legs are on each side of me and I let my hands slide up and over her hips to guide her movements. I break our stare because I have to watch how her pussy swallows my cock whole. Each time she moves up I get a glimpse of myself covered with her juices before I get tightly gripped by her walls, repeating the process over and over.

Confident enough she'll keep a delicious rhythm, I sneak one hand up to knead her breast and I tweak her nipple at the same time I let my thumb find her clit to draw small circles. Yeah, the desperate moan filling the air, along with the increasing squeezing of her pussy, is telling me she's close.

I lift my upper body and snatch her other nipple with my mouth, sucking hard and flicking it with my tongue while I hold it hostage between my teeth. Her fingers grip my head to keep me in place and she starts to fuck me. Rough. Riding me like there's no tomorrow and it makes my hips shoot off the mattress to meet her with the same ferocity.

Harsh breaths rip through the air, sweat coating our bodies until my name is bouncing off the walls as she collapses on top of me to let her body surrender to the pleasure. I grip her hips and shamelessly use her limp body to grind myself as deep as I can to fill her up with my seed. Maximum intensity, maximum pleasure, and for sure as fuck; maximum love.

Our raging hearts try to settle but deep down they never will. They will always stay wild to chase the love flowing around us. A smile spreads my face while I let my hand slide over the back of her head.

The softness of her hair along with her warm breath flowing over my damp chest makes me damn happy. Though I know my woman is sated, she'd still have the restlessness flowing through her, the same when she was standing in front of the window. And it's for this reason I ask, "Want to go check on Izzy?"

Her gorgeous head comes up and she stares at me with a load of adoration. "You don't mind?"

"Woman," I grunt. "You know I'd bring her inside our bedroom if that makes you happy."

A smile falling right from heaven paints her face when she says, "Because you want me happy."

"Because you make me happy," I murmur and brush my lips against hers.

"Happy, loved, cherished, understood…I never knew something like this existed until you made me feel good the second I met you." The words are spoken with a load of emotion and slide like a straight arrow into my heart.

I feel the need to lighten the mood and the first thing that enters my brain is, "Let the good times roll, along with my hips to find the perfect spot inside you to make things forever roll our way."

Her head tips back and laughter flows from her body, making it shake so my dick slides out of her.

She glances down at me and murmurs, "Forever…our way."

"Fuck, yes," I rumble and fist her hair to keep her head in place to give her a kiss.

One where she knows I will keep the promise I just gave her; good times will sure as fuck keep rolling our way. And I can't wait to experience what the future holds for us as we realize our dreams with fulfilled hearts.

COWBOY
BIKERS MC #8

By Esther E. Schmidt

Oak

I'm a biker in an MC located at a huge ranch which breeds both longhorns and quarter horses. I'm not just a biker, a cowboy, or a rancher, but I am a man of many trades and talents. And one of those is to protect the one who captured my attention at first glance.

Lottie

Being immature and reckless kickstarted my life at a very young age, but I never once let it define me.
I'm a single mother, running a bar while raising my daughter all by myself. Until a ruggedly handsome biker swoops me off my feet, offering me more than one scorching encounter. At a moment when my life feels perfect, a ghost from the past stumbles back into town putting not only my daughter's life on the line, but all those I love, including my own.

CHAPTER 01

OAK

I signal the barmaid, bar owner, sexy-as-fuck woman, to get me another drink. It's crazy for me to sit here this late at night during the week while ordering one water after another. That's right; no booze. Mainly because I'm not here to get shitfaced.

Not because I don't drink, which I do on occasion, but mostly because I like a clear head and need to work early almost every day. I should hate alcohol due to my stepfather being an angry drunk who liked to beat the shit out of my mother, but I don't. Luckily the fucker is history, and has been for over ten years.

I made him leave after I came home from work one day and found my mother bleeding on the floor. The fucker was bent over her body, ready to give her another punch while Anson–his sixteen-year-old, shit for brains son–helped by kicking my mother in the face.

I never knew what she saw in him but their relationship only lasted for two years or so. Two years of hell. Me and my stepbrother not getting along also didn't help. I was barely eighteen when I faced the two of them but managed to call the cops and get them away from my injured mother.

Like I said, that was ten years ago. And it's a good thing my former stepfather and his son left town that day before the cops came. I had to stay put to help my mother, because eighteen years old or not, I was ready to hunt them down and kill them with my bare hands. My life would have been different than what it is now if I did in fact kill them.

Good thing I didn't and that they never returned because I fucking love my life as I know it. My mother is still breathing and happily married to an okay guy who runs the post office while I'm a biker in a motorcycle club which is located at a huge ranch. A ranch where I work day in, day out breeding and training horses and taking care of other livestock.

But that's not what I'm doing right now. Right now, I've given myself the task to charm the pants off the woman who owns this bar, and hopefully have her wrapped around my dick once the bar closes. Easier said than done, but I'm a determined man on a mission.

Ever since I saw her for the first time–when I picked up Spiro last week when he was too drunk to ride home–I've found myself coming here every night, drinking water and ogling the beauty serving drinks and running the bar.

I know absolutely nothing about her, other than the fact she has owned this place for years. Funny how this woman only now caught my eye, but on the other hand I mostly stick to the ranch and if I want a good time, I usually go out of state to avoid running into a one-night stand afterward.

But I don't want a one-night stand with this woman; I want many of those lined up for the unforeseen future. I can't help it, the woman has a banging body, making me drool in two places at once; my cock and my mouth.

"Another water, handsome?" she flawlessly flirts without missing a beat.

During the time I've been sitting here for the past few days, I've been observing her every move. And during that time, I have noticed a difference in her flirting toward men. Most of the smiles she gives never reach her eyes and she doesn't linger; except with me. Yes, I'm aware I might just be hopeful she's into me, but like I said; I'm fucking drooling to have her.

I let the lust racing through my veins spill through my voice and eyes when I tell her, "Unless you're offering something sweeter."

Her gaze travels over the last three men occupying the bar until it lands back on me.

"And what if I am?" Her voice is husky and I can clearly see my own lust reflecting in her hazel brown eyes, the gold flecks surrounding her pupils flare up and it bumps her up to breathtakingly beautiful.

I lean in closer and rumble, "I'd drink you up and savor the taste to make it last."

Her eyes close when she takes a deep and steady breath. When they flash back open, she points at the glass of water. "You have a clear head so I won't have to repeat myself. No sleepovers, just sex. Understood?"

I'm sure my grin is all telling, but I can't help myself; I'm burying my cock into this hot woman like I've been wanting to do ever since I laid eyes on her.

"Understood," I tell her because I know she wants to hear the actual word.

Her head whips up and she bellows, "That's it, guys, the bar is closed!"

I swear all it takes is a few minutes and the whole place is cleared out.

She locks up, flips most of the lights off and stalks past me with the words, "Follow me."

Don't have to tell me twice.

I watch her curvy ass sway and I'm mesmerized by it, her hips, thighs, all curves and I'm about to get my hands on them. I don't think I've ever seen a woman with such a banging body. Maybe I've never paid any attention other than glancing at their tits, whatever. But this woman? Smmmokin'.

She enters a small office in the back and waits for me to walk inside before she locks the door. Somewhere in the back of my mind it strikes me as weird because she already locked the front door of the bar, but whatever; I'm about to get my dick wet.

Her hands are on me and slide downward underneath my leather cut until she reaches my jeans where my sleeveless shirt is tucked in. She rips it out to allow her hands to roam over my naked skin, nails raking my abs and I'm instantly hard as fuck.

I fist her hair and growl in a guttural tone, "Tell me your name so I know what to call out when your pussy is ripping the cum out of me."

That's right, the time I spent in the bar she's only called me "Handsome" while I used "Gorgeous." No more, time to get better acquainted since we'll be up close and personal within the next few seconds.

Her breath flows over my lips. "Lottie."

"Oak," I grunt and slam my mouth over hers.

Fire. My whole body is set ablaze at mere contact. Seems like I'm not the only one when she gasps, allowing me to swoop right in to swirl my tongue against hers. Our hands frantically roam free while tearing at our clothes.

Shredding every single piece, I'm now able to take in all the curves of her perfect body. Forget about drooling, this woman is more than mouthwatering; she's a sight to behold and all mine to taste, pleasure, and fuck for the unforeseen future until I'm too sated to move.

My fingers dig into her lush ass and she releases a tiny yell in surprise when I easily lift her up and plaster her back against the wall. She recovers quickly and grips my head and drags me into a hot kiss.

My movements are feverish and I'm moaning my heart out when I move one hand down and slide my fingers through the lips of her pussy. She's drenched and with her legs wrapped high around my waist I can easily fingerfuck her while brushing her clit.

If I thought she was kissing the hell out of me before, she's now taken the pitchfork from the devil himself and is leading hell. It's proven to be lethal love when she bites my bottom lip, and starts to moan while her pussy is strangling my fingers.

Fuck if I'm passing her pleasure on my mere fingers. I pull them out to grip my cock and ram inside her. She rips her mouth from mine and screams my name while I throw my hips back and forth to surge in and out without mercy.

My balls are ready to draw up, spine tingling with my upcoming orgasm, and in this moment, nothing more exists but to take the both of us into a steep wave of bliss. And that's exactly what's happening for me but I need her to come with me.

Without thinking I prod my–coated with her juices–finger up her ass and as she comes so beautifully, my cock starts to weep in violent bursts. Cum shooting out like it's an everlasting stream and I rumble her name over her sweat covered skin.

Motherfucking earthshattering and there's no fucking way this will be a one-night stand. Hell, I'm still buried deep inside her and I'm ready for more. And it's for this reason I balance her ass in my hands and turn to see where I can put her down to start over.

Another tiny scream rips from her and I'm starting to like the sound, knowing it's her "caught by surprise while making no objections to stop me" sound. From the corner of my eye, I notice a desk and it's perfect for what I have in mind next.

I place her ass on it and pull out. Her eyes go wide when my cum instantly starts to leak out. Yeah, worry is for later, pleasure is what's more important now. But I need her fully in this moment with me without thoughts wandering.

It's for this reason I tell her, "I'm clean and there's nothing else to worry about unless you're not."

"I'm clean, but–"

I cut her off by snatching up my shirt and wiping her pussy to clear most of my cum leaking out along with the words, "Then we're going to save any discussion for later and enjoy this moment. And with enjoy I mean fucking relish because you felt damn good wrapped around me and even if I'm going to taste myself, I'm still dying to eat this pussy."

A low moan comes from her mouth when my tongue slides though her pussy. Yeah, whatever worry or discussion was plaguing her mind evaporated with the first lick. Her hands are back on my head when I take her bundle of nerves between my teeth and start to nibble and suck.

"Yessss. Fuck. Suck. Yes. Oh…Oak. Keep…yes!" Her gasps between needy words filled with lust and awe tease my ears, make me rock-hard once again.

This time, when her third orgasm slams into her body, I'm not burying myself deep like I did the first time. Nope. I'm eating her pussy like a starved man to get my fill of her taste on my tongue. Only when she's sagging down onto the desk do I surge up, grab my cock and nudge her entrance.

"Lottie," I grunt between clenched teeth, holding myself back which is costing me a load of restraint. "Eyes on me."

Her gorgeous hazel eyes are filled with golden flecks when she flutters them open and glances at me with so much adoration, appreciation, lust, desire, whatever emotion she possesses because for sure as fuck she's as drunk on emotions as I am when I start to push back inside her.

This time I'm not on a rampage for pleasure, but a slow and sensual one to obtain all the feels and prolong what we have in this moment. And what a moment it is. Full tits jiggling back and forth with each slow stroke. Nipples dark pink and standing at attention.

Her face is flushed and washed with pleasure as I grip her hips to keep her from grinding and trying to slam back to up our previous pace. I'm in control and determined to make this last longer than the passionate, raw, and hungry fuck we just had against the wall.

"Breathe, Lottie. Breathe and fucking feel my cock sliding in and out of your pussy."

She moans and sneaks her arms around my neck to pull me close. I never kiss any woman; too intimate. But taking her lips in the same lazily, yet thorough kiss gives me the sense of possession that overtakes me and I realize I won't be able to let this woman walk away after one hot night.

Lottie drives the heel of her foot against my ass and shifts her hips while her pussy starts to clench and I know we're done for. No matter the strength to hold back, there's no stopping pleasure once it's hit overdrive. A wave of heat slams through me when our simultaneous orgasms bind us through bliss.

I can't even keep myself up and crash my full weight on top of her, but she merely grunts and tightens her arms to keep me close. I can feel her raging heart against mine and the both of us are panting like crazy to catch our breath.

The thought suddenly strikes me, "I haven't even had the chance to suck on your sweet tits."

Her giggle vibrates through her body and it makes me chuckle.

A weight falls off me when she says, "With what we just did, I'm more than willing to offer another round, another day. Not tonight, though. I'm beat and have to get up early. Shit. What time is it?"

Regretfully pulling out, I glance around for my jeans and snatch them up to get my phone from my pocket. "Almost four in the morning. Shit. Work starts at seven."

She's hopping off the desk and pulling on her panties when she says, "We have that in common then. I have to be up at seven as well."

The longing in her eyes is ego stroking when she glances at my half erect cock. Licking her lips, she shimmies into her pants and snatches her bra from the floor.

"No wonder you felt good," she muses and hides her gorgeous tits from my sight.

I palm my cock and let my thumb flick over the barbell while I shoot her a wink. "The piercing gives us both a little extra pleasure. But I'm betting your tongue will feel damn magnificent when I'm thrusting into your hot mouth."

She groans and mutters, "Stop talking or the both of us will be pulling an all-nighter."

Laughter ripples from my body as I pull on my boots and snatch my leather cut off the chair I threw it on.

"Best to recharge and get back together soon," I offer and step closer.

She's fully dressed now too and slides her hands around my neck. "Tomorrow night? Same time and place?"

I suddenly remember I have to deliver a horse to a client and regretfully tell her, "I don't know what time I'll be back from dropping off a horse."

Before she can say anything I take her lips in a slow kiss and when I pull back, I let her know, "Let me get your number and I'll give you mine. If I leave early, I might make it back in time when you close the bar."

"Sounds good." She takes her phone in hand and I rattle off my number.

I feel my phone buzz in my pocket.

"You have my number, and now you have to go." She starts to shove my chest and I fake being hurt. The giggle flowing over her lips strokes my ego when she says, "Till the next booty call, handsome."

At least we're on the same page, though I'm sure I want more and it's for this reason I let her know, "No fucking others for either of us while we have this booty call arrangement in place between us."

"Agreed." The venom ringing from that word gives me the knowledge we're definitely on the same page.

I give her one last scorching kiss and enter the cold, dark night but the fire this woman lit inside me is keeping me warmer than ever as I fire up my bike and head back to the ranch.

CHAPTER 02

LOTTIE

"You haven't finished your breakfast yet," I softly scold.

Clover, my nine-year-old daughter, is standing near the door with her hand on the doorknob. "But Mom, I'm late."

I check the clock and notice she's actually a bit early for her walk to school.

There's no need for me to use words; one rise of my eyebrow is enough for her to admit, "Now I don't have the time to watch the foals running into the pasture. He's always early when he takes them from the stables into the field."

"And who is he?" I question in the hopes she will finally tell me the rancher's name so I can talk to the man in question about not letting her get too close to the horses.

She shakes her head with force while her hand and mouth give me the "my lips are sealed" visual. And to make it clear she adds, "I can't tell you that or you'll talk to him and ruin everything."

I restrain myself from rolling my eyes at her overdramatic

reaction. But on the other hand, she's absolutely right, because I would talk to him.

"Just stay safe and don't be late," I tell her and stroll over to place a kiss on the top of her head.

"Later, Mommy." Such a cheerful tone and it's all because she's about to see the horses she loves to watch in the pastures she walks past on her way to school.

The door closes and my jaw drops to yawn without shame. I am so damn tired. Worth it, though. Just the reminder of last night makes my whole body tingle. I don't think I've ever had sex this consuming. I pour myself some more coffee and cup it with both hands as I take a seat on the couch. Curling my feet underneath my ass, I reach for my phone to check my messages.

There's only one from Alexi, a waitress who sometimes watches Clover for me and can run the bar if I'm sick or if I have something I can't get out of. But her message was just to let me know she's going to be half an hour late because she needs to pick up her cat from the vet.

It's probably an excuse because the woman is always late. Most times she partied a little too long or hitched a ride with some guy, had sex, and now has to figure out how to get home and to work on time. Yeah, she's a little wild and a free spirit who likes gossip, but still, when she's working, she's a good employee.

I shoot her a reply to let her know to take her time and after hitting send I stare at my phone and debate sending a text to Oak. Would it be weird to shoot him a message? He should be awake since he said he needed to work early. And what would I text anyway?

Last night was amazing. I woke up a bit sore but can't wait to get together again? Do you have time right now? Ugh. It might be better not to text and give him space because the way he looked–all inked muscle, rough biker with the kind of handsome, sexiness that lasts a lifetime–he sure didn't look like a man who likes a woman to be needy and running after him.

Hell, I bet they fall down in piles in front of him to get his attention. Shit. How could I've been so stupid to forget about a condom? Again. The last time–and also the first time I had sex–it resulted in getting pregnant at the age of fifteen and becoming a mom at sixteen. But that's a faint memory and Clover is my pride and joy.

Even if the guy I had sex with once left without a word after he pulled out of me and I never saw or heard from him again. I don't have a clue who he was or where he lived since I had just moved here with my parents. The only thing I remember about him was his first name and the fact he was missing the tip of his little finger on one hand.

My parents bought the bar when I was fifteen and we all moved here. The day I got pregnant, I was outside, bored out of my mind when this boy showed up. His father was in the bar drinking and we got to talking.

Feeling tough and daring we started kissing and before I knew it, we were awkwardly doing it in the old shed behind the bar. Reckless memories of the biggest mistake in my life as a teenager. The whole "don't talk to strangers," should have entered my brain with "don't fuck strangers."

My life might have been different if that moment in time didn't happen. But then again, I wouldn't have Clover and she really is my pride and joy. Not to mention, my parents were real angels. After I hid the fact of what that boy and I did, I couldn't hide my growing belly and eventually spilled my secret. They weren't angry but made sure I was prepared instead.

Dammit. My eyes start to burn and I know it's too early for a trip down memory lane. I miss my parents so much. Three years ago my father ran his truck off the road. They told us he had a stroke since no other cars were involved. And I think my mother died of a broken heart because she died five months later from a heart attack.

I've worked in their bar all my life so it was only natural to keep going when I inherited it. I moved out of my place and into the apartment above the bar, allowing me the chance to combine work and living to make it easier since being a single mom is anything but easy.

And that's where Oak fits in perfectly because the whole booty call thing doesn't involve spilling life situations. Though, it did sound nice he threw out the whole "not seeing any other people" near the end of our encounter. A smile spreads my face and it also makes me determined not to really overthink things and for once live in the moment. Like how I did last night.

I type out the message "Looking forward to a repeat of last night," and hit send. I take another sip of my coffee and feel my phone vibrate with an incoming message. A smile spreads my face when I see it's from Oak.

OAK:
Managed to swap my shift, see you tonight.

I want to shoot him a reply but decide against it, reminding myself not to seem too eager and needy. Releasing a deep sigh, I take the last sip of coffee and grab the file from the table along with a pen and go over the liquor supply I need to order. Back to the books it is for the next hour before I have to head downstairs and clean the bar to get it ready to open in a few hours.

Time slips through my fingers and I barely manage to clean the bar in time to pick up Clover. She can walk home from school herself but what good is being your own boss if I can't relish in the flexibility of it? Besides, it's a great way to clear my head and enjoy the day as I stroll past the large pastures Clover loves so much.

Her biggest dream is to ride and one day own a horse herself, but it scares the shit out of me. Those animals are huge and I will never forget the scary incident over seven years ago when I had Clover in a stroller and a horse was trotting past us and spooked. It jumped to the side and almost knocked into us.

I know it was just an incident but I felt I could have lost Clover. Overdramatic much? Maybe, but that kid means the world to me and it's the reason why I steer clear of those massive, unpredictable animals.

My eyes are glued to my right where a group of cowboys are guiding a herd of Longhorns into another pasture. The sight is extraordinary. The whole cowboy thing might be hot with two of them going full-speed, standing in their saddles, spurring their horses on, but it's the three men on their bikes that hold my attention.

One of them roars his bike, puts his foot in the dirt and lets the bike spin in place to take a sharp turn in an effort to guide a Longhorn back who escaped the herd. I can't stop myself from ogling the man and lean my forearms on the fence to make sure I don't fall down when I realize the man I'm ogling is Oak.

I recognize his dark leather Stetson, his inked arm, along with his build, and muscles...everything inside me screams it's him. The longing of feeling him against me slams through my veins at the same time Oak stops his bike and glances right at me.

He turns his head, barks out some words and roars the machine underneath him back to life as he heads straight for me. The determined grin on his face lights up my own and I can't remember if I've ever felt this giddy about talking to another person. Though I also have to admit, I've never met a man like Oak.

Turning off the bike and hitting the kickstand, he dismounts and closes the distance, leaving only the fence between us. Without a second thought he cups the back of my head and gives me a toe-curling kiss as if we've been lovers for months.

When he pulls back, he murmurs, "I needed that little taste, thanks for making home deliveries. Shame I can't taste your other set of lips standing out here in the open."

Laugher slips out and I have to admit, "You have to rectify that later today."

He leans in and places his lips next to my ear. "Or you can jump on the back of my bike and I'll take you to my cabin where I can give that magnificent pussy of yours all the attention it deserves."

My next breath comes out choppy and I'll definitely need a fresh pair of panties when I get home because the ones I'm wearing are now drenched.

Regretfully I tell him, "I can't. I have to pick up–"

My lips clamp shut and I wish I could put this moment on hold to have a little conversation with myself because telling Oak about Clover will change things. Yet, on the other hand what we have is a booty call so what does it matter if I'm a single mom? Though, over the years I've seen men who wanted to date me run the other way at the sound of me having a kid.

His eyes pierce mine with a curious look. "Pick up? What or who?"

I'm still debating what to tell him when I hear my daughter's voice, and I'm shocked through my soul when it's not me she's fondly greeting, but Oak.

"Hey, Oak. How's MayMay doing?" Clover steps onto the fence and holds her fist out to give Oak a bump; the both of them let their knuckles collide.

"No foal yet, Clover." The softness in his tone and the familiarity of calling my daughter by her name makes me realize this is not the first time these two have met. "Give me a moment to talk with the lady and I'll show you MayMay on my phone, okay?"

"Don't listen to her, don't talk to her either," Clover squeaks in panic, glancing from me to Oak.

Oak bounces his gaze between Clover and me and the corner of his mouth twitches.

To my surprise he leans in closer to Clover and fake whispers, "So…this is the mo–"

Clover slams her tiny hand over Oak's mouth and glances at me in panic while she whispers at Oak, "My mom. She's my mother, Oak."

Oak throws his head back and laughs. Clover keeps staring at him.

I know sweetheart, he's a sight to behold, believe me, I know.

Oak's eyes twinkle with laughter when they land on mine. "May I invite the two of you to check on MayMay?" I'm about to make up an excuse but Oak holds up his hand. "I'm sorry to say you can only watch from a distance and you won't come near any of the other horses. She can give birth any day, and I can't risk anything spooking her. It's why the rest of the stables are empty since the other horses are in the pasture."

Something about his words strikes me as fishy and when I glance at Clover she's begging me without any words. A sigh rips from me and I fall for her pleading looks.

I direct my attention to Oak and I feel like an idiot, but I need to know, "Is it safe?"

He leans over the fence and takes my hand, brushing his thumb over my knuckles in a soft caress. "Thrust me, Lottie. I wouldn't risk your girl. Like I said, the other horses are in the pasture and we won't get close to the one who's safely locked away."

"Please, Mom?" Clover's voice pushes me over the edge.

Instead of telling Clover, I tell Oak, "Just for a little glimpse."

"Yay," Clover squeals and wraps her arms around my waist. "Thank you, thank you, thank you."

"Yeah, yeah," I mutter and hug her back. "Come on, let's go. I have to open the bar in less than an hour and I have to fix you dinner and have everything set before then."

"You two can walk around and enter through the gate over there. I'm going through the pasture 'cause I have to take my bike back. We'll meet at the gate. Clover, you know the way, right?"

Clover bobs her head. Oak stalks back to his bike and I have to get my libido under control so I drag my gaze away from the sexy man and focus on my daughter to get all the details.

"Oak is the cowboy who you talk to most mornings?"

Clover takes my hand and we start to walk into the direction Oak told us to go.

"Uh huh. He's cool. Like I told you, he answers all my questions. He doesn't think I'm annoying. Unlike Dennis."

Dennis is a boy in her class who wasn't very nice to her. Though, it has been better these last few days.

I give her hand a squeeze. "Boys don't know how to behave

sometimes and say things before they think things through. Dennis might be a bit mean because he likes you and is having a hard time expressing himself."

"Dennis is a whole lot of mean and he doesn't like me. He says horses stink and how I stink too because I like them."

Okay, clearly I need to curve the conversation back to Oak because to me it seems like Dennis is a little punk, or he has a crush on Clover and is only saying things to get a rise out of her. I think it's time I have a little chat with the teacher if this continues.

"What does Oak say about Dennis?" I find myself asking.

Clover shoots me a grin. "That I should point my nose in another direction and ignore Dennis. Because if you don't like something, you have the choice to look or walk the other way."

I'm stunned and have no clue what to say to that.

We're nearing the gate when I finally ask, "And how does Dennis respond to you ignoring him?"

Clover grins. "He frowns a lot now and doesn't talk as much."

A smile spreads my face and I lean in to place a kiss on the top of my daughter's head. It also hits me how Oak gave his two cents to my daughter in a way to offer Clover a solution that seems to work.

My nerves flare up as soon as we get near the gate of this massive ranch. My fear of horses is creeping through my veins and I know I've allowed it to grow over the years without any real reason other than the one single incident.

But this is my daughter walking next to me without any fear. She's the only one I have and will protect her however I see fit. But on the other hand, I can't take away things that bring her joy. And the bright happiness shining from her face is warming my heart.

It skips a beat when Oak holds out his hand for Clover to take and they both head toward the stables. For the first time I see my daughter walking with a male as a picture perfect father and daughter moment and a burst of sadness drives away the fear.

My feet falter and tears sting my eyes. I have to swallow hard and close my eyes at the dreams and longing my body fills with. I'm crazy to let my mind run with this picture-perfect moment, because in real life, there is no such thing as perfect.

CHAPTER 03

OAK

Clover is rattling my ears off, as usual ever since I went over to talk to her a few months ago. She's been walking past our ranch for a long time, like many other kids on their way to school. But Clover always takes her time, picks a spot to climb the fence and sits on it for a full ten minutes and simply stares at the horses.

A few months ago, I was fixing said fence when she strolled past and I asked if she was going to enjoy watching the horses again, and that's how we got to talking each and every weekday. Her love for horses is clear, along with her sponge for a brain with the need to absorb every answer to her never-ending questions.

But I indulge her and it's become more of a routine for us to talk horses for a few minutes before she's off to school and I proceed with the rest of my day. After school, though? I'm most times working on the other side of the ranch so I don't catch her walking back home.

I shoot a glance over my shoulder at her mom. At Lottie. Fucking hell, what a coincidence. Clover has talked about her mother but never told me her name, just a load of information about her not liking horses at all. She also mentioned she doesn't have a father and now I'm curious to know more about Lottie because she raised this nine-year-old all by herself.

A fucking nine-year-old while Lottie looks to be in her early twenties, how old was she when she gave birth to Clover? Fuck. Many questions roam inside my head but when I take in the closed eyes and tears spilling down Lottie's cheeks I realize I have different matters to tend to.

I direct my attention to Clover who's oblivious to her mother and has her eyes set on the stables. "You can go inside and check on MayMay, but don't open the door to her stall, okay?"

Her head bobs as if it's going to fall off and she manages to timidly speed walk, making the corner of my mouth twitch. Such a smart girl. We've talked about no sudden movements or running when you're close to horses and for her to go where she's wanted to go for many months, I'd say she's keeping a clear head.

Now I can have my hands free, full, whatever, with her mom since I know she fears horses. It's the reason why Clover sticks to sitting on a fence watching them instead of interacting with the animals she clearly loves.

With Clover out of sight I cup Lottie's face with both hands. She gasps and her eyes go wide. They collide with mine as they fill with panic, switching to shame, and finally tear away from me to hit the dirt.

"Sorry," she mutters and takes her head from my hands to wipe away her tears and she clears her throat. "I'm having a crappy moment. I have to take a few breaths and I'll be okay."

"What happened to make your fear of horses this extensive?" I question.

She snickers. "I didn't spill tears from fear, it was from seeing you holding her hand and casually walking with her. Stupid, I know. Sorry. Wow. I'm rambling. Ignore me. Oh. My. God.

You let her to go inside the stable by herself?"

"Remember the whole 'take a few breaths' you mentioned earlier? Now is the time." I give her a comforting smile and she shoots me a glare in return. "No worries, like I said, the horses are in the pasture, the only one inside is the mare MayMay and she's safely locked away in her stall. Your kid knows a lot about horses because she's been asking my ass off every morning for months. She's smart. She won't open the stall nor would she stick her hand through the bars. Besides, the mare is a sweet one who's always calm no matter what. And how do I know your kid won't do something stupid? She just managed to speed walk timidly instead of running to something she's been wanting for a long time. Which allows me to give my attention to you. You know, because you're the monster who won't let her ride a horse or even pet one."

If I thought her eyes went wide a moment ago, they're now about to fall into the dirt.

"She calls me a monster?" Lottie squeaks in a harsh whisper and I fucking hate to see new tears well in her gorgeous eyes.

I glance over my shoulder to make sure Clover isn't watching us but I can't see her from here so I'm sure she's watching the mare.

It allows me to pull her mother into my arms while I try to lighten her mood. "Nah, she just mentioned you growl like one when she asks about her being allowed to take horse riding lessons."

Lottie's fists dig into my leather cut and a sob mixed with a laugh comes out before she adds the words, "I don't know if that's any better."

I slide my fingers into her hair to fist it so I can guide her head back. "From what I've heard and seen you've done your absolute best and I've known Clover for months. The handful of minutes every morning I talk to her is enough to know she's raised to be polite and respects the boundaries you've put in place. Every parent raises their kid differently and every person has their own set of values and beliefs. Not to mention, every kid thinks their parents are monsters at some point, especially if they're not allowed something they want."

Lottie narrows her eyes. "So, she does think I'm a monster."

I can't help it; I have to kiss the fuck out of her and I do just that. The moment my mouth slants over hers is when she greedily opens up and sinks into the kiss. For a few blissful seconds I get to indulge in the flaming need this woman rises inside me.

But she suddenly breaks the kiss and places her forehead against the patches of my leather cut while she grumbles, "We shouldn't kiss. Clover could see." Rearing her head back she gives me an intense look. "And why aren't you running away from your one-night stand knowing I'm a single mom? Most would, you know, not wanting the parent angle and not being free but tied to a kid."

And yeah, why aren't I? First, because Clover is a tiny person I've known for months and I happen to like her spirit. Second…this woman was one hell of a lay and her spirit and wit is more than intriguing. We already established it was more than a one-night thing and I now realize I wouldn't mind wanting more. If anything, I'm more interested in the woman standing before me than just using her body for sex.

And that shit does surprise the fuck out of me, but it doesn't hold me back from asking, "If I would ask you, knowing you have a kid, if you'd be interested in dating to see where this connection between us will lead…would you say yes? You know, with me breeding, training, and living with horses and won't stop either?"

She actually balls her fist and punches me in the shoulder. "The horses don't compare with having a kid."

"Nah, it sure doesn't. Though you fear horses the same way some men run from dating a single mom."

Laughter ripples through her chest and she mutters, "Touché."

"So, that's a yes?"

She gives me a look with a truckload of warmth when she ultimately says, "How about dinner at my place tonight? I'm sure Clover would love that since you already know her. Besides, it would be silly to hide us dating from her to prevent things getting more complicated."

"I don't do complications, I'm a simple man," I tell her and brush a kiss over her lips. "We're already compatible between the sheets, we agreed to be monogamous while putting it on repeat, I like your kid, and I'm open to a relationship long term."

"A simple man," she croaks. "I'm more than open to that."

"Good. Now let's handle your fear of horses because we're about to walk into this stable to see your kid loving the sight of a mare about to give birth any time."

"Great, get over one bump in the road to face another one," she mutters underneath her breath.

A bark of laughter rips from me and I shake my head while I guide her into the stables. "Get ready for some more bumps, gorgeous. Life is full of bumps. And I'll throw another one in front of your feet because I offered to talk to you about me giving Clover riding lessons. She wouldn't let me talk to you, though. But I now know who her mother is so I might as well put in the effort since the kid clearly loves horses to her very core."

I can feel her body go tense but she keeps walking. "Let's get through this moment first, and we'll talk about freaking riding lessons later."

Letting my hand slide to her hip, I give her a tiny squeeze. "That's all I'm asking."

Our talk would be futile. I know since the look on Clover's face will persuade any person with a heart, and Lottie clearly has a big one. She's even facing her own fear of horses when she steps closer to her daughter who is staring at the mare with bright happiness radiating off her.

Clover glances at her mother and starts to whisper little details I've told her about this mare. I keep my distance and give them both some space to allow Clover to draw her mother into the moment with her enthusiasm.

It doesn't take long before Lottie is stepping closer to the stall and is even gripping the bars to take a closer look. The mare is pawing and has been getting up and down a few times. It's a clear sign she's restless and though we thought this morning it could still take a while, we're also aware birth can start unexpectedly.

The mare swishes her tail and urinates again. Yeah, she's definitely close to giving birth. I grab my phone and shoot a text to Harlene, my president's old lady. She's a veterinarian and I know she's off today and would love to give me a hand. The quick reply I get shows it.

I keep my voice to a minimum when I whisper, "If you two would like to watch the foal being born, you'd have to keep quiet but I also have to admit, it can take a while."

Clover furiously nods but Lottie bites her bottom lip and regretfully tells me, "I'd love to but I also have to open the bar later. Normally Alexi can open for me but she's running late."

"If you like, and if you don't mind of course, I could keep an eye on Clover and bring her home after the foal is born. And if you would like to stay, I could ask one of my brothers to open the bar for you," I offer.

Lottie turns and steps closer to me, curiosity slides over her face. "How many brothers do you have?"

The corner of my mouth twitches. "Many, but not by blood. Though, a decade ago I did have a stepbrother but I never considered him as such. He was an asshole, like his father. Glad they're out of my, and my mother's, life. Anyway, as you can see," I point at the patches of my cut, "I'm a member of the Iron Hot Blood. Every member is one of my brothers. We're a family, a brotherhood. We look out for one another and the old ladies are treated like queens around here. And we also run this ranch together." I hear footsteps and assume it's Harlene. "You're about to meet one of the women, my president's old lady, Harlene, who is also a vet."

Her eyes go over my shoulder and a warm smile spreads Lottie's face. "Hey Harlene."

"Hey," Harlene quips, keeping her voice down. "Imagine meeting you here. Oh, hey Clover."

"Different setting instead of a girls' night out in the bar, huh?" Lottie chuckles.

Figures. I didn't need to explain shit. Lottie owns a bar, Harlene and the rest of the old ladies enjoy a night out every now and then and always stay close to home instead of hitting a bar out of town. I'm the odd one who hasn't been in her bar until recently.

"Are you two going to watch?" Harlene asks.

Regret slides over Lottie's face. "Oak offered but I also need to open the bar."

Harlene throws her thumb over her shoulder as she places her bag on the ground. "I saw Spiro heading into the clubhouse. He's watched the bar for you a couple of times. We could ask him to keep an eye out if you want."

My gaze swings to Lottie and before I can catch myself, I growl, "How up and close do you know Spiro?"

"Dude," Harlene snickers. "Rein in the neanderthal response. Spiro has kept an eye on us a few times when we went out and then asked Lottie to join us. Spiro takes over bar duty without a complaint since he's always sober when he's on watch duty," she easily explains.

Her eyes bounce between me and Lottie and they widen. "Oh…this is too freaking cute and so perfect," she gushes.

Clover has her full attention fixed on the mare and isn't picking up anything from this discussion.

I try to keep a handle on the situation and turn the discussion back to the matter at hand when I state, "You guys can chitchat later. MayMay and her foal have priority along with hopefully arranging someone to open the bar or I'll drive Lottie back home myself and bring Clover by later. Decision time, Lottie. What's it gonna be?"

Her eyes go to Clover and she gives me a determined look at the same time she shoves her hand into her jeans and offers me a set of keys. "Can you please ask Spiro to open for me? Let him know Alexi is coming in later than usual and I'll be there as soon as I can."

Clover might not have been completely oblivious to her

surroundings when she spins around to give her mother a hug and whispers, "Thank you, thank you, thank you," over and over.

I take the keys and head out to the clubhouse in search of Spiro with a fucking huge smile on my face. And it's for more than one reason. Mainly because I feel damn good about being in a relationship with a damn fine woman. And not your normal relationship either, one where my woman has a daughter I've known longer than the woman herself. And the kid in question is funny, smart, and easy to be around too.

They both might need some time to get used to the idea of having me around for good, because this feels fucking perfect and meant to be, which also drives my need to speak a claim and let everyone know Lottie is my old lady.

But for now we'll take it one day at a time. And this day isn't just perfect because Lottie and I are now together, it's also a breakthrough when it comes to her fear of horses; allowing her daughter to grow closer to the animals she loves.

Shit can't get any more perfect than this.

CHAPTER 04

Five weeks later

LOTTIE

I hold my breath and watch how Oak runs right next to the horse Clover is riding as she holds the reigns. Oak was holding them to, has been since he started teaching her, but he lets go and keeps jogging beside them. I feel someone place a hand on my forearm.

"You can breathe now," Colt chuckles. "Your daughter has been practicing every day for weeks on end. She has a talent that one. And you know Oak picked Cal, Garrett's old horse, for a reason. The animal is gentle, kind-natured, and doesn't get spooked by anything."

"I know," I mutter and keep an eye on Clover.

Weston leans to the side to look past me at Colt. "You should have been there the first few times Oak put her in the saddle. I think the imprint of Lottie's nails are still in the fence."

"Very funny," I grumble.

I've known some of these men for a while, especially the ones who come into the bar for a drink more often. Over the past few weeks, since I've been with Oak, I've gotten to know them a lot more. They're a great bunch of people. Each one of them is different but they all have the same goals, priorities, dedication, and loyalty.

Their brotherhood is solid and the way they treat the women, along with all the kids, is amazing; they're one big happy family. They have welcomed me and Clover with wide open arms. And when I agreed to let Oak give Clover riding lessons, he made sure he was never alone with her. He has at least one of his brothers there with them and one by the fence in case something happens.

Not that anything has happened yet, but Oak has done an amazing job in pushing down the fear inside me. With the security of help around him like I mentioned, but also by showing how tender and careful he is with my daughter.

And then there's Clover, so strong and eager to learn. She holds no fear at all and listens to everything Oak says. The smile on her face each and every day for the past few weeks has brightened my heart, and I know I made the right decision to move past my fear of horses for her.

Emotions overwhelm me when I think about how close those two have become; a bond similar to father and daughter. It must be because they have known each other for months and are now growing closer together by doing something they both love. And to top it off, the three of us spend a lot of time together every day.

And I do realize it's something Clover has been missing. Not to mention, he fulfilled her dream by giving her riding lessons and being close to horses every single day. A tear slides down my cheek.

"Hey now, everything is fine: nothing is going to happen, okay?" Colt rumbles.

I drag my eyes away from Clover and give Colt a smile. "Look at those two, how can I not spill happy tears?"

He throws an arm over my shoulder and gives me a sidewards hug. "You and the kid deserve it as much as Oak."

"Hands off my old lady," Oak bellows from a distance.

Laughter slips out while Colt mutters, "Possessive fuck. I have an old lady myself. One I'd never in a million years cheat on," and lets his arm fall away from me.

I let my eyes trail back to Oak whose eyes take me in. I give him a smile in assurance and he shoots me a wink in return before his gaze settles back on Clover. The rumbling of a bike drags my attention to a motorcycle driving through the gates of the ranch.

Weston mutters a curse underneath his breath and orders Colt, "Stay here while I handle this," and walks toward the man who is getting off his bike.

I give the stranger my full attention and when I take in his face, my whole body freezes. He might be a decade older but I do recognize the guy who took my virginity, and with it gave me Clover.

My gaze slides down to his hands in front of him as he cracks his knuckles. I shoot a desperate plea inside my head for this not to be true, but I notice the missing half of his little pinky, and I have my answer; Clover's father is walking toward Weston.

Panic sets in and I turn to Colt. "Can you please get Clover for me? I have to go. Right now."

He gives me a piercing look. "Everything is okay, there's no need–"

I shoot another glance at Anson and turn my attention back to Colt.

"I want to leave. Right. Now," I almost growl and am ready to jump over this fence and get Clover myself off the damn horse if that's what it takes.

This time Colt merely nods and jumps over the fence to get to Oak. They exchange a few words and Oak brings Clover back to me himself.

"Hey, everything okay?" Concern is written all over his face.

I have no clue what to tell him but there's no need when Anson starts to call out. "Come on, call off your boss and talk to me yourself, Oak. We were once brothers, man. Least thing you can do is…hey, that your woman? Are you married now?"

"Stepbrothers," Oak growls low in his throat and mutters, "Ten years and that asshole thinks he can come back here and ask for help like nothing happened."

My heart is slamming against my rib cage and it's a mixture of panic and fear. I don't want Anson to notice and recognize me, and for sure not make the link about my daughter and our one encounter a decade ago. But the stress of discovering Clover's father is actually Oak's stepbrother is consuming my every thought.

"I have to leave," I tell Oak in a low voice.

He narrows his eyes and it's clear he wants to ask me why but Anson is calling him again and is now making a scene because I can hear him growl at Weston to get his hands off him. Oak curses and joins Colt, who is running toward their president.

I glance over my shoulder to see the men pushing at one another and I take this chance to take Clover over to my car, thankful I decided to drive over today instead of walk, and hop in. I keep my eyes fixed on the road in front of me and don't look back as I make my quick escape.

During the ride home I lock out every single thought and concentrate on the ride, and on Clover who fired the question why we had to leave. Once I lied to her about forgetting something I needed to do, she started to rattle about how much she enjoyed today's ride, and it was a warm welcome.

She's always been the brighter side of my heart and hearing her rattle about her passion calmed me down. Though, parking the car and walking into the bar through the back makes reality—along with a decade ago memory—slam back into my brain.

Luckily Clover heads into her room because she wants to sketch about today's riding lesson. It's another passion of hers. She's very talented, and this is not just the mother inside me boosting her talent, but she really can create stunning art.

As for me, I sag into the chair at the kitchen table and rest my head in my hands, trying to grasp some sanity about what the hell I'm going to do. And not just about Clover's father situation, or Oak being tied to it. But I also realized this morning my period is a few days late.

Now I've been late more than once in my life but I haven't had sex in years. And the first time I had sex ten years ago, it was with Oak's stepbrother. What a shit-crazy tornado blasting over my life while I was finally happy and thought everything had fallen into place.

Dammit, one night without condoms while Oak and I have been using protection ever since. History might be repeating. I guess I shouldn't be surprised since my first time, ten years ago, was over in what felt like three awkward and painful pumps and nine months later Clover entered the world.

I groan and try to take a few more calming breaths. I should buy a pregnancy test and get this uncertainty out of my life. If I do turn out to be pregnant, I'll deal with what to do next. At least I know the man and have a relationship with him and we can face it together. Hell, maybe I'm just stressing about nothing and my period will hit tomorrow or tonight for that matter.

Great, now my mind slams back to seeing Anson. I finally found him–he found us–and I have a way to contact him and tell him about Clover. Will he be angry? Would he want to be in her life? Would he disappear as soon as he hears we made a daughter ten years ago?

My phone starts to ring and when I check I see Oak's information. It pains me not to answer but I have no clue what I should say to him right now. I wait for the ringing to stop and turn my phone off.

I glance at the clock and notice I have one hour before Alexi opens the bar. She offered to open on the days Oak only has time later in the day to teach Clover, and I'm not able to be back on time.

And yes, I've been there for every single lesson she had and not because of my fear or need to control her every move. I wanted to be there to watch her shine, because that's what she does when she's on the back of a horse; radiates happiness.

I should still have been at the ranch for Clover's riding lesson. Deciding to keep my hands busy and distract my mind, I stand and stroll over to the refrigerator and pull out a few things to make lasagna.

I'm putting the lasagna into the oven when I hear Oak knocking on my door and asking me to open up along with it. I know I owe him an explanation on running out on him the way I did, but on the other hand…my brain was kind enough to offer a plot twist about how Oak might have known Anson was Clover's father and is with us because of it.

Crazy and insane, I know, because we just got together and he couldn't have known. But the whole "why now" thing is running through my mind. Ugh. My brain is on overload and I have a lot to deal with. My shoulders sag as I open the door in defeat.

Opening my mouth to say hi, I'm robbed from doing so when Clover comes storming out of her room and jumps right at Oak, calling his name loud enough to let it bounce off the walls. And this is how she always greets him.

It's another reason why I don't want to lose Oak and the internal fears flowing through my head when I was making lasagna offered many scenarios. For one Oak running out if I am indeed pregnant. Another reason for him to run might be when I tell him Clover is his stepbrother's daughter.

I hear Oak rumble something and Clover replies but my thoughts are too loud inside my head to focus on their discussion. Clover is already skipping back to her room when I tune back in.

She throws the words, "I'll show you when it's ready," over her shoulder, and I'm guessing she's off to finish her sketch or make another one.

I swallow hard and face Oak. "I'm sorry. I freaked out when I saw Anson and then my mind jumped right into a pool of craziness how you might have known Clover is his daughter and then there's this thing where my period is late and I have no clue if I'm pregnant and should really go get a pregnancy test and—" Holy verbal-diarrhea on a stick where it just slides right off, did I really just rattle everything out?

I smack my hands up and cover my face. I really incoherently threw all of it at him without thinking things through. Swallowing hard, I risk a peek between my fingers. I don't know what I expect to see written on his face, but it sure isn't the patient and warm look he's giving me.

"Mind running it by me again, and this time a little slower? Though I did catch the 'might be pregnant' part. We kinda knew about it that first time I had to have your sweet pussy. So, no regrets or blame about that one. But the stuff involving Clover? Please repeat because you're not making sense."

"No regrets or blame?" I echo and feel my eyes widen. "I'm freaking out and you're wiping it off the table as if possibly adding a human life to this world is not a life-changing discussion."

His fingers slide over the back of my neck and he pulls me flush against his body. "We're together, you already have a kid who has crawled her way into my heart so I figure what's one more?"

I gasp and the man takes advantage by slamming his mouth over mine and thrusting his tongue between my lips to let it swirl against mine. I grip his leather cut and sigh into his kiss, allowing my ears to stop ringing and letting the warmth this man gives me enter my veins.

I could live in this kiss for many lifetimes but Oak pulls back and guides me toward the kitchen table. "Tell me, what was it you mentioned about Clover?"

I shoot a glance in the direction of her bedroom and lower my voice. "I've told you about how I got pregnant with Clover, right?"

"You were fifteen, the boy was sixteen, you two got to talking behind the bar, started kissing and one thing led to another, foolish teenager shit, but it ended with you getting knocked-up in the shed behind the bar. The boy left town never to be…motherfucker. Are you telling me it's Anson?"

I swallow hard. "In a nutshell."

Oak leans back in his chair and rubs his hand over his face.

I nervously start to wring my hands and blabber, "You never told me your stepbrother's name when you mentioned him. And that's basically all I knew, and I never told anyone since he mentioned he was leaving town never to return again. And no one knew about the pregnancy until my belly was too big to hide it. My parents did ask around when I couldn't hide the fact I was pregnant and spilled all the details but—"

"His father called him Junior, most people didn't even know the sonofabitch's name was Anson," Oak grunts.

"Then a man shows up at the ranch and he looked familiar and I realize who he is and then seeing the missing part of his little finger…I knew…I knew it was her father. I can't…I don't know…what am I going to do, Oak?" I croak and tears start to fall down my cheeks.

From all the things going through my head I only now realize Anson might try to take Clover away from me. Would it be possible? Oh. God.

"What if he's going to take her away from me?" At this point I'm close to hyperventilating but suddenly anger takes over and I jolt out of my chair. "I won't let him," I growl with determination.

"We won't let him," Oak says with the same determination and my heart skips a beat, realizing I'm not alone; I have Oak by my side.

Fear grabs my heart once more when Oak states, "But we do have a problem. Anson came back to town because he's running from another mess he made. He's demanding money and my help. And if he becomes aware of Clover…he might have reason enough to get what he wants or take her to force his way because he's a vile motherfucker."

My heart doesn't just sink. It's ripped right out of my chest and goes flying out the window.

CHAPTER 05

OAK

"Hey." I close the distance between us, not liking the fear and devastation marring her face. I need for her to understand, "Whatever we have to face or do, we'll do it together, okay? And I mentioned we had a problem because I think you are entitled to the truth instead of me hiding it and going behind your back to finish what he started. Because I will finish it. I won't have this asshole ruin Clover's life, or yours for that matter. I'm going to call Weston and explain. The situation Anson is in doesn't have anything to do with us and that's why we agreed in church we would keep out of it and kick him off our property if he came back. Clearly things are different now so we need a different approach."

Her forehead scrunches. "What kind of approach?" Her eyes widen and she gasps, "You're not going to kill him, are you? I don't want you or anyone else landing in jail because of me."

A bark of laughter rips from my throat and I pull her into my arms.

Burying my nose into her fruity smelling hair I murmur, "No one is landing their ass in jail. But I also can't tell you what the approach will be. Not because I can't, but due to the fact I have to bring it to the table. Me and my brothers will go over it and then decide."

Some of the tension slips from her body and her arms circle my waist. "Then we'll put that discussion on hold. But what about the possible baby in my belly?"

"There's a baby in your belly?" Clover squeaks.

Lottie jerks from my hold and stares at her daughter who is oblivious to her mother's panicked eyes.

Clover starts to ramble, "If there's a baby in your belly, Oak becomes a daddy. And if he's the daddy of my brother or sister…I really want a sister so you better make sure it's a girl… then Oak is my stepfather, right? When Dennis' dad's girlfriend had a baby they got married and she became Dennis' stepmom. Hey, are you going to get married? You are going to get married, aren't you?"

Lottie's trying hard not to look like a goldfish but she's failing drastically.

I have no clue how to answer Clover, but I do know one thing and tell Lottie, "Clover is rambling. She's happy when she's rambling, right?"

Lottie drags her gaze away from Clover and she gives her head a little shake as if she needs to clear it while she murmurs, "What? Right. Rambling. Yes, she's happy when she rambles."

I step closer to Lottie and repeat, "She's happy when she rambles." I make sure the next few words are for Lottie's ears only when I tell her, "I already mentioned liking the angle of adding to our family of three. Deep breaths, gorgeous. We can handle this, or anything else for that matter, together."

She takes in a choppy breath and declares, "Come on you two, let's take a seat and have some lasagna while we talk about it."

Lottie jolts into action while Clover steps up to me and wraps her tiny arms around my waist. "I really wish you'd be my stepdaddy, Oak. I really, really like you. And I really like our riding lessons, and all the horses you have."

"I'll always be there for you, kiddo. And for sure our riding lessons will continue no matter what, you're a natural and belong on the back of a horse. Go take a seat at the table and we'll see what your mom has to say because you know she's in full control about all of this stuff, huh?"

"Yeah," Clover huffs but instead of taking a seat, she shows me the sketch she finished.

Damn, this kid has some amazing skills. "You did a stellar job, we're going to have to frame this one. Look." I hold it out for Lottie to see. "The spitting image of Cal."

My chest squeezes when I see a smile sliding back on Lottie's face. She always needs to wear that smile, and I'll make sure she won't have anything to worry about. Anson is a fuck-up, just like his father. I kicked both out of my life many years ago, and over time Anson has tried to reach out once or twice whenever he needed something, but I shut him down each and every time.

Fuck knows why the idiot thought I'd come to his help this time. The fool probably thought with me being a biker, I wouldn't mind going head-to-head with another MC. Shit for brains I tell you, because he needs to face his own responsibilities. We were going to leave him be but clearly, we can't now.

There's a burning pit in my stomach, knowing he's Clover's father. The fantastic little girl doesn't need a fuck-up for a dad. The image of Anson and my stepfather beating the shit out of my mother is still vivid in my brain ten years later. Sure as shit I am going to protect Clover as if she was my own.

Hell, after months of knowing her and now practically living with these two for the past five weeks, I practically feel like we already are one family. And this realization also makes me aware I actually hope Lottie is pregnant, it'll tie the both of us together for life.

I take a seat and while Lottie places the lasagna on the table, I wait for her to connect her gaze with mine before I tell her,

"We should get married. You're already my old lady, we practically live together, I adore the fuck out of you and Clover, and it would give a solid foundation for if that asshole wants to start some legal shit."

Clover throws her hands in the air, "Yay! Say yes, Mom. You have to say yes. Wait. Does this mean I have to wear a dress when you guys get married?"

Lottie covers her face with her hands and slowly starts to shake. I'm worried she's gonna freak out on me because I should have asked her in private and not in front of Clover but when her hands fall away, I notice she's laughing.

She keeps shaking her head when she tells Clover, "You betcha I'm going to make you wear a dress." Her gaze lands on mine. "And yes, I would love to marry you because I've never met a man in all my life who is as amazing as you."

My ass is out of the chair with my next breath and I take her into my arms to give her a kiss.

"Gross," Clover mutters underneath her breath.

We break the kiss due to laughter and we regain our seats to enjoy the food along with some small talk. Good thing my proposal took away the whole baby discussion, solving a big chunk of our issues in one go. Though, she still needs to pee on a stick so we'll know for sure, and I have to call Weston and tell him what's going on so we can handle Anson.

After the delicious food, Lottie and I do the dishes while Clover watches some TV. I finally call Weston and get him up to speed. We decide it would be better for us to stay the night in her apartment while Lottie doesn't go to work. Spiro takes over the bar and handles it together with Alexi.

Tomorrow I will bring the both of them back to the clubhouse. It's a good thing Clover doesn't have school this week because we'll be staying at the ranch for a few days just to have some added protection in case Anson shows up and somehow figures out he has daughter, one I'm sure he would see as a bargaining chip.

Fucking hell. If he knew he'd have endless possibilities to

get what he wants. Force us to help him for one. Money or threaten to claim his rights as a father and demand visitation, whatever.

Yes, a father has rights, and I'm all for equal rights and no fucking way would prevent a parent from seeing their kid, but this situation is different. For one, Lottie didn't know who he was and he left town before she discovered she was pregnant.

Sure, she could have known it was a possibility with unprotected sex, but she was fifteen at the time, in a new town, had no friends, and she didn't want to tell her parents...too embarrassing, and they were busy setting up their new business, whatever, it's in the past.

But in my opinion Anson doesn't deserve to be in Clover's life. Clover is fucking sunshine while her biological father is darkness without any ability to shine. I knew and witnessed it from the time he entered my mother's and my life when he was barely fourteen. Our parents hooked up, until I kicked him and his father out when Anson was sixteen and fuck...it was the day he knocked up Lottie.

The main reason I don't think he's worth so much as being near Clover–and Lottie for that matter–is what the fucker did... what sent him running back here. The idiot thought he could break into a house, while a woman was at home for fuck's sake. He shot her in the leg to keep her immobile and walked out with some cash and a laptop, probably to get his next fix, who knows.

Now, the woman in question was Bark's daughter, Isabeau. Bark being the vice president of Lost Valkyries MC, I'd say the idiot finally ran into something he can't get out of without losing his life. Because Lost Valkyries MC are basically mercenaries for hire.

And the idiot not only broke into the woman's home, shot her in the leg and stole cash along with a laptop, but he also smacked her around and to top it off the idiot wasn't subtle about it because the woman in question was his fucking neighbor. Talk about idiocy at its best.

I guess he had some brain cells working that night because

he ran out of town and headed straight here. The fucker even confessed to all of it and thought I'd call Bark and make it right. As if. I wasn't getting in the middle of it and don't owe Anson shit.

But knowing he's Clover's father and the many ways things can go to shit because of it? Yeah, I'm handling his fucked-up situation for sure. Only not the way he thinks or wants, but if Weston agrees, we'll be delivering Anson to Bark on a silver platter; it'll solve all our problems in one go.

I release a deep sigh and tighten my arm around the woman…fuck. Around my fiancée. It was a spur of the moment thing, but it doesn't take away my integrity; to give them both a foundation if anything goes to shit with Anson. But it most definitely also is a longing from deep within my chest to make our bond official.

My mother is going to be ecstatic. She gave me my grandmother's ring when I was barely twenty and told me to think about dating someone nice to settle down with and give her a few grandkids.

I accepted the ring but told her I'd save it for if that special someone came into my life. But I sure as fuck wasn't looking or on the hunt for that matter. Turns out, the right woman entered my life when I least expected it, captivating me on first glance.

I make a mental note to give Lottie the ring when we go to my place tomorrow. Taking my phone from my jeans, carefully so I don't wake Lottie who has fallen asleep against me, I look up the website of a friend of Mayven.

Mayven is Ledger's old lady and she owns her own company. Through this company she met a jewelry designer and she created some amazing pieces for my brothers and their wives. I look up her email address and type out a message, hoping she can make what I have in mind or she might already have something in her collection that fits my needs.

I shove my phone back into my pocket, turn off the TV, and scoop up my woman. Time to get to bed and hopefully catch a few hours of sleep. We're going to need it to face whatever comes our way in the morning.

By the time my head hits the pillow I'm out like a light and wake up way too fucking early with Clover standing next to me, cheerfully stating, "Are we going to live with you now?"

"I need coffee to answer that question, sunshine," I mutter.

Lottie groans and chuckles right after. "Ain't that the truth."

"Okay," Clover cheerfully states and dashes out of the room.

Lottie throws an arm over her eyes. "I don't remember waking up that cheerfully as an adult. As a kid? Sure. Adult? Ugh. Too much worry and less simplicity in life."

I reach out and drag her over my chest so I can kiss the top of her head and feel our body heat mingle through the fabric of our shirts.

"Simplicity is overrated," I mutter and inhale her scent. "Let's snuggle for a breath or two before I head into the kitchen to make some coffee and hotwire our old bodies to start the day. You know, because we're adults and can ask one of my brothers to look after Clover so we have a moment to ourselves. One where I'll bend you over and fuck you from behind. Because that's what responsible adults do: get the most out of life."

Her giggle flows through the air and I know I've done my first job for the day; distract her from the worries our lives are wrapped with and point out the good things in life. In our life. And from now on I will make it my business to see her smile each and every day.

Coffee first. Packing a bag second. And then we'll handle the bar so she can hand it over to Spiro for the next couple of days or till I know the Anson situation is handled. Both Clover and Lottie will be staying with me on the ranch until that's set and done.

Relishing a few more heartbeats of our closeness, I let this moment sink into my brain. For damn sure am I dead-set to get the most out of life. And it's not just about the sex; it's about shared life, family, closeness…and the very foundation of life itself…love.

CHAPTER 06

LOTTIE

"Mom, can I wait outside with Oak?" Clover asks with her backpack in hand.

I'm still fussing over things because I'm not sure what to take with me, even if we're only planning to stay with Oak for a few days.

"Yes, but let Oak know and stay near him. He's outside waiting by his truck along with Spiro." The words haven't even all left my mouth and she's already rushing out of the house.

I huff and direct my attention at the refrigerator to check if there will be stuff going to waste if we don't return in a few days. Slamming the door closed I glance around the room. My bag is packed and I'm sure I have everything, but like I said, I'm fussing.

Glancing outside, I see Oak leaning against his truck, his head turned toward Clover who is practicing some dance moves, while Spiro is clearly talking to him. The way his protective gaze never leaves my daughter warms my heart.

I've fallen hard and fast for this man, and from everything he says and does, it's clear he feels the same way. Having a baby as young as I had has given a spin on my life and took away some of the things I might have once dreamed about.

For one a big wedding before having kids, that's for sure. But life's too short for regrets and looking back instead of aiming your eyes on what's right in front of you will only make you run into walls. At least, that's what my mom used to say.

A smile tugs my lips at the fond memory. I wish she could see me now, and most of all, meet Oak. She would love him just because of the way he is with Clover; always patient, caring, but stern when needed. I know I made the right choice to accept his proposal and I do hope the situation with Anson is handled quickly without any issues so we can move on with our lives together; as a family.

Shit. I have to swing by the store for a pregnancy test. I grab my backpack and throw it over my shoulder. Snatching the suitcase near the door, I walk out and lock up. Oak comes rushing toward me when he sees me coming down the stairs.

Spiro chuckles and shoots me a wink, muttering, "That man is head-over-heels for you," as he slips past me to enter the bar.

Oak takes the backpack and suitcase from me and stalks back to put them into the truck. Clover is oblivious to her surroundings and is still dancing. I now notice she's wearing earbuds which are connected to the phone she's holding in her hand. My attention is drawn away from her when I notice movement from the front of Oak's truck.

The air freezes inside my lungs when I hear, "Well now, look at you two pretty ladies."

Clover is still oblivious but Oak is clearly not when he brushes past me and growls, "Fuck off, Anson, there's nothing here for you. I told you to leave town, now fucking leave."

Anson clicks his tongue. "On the contrary, bro, I think there is. I was about to talk to the nice lady, might even buy her a drink."

"The bar is closed," I hiss, making Anson's gaze land on me.

Shit. I shouldn't drag his attention to me, but I guess it's too late now. He tilts his head to the side and I repulse every moment this man has his eyes on me.

"Oh, I know it's closed, babe. Hey…you look familiar," he mutters and points his finger at me. "Where have I seen you before?"

He taps his chin as if to appear in thought, but his eyes make me feel as if he's faking it. An eerie feeling overtakes me. His eyes and demeanor scream that he's playing us. The sinister smile alone makes me think he knows exactly who I am.

"At the ranch," Oak snaps. "Remember? Our conversation ended the same way it ends now: with you leaving."

Anson takes a step in my direction but Oak blocks his path.

Anson keeps his gaze on mine and the slimy asshole says to Oak, "Why are you protecting that fine piece of ass? She yours?"

"She is mine. And call my old lady a piece of ass again and I'll make sure you're pissing blood for days."

My head whips to Clover, hoping she's still oblivious about what's going on but to my horror she's staring at us and she is still holding the phone in one hand but has the earbuds in the other. I hold my hand out in a silent plea for her to come to me and she immediately walks over.

But Anson steps in front of her and lowers his face into hers. "You look like your mommy instead of your daddy. How old are you, sweet cheeks?"

"Nine," Clover blurts in a shrill voice and quickly dashes around him.

Clover worms herself between me and Oak and grabs his cut to hold tight. It warms my heart to see she feels protected by Oak.

"Nine," Anson murmurs and directs his attention back to Oak. "She's not yours, is she?"

"Get the fuck out of here," Spiro snaps as he comes to a stop next to us. He has a gun in one hand and is aiming it right at Anson.

Anson throws his hands, palms up, into the air. "Hey, now.

I'm just making conversation with my bro here. I'm not looking for any trouble."

"Guess trouble found you, asshole. Now run along 'cause this lady's bar is closed and even if it were open, you wouldn't be welcome anyway." Spiro does something with his hands, the gun makes a slight noise and Anson takes a step back.

His eyes slide to me one final time and I can tell the moment validation sets in before his gaze shifts to Clover.

Anson throws his shoulders back and appears to be growing a few inches when he says, "The kid is mine, isn't she? Yeah, she is. Nine. Nine years old and I fucked you." His bony finger aims in my direction. "A shy ten years ago behind this very bar you said your parents owned. And these two fuckers blocking you behind their backs, gun fucking blazing…yeah. No need to tell me shit, it's written over y'all's faces."

The sinister grin he's sporting grows.

"Oak, my bro…you've been fucking my baby momma. You can't deny my request now." He spins on his heel and waves as he walks away. "I'll give you some time to handle my request. No worries, I'll be back. Talk to you guys soon."

Oak curses and Spiro adds a few of his own. I pull Clover against me and tip my head down to place a kiss on the top of her head. Screw parental rights; no way am I ever going to let a man like that near her. He didn't even show an interest in Clover or so much as talk to me about visiting rights or whatever. No. This man was selfish enough to be happy about the fact Oak couldn't deny his request now. Not to mention, Oak told me all the details Anson did before he came back to town.

I keep Clover's head pressed against my belly and place my hand over her other ear when I whisper hiss, "I don't want him anywhere near her again."

"Agreed," Oak grunts. "Get in the truck, we're leaving. Spiro, call Prez and let him know what just went down."

Spiro nods and tucks his gun away and takes out his phone. I guide Clover to the truck and open the door for her. She hops in without a word and I quickly round the truck and get in the front at the same time Oak fires it up.

There's a loaded silence when we hit the road but Clover's soft voice rings out like a hit with a hammer when she says, "Who was that man? And why did he say those things?"

Shit, shit, shit. What should I say? Anson rattled out details and for sure she knows what they mean but it breaks my heart to explain them to her, and yet…she needs to hear the truth.

I've always told her she had a father. Only that the man left and I didn't know where he was or had a way to tell him about her, and how he didn't know how to contact us either. I mean, it was the truth. I glance at Oak and his gaze connects with mine before he aims it back on the road.

He reaches over to grab my hand in his, giving it a little squeeze before he says, "As soon as we're at the ranch we're going to explain it to you and talk about it. And don't worry, Clover. Everything is okay."

"I don't like that man. He scares me."

My heart breaks and I want to pull her into my arms, tell her there's nothing to be scared of and yet I can't, because I would be lying. Luckily the drive to the ranch is short. Oak parks the truck and to my surprise Weston, along with Roper, Decker, and Garrett are all waiting for us.

Garrett opens the door for Clover. "Hey, I heard you were coming over for a few days and I'm about to see Cal but I have to check on MayMay's foal first, care to join me?"

Clover's head whips my way. "Can I, Mom? Please?"

How easily kids are distracted sometimes. But in this case, I welcome it and give her a smile. "Sure you can. Garrett will come find us when you're done visiting the horses."

She doesn't even say goodbye or give us another glance and starts to skip into the direction of the stables. Garrett strides beside her and answers every question she shoots at him. That girl has an endless supply of horse-related questions.

Oak grabs our bags from the truck. Weston steps closer and those two seem to have a silent conversation, their eyes land on me for a mere second and the tension seems to build. I'm about to question what's going on but Oak places the bags next to him and sighs.

"Whatever it is, my old lady can handle it. Besides, she knows everything about me and I don't want any secrets between us." Oak holds out his hand and I take it to let him pull me close.

How does this man make everything in this world seem irrelevant and it's just us and the people we care for that matter the most?

Weston nods. "Me, Roper, and Decker discussed it last night after you called. We decided not to wait till morning to have a meeting but instead we reached out to Lost Valkyries MC right away. Bark, along with a few of his brothers, are on their way but I don't know how long it will take for them to get here. They might stop a few times since it's a long ride, he didn't say. But it will at least be a day or two before they show up at the ranch."

"And then there's the request they made," Roper says with a bit of a bite.

"What request?" Oak throws out the question that also crossed my mind.

Decker folds his arms in front of his chest. "They want us to grab and detain."

"We're not getting involved in this," Oak instantly replies. "I'm fine with handing him over for them to deal with Anson, but that fucking means we point them in the right direction. We can't have any of this blow back on us. On any of us."

My heart is pounding inside my chest. I have no clue what to say or if I even have a say in any of it. I do know Anson is not a nice person and can do a lot of harm. From everything I've been told, the man is a ticking timebomb.

And what if he does want to have some form of a relationship with Clover and he hurts her? Physically. Not just by making promises and not showing up, but the way Oak caught his stepfather and Anson beating his mother.

Worry overtakes my brain again but I'm pulled back into the discussion when Weston says, "Nothing is going to blow back on us. Decker called Nick and sketched the situation from one friend to another. We're covered in case it all goes to shit."

"Well," Decker drawls. "If I make the call as soon as it's about to go to shit or if it just went to–"

"Yeah, yeah," Oak grumbles. "We get the idea. We're in the clear if you keep the FBI in the loop."

"Bingo," Roper mutters, clears his throat and adds a little louder, "We don't know where the fucker is now, do we?"

"No. He walked away, but he'll be back for sure. He said he would because he knows about Clover and Lottie being my woman. The idiot thinks it's going to force me into doing his bidding. And what the fuck was that idiot even doing at the bar this time of day? Right when we were standing outside. It doesn't make any sense," Oak growls.

I thought the same thing. It was as if he came for us, to confront, as if he already knew...dammit.

"Alexi," I snap in anger and pull my phone from my pocket to dial her number.

Oak covers his hand with mine. "What are you doing?"

"I bet Alexi must have told him. Who else? She knows about me and Clover."

"Why do you think she told Anson? And how does she even know him?" he asks as he manages to take my phone from my hand.

"Because Alexi screws anything with a cock and no morals, especially strangers who are passing through town," Weston answers before I get a chance to say one word. Weston cringes and mutters, "Sorry. News like that travels fast in a small town."

I wave my hand and sigh. "Meh...I would have voiced the same thing because it's the truth. Not to mention she loves gossip and being the center point of all of it. Why do you think I wanted to call her out about that big mouth of hers? It can fit at least three dicks, no wonder the words fall right out."

All the men go silent until the air fills with barks of laughter. Roper holds onto his belly as he tries to stop laughing.

He eventually does and says, "I don't know about you guys,

but I truly needed a good laugh."

"Damn right," Weston chuckles. "It also shows these two can use some alone time. The kid too for that matter. Oak, let your old lady settle in and stay in the cabin. We have eyes all over the place and we're all on high alert. If anything happens or changes, I'll let you know."

"Thanks, Prez," Oak says and grabs the bags.

I give the men a warm smile. "Thanks so much, all of you."

They tip their hats and I follow Oak to his cabin, hoping Clover will enjoy her time with the horses before coming back. Because I'm not looking forward to having a conversation about her biological father.

But it needs to be done. Not only is she entitled to an explanation, but her not knowing can also put her in danger if Anson can somehow get close or whatever might happen. I just want her to know…to be prepared. If only I felt prepared.

CHAPTER 07

OAK

Lottie sighs and her eyes slide to me. A pleading look slides over her face. I feel her pain and frustration and I've been sitting here for the last half hour listening to her explain everything to Clover with utter patience, answering every question she shoots in return.

I don't know if Clover understands everything her mother just explained, but she sure looks confused. Mostly it's about the part where she doesn't understand the danger of all of it and it might be due to the parts we left out. But honestly a ten-year-old doesn't need to know how Anson has a past filled with assault, burglary, robbery, drug dealing, you name a crime and that fucker had a part in it.

I clear my throat to draw Clover's attention. "You know what happens when you shake your soda?"

Clover's eyes twinkle and she says without thinking, "It sprays all over."

"Right." I shoot her a grin. "And if you leave it be for a

while, letting it cool down so the bubbles settle, it all goes back to normal. The same can be said about Anson. We have to be patient. A confrontation like what you saw and heard today can't happen again."

She tilts her head. "Anson is like soda?"

Lottie snickers and quickly slams a hand over her mouth when I shoot her a glare before giving Clover my attention again.

"Something like that," I mutter. "We need to give him some time to cool down. Ignore and watch out because we don't want him to spray–"

"Bad words all over," Clover finishes while bobbing her head in understanding. "You were using a metaphor."

Lottie looks relieved and I think we finally came to the end of the discussion.

"Yes." I shoot her a proud grin.

"It's also like when you want to ride a horse but he's been in the stall for too long and you need to put him in the pasture to get rid of all the energy."

Lottie is now the one beaming pride. "Very good, Clover."

"I think we need ice cream," I state, earning me two pairs of hungry, twinkling eyes.

I head for the fridge while Lottie grabs us three bowls and spoons. With each of us sitting around the table–enjoying some icy goodness–it gives me a moment to reflect and appreciate where life has brought me to this point.

A knock on the door draws me out of the overwhelming feeling of being whole and complete. Heading over, I notice it's Harlene. I take the bag she's holding up and invite her in. I asked her to pick up a pregnancy test since I didn't want to stop when we left Lottie's place after our run-in with Anson.

And in the bag should also be the item I requested from the jewelry designer. She texted me back that she gave the item in question to Mayven, who in return gave it to Harlene. And I'm thankful for all the help because it's just the thing we need right now.

"Hey you guys. Oh, yummy, ice cream," Harlene gushes and

takes a seat next to Clover. "I came by to ask your mom if it would be okay for you to come with me. The farrier is coming and I thought you would like to see her work on some horses."

Clover nods with great enthusiasm and whips her head toward her mother. "Can I Mom? Can I? I have to know all these things because if we're going to live here and I have my own horse I have to know, and I've never seen it. Can I? Please, Mom, please?"

A chuckle flows from me when I see Lottie's panicked face. She's surrendered to the fact her daughter now rides horses, but her fear hasn't completely faded. I've tried to involve her more with every riding lesson but overcoming fear isn't something you can force and going slow is the key.

And her daughter's enthusiasm isn't helping, neither is her rambling of getting her own horse and living here. While we have been together for the last couple of weeks, going back and forth between my place and theirs, add our engagement to it along with it…we haven't exactly had the time to discuss future living arrangements.

I hold up my hand and tell Clover, "Slow down, kiddo. You have to learn everything first, become a good rider, and prove you have the patience and ability to care for an animal. It's only then you can ask your mother if it's okay I find you a horse that fits your needs. And that's something that takes time too: finding the perfect horse."

The exciting gleam in Clover's eyes hasn't faded and she's nodding in agreement. Lottie shoots me a thankful look. While her daughter didn't hear a "no," her mother heard me buying her a load of time to process and work to the inevitable point where we will buy her a horse.

Me being a rancher with a great love for horses and becoming the kid's stepfather, for sure as hell will she get her own horse at some point. Though Lottie is her mother and will be the one deciding when, because she knows the "if she gets a horse" is the inevitable.

I reach in the bag and pull out a small velvet box. I hold it up for Clover to see. "I have something for you."

She steps closer and she lets out a loud gasp when she sees the tiny silver horse dangling on a chain. Clover glances to her mother and she gives her a little push for Clover to move closer to me and take the gift.

Taking it from the box, I hand it to Lottie instead who in return easily puts it around Clover's neck. She caresses the tiny horse with her fingers while glancing at me with a load of adoration and thanks.

I give her a smile and tell her, "I can't give your mother a ring and not give you any jewelry, right?"

She fiercely nods and launches herself at me to give a tight as hell hug.

"I guess you have to go with Harlene then to see the farrier work," Lottie says. "And keep your distance so you can observe and learn."

Clover pulls back and dashes to her mother to throw her arms around Lottie's neck, squealing "thank you," over and over.

"Okay, sweetie. Bring your bowl to the sink first."

Clover doesn't need to be told twice.

"I will keep my eye on her at all times," Harlene assures Lottie.

I haven't met the new farrier yet. Though, she isn't quite new to us since we've worked with Seger, her father, for years. She recently took over her father's business when he was murdered. Sad to say the man was killed on our property by the father of Garrett's old lady.

To make a long story short, Raney, Garrett's old lady, had been kept underneath her father's thumb all her life until she ran into Garrett. Before she met him she didn't even have a damn birth certificate or social security number. She basically didn't exist other than to her parents where she needed to work her ass off and sleep in a fucking barn.

Her asshole father thought he could come here and take her back to his ranch. He used Seger and his van to get onto our property unnoticed. So, Seger was at the wrong place at the wrong time and paid for it with his life.

"How's she doing?" I ask Harlene.

Sadness washes over her face. "Okay, I guess. She's always been all business and less talk: the woman is tough."

Harlene is a vet and has worked with both Seger and his daughter for years.

"I'm ready," Clover claims enthusiastically.

The both of them head out and I'm sure Clover will be occupied for the next few hours. And this gives me the opportunity to give Lottie something I should have given her when I proposed to her.

"Come on," I gruffly tell her and hold out my hand for her to take. "I want to give you something."

She shoots me a questionable look but slides her fingers over my palm anyway. I take her with me to the bedroom and come to a stop near the bed.

"Clothes off," I order.

Her head rears back. "Clothes off? I thought you wanted to give me something." A giggle slips past her lips when she grabs the hem of her shirt and pulls it over her head. "I should have known it was your dick you wanted to show me, though I've seen it before, you know."

I don't give her a reply but cross my arms in front of my chest and enjoy the way she strips her clothes away until she's standing before me, gloriously naked and all mine.

Her eyes go thoughtful. "Aren't you going to strip?"

I slowly shake my head and take a few more breaths to enjoy the view of seeing my woman standing comfortably naked in front of me.

"You're fucking gorgeous," I croak. "But I have something that will make you even more stunning than you already are."

Her eyes fill with heat and she steps closer to place her palm on the patches of my leather cut. I wrap my fingers around her wrist and pull back, softly letting go so I can take her hand in mine as I reach behind me.

I grab the box with my grandmother's ring and hold it

between us, popping the lid at the same time her curious eyes land on the item I'm holding. The tiny gasp and the ripping of her hand from mine to place it over her mouth as her eyes fill with happy tears is all I need to know she loves the ring. Taking it out, I let the box drop to the floor while I take her hand and slide it on her finger.

Her eyes are fixed on the band around her finger when I tell her, "My mother gave it to me a few years ago with the instruction to find myself a woman and give her some grandkids. I knew there would come a time I had the opportunity to give this to the right woman. Never in a million years did I think I'd deserve someone as perfect as you. And don't give me that look. You are perfect in all ways because you make my heart race with excitement, my brain overload with each and everything I want to experience with you, while my body fills with the heat of feeling your body next to mine. Bonus points for already being a brilliant mother, allowing us a head start at being a family where my mother is already graced with one grandkid. But I do hope we can soon add to that number."

Her tears are now spilling down her cheeks as I pull her close and take her mouth. The sensual kiss is meant to add the feelings I can't express with words. Telling her I love the fuck out of her isn't enough; she needs to be worshipped and feel my love in every fiber of her being.

I lift her off her feet and gently put her down on the bed. Dropping to my knees, I let my hands slide up her legs and spread them wide to bare her pussy to my hungry gaze. My mouth waters and my cock goes rock-hard when I see my woman cover her center with the hand wearing my ring.

Her gaze radiates possessiveness when it hits mine. Inching closer we stay connected as her fingers spread the lips of her pussy, allowing me to pierce her with my tongue and let her taste enthrall me even more.

Her other hand moves toward my head to pull me tighter against her as her head falls back, a low moan ripping from her body as I start to suckle her clit. Both her hands fly to her side where she grips the sheets, throwing her hips off the bed as I tighten my fingers deep into her flesh to keep her pinned.

She's damn responsive and I love the way the pleasure flows from her body in hushed pants and low moans. I take my time licking, sucking, nibbling, and drive her to the brink of insanity before I let her tip over.

"Oakkkkk…fuckkkkk," she moans when her pussy starts to ripple.

I stare at her curled body as she pushes her magnificent tits into the air, fingers plucking at her nipples while I catch a glimpse of the ring on her finger, marking this gorgeous woman as my fiancée.

Ripping my mouth away, I jump off the bed and shed my clothes in the blink of an eye. I palm my cock and squeeze to take away some of the pressure. I'm so damn hard for this woman, but blowing my load the second I'm inside of her isn't what I'm planning on.

We only fucked bare the first time we were together and have been using condoms ever since. We're both clean and at this point in our lives, engaged and we might already be pregnant, there is no need for a rubber barrier. I place the fat head of my dick at her entrance and with one hard thrust I slide deep.

"Fuuuuuuckkkk," I groan and glance at the heavens above to relish in the perfect way this woman feels wrapped around me.

Slowly pulling out, I glance down to where we're connected to see my dick–covered with her juices–moving within her. I have to tear my gaze away otherwise I will blow my load in the next two thrusts.

I place a hand on her shoulder to keep her body in place with the fierce way my cock is tunneling in and out of her body. This is what we will have for the rest of our lives; connected, together, forever.

The heat in her eyes tainted with love and affection along with a load of desire for more is both thrilling and captivating. Sex may be sex but when you add feelings and the realization your body and soul belongs to the right person it adds to the chemistry inside you to experience a whole different level of lovemaking.

A perfect fucking way we will enjoy for a long damn time, and that's good since my orgasm hits out of nowhere and I take my woman with me into a sea of bliss. Our groans of pleasure mix when the cum rips from my body and enters hers.

Collapsing on top of her, I can feel our raging hearts beat tightly against one another as the both of us try to catch our breath. Her hand slides up and down my back and the soft touch is caressing my heart at the same time.

I pull back to connect our gaze and give her the words, "The love I hold for you might be young but I know damn sure it will only grow stronger from here on out. And I'm never letting you go, you hear me? Never."

The coy smile I get in return makes my dick twitch, but the words she gives me next fires my dick right back up.

"Good, because I love you already so much, I won't ever be able to let you go."

I take her mouth and slowly rock my hips, taking our time to enjoy this shared moment and make it more special, knowing there will be many special moments to come.

CHAPTER 08

LOTTIE

I would like to say it's been one blissful day after another, but only one day has passed since Oak slid the ring on my finger. It feels longer because it feels right. Staying here on the ranch, and not to mention, Clover smiling all the time due to spending every second she's awake doing what she loves; being around horses.

And it's also what she's doing right now. Decker picked her up bright and early this morning for a riding lesson. Oak explained to me how letting his other brothers teach her also adds to her skills because each one pays attention to different things.

And I've seen some of them work with horses and my daughter and know how sweet they all are. A funny thing to say about this bunch of cowboy bikers who are all muscled with rugged appearance.

I bring my cup of coffee to my lips and take a sip before putting it back down. A smile spreads across my face when my gaze lands on my ring, letting warmth spread through my body.

324 Cowboy Bikers MC: Collection Books 5 - 8

Even with the mess I'm in with Anson, it doesn't diminish the happiness I feel in this moment.

And it's all because of the man who is currently taking a shower. We're heading for the clubhouse in about fifteen minutes. Weston wanted us to be there since the guys from Lost Valkyries MC can show up any minute and we need to talk some things through.

There's still one thing bothering me in all of this, and that's Alexi. Normally she would text me every day. She might be my employee, and we're not tight friends, but there's always something for her to shoot me a message about. Mainly because she's always running late.

But not a peep today nor yesterday. I also wanted to call her to see if she had anything to do with Anson showing up at the bar and instantly knowing about Clover. But Oak didn't think it was a good idea and with the whirlwind of events it didn't cross my mind again until now.

Oak steps into the living room, looking handsome as ever with a sleeveless, gray-white checkered shirt, and his jeans riding low on his hips. He's holding his leather cut in one hand and his boots in the other as he walks toward the couch.

Instead of ogling him some more, I let him pull on his boots and cut as I reach for my phone to see if I have any messages. Still nothing. I dial her number but it goes straight to voicemail. Strange. I grab my empty cup and head for the kitchen. Oak comes up next to me to grab my cup before I can wash it and pours himself some coffee in my cup.

He gives me a mischievous smile at the same time I ask, "I still would like to reach Alexi. It doesn't sit right if she had something to do with Anson knowing about Clover. I know she gossips a lot and sleeps with every guy who is willing to give her a good time, but…I don't know. She didn't text me today either and I just tried calling her but it goes straight to voicemail."

Oak puts the cup on the counter and grabs his phone, jamming his thumb over the screen before he holds it to his ear.

"Hey, Spiro, sorry to wake you. Did Alexi come into work

yesterday? Yeah. No, stay put, he might show up there again. Okay. Talk later."

Oak disconnects while he shakes his head. "She didn't come into work. Spiro didn't let us know since it was a slow night and was going to give her the night off anyway. If she showed up that is, since she's always late."

"Yeah, but she always messages me if she's late," I muse.

Oak swipes his thumb over the screen of his phone again. "Decker, mind calling Nick and have him swing by Alexi's place? You know, the waitress that works for my old lady. Lottie thinks she might have something to do with Anson finding out about Clover so quickly and now the woman didn't show up for work yesterday and didn't text or call in sick, and she isn't answering her phone either, it goes straight to voicemail. Thanks. Yeah, let me know."

He tucks his phone back into his pocket and cups my face with both hands. "Decker will call back as soon as Nick knows more. I'm sure there's a logical explanation. Maybe she partied a little too hard and decided to skip work and sleep in late. Hell, she might have met her next man to toy with and is still in his bed."

"You're right," I mutter. "All of those things have happened many times in the past."

And it actually makes me cringe to say this because it's the truth. It might make her a bad employee but at the same time she does one hell of a job when she does show up. Late or not, she also earns me money since most of the customers are older men who enjoy the sight of her serving drinks and her flirtatious ways.

Oak leans in and brushes his lips against mine but pulls away all too soon. "Decker will get back to me when he hears from Nick. Let's head over to the clubhouse and talk to Weston or we could check on Clover first."

I love how he always puts my daughter first and like with me, she's never completely out of thought.

"We could do both if we go through the back. Decker is

working with her in the pasture to the right of the stables, or so he told me."

Oak nods, laces his fingers with mine, and grabs his keys from the counter before we head for the clubhouse. From a distance we see Clover riding Cal. My heart still skips a beat when I see her riding that big horse without anyone but her holding the reigns.

Though, I know she can handle the older horse and when they let her gallop the first few times, they were running beside Cal while holding on so Clover could focus on the feel and her posture. I thought I would die the first time I saw Oak do it. I was holding my breath for too long and went dizzy before I realized I needed to keep breathing.

She hasn't fallen off yet and the way these guys take great care in teaching, I have to let go of my fear once and for all. Especially when I see her radiant smile from miles away. Why should I hold her back when something as precious as riding a horse brings such pleasure?

I loved the way Oak told her all about the steps she needs to go through to be able to get a horse for herself one day. But the pressing matters we're wrapped in also makes me realize how short life is and one day can be all you have left on this Earth.

I glance at Oak who has his eyes set on Clover as we walk toward the clubhouse. I place a hand on his forearm and bring him to a stop. He shoots me a questionable look while I think over my words.

Eventually I tell him, "Maybe we could look for a nice and calm horse for Clover. I have no clue how much one costs, but I do need your expertise on health, character...hell, I have no clue where one needs to pay attention to when you're buying a horse."

A squeal rips from my throat when Oak grabs me by the waist to hoist me up and twirls me around.

"You're fucking amazing, you know that?" He lets me slide down his body. "She's going to be as thrilled as I am. You make me damn proud, stepping over your fear of horses to give your daughter what her heart desires."

I lift my arms to sneak them around his neck. "That's because a certain man gives me what my heart desires and has helped me see past my fear."

We're about to kiss when Oak's phone starts to ring. We pull apart and when he answers his gaze swings to the pasture where Decker and Clover are. I follow his gaze and see Decker holding his phone to his ear. Clover is still on Cal's back and they are riding at a very slow pace.

My eyes go back to Oak when he grunts, "Lesson is over, I want Clover with us. Okay. Thanks."

He hangs up and his eyes go to me. He's about to say something but there's a loud whistle dragging both of our attention to the pasture where Decker and Clover are. I see Decker who is waving us over. I see Cal. But the saddle is empty and Clover is missing. I start to jog in their direction and scan the ground but don't see her.

"Did she fall? She fell, didn't she? Where is she?" The questions rush out in a desperate tone.

My heart races as Oak picks up his speed and easily runs past me with his phone glued to his ear. "Prez. Nick found Alexi dead and now Clover is missing. She's not on the horse she was fucking sitting on a moment ago. Help look, dammit." He shoves his phone back in his pants, his head swings toward Decker and he bellows, "Where the fuck is she?"

"I don't know," Decker bellows in return. "I was looking at you for one fucking second and she was gone."

We all took our eyes off her for one freaking second, my mind offers. But it was enough to let her slip through our fingers.

Decker grabs Cal. "She's not here."

He glances around himself and I'm panting like crazy, my lungs are burning and I whip my head around so fast, it might rip off any second. There's no trace of her. It's as if she vanished into thin air. I peer at the bushes near this pasture. There are a few trees and...my heart sinks when I see Anson step out from behind the tree.

"Where is she?" I screech.

One of his arms is stretched out and aimed at the tree. Oh. God. He has a gun and I now notice Clover's riding boots. She's lying on the ground? Why is she lying on the ground?

"What did you do?" Oak's deadly voice flows from beside me.

"I figured I'd get some leverage when I came to ask if you had an update for me. Did you arrange for those Lost Valkyries MC fuckers to back off?"

"I'll give you an update when you give me my–"

"Your what?" Anson sneers. "Your daughter? You know damn well she's mine. You might have played house all this time but her fucking DNA is a part of me and that bitch took it."

"You were sixteen years old and blew a fucking nut, leaving town right after," Oak growls.

"And why the fuck do you think I left town?" Anson bellows, swinging the gun in Oak's direction.

My heart thunders in my chest. Why is Oak taunting Anson when he has a gun aimed right at him? Slight movement behind the tree catches my attention and I notice Weston is inching closer toward the tree that Clover is lying behind.

I'm afraid to take my next breath because the vicious man standing in front of us has his gun aimed at the man I love while he's just hurt my daughter. My heart feels as if it's about to be ripped in two, shattered beyond repair if he kills Oak or has hurt Clover more than I already fear he did. At this point I don't care about myself because I know Oak or any of his brothers will be there for Clover.

It's for this reason I replace fear with anger and screech with everything I have in me, "I hope you fucking die and if you don't? Then you'd better fucking kill me right now because I will hunt you down like the rabid dog you are and kill you with my bare hands. You hear me, asshole?" His head turns to me and I take a step forward, earning me his gun aimed at my head. "That's right. Come on, pull the damn trigger."

"Lottie," Oak hisses. "Cut it the fuck out."

"No," I snap. "I won't. You know why? Because I love you, that's why. And this no good sonofab–"

I'm roughly shoved to the ground, pain shoots through my side as I see Oak launching himself toward Anson. But before he reaches him, there's another gunshot followed by another one. I watch how Anson's head whips back, a hole appearing right between his eyes as he stumbles back and crashes to the ground.

Oak jumps over his body and squats to his knees. The pain in my side demands my attention but I clench my teeth and drag myself up. Stumbling, I reach Oak, he's cradling Clover against his chest.

I drop to my knees and ask the dreaded question, "Is she okay?"

"She has a bruise on her left temple and she's scared shitless. I think she's okay but we're going to take her to the…fuck, you're bleeding, woman. Weston, a little help here."

"Ambulance is on the way," a guy from my left says.

"Thanks, Nick," Decker says.

I drag my gaze away from him and focus on my side to see where the pain is coming from. I still have my hand pressed against it and when I pull it away, I actually sway on my feet at the sight of crimson spread all over. Weston balances me and mutters a few curses.

Oak is suddenly standing in front of me and it makes me question, "Where's Clover?"

"Decker has her in his arms. Fuck, stay with me, Lottie, eyes open."

"I'm a bit dizzy, but I think I'm okay. It does hurt, though," I mutter and try to see where Decker is standing.

Black spots appear in my vision and I can only give in to the oblivion where there's silence, no pain, and no worries. I keep fading in and out until I wake up in a hospital bed. I'm completely disorientated but there are voices drawing me back to the here and now.

I recognize Weston's voice when he says, "We have to stop letting people die on our ranch. Fucking hell, I bet even the FBI is noticing the body count."

Blinking a few times, I see Decker standing beside Weston. "You forget how the body count adds to their cases being solved, that balances shit out, you know. Hey, you're awake."

"Where's Clover? Oak?" I croak, my throat scratchy and dry.

Weston grabs a cup from the table beside me and places the straw at my lips. "Harlene is with your old man and Clover. I will let her know you're awake. Oak didn't want to leave Clover. He said something about you wouldn't be leaving her either and since they had to pull the bullet from you and he couldn't be with you anyway, he asked us to keep an eye on you while he stayed with Clover. She's okay, though. They wanted to make sure she didn't have a severe head injury."

I swallow a few sips of water and pull back. "Thank you."

He gives me a nod, places the cup back on the table and takes his phone to shoot a message to Harlene.

"Always. You're family, Lottie. We always take care of our own, no matter what," Weston mutters while he's typing away on his screen.

"Even when it adds to the body count?"

His eyes meet mine and there's a smile tugging his lips when he says, "Even more then."

Decker chuckles. "Don't worry about it. Nick has everything under control." His face grows sad when he adds, "My condolences regarding your employee Alexi. Nick found her with two gunshots to the chest. It looks like Anson killed her. They're still processing the scene and we might never know why he killed her. Maybe she regretted telling him about you and wanted to go against him, or maybe he took his anger out on her, who knows? Fact is, she's dead. And it's a good thing Lost Valkyries MC showed up after everything went down. They kept their distance and were satisfied when we told them Anson stopped breathing. You can rest assured nothing will blow back on you or Clover for that matter."

I mindlessly nod and try to process everything. I'm thankful to still be alive, that my daughter is still alive along with the man who has completed our lives and hopefully we can move forward from here on out.

I'm drifting away when I hear Clover's voice, making me snap my eyes wide open as I swing my head toward the door.

"Mommy," she squeals and Oak scoops her up before she can launch herself at me.

"Okay there, little dynamite, calm down. Mommy is hurt and pregnant on top of it so you can't launch yourself at her," Oak softly reprimands.

Stunned, I keep my eyes on his, a smile tugging his face when he adds, "You heard me. You might not have taken the test we had in the cabin but when they started to move you into the ambulance, I let them know about the possible pregnancy. They ran a blood test and it showed you are in fact pregnant. Don't worry, they took all the necessary precautions. The baby is okay and you're okay. They took out the bullet and the doctor is supposed to swing by to see you, and if all is fine we can take you home later today."

I'm hugging Clover with one arm and I can't stop the happy tears from spilling. This magnificent man kept Clover safe and knew exactly what was going on with me. He truly is one of a kind and I'm thankful he's a part of our lives. And I can't believe I'm pregnant.

New life, our family expanding; a new start. And I owe it all to the man who is rooted deep in my heart.

EPILOGUE

Four years later

LOTTIE

I slide my palm over Cal's coat one final time and stroll out of his stall, locking him safely inside. It's taken two years for me to ultimately give in and get on that saddle, but it was another heartwarming change Oak gave me.

Leaving my fear of horses completely behind me, I'm able to enjoy riding together with my daughter and with my husband or all of us together for that matter. It's also brought Clover and I closer, allowing us to both enjoy spending more time together. A warm welcome between her headstrong, teenage ways.

I'm so proud of my young lady, to be able to balance school and taking care of her own horse. She gets up early each day to take care of Jessy, the mare Oak bought for her four years ago. And after she's done with school and homework, she's back in the stables to groom and ride.

Clover's only struggle these days is not being sure what she wants to become, either a veterinarian or a rancher. She's intrigued by the club's dynamics of breeding horses but also loves helping Harlene and Cassidy at the clinic.

A smile forms on my lips when I remember Harlene telling her how she could become a vet and marry a cowboy biker like she did, so she'd have the best of both worlds. The look Weston gave his old lady was priceless. Such love and affection.

And that's just it. The moment Oak came into our lives four years ago gave a spin on the world as we knew it, one where we were thrown through danger from the past and moved past it to the steady family life.

So much has changed. Four years ago we got married and I decided to make Oak a silent partner in the bar so it also became club business. This gave me a lot of breathing space while still having the fifty-one percent to keep what my parents worked hard to build, but also more time to relax and spend with Clover, and Oak for that matter.

Mayven walks up to Oak, who is still on his horse and has our three-year-old son, Cedar, sitting in front of him. That little man was riding a horse before he could walk, giving me heartburn the first few times Oak held out his arms for me to hand him over.

But Cedar loves riding with his daddy. Oak is a skilled rider, always making sure he picks one of the calmer and older horses when he takes Cedar to ride with him. I'm proud to call him the father of my children and it warmed my heart when he officially adopted Clover as his own. When he showed her the adoption papers she threw her arms around him and didn't let go for the longest time.

Mayven takes Cedar and puts him with both feet on the ground. He instantly walks over to me and holds his hands up. I oblige and lift him up on my hip because he might want to give me a hug, but the main reason for wanting me to lift him is because he can glance into the stall and pet Cal. Yes, this boy is like his father; the love for horses is in his DNA.

"Harlene and Cassidy organized movie time in the barn with all the kids," Mayven says as she comes to stand next to me. "She asked Clover to help and I said I'd help out too. I could take

Cedar if you two want to have a few hours to yourself?"

I give her a thankful smile and instantly nod. "That would be heaven. Thanks."

She shoots me a grin and holds out her arms. "Want to check on the other horses with me, Cedar? And when we're done, we'll watch a movie with Parker, Heather, Rose, and all the others, what do you say?"

Cedar instantly leans in and curls his tiny arms around Mayven's neck to start babbling about all his friends. I inhale deep and again a smile forms on my lips when I realize how many good things my life consists of.

The level of friendship, brotherhood, loyalty, and devotion is high with all the people we're surrounded with. Living on the ranch doesn't just make it easier for Oak to be close to his work and friends, it also gives us the ability to be surrounded with family.

And it doesn't matter if family isn't blood. The title of being a father can either be through DNA or through some writing in black and white, but the bottom line is the actions that gives a child the heartfelt connection of having a father. Oak is a father to both Cedar and Clover. There is no difference or bigger love, there is only the unconditional bond and I love him even more for being the great man he is.

"Is Mayven taking Cedar to movie time with all the other kids?" Oak asks, his eyes pinned on his son who is on Mayven's hip while they head for another stall.

I step closer to him and let my hand slide over the patches of his leather cut. "Yes, Clover will be helping out too."

His eyes hit mine and they fill with lust, a sly grin spreads his face and he huskily says, "Is that so?"

I hum low in my throat and lean in next to his ear to whisper, "Let's make the most of the time we have to ourselves tonight."

I instantly take off running and hear my daughter snap, "No running in the stables, Mom!"

There is no time to reply when a strong arm catches me around my waist, spins me around and Oak throws me over his shoulder.

He smacks my ass and grunts, "You heard your daughter, no damn running in the stables. I think you need some kind of punishment so you won't forget next time."

I should laugh but the husky promise in his voice makes my pussy tingle with anticipation. The fire in our connection never fades, it only simmers and flames hot each and every time. We might have days where work, taking care of the kids, and every other responsibility overtakes us, but we always make time for one another.

Even if it's just to lace our fingers while they are resting on the back of the couch when we're surrounded by our kids, watching TV as a family. We don't have to have sex to keep our relationship functioning, it's an added element because there wouldn't be any sex if our bond wasn't strong enough.

And yes, we each have our frustrations, displeasure, crappy days, and annoying quirks, but life isn't perfect and neither is any person walking this world. But I like to think Oak and I are a perfect match in and out of bed.

Though right now it's in bed where my hands roam over his naked body. I can never get enough of his hard, inked muscles. My fingers trail down and over his abs to his happy trail which leads to dark, trimmed curls where his cock is nestled. He's already hard and aimed right at me and my mouth waters at the sight.

Leaning in, I palm his cock, letting my thumb play with his piercing before I close my lips around him. His fingers slide into my hair and a groan ripples from him at the same time his hips thrust forward. I hum low in my throat, knowing it drives him crazy and he instantly falters with sliding his dick in and out of my mouth.

Curses ring out and the blow job is instantly forgotten when I'm being hoisted up and thrown on my back. My legs are shoved apart and I use my next breath to scream when his mouth covers my pussy while his tongue assaults my clit.

My heart is racing and desire laced with lust is flaming hot through my veins. My nails rake over his skull, egging him on. He shakes his head gently to stimulate my pussy, driving me crazy and I'm already balancing on the edge of pleasure when he surges up and slams into me with one stroke.

He lifts one of my legs over his hips to pound deeper inside me. His hand circles my neck, locking our eyes as he dominates me in the most delicious of ways. Just the sights of this man hovering above me, his harsh grip on my thigh to balance himself as he drives his dick in and out of my pussy is overwhelming.

"I'm fucking close," he grits through clenched teeth. "Touch your clit."

I follow his demand and it only takes a few strokes for pleasure to hit. I moan his name and relish in the way I hear his grunts between my name falling from his lips in a guttural tone as his seed fills my pussy.

For a moment in time our world only consists of our connected bodies while pleasure consumes us. It's a delightful bliss we chase on a regular basis and it gives our hearts what our bodies desire.

Being young and reckless kickstarted my life and threw me into adulthood face first, but I never once let it define me. It's all about your outlook on life and the loving people you have around you. My parents when I was young, and Oak as I reached a point in life where it was the perfect time for the next step; adding to a new family and to let our hearts expand along with it.

"I love you," I struggle to push those words out with my raging heart as it takes effort to catch my breath from the intense lovemaking.

"Love you more," he grunts and loses his balance, crashing on top of me with all his weight.

"Can't. Breathe," I fake gasp, making him chuckle.

"Not getting rid of me that easily," he mutters and wraps me in his arms as he rolls to the side, taking me with him.

"As if I would ever want to get rid of you." I snuggle against his chest.

"Our ride will always be at full speed, on a road to forever while we're still able to enjoy the scenery because we're all about the fast life."

Laughter erupts inside me. "The fast life, you're talking about the handful of minutes of sex we just had?"

I'm not on top of his chest any longer, but I find myself pinned underneath him while he stares at me intently.

"It was more than a few minutes," he growls.

I can't help but tease and tell him, "Are you sure? It felt like a fast ride."

He pulls back, grabs my hips, puts me on all fours and slams back inside me, his piercing deliciously rubbing in all the right places. Smacking my ass, he rumbles, "I'll fucking show you a hard and fast ride."

And yet again, I have no complaints about our lives. Not a single one.

Thank you for reading Cowboy Bikers MC: Collection Books 5 - 8

More Cowboy Bikers, standalone stories, can be found here:
books2read.com/rl/cowboybikersmc

If you love some crime fighting added to your stories, check out: Cowboy Bikers MC Lawmen They have a keen eye for justice and catching killers, but also for finding the one woman who jolts their heart at first sight.
books2read.com/rl/Lawmen

If you enjoy reading paranormal stories, you will love the paranormal Cowboy Bikers series:
books2read.com/rl/CowboyBikersMCPNR

Dive into an all new, standalone, cowgirl biker romance series with an MC filled with "sisters" instead of "brothers."
books2read.com/CowgirlBikersMC1

Gaining exposure as an independent author relies mostly on word-of-mouth, so if you have the time and inclination, please consider leaving a short review wherever you can.

Even a short message on social media would be greatly appreciated.

Be sure to check out all my other MC, Mafia, Paranormal MC, and Contemporary Romance series!
books2read.com/rl/EstherESchmidt

Signup for Esther's newsletter:
esthereschmidt.nl/newsletter

SPECIAL THANKS

My beta team; Neringa, Tracy, Lynne, Tammi, Wendy, my pimp team, and to you, as my reader…

Thanks so much!
You guys rock!

Contact:

I love hearing from my readers.

Email:

authoresthereschmidt@gmail.com

Or contact my PA **Christi Durbin**
for any questions you might have.
facebook.com/CMDurbin

Visit Esther E. Schmidt online:

Website:
www.esthereschmidt.nl

Facebook - AuthorEstherESchmidt
Twitter - @esthereschmidt
Instagram - @esthereschmidt
Pinterest - @esthereschmidt

Signup for Esther's newsletter:
esthereschmidt.nl/newsletter

Join Esther's fan group on Facebook:
www.facebook.com/groups/estherselite

Join The Cowboy Bikers group on Facebook:
www.facebook.com/groups/CowboyBikersMC

Printed in Great Britain
by Amazon